Susan Sallis is the number one bestselling author of over a dozen novels including *Daughters of the Moon*, *Water under the Bridge*, *Touched by Angels*, *Choices*, *Come Rain or Shine*, *The Keys to the Garden*, *The Apple Barrel* and *Sea of Dreams*. She lives in Clevedon, Somerset.

www.**booksattransworld**.co.uk

TIME OF ARRIVAL

Susan Sallis

CORGI BOOKS

TIME OF ARRIVAL
A CORGI BOOK : 9780552149037

Originally published in Great Britain by Bantam Press,
a division of Transworld Publishers

PRINTING HISTORY
Bantam Press edition published 2002
Corgi edition published 2002

3 5 7 9 10 8 6 4 2

Set in 11/13pt New Baskerville by
Kestrel Data, Exeter, Devon.

Corgi Books are published by Transworld Publishers,
61–63 Uxbridge Road, London W5 5SA,
A Random House Group Company.

Addresses for Random House Group Ltd companies outside the UK
can be found at: www.randomhouse.co.uk
The Random House Group Ltd Reg. No. 954009.

Printed and bound in Great Britain by
Cox & Wyman Ltd, Reading, Berkshire.

The Random House Group Limited supports The Forest Stewardship
Council (FSC), the leading international forest certification organisation.
All our titles that are printed on Greenpeace approved FSC certified paper
carry the FSC logo. Our paper procurement policy can be found at:
www.rbooks.co.uk/environment.

Mixed Sources
Product group from well-managed
forests and other controlled sources
www.fsc.org Cert no. TT-COC-2139
© 1996 Forest Stewardship Council

To my family

One

It was 1951; the Festival of Britain would be officially opened in May and now, in April, there was a mood of expectation in the country. People were going to London to look at the newly completed South Bank before the crowds got in the way. Summer was in the air, hope too. Surely, if we really had won the war, things would soon get better.

The huge steam engine stood at the head of the eight forty-five train from Temple Meads, Bristol, to Paddington, London. It was already fired up from the previous trip and though the pressure gauge was low, it seemed to be breathing in energy slowly and surely. Albert Priddy, the driver, and Wilfrid Pickering, the fireman, were already in the cab. Albert was wiping over the controls with a piece of cotton waste and keeping an eye on the gauge; Wilfrid had slammed the door shut on the firebox after frizzling his breakfast bacon on the shining shovel. He slapped the smoky rashers between two hunks of bread and devoured it like a starving animal. Albert had breakfasted at home and had a lunchbox in his satchel anyway.

While Wilfrid chewed at his rinds, Albert leaned out of the cab, checking on the coal tender, the gleam of polish from the engine, the dull gold of the nameplate. He grinned, suddenly happy. The engine was the *Prince Albert*. That would please Gertie. She was a great one for names – nobody but Albert called her Gertie, to everyone else she was Truda – and she would make something of this coincidence. Albert driving the *Albert*, she would say. And the *Prince Albert* at that. Didn't that give him a feeling of importance? Didn't he realize now that he was better off with his full name of Albert rather than Bert? Or *Al*, as That Woman Next Door called him.

His grin widened. He liked it that Gertie was jealous. It had to mean something. It made up in a small way for the fact that over the past three months she hadn't liked anything 'happening' in the bedroom. Or the living room, bathroom, kitchen. Anywhere. He knew she must still love him because they got on as well as ever, so long as he didn't try to cuddle her. The day after the awful row, when he was still on the Birmingham run, she had put his usual carnation in the special box next to his sandwiches. At first he had thought she'd bought it the day before

8

the upset and had decided to pack it as usual. But the carnations hadn't stopped. And at this time of year they weren't cheap. If she didn't love him, surely the flowers wouldn't have been there. Besides, she began to josh him again like she always did. 'Wish you knew your way around the kitchen same as you do a driver's cab!' she would say, whipping the tea towel out of his hands in order to dry and put away the crocks herself. She knew he could do it as well as she could, but since she had given up work, the kitchen was her domain just like the cab was his. It was her jealousy – her jealousy of Wendy Watkins next door – that reassured him that somethere, deep down inside her, she still loved him . . . in *that* way. Otherwise why would she care at all whether he looked at Wendy Watkins?

He knew there was a lack of logic about his reasoning but he was feeling strangely optimistic today. Maybe tonight Gertie would relent and let him kiss her; and then perhaps tomorrow, especially if it was her fertile time, she might turn towards him in their brass bed in the way she had when she was interested. She might, just possibly, let him take off her nightie. But then again, probably not. He sighed as he drew back inside the cab and tried not to remember the last time something had 'happened'. She had told him he should be ashamed of himself, and he was. Probably always would be.

He glanced down at Wilf and wondered how

he and his wife managed. They were both in their sixties: did that mean they were too old for anything to happen? Or did it mean that they were too old to be ashamed about it? Wilf was always full of someone else who was 'doing it'. Maybe that was because he was too old to do it himself.

Wilf met Albert's gaze, finished chewing, grinned and straightened luxuriously. 'Ready when you are, driver,' he said.

That was another thing about Wilf. He never called Albert anything but 'driver' and he always referred to Maisie Pickering as 'the wife'. Albert made a mental note to tell Gertie about Wilf and his depersonalization of everyone close to him. That was a word she would enjoy: depersonalization. She was a woman of many parts, was his Gert, and he loved her. He felt himself blushing as he leaned out of the cab again as if to leave such sentimentality behind.

Under the canopy of platform three it was warming up already and easy to ignore the spring rain drifting lazily above the *Prince Albert*. Albert thought with some amusement that it would doubtless be the worst summer for God knows how long simply because it was the Festival of Britain. Meant to cheer them all up or something. He sometimes thought that the powers that be, whether they were called Tories or Socialists, had no real idea about the rhythm of things. All right, so the war had been over for six years, but people needed a bit longer than that. He frowned, thinking about it. Maybe when the sixties arrived they'd be able to enjoy parties and festivals again. Not yet. No, by gum, not yet.

He sighed and looked down the curving length of the train. The crew had not yet put in an appearance; guard, ticket collector and buffet car staff were all doubtless in the staff room. A good mix, a crew to be proud of. Harry Blackmore was one of the youngest guards on the new British Railways network, but he was solid stuff. The head steward was an Indian chappie called Ahmed, named after a sultan or some such. Names again. He must tell Gert that one. Albert respected Ahmed in the same way as he respected Harry Blackmore; he was not only superefficient, he put his soul into the job. Someone – probably Wilf – had told him that Ahmed was a refugee. Also a prince back home in West Bengal. But then, that could be just Wilf talking. But he had dignity, did Ahmed, and he brought that dignity with him onto the train. Other train crew members might well have questioned his authority, but after the first shock of seeing his black skin they naturally deferred to him, recognizing his innate command. Passengers often looked surprised at the sight of him standing so regally behind the bar, but once they saw his complete competence they, too, accepted his presence without question. The service had been chosen for a bit of an experiment, which seemed to be working very well. British Railways had decided that it was not worth opening the restaurant car for such a short journey and they had approached various caterers for tenders to run a buffet service. Ahmed and two others formed a team. It would be interesting to see how it worked over the next few months.

Albert wasn't sure about the two other stewards. He did not know them well. He would have to rely on the look of the passengers when they arrived in Paddington to judge their performance: you could always tell from the way passengers stepped down onto the platform and picked up their luggage whether they'd had a good trip or not. Then there was the ticket collector. Albert did not even know his name but he was aware of his reputation. Old Misery Guts, Wilf called him – and so did the rest of the crew. Oh well, there was always one.

The eight forty-five was the return trip of the early five thirty from Paddington and the stock was still being cleaned. A few early passengers waited with a kind of stoical resignation for the announcement that would allow them to open the doors and settle themselves into the warmth of the train for the two-hour trip. Ahmed would send one of the stewards through the first-class coach to offer the personal service expected for the extra fare, and the buffet would be busy. There would be room – at least until Bath – to spread out a bit, to do some work. Albert's grin settled into a smile of satisfaction. He was of the old school, he liked his passengers to enjoy their trip.

He turned to the black satchel hanging at the back of the cab and foraged inside it for the first sandwich of the day. Gertie did some grand sandwiches; whenever he asked her what he'd got that day she always said airily, 'Oh, this and that. More of this than that but quite enough of both.' There was always cheese, of course, but depending on the time of year there might be egg and cress or even salmon if she'd opened a tin to make fish cakes for supper. He took a bite of the first one and felt his tastebuds respond happily to corned beef and chutney. Thank God they could buy tinned food again without those blessed ration points. He delved again for the box that would contain that day's buttonhole. Not many drivers wore buttonholes but his father always had and Albert did too. The bag had belonged to his father, who had driven engines for 'God's Wonderful Railway' before the war and before the old Great Western had become part of British Rail. He'd worked past his retirement age – Albert had been in the army and Walter Priddy had wanted to do his bit too. Then, when Albert was demobbed, he had said, 'Enough's enough, lad. I'm going now.' And he had retired from his beloved railway and shortly afterwards from life itself. Albert and Gertie had not been surprised. 'The Great Western *was* his life,' Gertie had said.

Albert had loved his dad. Even now he felt his throat thicken at the thought that the world no longer contained that upright, proud figure. Walter had been so sure of himself, of his place in the world. He had known that his place was unique; simple as that. Albert tried to be like his father in that way; it was good for self-respect.

He settled his cap well down on his head and fixed the carnation in his buttonhole. Gertie, too, had loved his father and when she heard that he had always worn a carnation in his uniform jacket she had made certain that Albert had a fresh carnation daily. Even in the dark days of winter the Bakelite box would contain a fresh bloom. Albert lifted his lapel and sniffed. The combination of flower scent and corned beef was wonderful, and his smile became beatific. He finished the sandwich and leaned out of the cab again just as the tannoy pinged and the announcement blared out.

'The eight forty-five to London Paddington is now ready for boarding at platform three. Calling at Bath Spa, Chippenham, Swindon, Didcot, Reading and Paddington. Due to arrive in Paddington at ten forty-five. The eight forty-five is ready for boarding on platform three.'

Albert watched the first arrivals board the train. There was that young railway widow – he had forgotten her name but the magazine had been full of her when her husband died. Pretty girl, bad leg, she wore a caliper. Her husband had been management and she had been his typist. They'd been married little more than a year when he died of cancer. Albert sighed and wondered what kind of justice there was in matters of life and death. It seemed pretty random as to who went into old age and who didn't, who had children and who didn't.

He switched his thoughts quickly and looked beyond the girl. A woman got up from one of the platform seats and seemed to steady herself before walking forward. She was dressed severely in a navy linen suit and could have been anywhere between forty and fifty years of age. It was her hair that took Albert's attention. It cascaded around her shoulders, brown and plentiful. He knew that Gertie would say it should be tied back because it looked a frizzy mess, but he rather liked it. It made her look not exactly beautiful but very striking. She was walking oddly, pausing every other step and staring around her. Surely not drunk at this hour of the morning?

The door to the trainmen's office swung open and young Harry Blackmore emerged, adjusting the lapels of his uniform jacket as he made for the guard's van. He looked up, saw Albert and held up a hand in greeting. Albert gave his usual small grin. Harry, too, was wearing a carnation.

Gertie was right again: set a good example, she always said. When people follow your lead, it gives you a sense of importance. Albert sucked in his lips; he wasn't sure about feeling any more important but Harry's carnation made him feel good. Especially when Harry gave the woman with the hair a helping hand. She could easily have slipped down on the line the way she was going.

Jenny Price knew she was late but it was not fair of Ahmed to make her look a fool in front of all the station staff. He and Marvin were loading the drinks into the buffet car as she dashed up. Ahmed was on the top step and looked over Marvin's head at her dishevelled figure.

'Late for duty and improperly dressed,' he said in a monotone as if to himself. Marvin loved it. If Marvin spent two hours getting ready for work he would still look a mess with a face full of acne and horrible teeth.

Jenny gasped, 'Sorry.' The guard was passing and heard everything. Jenny had worked with him before; his name was Harry Blackmore and he was the absolute opposite of Marvin. She could have wept. 'I'm all right underneath,' she said. Marvin guffawed and Ahmed looked as if a slug had appeared under his nose. 'You know what I mean,' she protested desperately. 'I rode my bike down and I had to put Granddad's mac over everything because it was raining.'

'Fetch the sandwiches,' Ahmed ordered. 'Leave the mac in the staff room.' He looked her up and down. 'And do your hair,' he finished despairingly.

She drooped away, barging into a passenger as she crossed the platform, apologizing profusely, sensing Ahmed's disapproval escalating before she disappeared. But he was right: she did look a mess. Her old school scarf, intended to keep her hair dry, made her look like one of the black-haired gypsies who had sold pegs around the villages last winter. When she took it off, her hair was still wet, plastered to her head, her ponytail fraying out of its black ribbon. She ripped the thing off and hung her head, combing her hair upside down until the blood rushed into her face. Then she flung back her head and secured the hair so high that it bounced from ear to ear and made her look like a cheeky schoolgirl.

She pounded back to the buffet car carrying two boxes of sandwiches, dumped them on the counter and ran back for more. Then she went for biscuits, coffee and tea.

'You're keen, I'll give you that,' Ahmed said as she started to load the first-class trolley. She flushed brilliantly; coming from him it was high praise. Then he spoiled everything. 'You might sound like an elephant stamping about, but you can't help that.' He was referring to her legs. Granddad said she would make a good rugby player with legs like hers. But at this time of the year with fine stockings and her new strap shoes, she had imagined they weren't that noticeable. Her flush deepened with shame and she bent over the counter, stacking the cups with unnecessary diligence. But Ahmed had already forgotten her and was muttering about the bloater paste sandwiches.

Marvin appeared from the kitchen with a jug of boiling water.

'Hold her steady,' he said in what he thought of as his nautical voice. 'Avast there, me 'earties . . .' He poured the water carefully into the trolley's urn and turned to grin at her. She saw he was wearing a brace. 'D'you know what the doctor said to our mam when she was about your age?'

'No, but I can see you're going to tell me.' Why couldn't she stand up to Ahmed as easily as she stood up to horrible Marvin?

'He said that men liked women with big hips 'cos they could have babbies easier.' She stared at him incredulously and he added, 'Well . . . yeah. OK. It was the dark ages, remember. And he was a doctor . . .'

'It's as if you think a woman's only goal in life is to find a man!' Jenny spluttered. 'That's what is so . . . so . . .' she recalled a phrase she had heard on the wireless one night this week, 'so utterly demeaning!'

'Oh Gawd. Are we back to all that stuff? I'm

off.' He eased himself back into the kitchen then stuck his head out again. He was grinning and looked like the villain in an Alfred Hitchcock film. 'I still like your hips. As for your legs . . .' He rolled his eyes hideously and she flapped her dishcloth at him just as Ahmed rolled up the shutter of the serving hatch.

'Jennifer Price!' he hissed. 'The aim of the catering company is to promote an image of dignified courtesy! And here you are, behaving like the schoolgirl you are, letting us all down! Why Mr Beauchamp insisted on employing an eighteen-year-old girl on the London trains beats me.' He stared at her, wide-eyed and perplexed. 'I simply do not understand it!'

'I'm sorry, sir. I wouldn't have done it if anyone had been about . . .'

Harry Blackmore appeared, the epitome of dignity with his lapel boasting a white carnation. 'Everything all right?' he enquired, edging past the bar. 'Two minutes to go. Everybody appears to be on board. I'm about to make the announcement.'

He disappeared and Ahmed snapped, 'You heard the guard, Miss Price. Finish stacking that crockery and then make sure everyone in first has a newspaper!' Ahmed was very conscious that he and his team were a flagship for the new system. It was he who had suggested that the first-class passengers be given free newspapers and a complimentary coffee. Mr Beauchamp had congratulated him only last week and told him it was 'paying off'.

Harry Blackmore's voice came from the platform, clear and precise. 'The eight forty-five to London Paddington is ready to leave. Please close all doors. The train will call at Bath Spa, Chippenham, Swindon, Didcot, Reading and London Paddington. Refreshments are available from the buffet car which is situated next to the first-class coaches . . .'

Jenny felt her heart swell with pleasure. Harry Blackmore was such a gent. Her grandfather used that word all the time and she had thought it was completely outdated and showed a horrid pre-war subservience. But she knew now what he meant. Harry must have heard Marvin and then Ahmed going on at her and had probably agreed that a girl like her, straight from school, should not really be in charge of the comfort of the first-class passengers. Of course what he did not know, what no-one on the train knew, was that the school she came straight from was for children with special needs. And that her granddad had known Mr Beauchamp when he was the landlord of the local pub.

Mary Morrison settled herself in her seat facing the engine and adjusted the blind so that the morning sun would not be full in her eyes when the train drew out of the station. She chided herself silently; she had been delighted with the soft spring rain as Andrew drove her down into the city, and he had hated it because he was working out of doors all day. But for some time now the sun had not been welcome to Mary. Her left eye seemed to jump nervously at any strong light, and though the local optician had tinted her glasses accordingly she still found herself closing one eye, holding up a protective hand, drawing a curtain against bright sun. She sighed sharply; it would be good to get this visit to the specialist over and done with. Whatever the result, she had made up her mind that she would tell Andrew she was going to be all right. And then he would feel free to go. Lead his own life. She sighed again and wondered why pity was such a horrible and impossible thing to accept from someone you love.

She became aware that somebody had stopped outside her compartment. The door slid open and a voice, a young voice, said, 'Would you like something to drink, madam? Tea, coffee, lemonade?'

Mary tried to focus her gaze on the source of the voice. 'I don't think so. Thank you.'

She sensed a hesitation about her, then the voice said, 'Are you all right? You look quite peaky.'

It was a word Mary's nanny had used, many years ago. It brought back memories of childhood and warmth and security before everything had gone wrong. She smiled widely.

'My goodness, I haven't heard that word for many a long year! I'm fine. It's just that I don't see very well.'

Suddenly a face swam into view. It was a schoolgirl's face, dark and alive with concern; a rope of hair swung from ear to ear. 'My best friend at school can't see very well. Can you see me now?'

Mary nodded. 'Yes. I like your uniform. And it's good to see a woman doing this job.'

'Oh, thank you. It's a new idea. I hope it works because I enjoy doing it very much.' The girl's face withdrew slightly. 'My friend at school, she used to call me her eyes. I used to tell her what was happening – told her anything I could see really. She was bright, very clever. I wasn't. So I used to look at things for her and she used to work them out for me!' The laugh was unaffected and made the girl sound about fifteen. 'I live with my granddad and he says that word sometimes. Peaky. It's funny, isn't it? I never thought about it before. Peaky.'

'My nurse used to use it too. And yes, it is funny. But you know instantly what it means. Perhaps when one is not well one's face becomes pointed.'

'Could be.' There was another pause while the face hung in mid-air. Then the voice said, 'Have a coffee. It's free. And it might make you feel better.'

'I'm fine. Honestly.' Mary sensed disappointment. 'But all right. I will have a coffee. Thank you very much.'

'Won't be a second then.'

The face disappeared, the door slid shut and Mary put her head against the linen headrest and closed her eyes. She could remember being that young. If only she had met Andrew then . . . She checked her thoughts and tried to smile. When she was that age Andrew had probably not been born.

The door slid open and the girl pulled out a small table from beneath the window. Mary could see her hands: scrubbed hands, unmanicured.

'You seem so young to be doing this job.'

'I'm eighteen. Nearly nineteen actually. This is my first job because I stayed at school until I was eighteen.' She placed a paper napkin between Mary's hands. 'Most of us did in my school.'

'I understand,' Mary said politely, though she didn't really. Maybe the girl had failed her highers and had had to take any job that came along. There was no answering comment so Mary filled the awkward silence by saying, 'You've done very well to get a responsible job like this, haven't you?'

There was a long pause before the girl said quietly, 'How did you know?' Then, quickly, 'I don't mind you knowing. Really. But will the others know? Ahmed and Marvin and – and Mr Blackmore? The train crew? What did I say that sounded funny?'

'My dear girl!' Mary was appalled. 'What did *I* say? Obviously I've put my foot in it, but not deliberately, I do assure you. You're doing your job impeccably and with the kind of sympathy that one rarely finds these days. If I sounded in any way critical or – or patronizing, please forgive me!'

There was another pause then the girl gave a small laugh.

'Oh, you didn't. I just thought . . . it sounded as if you knew.' Suddenly she eased herself sideways and sat opposite Mary with a thump. 'I don't mind you knowing. I mean, it doesn't matter because on train journeys . . . well, we shan't see each other again, shall we?' She paused and Mary made what she hoped was a reassuring sound. The girl puffed a little embarrassed laugh. 'I went to a special school, you see. I was thick and my friend, Lydia, was almost blind. And I *was* lucky to get this job, you're quite right. But I sort of lied. No, not lied because Gramps wouldn't let me do that. But I haven't told anyone. Not about Winderslake. And actually, I'm not . . . what you said. Peckerble. I'm not very good at the job at all and I think if Ahmed found out about Winderslake he'd get rid of me.'

Mary could see her better now. Her hair was parted in the centre and swept over her forehead in Brontë-like wings. Her face was heart-shaped and perfectly symmetrical.

'I live at Winderslake,' Mary said, surprised. 'And I've been to fêtes and things at your school. How strange. What a small world.' She smiled again. Andrew had said once she had a 'blinder of a smile'. How ironic that was now. 'I suppose Ahmed and Marvin work in the buffet car too, do they? They would be very foolish to risk losing you. I think you're excellent at your job. I mean that.' Mary reached across the table and touched the girl's hand. 'And you got it, didn't you? There must have been quite a bit of competition in this day and age.'

'Well, that's it. There wasn't. Mr Beauchamp runs the buffet car. And he owned a pub – a lot of pubs – so he knows about the business. He did a sort of deal with the British Railways man . . . I don't understand it but he, Mr Beauchamp, I mean, runs the buffet car like a little shop. He's not allowed to have the full restaurant car but on short journeys . . . Anyway, my granddad knows him and he said – well, you know.'

'Then you are proving him right,' Mary said sturdily. 'Both of them. Your grandfather and Mr . . . the man who runs the shop here. They had faith in you and you're proving them right.'

'Ahmed and Marvin don't think so. They see through me. My legs and my hair and things.' She stuck a leg out and kicked the opposite seat. 'I'm ever so clumsy,' she concluded.

Mary laughed. 'How do you think I manage? And your friend. Lydia, was it? We have to train ourselves not to be clumsy. And that's what you will do.' She laughed again. 'I bet you won't kick one of the seats again – you've probably learned that it hurts!'

The girl laughed unwillingly. 'There are other things too. They want me to sort of act. Like they do. And Granddad says to be like myself.'

'I think he's right. You've been yourself with me, haven't you?'

'Yes. But you're nice.'

'Most people are. And the ones that don't seem very nice have surely got a tiny bit of niceness somewhere. Just talk to that bit and try to ignore the rest.'

The girl thought about it and then nodded and her ponytail almost flipped upside down. 'All right.' She glanced sideways. 'Oh, we're almost at Bath! I must go. Loads of people get on at Bath but I'll come back and take away your cup.' She got to the door and turned back. 'I almost forgot, have a good journey.' She had obviously learned that phrase but then she added in a normal voice, 'Thank you for talking to me.'

Mary realized she hadn't thought of Andrew or her appointment with the eye specialist since the train had drawn out of Bristol.

'Thank you for talking to *me*,' she said. But the girl was sliding the door shut again and Mary could no longer see her. She sat back, still smiling. The coffee smelled good. She stirred it contentedly and remembered something from *Anna Karenina* about journeys. Hadn't one of the Oblonskys decided that it was only on a train journey that one had time completely to one-self?

Harry Blackmore went from coach to coach making his announcement about arriving at Bath Spa and would any passengers alighting wait until the train stopped at the platform before opening the doors. Then he stuck his head through the window of the brake van and as the train ground to a halt he looked across the heads of the waiting passengers for anyone who might need help or, indeed, might cause trouble. There would certainly be no cause for complaint today unless it concerned the ticket collector, old Misery Guts, but then, everyone expected a ticket inspector to be unhappy. The three stewards who were running the buffet were excellent. He knew Ahmed of old, a regally suitable figure if ever there was one. And the lad, Marvin, was shaping up nicely as a barman. He had come across the new girl, Jenny Price, before. Very keen, anxious to please . . . not too pretty or glamorous. He had watched her and wondered whether she was spending too long talking to the woman with the eye trouble, but Harry had noticed the 'blinding smile' and had known that Jenny had done the right thing. He tightened his lips; after that business with Corinne he must guard against getting involved.

The train drew to a halt and he leaned out to open his door and swing onto the platform. A clutch of grey-suited men made for the first class and he stood back, smiling a welcome. They were regular travellers and would sort themselves out and immediately open their briefcases to start work. Behind them a young couple arrived at a trot. They were smothered in damp confetti, laughing helplessly. Must have been married yesterday, the register office wouldn't even be open yet. A gaggle of guests followed them with luggage. There was a lot of screaming, pushing, shoving cases into the corridor. Harry took a last look along the platform. Next to the engine, a man and woman were getting into the first coach; not much luggage but they seemed to be having difficulty with boarding. Behind them a late arrival ran across the platform, a knapsack joggling on his back and paper carriers swinging from each hand. He looked shabbier than the man and woman and . . . aggressive. Harry had met his sort before and felt a certain sympathy with him. The war had made men like Albert Priddy and Harry Blackmore deeply thankful for their ordinary lives; there were others who had inherited a full cup of bitterness.

Harry watched as the three of them struggled onto the train and slammed the door, then he mounted the running board himself. At his side the young bridegroom said desperately, 'We've got first-class reservations somewhere . . . never travelled by train before . . .' Harry smiled at the guests, who were jumping around as if on pogo sticks, and held his green flag aloft. Albert Priddy acknowledged the signal.

Albert had noticed a middle-aged couple with a child – grandchild? There weren't many kiddies on this early service and it touched him that this child was asleep and held beneath her grandfather's summer mac. There was something so tender and protective about the two of them as they clambered aboard the first coach. Albert watched them, leaning right out until they closed the door. They were having difficulty, trying not to wake the child. If he and Gertie ever had a baby, that's how they would be. Especially Gertie. Gertie would be a wonderful mother. He hoped Harry Blackmore would keep an eye on this couple and their small charge.

Albert grinned. Harry seemed to be completely involved with some newlyweds. When the green flag flipped at him, Albert acknowledged it and pulled the whistle. The driving wheels spun then gripped: they were off again.

Harry smiled at the young husband. 'Shall I take the labelled case into the luggage van while you say goodbye?' They took his place at the window while he stowed the case next to two others.

'It will be safe there, sir,' he said when he returned. 'Your other luggage will go into the luggage racks in your compartment. May I see your reservation number?' He led them down the corridor to the empty compartment next to the woman with the hair. She was still alone. 'Here we are, sir. Madam. The stewardess will be around in a moment and here are your morning papers. One each.'

The girl was reassured; she smiled at her husband and said, 'Oh darling,' and he reached for her hand and put it to his lips. Harry liked that. It was loving but it was also respectful. There wasn't enough respect around these days. Albert Priddy had it and so did Ahmed in the buffet car, but old Misery Guts was already in the third class now demanding to see tickets as if he expected everyone to be trying to cadge a free ride. There was no carnation in his button-hole either.

'I hope you have a comfortable journey,' he said to the young couple and moved on towards the buffet car. He'd ask Jenny Price to look after them, she'd make a good first impression. He flushed slightly, remembering Corinne of the blond curls and ridiculously long fingernails. She had been like a flame walking down the aisles and he had been like a moth. He would have died for Corinne but she would never have fitted into his life and when one day she pushed open the door of the toilet and asked him if he needed a cold shower, he had known he must have been behaving like a lovesick dog and nearly fainted with embarrassment. Luckily, the job proved too much for her nails and she left to demonstrate false ones in a local department store and Ahmed took on Jenny Price. Yes, Jenny would enjoy looking after the newlyweds. And he would ask her to try to find a moment to walk through the third class and check up on Sylvia Pemberton who had been married to Pem Pemberton in the planning department; she had a bad leg and might well need help at Paddington. And there was the couple who had had such difficulty in boarding just now; Jenny would be tactful with them too. He must warn her about the aggressive-looking young man, however; she would not stand a chance with him. He smiled gently as he experienced the feeling of being in complete control of his train. Albert Priddy and Wilfrid Pickering might well be driving the enormous locomotive, but the passengers and the rest of the crew were his responsibility. He felt good about that. Very good indeed.

Jeremy Kemp – or Joe Kemp as he preferred to be known – boarded the train at Bath as he did most months after a weekend with his parents. His mother always sent him a postal order to cover the cost of a first-class ticket, but Jeremy did not believe in the class system so he always

bought a third-class ticket and used the difference to supplement his dole.

He felt a little better than he had last Friday,
which was doubtless due to his mother's cooking,
walks with his father along the Avon, and
dream-free nights in his old attic room with its
panoramic view of the city. The thought of his
bedsit in Kilburn with the trains rattling at the
bottom of the yard and the smell of hot fat
seeping up from the chip shop below was not
enticing. His mother had said, as she always did,
'Darling, you can write plays here, surely?' And
he had smiled and shaken his head. 'It would
compromise my principles, Ma,' he said half
humorously.

At one time she would have come back at
him in the same vein. 'Principles don't fill the
stomach', or 'Principles be bothered!' She gave
that up eighteen months ago after she had read
his first play. He did not let her read his stuff
now; he was frightened that if he was going mad
he might drag her with him.

The train was full and people were standing in
the corridors. Jeremy had his gear in an old
pre-war knapsack and was carrying two bags
containing goodies from the Kemp kitchen.
He shuffled sideways, thinking as always how
ridiculous it was to fit eight seats into a third-
class compartment and only six into a first-class
one. Were third-class passengers thinner than
first-class ones? He smirked at the thought and

decided to put it the other way around: first class must be fatter cats than the third class.

His smirk widened into an apologetic grin as he met the ticket collector head on between carriages. He lifted his bags to show he could not get at his ticket.

'All tickets, please,' the man said woodenly, blocking his way.

'Can't it wait till Chippenham?' Jeremy said irritably.

The ticket collector did not even deign to reply. With much huffing and puffing Jeremy put his bags on the floor and found his ticket inside his jacket. For once he wished he had bought a first-class ticket so that he could wave that at the man. The clippers looked like medieval instruments of torture; they punched viciously at his ticket so there was no hope of his using it again. He'd read somewhere that in Russia all public transport was free. Well, next trip home, he would hide in the toilet and hoard his ticket for a second trip. That would show them.

He sidled on into the next coach and at last found a compartment with only seven people in it. He slid the door open. 'Anybody's seat?' he asked truculently of the three people sitting along one side. They had spread themselves so that no spare seat was visible but he knew his rights.

'Oh . . . oh, I'm sorry. Yes, of course.' The girl

who was sitting in the seat next to the corridor began scraping together some papers and piling them on her lap. She glanced up and smiled apologetically and then moved as far away from the corner as she could. Everyone else made little jumping movements full of resentment. The girl patted the space next to her. 'Can you manage?'

'Perfectly, thank you.'

He put his mother's bags into the luggage rack, eased out of the knapsack and sat down. At least then he could not see the girl; she was everything he did not like, from her neat white blouse and long new-look floral skirt, to her ridiculous straw hat wreathed in flowers. Was she going to a wedding? Even for that the hat was too much. He glanced at the papers in her lap: a list of names and on top was a staff rail ticket. First class.

She said, 'There's not really enough room for four people, is there? If I just move my leg a bit . . .' She caught hold of her knee and dragged her leg away from his. And he saw it was calipered.

Sylvia Pemberton sat very still next to the young man and wondered what could have happened to him to make him so full of rage. He emanated anger; the air around him was hot with it. She shrank as far away as possible and tried to turn her thoughts away from it. She still had the petition on her lap and she pulled it out and let her gaze run over the reassuring length of it. But she knew very well that petitions meant little unless they were backed by good, cogent arguments and it seemed to her that she was the last person in the world to present logical arguments. The fact that she was wearing her best suit, a new blouse and her wedding hat would stand her in good stead, surely. The hat was especially lucky; she'd worn it for her wedding to dear Pem and he'd said she looked entrancing, like someone from a Hardy novel. She sat upright so that the brim would not catch on the back of the seat and send the whole thing askew. In another two hours she would be there. The Houses of Parliament. People were depending on her. But why on earth had they chosen her?

She took a deep breath and let it go slowly. The angry man next to her fidgeted and then began to inch forward in his seat. She wondered whether the MP who had agreed to accept her petition would be like this: prickly and irritable and ill-disposed.

And then he said, 'I'm going to get myself a coffee. Would you like one?'

She was astonished and was about to say no when she noticed his dark, haunted eyes.

She nodded. 'That's most kind of you. Let me find some money.'

'Certainly not. I won't be long.'

Jeremy stood up with difficulty and forced his way into the corridor. It was the least he could do, after all; the poor girl couldn't walk down the corridor with her leg in a caliper. Luckily his mother had slipped him a ten-shilling note when he left that morning. He glanced back into the compartment and saw her settling the blasted hat on her head. He was despicable; people had died, most of the men he knew had died, so that he could live. He wished he had died too.

In the front coach, the shabby couple who had stumbled onto the train at Bath with the sleeping child had found an empty compartment. Gratefully they collapsed and the man put the child between them. She was not asleep; her small face was expressionless.

'Aren't you hungry, my love?' the woman said in a low voice. 'Daddy will get you a nice drink in a minute. Have a biscuit. Yes? There's a good little girl. There's Mummy's good little girl.'

The girl, who appeared to be about four until you saw the set face, waited until a biscuit was removed from the packet and actually put into her hand. Then she ate it furtively, hanging her head above it and nibbling it quickly, her cheeks widening as she pouched it like a hamster.

The man looked across the roughly cropped head and met his wife's brown eyes. 'What have we done, Ilse? What the hell have we done?' he asked in a low voice.

She pressed her lips together. 'We had no option, Ray. It was meant to be.' She leaned over the child. 'Wait till that one has gone into your tummy, sweetheart, then you can have another one.' She looked up again and smiled brilliantly. 'Isn't it wonderful, Ray? We've got our little Caroline back again.' She kissed the crop of dark hair. 'Oh Carrie, we do love you so.'

The child took another biscuit and started to dispose of it. The name obviously meant nothing to her. The man called Ray closed his eyes as he felt them fill with tears. His sister had told him in her stern I'm-older-than-you voice that Ilse wasn't 'quite the ticket'. He knew that she was right. He also knew that there was no turning back now.

The train rattled over the rail joints in a steady rhythm, ABCD, ABCD; every joint taking them nearer to the anonymity of London.

Two

Albert applied the brakes gently and came to a stop so that the train was alongside the passengers waiting to get on at Swindon. Wilf leaned on his shovel and wiped his forehead with the back of his hand.

'On time, driver?' he asked.

Albert wrapped a piece of cotton waste round the drive lever then fished out his watch, glanced at it and nodded. Wilf started going on about one of the controllers in the Bristol office. 'Thinks 'e's God almighty because he's a white-collar man.' Wilf lifted his shovel, spat on it and watched with some satisfaction as the saliva instantly bubbled away. 'They dun't know what work is. I've allus prided meself on keeping my shovel red-hot. Red-hot Wilf they called me when I started. And nothing's changed.' He had a titbit of gossip to impart about the controller. He was part of the old Whiteway Colony up in the Cotswolds. 'He still goes up there, it seems.

Dances round the maypole as naked as the day he was born!'

Albert had heard it all before; Wilf probably made up half the stories he told. Good job he was retiring soon. Albert stopped listening and gazed across the platform to the workshops. The enormous brick façade was pierced by arrow slits of windows and reminded him vaguely of pictures he had seen of old Moorish forts. He had taken Gertie and Janie around the loco sheds once but Gertie had shivered and said they reminded her of hell.

Janie lived next door and worked in a junk shop sporting tin baths and prams on the pavement and old clothes inside. Of course she had the pick of everything and went through the clothes with a fine-tooth comb for anything in a size sixteen. She and Gertie washed and pressed any 'finds' and matched things up into ensembles fit for royalty. Albert told them so, often. It helped them when it came to dealing with the other neighbour, Wendy Watkins, the one who called him Al. He thought of 'That Woman' now and smiled slightly. She never looked like royalty. She wore very tight clothes, probably a size ten, and she had what Janie described as an hour-glass figure. Albert almost laughed out loud at the thought of Wendy Watkins looking like their egg-timer. His dad would have called her common as muck. But then, his dad could be a bit uppity at times.

Albert felt a stab of remorse at his disloyalty and stopped wanting to laugh.

He leaned out of the cab to watch Harry Blackmore ushering the last of the Swindon travellers onto the train. The spring rain had almost stopped and the sun was striking off the glass canopy and showing up the hanging baskets to perfection. Good to see that the station staff looked after the platform so well. The parcel trolleys were parked in a dead straight row at the end of the platform and the platform inspector had his whistle in his mouth, ready to scurry the passengers along like sheep into a fold. The whistle blew, the green flag flashed, Albert held out an arm in acknowledgement then pulled the drive lever gently towards him, smiling as the *Prince Albert* snorted, her driving wheels slipping momentarily on the damp, greasy rails. Next stop, Didcot. He stopped thinking about Wendy Watkins and thought about Gertie. Wilf flipped open the lid of the firebox and started shovelling rhythmically; it was too noisy to continue his tale of the wayward nudist controller. A kind of rowdy peace isolated them. Albert noted that the distant signal was clear, held the drive handle and leaned to his right to catch the Wiltshire breeze. Every county produced its own special brand of air. Wiltshire's smelled of hay and ancient fields wrapped in a hazy blanket of mist.

Basically, the trouble with Gertie was that she had the same kind of morals as his dad.

As soon as the thought came into his head, he was aghast at himself. The *trouble* with Gertie? What was he thinking of? And . . . *like his dad*? What on earth did he mean by that? That his dad was not perfection?

He fingered the carnation in his buttonhole and blinked hard as they flashed beneath a gantry of semaphores. His dad had been . . . an example, revered, and loved. Yes, definitely loved. In a world where values were highly prized, he had values that were right at the top of the scale. Nothing wrong with that, surely? You knew where you were with a man like that. No grey areas. Black and white. Right and wrong. Nothing . . . hidden. What you saw was what you got. People were like that in those days. Well, except for bigamous Uncle Ernie whose other wife had turned up at the funeral and demanded her share of what she called the 'profits'. And maybe Aunt Cissie who had got through several husbands so quickly she boasted she had never had to buy fresh mourning black, not once. Something had gone on there. One Christmas, long before the war, when Albert was ten and the whole family had gathered at Aunt Cissie's very comfortable home, Uncle Ernie had poked around at his dinner plate and asked her whether it was safe to eat. After Aunt Cissie had gone to lie down, in tears, Uncle

Ernie had defended himself by averring that 'Something must have gone on.' He helped himself to his fourth whisky and added jovially, 'To lose one husband is bad enough but to lose three is downright careless!' Albert had been coated, hatted and removed from the house very speedily. Dad – and Mum – had both insisted he should take no notice of what had happened that day. It ensured that he never forgot it.

Mum had had values, of course she had. But they weren't the same as Dad's, though it was difficult to pinpoint exactly where and how they were different. She had still been alive for Uncle Ernie's funeral and when the other wife, threatened with police action, had drooped away, Mum had gone after her and given her all the money she had on her. Albert remembered Dad's horror when she returned to the hearse, penniless. Mum had said, 'But, Walter dear, she had no money for her bus fare back home! And she has children. Ernie's children, remember. It was the least we could do.'

'You're too kind for your own good, our Edie.' He had taken her hand but had added, 'Don't you see that by your action you are condoning a sin?'

But he *had* taken her hand; Albert remembered that thankfully. Dad had not been a cold man; he had not been unforgiving. He must remind Gertie of that fact. Next time she brought up Dad as an example, he must remind her that Dad was not unforgiving.

He checked that thought too. Did he mean – did he think – that Gertie was unforgiving? Just because she wouldn't let anything happen since that time, that one time . . . was it four months ago now? It was. Four months almost to the day. It had been one of her fertile periods and he had almost dreaded going home to the strained business of lovemaking. He remembered it because it was just after the New Year's Eve party when he had so nearly – so very nearly – gone into the garden shed with Wendy Watkins. And since that time, Wendy had practically haunted him. She had a kind of honesty too; no values whatsoever but at least she admitted that. She'd said, 'OK, Mr Pretty-Priddy. You've escaped me this time but be warned. I'm going to be on your back until you give in. Understood?' And she had, almost literally. He would wheel his bike down the back alley when he finished work and open the gate to the yard, turn round to close it and there she'd be in her black skirt and pink drawstring blouse with her yellow curls all round her face, grinning like a monkey. It was usually late at night, the alley lit with a single street light, and the whole scene reminded him of the wartime song, 'Lili Marlene'. Lili of the lamplight. Dad had always switched the wireless off when that song came on. And when Albert had been posted to North Africa to drive a tank instead of a train, he had specifically told him to avoid the 'Lili Marlenes'. Albert had grinned. 'I think she lives in Germany, Dad,' he had said. But Walter had been adamant. 'Lili Marlenes are all over the world, lad. And don't you forget it.'

Well, Dad was right about that too because Wendy Watkins was a Lili Marlene, that was for sure.

Anyway, Wendy Watkins was probably coming home from work too, not dogging him at all. All she said was, 'G'night, Al. See you tomorrow!' When he mumbled something back she always laughed. Just as if he'd said something funny, which he certainly hadn't.

It must have been around the second week in January when he stopped mumbling and managed to say goodnight to her. The thing was, the stupid thing was, he called her Lili. It just slipped out and was totally ridiculous because it was only four o'clock and the lamp above the wall wasn't even on. She said, as per usual, 'G'night, Al.' And suddenly, freed of his stupid embarrassment, he came back with, 'Night, Lili.' He didn't even realize what he'd said till she checked her usual laugh and spluttered, 'What was that you called me, Al? Lili, was it? You got a secret love or something?'

He hung on to his bike, one hand on the gate, ready to close it and go on in to the homeliness of Gertie.

'I was thinking of that old wartime song. You know, "Lili Marlene".'

She was thrilled. 'You getting me mixed up with her, were you?' She leaned dramatically against the wall, her coat falling open, showing a top with a deep V neck. She took on a swooning attitude. 'Lili of the lamplight, my own Lili Marlene . . .' Her voice was light and much too high for the song. She giggled. 'Don't reckon I'm much like Marlene Dietrich. It was her, wasn't it? The song was about her?'

'I don't know.' He could feel his face red and hot right down to his shoulders. But he didn't close the gate.

She said, 'You know, we're the same sort, aren't we? I like pretending things and so do you. They call it fantasies nowadays. But it's only like being big kids, isn't it?'

He said hoarsely, 'I'd better get on. Gert will have my tea on the stove.'

'No, but really. It's like me calling you Al Capone, you calling me Lili Marlene.'

'It was just a slip-up.'

'Fun though, isn't it? Tell you what, you'll always be my Al Capone. And I'll be your Lili Marlene.' She was laughing hysterically as she went into her yard. He heard her shove the bolt across the yard door, still laughing. Then she called over the wall, 'Sleep tight, Al. Keep your gun at the ready!' And then she really did have hysterics. He waited until the screaming whoops were cut off by her closing her kitchen door, then he carefully fastened the gate, put his bike in the old wash house and went into the house.

Janie was there from the other side, having a cup of tea before she went home to cook her tea. That was a nuisance because Gertie wouldn't start cooking their tea until Janie had gone and the cups were washed up. He went to the sink and began to unpack his lunchbox.

'Whatever was up with That Woman?' Janie asked. 'We could hear her from in here! Braying like a donkey, she was. What on earth did you say to her?'

'Nothing.' He was blowed if he was going to tell Janie McEvoy that he was playing kids' games. Maybe later he could tell Gertie. Maybe.

Gertie was picking up the teacups and stacking them in a bowl as a signal to Janie to go. 'Did you have a good day?' she asked, putting the bowl next to his satchel on the draining board. She picked out the box which had contained his carnation and put it on top of the fridge. 'Still on the Birmingham run?'

'Yeh. Not bad. Not bad at all.' He tried to recall some little thing to tell her but all he could think about was Wendy Watkins playing at being Lili Marlene.

Janie stood up obediently and pulled her cardigan off the back of the chair. 'Suppose I'd better get on. I'm dog-tired.' She yawned widely as if to prove the fact then apologized. 'Sorry.

Sorry, folks. I've been in the back sorting today. Must be something in the clothes that makes you tired – we were all the same.'

'It's the weather,' Gertie said. 'Get February over and spring's just round the corner.' She ushered Janie through into the living room and then the hall. Janie said something in a low voice and Gertie said briskly, 'I told you, Janie. Not just yet. I want to give it a proper try before I start thinking of anything else.'

He finished cleaning up his satchel and swilled his hands under the tap. He knew what that was all about, of course. Gertie had given up work over a year ago to start a family. It had all been planned so carefully: they had waited for the war to finish before they got married; then she would work for five years and they would save like mad. Then they would have a baby. Sometimes she cried about it. He'd said to her a long time ago, 'Listen, love, you make too much of the whole thing. We only do it at those special times. It's all so contrived . . .'

'You think we should be at it like rabbits, do you?' She had been angry. Her next breath was being saved to tell him that he'd always been the same, sex mad.

He got in first. 'Listen, our Gert. The doctor told us the key is relaxation. There's nothing very relaxed about the way we make love. Admit it. Go on.'

She never would. And now that Janie wanted

her to go and do some work at the shop – 'to take her mind off it' – she was still hanging on in case one of their infrequent sessions 'took'. Sometimes when he came home the next day she would be practically upside down in an armchair in the hope of helping the sperm in the right direction. Not that she would ever have put it like that. He doubted that she would know what the word 'sperm' meant. He smiled. It was funny really. Not the sort of thing Lili Marlene bothered about.

Gertie came back and bustled around getting the tea. It was liver and onions, his favourite. And she was in a happy mood, talking aloud to herself as she cut the onions – 'No tears now, Truda, just another couple of slices . . .' and pouring him a cup of tea – 'It's still hot enough, Albert. Take the weight off your feet . . .'

He sat down willingly. 'I was going to get washed upstairs.'

'Tea first.' She smiled as she stirred the hissing onions. 'Sorry about Janie. She had a dress she thought would do for the spring. But I didn't bother.'

'I don't mind Janie. You know that.'

'No. You're very good. Her husband is a tartar. If anyone visits her when he gets home from work, they're sent packing.'

'Poor old Cyril. His home is his castle and no mistake. But she thinks the world of him. You can tell.'

'Oh yes. Not every marriage is made in heaven, but it still works if you're willing to stick at it.'

'That's true,' he agreed comfortably.

She floured the liver and put it in the pan then turned with a flushed face. 'What d'you mean by that?' she asked jokingly.

He played along. 'Well. It's like you said. Hard work at times.' He looked up from his cup roguishly.

She turned the liver expertly. 'That's good, coming from you sitting at the kitchen table with a nice cup of tea while I'm hanging over a hot stove!'

'Breadwinner's perks.' He had gone too far; he knew it even as he said the words. Gertie had run the house and done a job for five years so that they could afford to try for a baby. He said quickly, 'Tea was lovely, our Gertie. I'll lay the table, shall I?'

'No. You go on up and have your wash. D'you want a tin of peas with this?'

He swallowed. 'Mash, is it? No, then. I'll have some sauce though.'

'All right. Go on – off you go.'

She didn't turn round again and he knew he mustn't even stop to put his cup in the sink. He went into the living room and then the hall and shut the door behind him with a definite click. Then he opened it quietly and went back. Sure enough Gertie was sitting at the table, head in hands, weeping quietly. He couldn't bear it. He swept her into his arms and held her close. 'Oh my girl, my dear girl. Don't cry then. I'm here, don't cry . . .'

She pushed at him weakly. 'Don't be silly, Albert. I'm all right . . . I'm really all right . . .'

'No you're not. I shouldn't have said what I said – I was joking. It was just a silly joke. I'm sorry, honey, so sorry.'

She got worse. 'You've never called me honey. What made you call me honey?'

'Play-acting again.' His lips were in her hair, he could have cried himself. 'I was pretending to be Al Capone. American. You know.'

He sat down and pulled her onto his lap. She curled up like a child. He wanted so much to comfort her and he did not know how.

'The Americans have got some good pet names, haven't they? Honey. You're as sweet as honey, our Gert.' She managed a little gaspy laugh and he smiled into her head. Gertie was not sweet, not really. She was straight as a die, honest and good and true and loyal . . . not sweet. She was a bit like a sharp apple. He stroked back her hair. 'You're like an apple. Shall I call you my apple?'

'Don't be daft, Albert,' she mumbled into his chest. 'I wish you'd call me Truda. Gertie is horrible. And our Gert is even worse.'

'Yes, but pet names are . . . intimate. Special and private. I know, I'll call you baby.' He felt her stiffen even as he spoke and he held her tightly to him. 'I'm Al Capone and you're my baby. Babe.' He laughed again. 'Babe Priddy. Sounds kind of racy, doesn't it?'

There was a long silence. She had stopped crying and he could almost hear her brain ticking over. He continued to hold her and kiss her head and make soothing noises as if nothing was wrong. As if he would, in a few minutes, go upstairs to wash and then come down for tea.

She spoke at last, her voice very low. 'Al. Al Capone. That's what That Woman calls you. I didn't realize . . . Al Capone. That's why she was laughing.'

'Now, now.' He held her slightly from him and looked into her drowning eyes. 'Come on, our Gert. What's brought this on?'

'You said something to her tonight. You don't usually but you did tonight. That's why she was laughing like a hyena. What did you say to her?'

'I just said goodnight to her. That's all.' He held her gaze with some difficulty. It wasn't a lie but it was certainly only half the truth. She knew it too; she could read him like a book.

She said slowly, 'Did you call her baby? That would have made her laugh all right. You called her baby, didn't you? And now you're calling me baby! You've got babies on the brain!'

The sheer injustice of this almost took his breath away. 'I called her Lili, if you must know!' he blurted.

She stared at him, astonished.

He babbled on helplessly. 'It slipped out. Damned silly. I've thought it often. When it's dark she stands underneath that lamp looking like, well, you know what she looks like. And I thought of Lili Marlene. And tonight I just said it. Off the top of my head. No wonder she laughed!' But she hadn't had hysterics about that, not really. It was when she rapped out that innuendo about keeping his gun ready. Yes, she was coarse, there was no doubt about it.

Gertie said, 'It's a form of flirting. That's what it is. You're playing silly games with each other. My dear Lord, you've got more in common with her than you have with me!'

He stood up suddenly, horrified because in a kind of way – the way his father would have called lustful – there was something between him and Wendy Watkins. No, between Al and Lili.

Gertie slithered off his knees and would have fallen if she hadn't grabbed his arm. She was sobbing again but with anger this time.

'You know what tonight is too, don't you? Tonight of all nights you have to start mucking about with Wendy Watkins! I can't believe this is happening!'

'Neither can I! You must be damned serious to call her by her name and not your usual That Woman!'

'Don't you swear at me, Albert Priddy!'

'God, if you could hear some of the language at work—'

'Well, I can't, thank you very much. And I'm certainly not going to hear it in my own home. So I'll pop round to Janie's while you cool off! We'll forget tonight!'

He grabbed her shoulders. 'Oh no you don't, my girl. Not before we've sorted this lot out. It's nothing to do with Lili Marlene or Al Capone or any of that nonsense, is it? It's the baby business again. And we're not going to waste tonight just because you're in a state. Tonight is one of the special nights and we're jolly well going to make sure we do the job properly!'

It wasn't the best way of putting it and he was hardly surprised when she covered her face with her hands and wailed, 'I can't bear it! I can't bear it!'

He said grimly, 'You ought to take a leaf out of next door's book, our Gert. Stop thinking about it all the time – yes you are! Don't shake your head like that! You don't think of anything else!'

'Let me go, Albert!'

'All right. Sit down here,' he turned her and pushed her into a chair, 'and stay put while I get the tea. I mean it, our Gert! You're not going to go off to Janie's in a huff.'

'Huff!' she repeated, outraged.

'That's what it amounts to. And it's not you.' He slammed cutlery down, stirred the frying pan, stuck a knife into the potatoes. It was as if he *was* Al Capone, a bully, used to making his women do what he told them to do. He strained the potatoes against the side of the saucepan lid and grabbed the masher. 'And after we've eaten—'

'You haven't washed, Albert!'

'No, because if I leave you for one minute you'll be gone. And I'm not having it. After we've eaten, we're going to do it – ' she gave a little scream – 'sorry, we're going to make love. Here. On the floor. And we're not going to wait each time for these special dates. That's not how it's done.' He slapped a spoonful of mashed potatoes onto her plate. 'All this bloody stupid business of disturbing the foetus. I've never heard such rubbish in all my born days. Men and women who love one another show their love in certain ways.'

'You sound like that awful Uncle Ernie of yours. I remember your father telling me—'

'And that's another thing. Dad was Dad. We're us. OK?'

She said nothing, just stared down at her plate where the liver sat inelegantly on top of the mashed potatoes with the onions splattered around the edge. He sat opposite her and began to cut up his liver with something very like savagery. She watched him covertly as he put a forkful of food into his mouth, then very tentatively she picked up her cutlery and started to eat.

He almost caved in then; she was never docile

54

and it touched his heart that she was so confused and unhappy that she was doing what she was told. But he said nothing. If this was the only way to get them out of the rut they were in, then so be it. He could go on playing Al Capone for as long as it took. But he hadn't expected to have to go the full distance.

She wept afterwards, lying spreadeagled in front of the stove, looking simply terrible with her hair a mess and her clothes half off, which was all he had been able to manage, what with her flailing arms and legs, and her teeth – yes, she had bitten him at one stage.

He leaned over her, Al Capone retreating into the shadows, contrition weighing him down. 'Oh Gertie, I'm so sorry . . . I had to do it. I can't talk to you, and I had to show you that I want you as a woman, not just as a container for a child. I love you, our Gert, I love you.'

She said through her sobs, 'You should be ashamed of yourself, Albert Priddy. If your father knew he'd turn in his grave . . .' He tried to arrange her clothes and she slapped his hand away. 'You didn't even clear the tea things away – you didn't even *wash*!'

He knelt above her, looking down, and suddenly he started to laugh. It was a Wendy Watkins laugh, unstoppable and near hysteria. It made Gertie angry and she sat up and began to tidy herself.

'I'm glad you find it a joke! You do realize what you've just done, do you? There's a word for it, you know!'

He leaned against the table leg, spluttering helplessly. 'You won't say that word though, will you? You wouldn't let it soil your lips!'

'I didn't encourage you – didn't want it . . .' She knelt, adjusting her clothes furiously.

'Al Capone wouldn't have let that stop him,' he said.

'Oh my dear Lord.' She stood up. 'It was all a game. That's what it was to you, wasn't it? Just a game.' She looked down at him and for a moment her face was full of grief. 'Oh Albert,' she said. And then she left the kitchen. He heard her go upstairs and then the roar of the geyser and water running into the bath.

He sat still for a long time, one leg straight out, the other tucked beneath him. He knew he had really done it this time. And in a way it served him right because that's how it had started, as a game. Invented by that bloody woman next door. And he and Gertie didn't play games.

He leaned out of his cab at Didcot and watched as a handful of people got off the train and others boarded. Yes, four months ago. And he was ashamed of himself, that much was probably good. After all, he had done a shameful thing. His father would have hated it, been disgusted with his only son. Maybe he did take after Uncle Ernie. In which case, what was stopping him going into Wendy Watkins' garden shed?

He knew the answer to that one too. He was in love with his wife. She was his apple, strong, white and acid-sweet. Wendy Watkins was . . . Lili Marlene.

Three

Jenny Price was happy. She felt a surge of confidence because of Harry Blackmore. A few of her self-doubts were laid to rest, her ponytail swung like the pendulum on her grandfather's old clock and her smile was very white and infectious. Harry Blackmore had asked her especially to look after the newlyweds in the reserved compartment, plus check on a lady in the third class who had a bad leg, *plus* make sure there was nothing wrong with a couple in the front coach – and that could mean only one thing: *he* thought she was good at her job. And if Harry Blackmore thought so then who cared about Ahmed and Marvin?

She carried a tray carefully along the corridor. The door of the first compartment was pushed wide and, inside, the lady with the pretty hair seemed to be staring into space again. She lifted her head as Jenny approached and gave a lovely smile. Jenny stopped and asked her if she would like another coffee.

'No, thank you.' The smile widened. 'You're not a bit clumsy, you know. You're doing awfully well with that tray. You're standing against the light and I can see you perfectly.'

'Oh.' Jenny flushed happily. 'Well . . . it's not hard really.' She liked this woman, there was something special about her. 'Can I get you a sandwich or something?' she persisted.

'I don't think so. I might go along to the buffet car later. It would do me good to move.'

That would mean she would meet awful Marvin. Jenny said, 'No need. Just let me know.'

The smile widened again and Jenny moved on with an even lighter step, her rugby player's legs forgotten.

The couple were in the next but one compartment, sitting on the same seat, side by side, almost welded together. They did not look up until Jenny tapped lightly on the glass and slid their door across. She smiled. 'Would you like a hot drink? Biscuits?'

The girl turned her head, startled. She was blond with one of those very short bubble haircuts immortalized by Ingrid Bergman in *For Whom the Bell Tolls*. It showed her ears and they were like shells, almost translucent. Her eyes were very pale blue and she'd put on a lot of mascara to darken and emphasize them. Jenny thought – surprised at herself – that the girl would be beautiful without so much stuff on her

face. Like an ice queen. But then, perhaps she
didn't want to look like an ice queen, any more
than she herself wanted to look like a rugby
player.

'I'd kill for a cup of tea,' the girl said and
Jenny almost laughed because she sounded just
like anyone else. Ordinary. Nice.

Jenny fetched a tray of tea and put it on
the little table by the window. The man – boy
really – had the same. She had known he would.
Whatever one had, the other would follow. He
tried to find some money and it was good to
be able to murmur, 'Complimentary, sir'. They
were both overwhelmed.

'This is all so – so great!' the girl said.

Jenny smiled. 'I hope you'll be really happy. If
this is a good start . . . well, it is great, isn't it?'

'Oh, thank you . . . thank you.' They were
talking together, laughing, intertwining their
arms to breaking point. Jenny got the impression that the wedding yesterday had been a
bit tricky; apparently the best man had fallen
over and the bride's mother cried all the time.
But now they were on their own and everything
was simply . . . great.

'I'm so glad,' she said, beaming at them as
if she were an old hand at all this. 'Can I get
you something else – a sandwich? We've got all
sorts.'

He said fervently, 'We've got everything we
want. But thanks.'

She was grinning inanely all the way down the two first-class coaches, pouring tea and coffee and handing out biscuits and newspapers. She wished she could go on through into the third class as well. It didn't seem quite fair that they had to queue up at the bar and be served by awful Marvin. Though of course they might get dignified Ahmed. She went back to her station at the side of the bar, smiling still, practically walking on air.

Jeremy Kemp could not quite believe what he was doing – basically, acting like an ordinary human being. First of all the coffee, then the introduction.

'I'm Jeremy Kemp, by the way. Going back to London after a weekend with the parents.'

Sylvia Pemberton could not believe it either; though there were little spurts of irritability, the overpowering aura of anger had gone. She turned slightly to look at him; he had a good face, a long nose and a bit of a lantern jaw but when his dark eyes weren't full of nightmares they were . . . polite.

'I'm Sylvia Pemberton. Going to London.' She giggled. 'Not exactly to Buckingham Palace but the next best thing. I'm going to the House of Commons.'

He hated the name Sylvia and he did not like women who giggled and showed off. He said, 'I see.'

She sensed the change and tried to explain. 'I belong to a group of people who . . . who . . .' She was floundering, just as she would when she saw the MP. She was no good at this sort of thing; she'd never do it.

He glanced at the paper on her lap; of course, a petition. He said with exaggerated patience, 'You're representing a group with a grudge. You want to save a building that should have fallen down a hundred years ago? The flowerbeds in your municipal park are full of weeds? The roads need repair? What is it?'

She should have kept completely silent, cut him dead, maintained an icy dignity. But unexpectedly she was not cowed by him and her dignity did not seem to matter much. She almost spluttered with a rage that outraged his.

'How dare you talk like that about things you can't know anything about!' She paused and rephrased furiously. 'Of which you know less than *nothing*! I suppose just because you bought me a cup of coffee you think you can say what you like!' She took a deep breath. 'If you must know, I represent a reading group!'

He was completely taken aback. 'A reading group? Did you actually say you represent a *reading* group?' He barked a laugh. 'Well. That piece of information was scarcely worth the price of a coffee!'

She fumbled in her purse and found half-a-crown, at least three times the price of the coffee. She flung it into his lap and it rolled onto the gritty floor.

'Take it!' she snapped. 'And I don't want any change.'

The door slid open and the ticket collector stood there watching impassively as Jeremy grovelled for the half-crown. 'I don't want it, change or no change!' He realized they were sounding exactly like a couple of kids in a playground and he didn't care. 'Here. Put it away, for God's sake!' He actually put his hand containing the half-crown on her knee and she shrank away as if he were about to rape her.

The ticket collector said in a monotone, 'All tickets, please.'

'You've already clipped mine,' Jeremy snapped, scrambling back onto his seat.

The ticket collector looked at everyone's ticket and then Sylvia Pemberton's pass. He made no comment but left the door open and made his way down the train to where he knew Harry Blackmore would be. If he had anything to do with anything, that man would be put off at Reading.

Jenny waited in the kitchen for instructions from Ahmed, maybe even a nod of approbation. Instead he turned on her almost hissing, rather like the geese at the school farm.

'Where have you been? We're very busy. Even the guard was asking where you were. Dawdling

63

along with that tea and coffee tray as if you're in another world. Get on with the washing up, *if* you please!'

She came to earth with a bump. It was Harry who had told her to pay special attention to the newlyweds and now he was asking Ahmed where she'd got to; she felt as if he'd stuck a knife in her ribs. And Marvin was grinning like a cat; he seemed to thoroughly enjoy witnessing her telling-off. She drew off some water from the urn and nearly scalded herself, which actually made Marvin laugh. Ahmed ignored her. He was busy dispensing sandwiches and crisps, taking money, giving change, all with such obvious efficiency she could have wept if there had been time. But of course there wasn't; people were topping up their breakfasts, making sure they could work right through lunchtime. It would continue like this until Reading and then it would be clearing-up time. She made more sandwiches and thought of the newlyweds and wondered whether she would ever be married and go on a honeymoon and maybe even travel first-class to get there. Lydia had been so keen about getting married; she had seen it as the final freedom. 'I don't *care* if I'm half-blind,' she had declared, putting a sneer into those last two words. 'I've got as much right as anyone to lead a normal life! I can marry, have kids, bring them up . . . I can rule the world if I want to!'

Jenny smiled to herself. Dear Lydia, always

64

looking for a battle. She had never got one with Jenny who was genetically peaceful. Jenny had not been interested in getting married. Not then.

She thought she might like a winter wedding. That way she could wear boots and a long sort of Russian coat to hide her legs. And one of those fur hats would be nice too. Maybe she would have her hair done in a lot of loops and curls at the back and the hat would go in front of them.

She could hear Harry Blackmore coming along the corridor, telling the passengers that the train was approaching Reading station. He was sliding back the doors with a kind of rhythm: 'We hope you have enjoyed your journey . . .'

She packed the last sandwich in greaseproof paper and glanced sideways to the other end of the bar. Marvin was serving tonic water – ice, a twist of lemon. He fancied himself as a barman, did Marvin. She heard him say, 'Are you all right, madam?' and leaned forward to look at the customer. It was the lady with the hair. She was hanging on to the edge of the bar for dear life.

Jenny swilled her hands quickly and turned to go out of the tiny kitchen and help. She heard Marvin lift the flap and say, 'Let me . . . I'll take that. Lean on me . . .' and she rushed out protectively, knowing that Marvin would snigger afterwards and say, 'One too many.' And it was nothing of the sort.

Harry Blackmore blocked her way.

'Ah. Jenny. You did a good job with that young couple – thanks.'

'It was nothing. Really. I have to go and help one of the passengers—'

'Miss Morrison? She's very unsteady on her feet. But the lad is looking after her and I've got another job for you, if you can be spared.'

Ahmed was behind her, come to see what she was up to, presumably.

Harry said, 'Is it all right if Jenny clears up the third class now? It's just that we might well have some kind of troublemaker on board. The ticket inspector has reported a man behaving oddly towards another passenger – the widow of one of our managers. I wondered whether Jenny could make sure she's all right. Maybe pour some oil on troubled waters.'

'*Miss Price* will be clearing all the coaches during the next forty minutes,' Ahmed pronounced. 'So that will be in order. But I really do not see how she can be expected to identify your troublemaker.'

Harry smiled. 'She won't have any trouble finding Mrs Pemberton. She has a nose for people. I imagine that is why you employed her. Her natural empathy.'

Ahmed looked astounded and Jenny blushed gaudily.

She blurted, 'It's just that . . . I think that passenger, Miss Morrison, would appreciate a woman . . .'

Ahmed said swiftly, 'Marvin is probably better at coping with that particular problem, Miss Price. If there is some small way in which you can help Mr Blackmore, I am only too happy to release you from normal duties.'

Jenny found herself ushered into the third-class coach. Harry said in her ear, 'She doesn't look old enough to be a widow, Jenny. Rather pretty . . .' He blinked and added quickly, 'Not that I noticed much about her. But she used to work in the office and . . .' He abandoned further explanation and said, 'If she looks bothered, ask her to come with you as I want a word. But I don't think it will come to that.'

Jenny felt quite nervous. 'Well . . . if I can find her. I'll do my best.'

Harry had a flash of inspiration. 'She's wearing a hat. Straw with flowers around the brim. You can't miss it.'

'She'll have taken it off by now,' Jenny objected.

'She had it on when old Misery Guts looked at her pass. That's how he knew she was staff – she's got a first-class pass. Come on, Jenny. You don't have to do anything if you don't want to. Just keep your eyes peeled and let me know if there's any difficulty.' He glanced at his watch. 'You've got to clear the decks anyway.' He grinned at her and she thought her heart might be melting like in the magazines Lydia read.

She stared at his carnation then lifted her eyes to the round, intelligent face. He was so absolutely completely . . . *nice*. She took a firm hold of her tray and edged past the people who were standing in the corridor. She turned and grinned across their heads. 'Well, here goes then,' she said. And then blushed vividly as he grinned back.

Sylvia knew that she should have been icily silent before now but perhaps it was not too late; she stared out of the window as the river came into view. It was a delightfully calm picture of the Thames; Sylvia did not feel calm but at least she could be silent. She breathed as evenly as possible and thought she could hear her heart slamming against her ribs.

Jeremy discovered he was unbearably provoked by being so obviously sent to Coventry. How dared she? Sitting there in her Queen of the May outfit, ignoring him for the rest of the passengers to see. He searched his mind for something to say that she could not ignore. 'Tell me, why are you not using your first-class pass? Enjoy slumming it with the proletariat, do you?'

She abandoned her dignity with her silence and turned on him almost hissing. 'If you must know – you *horrible* man – this is my husband's staff card. He earned this status. Not me. All right?'

'Doesn't extend the privilege to his wife, eh?'

She stared at him for a moment. Of course he could not possibly know that Pem had gone and there was no need to tell him. But suddenly, for Pem's sake, she could not let it go. Her petty anger drained away. 'He's dead,' she replied quietly. 'He extended to me every privilege he possibly could. There are some I simply cannot take, even now.'

At last Jeremy was brought low. Aghast, he realized he had insulted a widow. And a crippled woman at that. How could he possibly have behaved so boorishly? He thought of his mother and of how appalled she would be.

He said, 'Oh God . . . I'm so terribly sorry. I don't know why . . . my behaviour has been absolutely unforgivable.'

She said in the same quiet voice, 'Yes. Yes, it has. But I expect there's a reason for that. So let's forget it.' She turned away again and looked at the view. The mist had cleared completely now. It was going to be a beautiful day.

Jeremy swallowed, then cleared his throat, then glanced surreptitiously around the compartment. Everyone was studiously ignoring the two of them.

He pitched his voice as low as it would go. 'Listen. Please talk to me. I'm a complete failure – everything I do goes wrong. I know you can't possibly forgive what I said just now, but . . . can you tell me about this – this reading group? Just talk to me. Please. Sylvia, please.'

She was incapable of sustaining anger and she had already registered the nightmares behind his dark eyes. She turned and studied him very deliberately. She saw a young man, probably the same age as herself so he had doubtless seen action in the war; a very intelligent young man who was hurt. Not physically injured but somehow as crippled as she was herself. He bore her inspection but a muscle twitched in his jaw and she saw him swallow.

She took a deep breath, let it go and said, 'Call me Sylvie. No-one uses Sylvia and it sounds odd to me.'

'Sylvie.' He said the name experimentally. It sounded quite different from Sylvia. No longer pretentious. 'My name is actually Jeremy, but I prefer Joe. If you could . . . you know.'

'Well, Joe is certainly not pretentious!' She smiled. 'That's what this is about, isn't it? You think I'm pretentious. Is it my hat?'

'Of course not!' Though he had found the hat ridiculous at first. Now it seemed to go with the new name: Sylvie. A truly sylvan hat. 'And I don't think you're pretentious at all. I think . . .' He frowned slightly, concentrating. 'I think I was jealous of you. Because you seem to know what you're doing. And I don't.'

She laughed; a proper laugh, not a giggle.

'Nothing could be further from fact!' She stopped laughing and sighed. 'I've been chosen to present this petition and to put forward a good case and I'm the last person to do it properly. I'm a background person. Not a front one at all.'

Jeremy – Joe – was fascinated. 'So that's why you dressed up?' He realized he was being rude again and added quickly, 'I mean, you're looking the part. Of a front person. I mean—'

She laughed again. She had a good laugh, not loud but full of amusement.

'You're sounding like me! Not saying what you really want to say. Because you're nervous.'

He was about to deny that emphatically and then knew she was right. He was nervous because he wanted to make a good impression and he couldn't remember the last time he'd wanted to do that.

He smiled and nodded. 'But we were both very much to the point when we were angry just now. Is this petition something you can get angry about?'

She considered the question. 'I'm not sure. This MP – Roger Hargreaves – has been so co-operative, on our side, really. I can't very well get angry with him, can I? He said he would accept the petition outside the House and the newspaper people would take photographs and then ask him questions and I would get a chance to put our point of view.'

He smelled a publicity exercise.

'Tell me about it. Pretend I'm the MP and tell me about this reading group.' It still sounded so silly.

She took another deep breath. 'Well. We're all damaged in some way. And there are lots of clubs and things for people like us but we wanted to *do* something – not just drink coffee and play cards. D'you see?'

'Certainly. So you formed a reading group.' It was making sense.

'Yes. And we choose a book, read it, tell the others what we think . . .'

'Sounds good to me.'

'Well, we want to do other things. And they're building a new swimming pool. It would be really good for most of us. But we won't be able to use it. We've seen the plans and there are steps up to the doors and no handrails and the cubicles aren't big enough for wheelchairs and the toilet facilities are inadequate.'

'I get it.' He did get it; injustices were his speciality.

'Nothing to be angry about, really. Unless they turn down our revised plans.'

'You've done revised plans?'

'Yes. One of our group is a civil engineer. He built bridges in France and Germany during the invasion. He lost both arms.'

'Oh my God. How can he draw?'

'I do it for him,' she said simply. She smiled. 'I

told you I was a background person. I put the pencil on the paper and have a ruler in my left hand and he tells me where to go and how far to go and when to turn an angle. I quite liked geometry at school, so we manage.'

He had a vision of the two of them poring over graph paper.

He said, 'Get that story into the interview somehow. Human interest. The newspapers will snap it up. There will be a picture of you without the bloody MP – whatever his name is – and the publicity will be centred on you and not him.'

She flushed slightly. 'I don't think I want that, Joe. I told you—'

'A background person. I know.'

'I think if I give the broader picture—'

'You'll get bogged down. Lost. Whereas if you paint a cameo of an armless man guiding a girl with a bad leg—'

'Joe. Stop it. Listen to yourself.'

He paused. 'Was I being offensive?'

'Yes.'

He gnawed his lip. 'I'm sorry, Sylvie. I didn't mean . . . I do it quite often apparently. Or so my parents tell me.'

She looked past him and he glanced up and saw that a girl in uniform was standing by the open doorway. The girl avoided his eye and spoke to Sylvie.

'Everything all right, madam?'

Sylvie nodded. 'Yes, thank you.'

'The guard wondered whether you might need some help at Paddington.'

Sylvie said, 'That's most kind.'

Jeremy blurted, 'I'll take you to Westminster. Get a taxi.'

Jenny said very firmly, 'The guard asked me to tell you that there are plenty of first-class seats available.'

Sylvie spoke even more firmly. 'I can manage perfectly well.' She smiled at Jenny. 'Please thank the guard for me.' She waited until Jenny had gone then said, 'Look, Joe. I would rather do this thing by myself. It's very important to me. Can't you see that?' She shook her head at him so that the flowers on the hat bounced. 'Change the subject. Tell me what you do.'

Joe looked at the flowers then at the grey eyes beneath the hat brim.

He said, 'Nothing much. I try to write plays. But no-one thinks they're any good.' There was a long pause; she was waiting for more. He said, 'I was in the RAF. I was lucky. Not many were. I feel . . . I have to do something for them.'

'Are your plays about them?' she asked.

'In a way.' He stared at the dirty floor. Then he said, 'They thought they were dying for a better world. Look at the world. Do you think it was worth dying for this . . . dump?'

She was silent for a long time. Then she said quietly, 'You told me to paint a picture – a

74

cameo you said. Could you do that? Just a small bit of what you've told me?'

'How do you know I'm not doing that?'

'I don't of course. But . . . you're somehow letting all that awfulness, that sacrifice, become a millstone. Drag you down. Swamp you. If you could find something small that might be sad or funny or hopeful or not hopeful . . .'

He stared at her. 'How can you know? About the millstone? I haven't said enough for you to *know* . . . have I?'

She lifted her shoulders. 'You must have done.' She smiled. 'Anyway, I know now what you meant about the picture – the cameo. A small thing can show a big thing – is that it?'

He nodded. 'That's it exactly, Sylvie.'

She fumbled under the seat and came up with two sticks. 'I must find the toilet before we run into Paddington,' she said, folding up the petition and slipping it into her jacket pocket.

He started to help her and then stopped and was rewarded with another smile.

After she had gone he thought about something his mother had said. It was when she was trying to interest him in her friend's unmarried daughter. He had refused utterly to co-operate and she had nodded, understanding exactly. 'It's got to happen naturally, hasn't it, Jeremy? One day you'll meet someone. On a bus or a train or in a shop.'

The image of Sylvie's petition stayed in his mind. He would go on thinking about it.

Marvin said, 'Now, you're sure you're OK? Jenny will be along in a minute to tidy up, so if there's anything you need, just let her know. I'll ask the guard to see you onto the platform at Paddington.'

Mary smiled. 'I'm so terribly sorry. You're all very kind. I can't thank you enough.'

Marvin flushed, which he knew emphasized his acne. 'Just doing my job,' he mumbled.

'I expect you're busy.'

Marvin knew he should be cleaning up the bar but this was a much better option. His feet were killing him and Jenny had been practically shoved into the third class with her tray so Ahmed would have no-one save himself on whom to inflict his notoriously high standards.

So he smiled benignly. 'I'm busy doing my job here at the moment,' he said.

Mary was enchanted. She could not see his acne or his brace.

'Why don't you sit down for a moment?' she suggested. 'The young stewardess sat down for a few minutes. I think it's good to rest your legs now and then.'

He was amazed; Jenny was never still. He sat down gratefully.

'That would be Jenny,' he said.

'Jenny . . .' Mary savoured the name. 'It suits her.'

'She's new. Very keen.' He stretched his long legs sideways so that there was no risk of touching hers and felt his flush abating.

'Yes. And enthusiastic. Interested in what she's doing, the people she's helping. I hope she doesn't lose that.'

Marvin glanced at the woman covertly: dammit, she was beautiful. He flushed again because she caught his eye but then her gaze wandered off behind his head somewhere.

She said, 'I think she's wrong about herself though.'

He blinked, wondering whether he had missed something. 'Sorry?'

She smiled. 'She thinks she's clumsy and after that little performance with my drink, I know I am!' She tried to laugh and he thought for a dreadful moment she might be on the verge of tears.

He blurted, 'Anyone can stumble on a train. It's like a boat. You've got to get your sea legs.'

'Yes. You're probably right.'

'It's the same for Jenny. She's not really clumsy. She'll get used to doing two things at once!' He laughed. He felt in control of his face for once. 'She's steady enough really. Strong. She's got a good shape – d'you know what I mean? Sort of . . . I don't know. How it should be.'

The woman focused on him, her wide smile becoming understanding.

She said, 'Are you an artist by any chance?'

He guffawed. 'Failed art at school. Failed most things really.'

'It's the sort of thing artists notice. Shapes. Good ones and not so good. And you're right. I didn't see her very well but Jenny has a good shape.'

He was surprised but delighted. Here was this woman – a beautiful woman – talking to him properly. And not about food and drink either.

He said, 'Are you an artist then?'

'I was. Not any more.'

'But you still know about shapes and things.'

She laughed. 'I suppose I do. Yes. That's good. It's not all wasted.' She paused. 'I didn't think I had anything else to give. But yes, I do know about shapes and things.' She sat back. 'You are a very reassuring young man, thank you.'

He was embarrassed but not hotly. He said, 'I usually say the wrong thing.' He sighed. 'I told Jenny she had good hips for babies. She was really upset.'

There was no response for a moment and Marvin could have kicked himself. Why on earth had he told her that? He must be mad. She would complain to Ahmed and he would be out of a job and he wasn't in any union and—

'If you said it in one way,' she said quietly, 'it

might be hurtful. But in another way it could be the biggest compliment a woman could have.'

'I meant it like that,' he said quickly. 'A compliment. Because she is such a good shape. But it didn't come out right or something. She was angry. It's my fault, I'm hopeless. She thinks the world of people like Harry Blackmore, the guard. He doesn't wear a brace and he probably doesn't know what acne is!'

There was another little silence then she leaned across the table. 'You think a lot of Jenny, don't you?'

'She . . .' he fumbled for words. 'She's like we were saying – right. A proper person. Someone to be by you. Always.'

Dammit, the woman looked suddenly sad. Why the devil did he always say the wrong thing? He tried to apologize even as he was getting to his feet but she waved a hand at him.

'No, no. It's not you at all. Please.'

'I have to go. Really. I didn't mean to upset you.'

'You haven't.' She seemed to make a gigantic effort and gave that wide smile again. 'Honestly. I want to wish you luck. You deserve . . . well, good luck.'

'And to you,' he said meaninglessly.

But it cheered her up still more and she said, 'What's your name?'

'Marvin,' he said.

'Mine is Mary Morrison. Good luck, Marvin.'

79

'Good luck, Miss Morrison.' He had never in all his life spoken to an older woman like this. Especially one who was obviously, well, special. He went back to the buffet car swaying easily with the motion of the train. Ahmed was already in the kitchen counting money. The narrow, clever face turned to him as he went through.

'Well done, Marvin,' Ahmed said.

Marvin nearly fell through the hatch. This really was his lucky day.

Mary Morrison closed her eyes and let the rhythm of the train take her over. It wouldn't be long now. If she sipped her drink slowly and then went along to the toilet, they would be running into Paddington. She would go straight to the taxi rank, get herself to Harley Street and then . . . Well, she could surely find somewhere to have lunch, and afterwards there was the exhibition. She did not need to go to that although she knew that it gave the whole thing a certain cachet if she was there to talk to people. In fact Davis Bryson, who ran the gallery and had arranged the exhibition for her, had said something about a short talk introducing the retrospective. She had turned him down instantly. 'You know I'm a private person, Davis. If you're hoping to get me on the lecture circuit, think again!'

She smiled as she recalled his instant retort. 'Lecture circuit be damned! I'm asking for some personal comments on your work over the years.

To a handful of your fans. That's all. Is it too much to ask?'

Of course it wasn't. Davis had been a constant support over the past twenty years. Mary had never been – was never going to be – the sort of painter whose work was known by everyone, art lovers or not. But she had a following; there was no doubt about that. And that was probably due in some part to Davis Bryson and his Cork Street gallery.

Her eyes were burning and she opened and closed them gently to stimulate the tear ducts just as that specialist had told her to do. What was his name? Something beginning with Y. She felt a moment of panic because she simply could not remember and now that her eyes were going she suspected other faculties as well. It became imperative that she should recall the name of the eye specialist. She searched her mind. When had she last heard it? From Andrew. Yes, Andrew had spoken his name only an hour or so ago. Andrew had left her on that platform seat saying, 'Give my regards to old . . .' To old who? And why had Andrew left her there like that? That question, which she had avoided so carefully, burned into her mind. When the announcement had come over the speakers that the train was ready for boarding, the walk across the platform had been a nightmare; she had had no idea where the doors were. If it hadn't been for that nice guard with the sweet-smelling carnation in his buttonhole she would still be waiting on the platform.

Tears flooded her eyes and she blinked them away, furious with herself for self-pity. Andrew was not her husband, thank goodness – no sense of duty to tie him to an older wife. And anyway, he had no idea how far her sight had deteriorated. She still went to her studio each day and she could find her way around the house blindfold. She smiled at the metaphor. That's all it would be, after all. Blind man's buff. And then she stopped smiling because so many children's games were cruel. And blind man's buff was certainly no exception. This morning, the game had not been fun at all. *Why* had Andrew gone like that? Even if he did not realize how bad she was he certainly knew she would have difficulty finding her way to the train. She had fought against his pity all these months. Perhaps she had won. Perhaps this morning was his way of telling her he could not cope with her going blind.

She shivered suddenly. The thought of life without Andrew was unbearable. She would not be able to fill her days with work – with anything. She closed her eyes tightly in a frantic effort to control herself and a voice said from the open door, 'Oh dear. Are you all right?'

She mumbled something and the voice became concerned. 'You look so white. Can I do anything?'

Mary opened her eyes and a face swam into view. Blond hair and blue eyes, an aura of youth. But not like Jenny. Not innocent like Jenny.

She murmured, 'Could you pass me my drink?'

The girl did so and laughed. 'Nothing like a gin to get you going, is there? I had to have three before I could go to my wedding yesterday.'

Of course. The newlyweds. She had heard them come in, shepherded by the guard. The very blue eyes came closer. 'Are you sure you're all right?'

Mary managed a smile and a nod. 'I'm naturally pale.'

'Oh, so am I! It's quite a problem, isn't it? I've got an inch of pancake on for today!' She laughed and went on towards the buffet car and Mary sat up straighter and told herself not to be such a self-pitying fool. And then it came to her. 'Give my regards to old Yorke,' Andrew had said earlier. That was his name. The eye specialist. Mr Henry Yorke. She forced one of her smiles. At least she wasn't losing all her marbles.

Jenny skipped the rest of the coaches and went back to Ahmed who was doing the books.

'I think everything is all right with Mrs Pemberton,' she said. 'I'll report back to Mr Blackmore. Is he in the brake van?'

He nodded. 'You still have to clear the first class, Miss Price.'

Behind him, Marvin checked bottles but took a moment to look over his shoulder and wink at her. She tightened her lips and went on through the buffet car to the first class. Her grandfather said that men who winked at women had no respect for them. She could believe that of Marvin.

She started off at a run down the first-class corridor, her tray held in front of her like a shield. If she hurried she would have time to tell Harry that she would keep an eye on Mrs Pemberton when the train arrived at Paddington. He would surely give her another of his compliments and the glow from that would last her for the rest of the day.

But the door to the first compartment was open and the lady with the gorgeous hair was staring out of the window, pale and set-faced. Jenny hesitated and then stopped.

'I wondered, would you like some help at Paddington? I could walk round to the taxi rank with you.'

The lady looked round, startled.

Jenny saw with a shock that the lady's eyes had filled with tears. She blurted, 'I'm so sorry, I didn't mean to make you jump.'

'It doesn't matter . . .' The lady controlled herself with an obvious effort and forced a smile. 'It's just that I've met with such kindness today.

It makes me feel . . . humble. Is that the right word?'

Jenny said, 'I don't know. But I do know what you mean. Like crying when you're happy.'

'Exactly. The guard was wonderful when I got on the train this morning. And then you came along like a ray of sunshine. And then that dear boy from the buffet.'

Jenny coughed loudly. Marvin? A dear boy?

The tears were mopped up with a surprisingly large handkerchief.

'That's better.' The smile was back in place. 'I have to tell you about the gaffe he made this morning.'

'Gaffe?'

'Mistake. No, not a mistake. A bit of a blunder. I understood it because I used to be an artist. You are perfectly proportioned. You are strong and capable. You are content with yourself. You are caring. You are everything a woman should be. That's what he meant when he said about your hips being good for childbirth. I can see it must have sounded just dreadful. He knows that now and feels so embarrassed.'

Jenny said, 'You're talking about Marvin? The barman? He has a brace.'

'I didn't notice the brace. He told me about it and about his acne. He feels very self-conscious about himself.'

'But – but he's always so rude!'

The lady said quietly, 'That's self-protection,

85

Jenny. It's his way of dealing with how he feels.' She smiled. 'I understand because I'm feeling like a snail without its shell at the moment.'

'Are you?' Jenny said, surprised. Then she noticed that the girl with the ice-blue eyes was leaning out into the corridor, making signals. 'Oh dear. I've got to get on. But I'll be back when we get to Paddington.'

She put Mary Morrison's glass on her tray and made her way down the corridor. The newlyweds had untangled themselves and tidied their own table.

The girl said, 'Are we nearly there? Should we get our things together? Will the train start back straightaway?'

Jenny reassured them as best she could. Her mind felt woolly just like it did when she used to do tests at school. Thin, lanky Marvin? Talking about her to the lady with the hair? Marvin who always sniggered when she got into trouble with Ahmed? Marvin who winked at her knowingly and told her she had big hips? How dared he discuss her!

She went on down the coach and there was Mr Blackmore, in charge, capable as ever, ready to be first on the platform and make certain every passenger got off. She felt a pang that it had not been him who sat by the lady with the hair and talked about her. Mr Blackmore was the sort of man she and Lydia used to dream about. Lydia might not have had much physical sight but her inner vision was amazing. 'I don't want any white chargers, Jen,' she would giggle. 'A nice big limousine will be perfectly all right by me. And as for knights in shining armour, who wants to knock their elbows on chain mail every time they turn round?' She had waited for Jenny to stop laughing and clutching her stomach and said soberly, 'Seriously, I want someone who is kind. That's the main thing. And after that, I'd like them to have a bit of dignity, a bit of, I dunno, authority. Like Mr Cousins.' Mr Cousins was the headmaster. 'So,' Lydia went on, screwing up her eyes in concentration, 'they'll have to be clean and tidy. Not dressy exactly but their clothes must show they care . . .'

Of course that could apply to Marvin. His uniform gave him a bit of authority. But kindness – Jenny had never considered him kind. He was too quick with the quip and the dig and the need to be clever. No, it was Harry Blackmore who fitted all Lydia's requirements – and Jenny's too. The carnation was the finishing touch.

She said breathlessly, 'I think everything is all right with Mrs Pemberton, sir. I found her straightaway because of the hat. With flowers on it. The hat I mean. And the man is still with her, but he's not shouting any more.'

Harry Blackmore grinned congratulations.

'Jenny, you're a good influence. You're going to go far in this job. Well done.'

Jenny was overcome. 'Oh, Mr Blackmore.'

'Ahmed told me you had qualities. And that's high praise coming from him.'

'Oh, Mr *Black*more!'

'Credit where credit's due, Jenny.' He scraped past her. 'I'll go up the train before we arrive. Check on her and the couple in the front coach.'

'Good luck, Mr Blackmore.'

'I'll stay up that end for the last announcement and see to Mrs Pemberton. Could you keep an eye on Miss Morrison? She'll have difficulty getting onto the platform.'

Miss Morrison. So that was her name. Jenny stood and watched him negotiate the doors; she knew she was smiling and she knew it wasn't anything to do with Marvin.

In the driver's cab, Albert Priddy was hanging out, checking the signals as the lines quadrupled and branched off towards Uxbridge. The morning sun was strong now and shot small rainbows off the side windows of the signal boxes. On his left some newly painted scrawls blazed a greeting on the concrete embankment and above that, homely-looking laundry blew on the balconies of the council flats.

Albert smiled quietly to himself. These were the sort of signs that made him feel at home wherever he went. Big cities might be run by clever and self-important people, but they were inhabited by protesting youth, women who ran homes and men who loved them. He must be feeling maudlin this morning because suddenly he felt he loved all the women in the world who did the laundry and made homes. How daft could you get?

The train roared beneath a gantry and he realized that he had not registered the signal. It did not horrify him; he would have known instantly had it been at danger. Even so he applied the brakes gently for the home signals and said aloud, 'Home signal. No hold-ups then.'

Wilf was leaning on his shovel, looking out the other side. He turned and grinned and said, 'On time again. We're too bloody good, that's our trouble!'

Albert grinned too but registered the bloody. Gertie was right, it got into a habit if you weren't careful. No need for it after all. Wendy Watkins used it casually whenever she opened her mouth. Actually, it made him laugh, and he laughed now to himself. Yes, he had to admit it. He loved her too. He wished he could be honest with Gertie and tell her that because he loved her so much, he loved Janie next door and Wendy Watkins the other side who called him Al Capone and all the unknown women in the flats above his head who were hanging out their washing above the smuts of the busy rails. It occurred to him that he was very close to understanding . . . things. Life, perhaps.

Four

Jenny had never been a quick learner. After her parents were killed in the Bristol raids and she was pulled out of the rubble that had been their house, miraculously alive and intact, she turned against school and for a whole year she did nothing but run away. Her foster mum was lovely and she longed to be able to help Jenny in some way but the more she talked to her, the worse it seemed to get. Jenny did not know why she kept running off, and she had no idea where she was going. She always maintained that she would know when she got there. Meanwhile, each time it happened, they put her into a big house called a hostel where they could keep an eye on her and then she went back to her foster home and it would all start again. They asked her whether her foster mum smacked her or got cross with her. She always told them the truth, that Mum was lovely and always tried to talk to her and find out what the trouble was. The real trouble was that Jenny did not know what the trouble was. And as her efforts to explain got more and more convoluted, she gave up and hardly spoke at all.

It got worse when she went to the 'big school'. She hated the remedial class and everyone in it. She ran away from there to escape, as well as to find something else. Then, at the age of fourteen she was referred to an educational psychologist and told she was a special child and that she was going to be sent to a special school in the country where she would be very happy. She would live there during term time and go home to her foster mum for the holidays.

Winderslake *was* lovely, she could see that. Just as her foster mum was lovely. But Winderslake was better than the foster home and the hostel. It was in the country and she knew that it was the countryside she was running to. She was nearer her goal and maybe she would find it somewhere near the school. The headmaster, Mr Cousins, was assisted by two teachers and half a dozen helpers. Jenny never remembered the names of the teachers but two of the helpers were called Maisie and Marcia. Like a singing duo on the radio.

She shared a room with a girl called Lydia Brahms and at first she thought it was going to be awful because Lydia was the tidiest person she had ever met and Jenny – according to her real mum – took after her real dad who could never find anything. 'I put it down here,' he would say plaintively. 'And now it's gone.'

'Are there rules about being tidy?' Jenny asked Lydia.

Lydia laughed. 'We make our own rules in Winderslake. And my rule is that I know exactly where everything is.'

Jenny said, 'I've never been anywhere where you made up your own rules. Supposing we say we're not going to any lessons?'

Lydia shrugged. 'Then we don't go.'

'But then it wouldn't be a school. We wouldn't learn anything.'

'We might learn that it's boring to have nothing to do.'

Lydia Brahms had a lot of hair which hung over her face so that you had a job to see her expression but Jenny could tell instantly that she was clever. Even so, there had to be a flaw in what she was saying.

'Supposing you found something else to do. And you weren't bored.'

Lydia pulled some of her hair straight down over her nose and held it taut. 'That would be OK,' she said and stuck the end of the hair in her mouth.

Jenny still did not believe her. 'They'd come after me and bring me back,' she said.

'So you'd run away. You've done it before.'

'How do you know?'

'Because you've learned something. You've

92

learned that the authorities come after you and bring you back.'

'Well, yes. And they'd do it here too, wouldn't they?'

Lydia shrugged. 'Dunno really. But you could go for a walk and come back yourself. That would be OK. That would be your own rule. You go out. But you come back.'

Jenny was enchanted. 'Really?' She still couldn't believe it even when Lydia swore a dreadful oath that made her giggle. 'They'd say I was a danger to myself.'

Lydia sighed deeply. 'You haven't got any imagination. You start off by going into the village. Back and forth for a week. Pick a few flowers. Press 'em. Make a collection. Get a reputation for being a botanist.'

'A bottomist?' Jenny collapsed onto her bed in a heap of giggles.

'Haven't you heard of botany?' Lydia asked in disgust, actually flipping her hair over her shoulder. 'It's when you're interested in plants and flowers. Nothing to do with your bottom, you ridiculous child!'

Jenny sobered. 'Sorry. I do like flowers. I didn't know I was a botanist.'

'Learned something already and you haven't been to one lesson!' Lydia was grinning, her black eyes snapping at the ceiling. Jenny glanced up. Nothing there except the light fitting.

'What are you looking at?' she asked.

'Nothing!' The head came down and the hair hung before it again. 'Anyway, why are you so anxious to run away all the time? Where are you going?'

'Everyone asks that. I don't know. But there was a garden once, with kidney-bean poles. I used to hide inside them with a cat called Tompkinson. Mum and Dad would tell me to come out and someone said leave her alone.'

'Are Mum and Dad dead?'

'Yes. They would have taken me with them. I know they would. But they weren't allowed.'

Lydia said nothing for a long time and Jenny went on unpacking and trying to keep everything tidy. She had three pairs of shoes and a pair of wellingtons. She put them in a neat row.

Lydia said, 'You could borrow mine if you like.'

'Borrow? Borrow what?' Jenny looked at her line of shoes again. It was satisfying to be tidy.

'My mum and dad.'

Jenny did not know what to make of that. She said a polite thank you and wondered whether Lydia was even more special than she was herself.

Lydia seemed to know what she was thinking because her voice became belligerent. 'I'm not as daft as you think, Jenny Price! You'll need a mum and dad when you get married. To arrange the wedding and give you away and things.'

Jenny gaped. 'Married? I'm not getting married!'

Lydia spat out her hair. 'You will one day! Just because we're in a special school doesn't mean we can't get married and have babies and everything. I bet you don't even know where babies come from, do you?'

'Yes I do,' Jenny said. 'I didn't run away for that lesson. Anyway, everyone knows where babies come from.'

Even so, Lydia told her again and then asked, 'Don't you want babies?' Jenny said she had never even thought about it and Lydia told her to think about it now. 'We're no different to anyone else. An' if we want to get married then we should be allowed to get married.'

'I thought you said there was no allowing and no rules.'

Lydia stopped waving her hands about and grabbed her hair again. 'Not here,' she said. 'But out there.'

Jenny said, 'It doesn't matter to me. I don't want to get married. Ever.'

'I do. I want to marry someone who thinks I'm the best in the world – the cleverest, most beautiful. Et cetera, et cetera.'

'Oh.' Jenny tried to peer inside the hair. The dark, dark eyes seemed to be closed. She said, 'Well, all right. When the time comes, you've got a mum and dad ready.'

'Yes. Well. They're the trouble. Over-protective. That's what they are. They think I should stay at home and smile and be looked after.'

'Oh.' Jenny was completely bewildered.

Lydia went on gloomily, 'All mums and dads think that people who have got something wrong with them ought not to get married and pass on their . . . their thing to babies. But I just thought if there were two of us and we badgered enough, well, between us we might talk them round.'

Jenny nodded, then realized Lydia's eyes were still closed and said comfortably, 'All right. I don't mind badgering.'

Lydia stood up impatiently. 'You don't *have* to agree with me, you know. Anyway, I'm going down for tea now. Cheerio.'

She made for the door and fell over the line of shoes.

Lydia refused to speak to Jenny until the evening of the next day. When Jenny kept apologizing, she put her hands over her ears. At breakfast the next morning Jenny tried to steer her into the dining room and got a cuff on her ear for her pains. At her yelp of pain, Maisie, one of the helpers, said, 'Hey. What's going on?' And Jenny said, 'Just knocked myself on the door.' Maisie said, 'Your foster mum said you were clumsy. That's why we put you in with

Lydia. She'll force you to be neat-fingered.' And Jenny, who had been hoping they would move her to another room, said, 'Oh . . . good.' And Lydia gave a bark of a laugh.

That night Lydia had a bath and came out smelling of something sweet. Jenny sat cross-legged on her bed watching her like a hawk, ready to pounce if anything was in her way. Now that she knew about it, it was so obvious that Lydia couldn't see much even though she swung confidently around Jenny's bed and over to her own. She said conversationally, 'It's Aroma of Arabia. Had it last Christmas.'

Jenny gulped. Then said quickly, 'It's very nice.'

'It's filthy, actually. Cheap stuff. Because my aunty thinks if I can't see I can't smell either.'

Jenny said desperately, 'I didn't realize. I could have guided you or something. I didn't know.'

'Everybody knows. And nobody guides me unless I ask them. And I never ask them.'

'Look. I'm sorry. I really am. I *didn't* know. You kept pulling your hair over your face . . . I just didn't know. I mean, I'm here because I'm thick, so that's probably why I didn't know.'

Lydia jumped on her bed in sudden fury. 'You are not thick! How dare you call yourself names! I'm a brilliant conversationalist and I was just enjoying the fact that I'd got someone decent to talk to when you go and humiliate me.'

'I didn't know. I told you a hundred times. I didn't know you couldn't see!' There was a little silence and she added miserably, 'I can't read or write or add up and my logical processes are no good.'

Lydia put her head back, stared at the ceiling and screamed. While she took breath, the door flew open and Marcia, the evening helper, stood there.

'What's going on?' she said, staring from bed to bed.

'I screamed,' Lydia explained.

Marcia visibly strived for patience. 'Any particular reason?'

'I was very frustrated. And it helps the blood pressure to express frustration in one form or another.'

'Not relaxing for anyone else in the vicinity however,' Marcia said.

'Better than messing up the room which, if I could see, I might well have done.'

Marcia said, 'Well, I'd better count my blessings then, hadn't I?' She glanced at Jenny. 'You all right, love? You don't take any notice of this crazy person, I hope.'

'I'm fine,' Jenny said in a small voice.

'Takes a day or two to settle in here. It's so different. Think about tomorrow and what you would like to do. Weather forecast is good and the autumn colours are wonderful round here.'

'Thanks, Marcia,' Lydia said from her bed.

'You could take this one off our hands for a couple of hours.' Marcia nodded at the other bed. 'Describe them to her. Get some fresh air into her lungs.'

'Thanks, Marcia,' Lydia said again.

'I'm serious. You two should get to know each other. Cousins thinks you'll get on well.' She sighed. 'I'm not so sure. But then, he doesn't have to hear you scream and threaten vandalism.' She closed the door with a click.

Lydia said, 'It drives me mad when she gets the last word in. Notice she closed the door so that I'd hear and know the evening's entertainment was over!'

'D'you always go on like this?' Jenny asked.

'Yes,' Lydia said absently and sniffed beneath the sleeve of her pyjamas. 'D'you know, I think I'll have another bath and get this dreadful smell off me.' She drifted towards the door and Jenny leaned forward and checked that the floor was clear. Lydia grinned. 'I know what you're doing. It's all right, you'll never leave stuff on the floor again. That's how you learn.' She opened the door and stood there for a moment. Then she said, 'Listen. You're not thick. You haven't learned anything because you're always running away. I can teach you Braille. It's fun. You'll be able to write ordinary stuff easily then.'

Jenny felt herself flush. 'I don't think . . . you don't understand. I've been tested. I am not able to learn things.'

'Tested. Psychologists. Doctors. What do they know? I'll teach you. Part of the deal, OK? I teach you and you tell me things.'

'What things?'

'First, the colours of the trees. When we go for this walk looking for this little bit of heaven you're after, I come with you and you tell me about . . . everything. I'll help you to find your kidney-bean heaven. What d'you say?'

Jenny did not know what to say. Lydia started fidgeting so she had to say something.

'You mean I'll run away – we'll run away together – and it won't be running away?'

'Well. Yes. More or less.'

Jenny grinned across the room. 'I say yes. Yes, yes, yes.'

'I think I've got it.' Lydia went into the hall and called back over her shoulder, 'Don't wait up, darling. I might have a couple of drinks while I'm out.'

Jenny looked at the closed door and felt a great wave of laughter sweep over her. It was lovely. She snuggled under the covers and reached over to put out the light.

They went out every day that week. Lydia called it 'Beating the bounds' but really it was to get everyone used to them disappearing each morning and to give the people around the village the opportunity to know them.

'If we leave it till the afternoon, we might be roped into something else,' Lydia said sagely.

'Also, it's getting dark earlier and earlier. Besides,' she appeared to be looking Jenny straight in the eye, 'if I do my bit of the bargain first, you're morally bound to do your bit. Got it?'

'Got it,' Jenny said without enthusiasm.

But strangely enough she didn't mind too much settling at one of the tables in the library and following Lydia's fingers over the ups and downs of her latest Braille book. It was so different from anything she had ever done before and Lydia did not mention the word 'reading'. 'Just get the letters. It's like a game. Like a typewriter inside your head. You print up the letters and they make shapes. Don't try to write them down. Just see them against the back of your eyes. I'll do the reading for you.' And after Jenny had laboriously identified each letter and each group of letters, she did the whole thing again while Lydia told her what the groups of letters said.

'He pressed her fevered body against his.'

Jenny gave a small, shocked laugh. 'You're making that up!'

'No. Someone else made it up. Not me. It gets better.'

'Go on then. What does it say next?'

'That's all you did. The first line. Now run your fingers gently over each word – come on, I'll guide you – and say them. Say the words. Go on.'

'He pressed her fevered body against his,' Jenny said woodenly.

'No. You're going too fast. We've only got to "pressed". Do it again, word by word.'

'But I can remember what you said!'

'Never mind. Just do what I'm asking. OK? It's part of the bargain.'

Jenny took the sentence word by word. 'Go on. What's next?'

'You haven't got this yet. You're too wooden. Do it again. Properly.'

Lydia was a hard taskmaster. By the end of that first week Jenny had 'read' three sentences. In return Lydia struggled along the autumn lanes, falling into cowpats, suggesting new routes, making Jenny describe every inch of the way. The girls forged a relationship which was acerbic yet mutually dependent.

A day came when they were resting on their beds before supper and Jenny picked up one of the magazines which circulated the school and stumblingly read the first letter of the letter page.

Lydia said slowly, 'My God. Yes. So what is the advice?'

Jenny blinked and stared and then started to read in a monotone. 'Dear Chrissie, true love between a girl and a boy is based on re-re-something.'

She spelled out the letters and Lydia said, 'Respect. Based on respect. My foot.'

Jenny looked up. 'Did I get it wrong?'

'No. You're coming along really well. Marcia will never read the readers' letters to me. This is great.' She rolled back on the bed. 'Sorry. I sound like a teacher, don't I? What a patronizing prig I am. I don't mean to be. Honestly. I've never had a proper friend before so I'm just a beginner.'

'I think you're great. Like my mum actually. She was my best friend.' Jenny pulled her own hair forward and tried tying it under her chin. 'It's working, isn't it, Lydia? I'm reading and you're getting lots of exercise just like Marcia said.'

Lydia frowned and turned her head towards Jenny. 'What do you mean, I'm getting exercise? I thought we were on a quest.'

Jenny said, 'Well, yes. But if we don't find the cottage, then I suppose we're having some exercise.'

'I smell a rat! You've been cooking this up with Marcia just to get me outside, haven't you?'

'No! It's not like that at all! I promise.'

'I don't believe you.'

'You don't have to!' Jenny felt the awful hopelessness that had so often overwhelmed her in the past. 'I don't want to look any more anyway. It's a waste of time. And I don't want to learn to read.' She slid off her bed. 'I think I'd like to go to bed now actually.'

'Oh, actually you would, would you? No reading out the rest of the letters either. You're just too kind!' She said this at the top of her voice, working up for another scream, but before it came to fruition, there was a knock on the door and Marcia's head appeared.

'What are you two going on about now? This landing is full of quiet well-behaved civilized—'

'Like heck,' Lydia interrupted. 'Listen, Marcia. Jenny and I did a deal. She took me for walks and told me about things. And I taught her Braille. Now she says it's all off.'

'What am I supposed to do about it?' Marcia asked, coming into the room and sitting on the end of Jenny's bed. 'Is she ill?'

'Probably.' Lydia stuck out a petulant lower lip. 'Tell her, Jenny. Go on, tell her what ails thee.' Jenny said nothing so Lydia sat up straight and said loudly, 'I'm going to tell Marcia. What have you got to say about that?'

Jenny smiled wanly. 'There's nothing to tell, is there? Wish there was.'

Marcia said, 'Shut up, Lydia. Just for five minutes. Let Jenny tell me.'

Unexpectedly, Lydia shut up. Jenny looked round, surprised, then back to Marcia. She shrugged helplessly. 'Well, it's not anything. Really. I've been looking for somewhere – someone – for ages now. And when I came here, it seemed like I was near it. But I think I've learned something since I came here because now, tonight actually, I sort of know that it's no good.'

Marcia said gently, 'That's why you used to run away and now you go out every day. You're searching for something.'

'Yes. But I don't know where it is.'

Lydia said in a very small voice, 'She'll know when she finds it though.'

Marcia looked from one bed to the other. Then she said, 'Any clues? House? Tree? River?'

'Garden really,' Jenny said. 'And . . . and a person.'

Lydia said, 'You never told me about a person.'

'I'm not sure . . . a man . . . he lived in the house with the garden.'

'Don't forget the kidney beans,' Lydia reminded her.

'There was a tunnel of kidney beans. I hid in it.'

Marcia waited but nothing else was forthcoming. She stood up. 'Leave it with me for a couple of days. I need to think.' And she left.

Lydia exploded. 'That woman is so – so *annoying*.' She rolled away from Jenny. 'I'm going to play a record.'

'All right,' Jenny said. She felt slightly better about everything. There was an air of assurance about Marcia. She might not be able to solve the problem but she would think about it, for tonight at least. 'Is it all right if I have my bath now?'

Lydia kept her back to Jenny and grinned. 'Oh, all right then,' she said.

It was a week later. They'd taken some half-hearted walks and Jenny had managed to read an article about the right way to apply make-up but somehow the sparkle had gone out of things. Neither of them believed in the 'quest' any more and Jenny no longer needed Lydia's help with reading; she was managing better than she had dreamed possible.

That particular night they'd had supper and Lydia had gone off with a girl called Mary Soames to listen to *Dick Barton Special Agent*. Jenny sat over her glass of milk, staring into space. Marcia arrived for her night duty and came into the dining room still in her outdoor clothes.

'Ah. I was looking for you. Have you got plans for this evening?'

That usually meant Marcia was after someone to help tidy the playroom.

'I'm going to practise my reading,' Jenny said, with sudden determination. And then, because she liked Marcia so much, she smiled. 'All right. I'll help you. I can read later.' She finished her milk and stood up. 'I found a new magazine in the common room. It's called *Chat*.'

'It's rubbish,' Marcia said flatly. 'You're only interested for Lydia's sake.'

Jenny made a face. 'She's a bit fed up lately. I've let her down.'

'Oh, Jenny.' Marcia shrugged out of her coat and slung it over her arm. 'She thinks the world of you, you know.'

Jenny laughed, not even embarrassed.

Marcia said, 'She can't tell you so. She's built up this defensive wall – her parents can't cope. You're the only one who can get through. I wanted her to be with you tonight. And she's decided to do something else. Typical.'

Jenny was silent, looking at Marcia for clues, knowing something had happened.

Marcia said slowly, 'I want you to meet some-one. He's waiting in Mr Cousins' office. It might be nothing – eight years is such a long time for a child. Would you like Lydia with you? I'll drag her in by her hair if necessary.'

Jenny frowned. She didn't get it. If it was someone from Social Services, what difference would eight years make? Unless something had happened to her foster mum. The kindness that had protected her for eight years – had that gone too?

She swallowed. 'I'm all right. I can see him by myself.' She looked at Marcia. 'Or with you.'

'All right.' Marcia dumped her coat on a chair. 'Come on then. Let's get it over with.' She took Jenny's arm and they went into the corridor and down past the teaching rooms to the office. And waiting outside Mr Cousins' door was Lydia.

Jenny said, 'I thought you were listening to the wireless.'

Lydia said, 'Mary Soames keeps talking and she's just about as interesting as a doormat. But she did manage to tell me that Marcia had a man with her and that they were going into Cousins' office.' She turned slightly. 'I know you're there, Marcia. And I know something is going on. And now I know it's to do with Jenny. Is she being sent off somewhere? Because if so, I'm going as well. We're a team now. She sees and I talk.'

Marcia said, 'Too much at times. But I'm glad you're here. If this is all wrong, you'll know. Could you shut up and listen? We'll talk about it after.'

Lydia pushed her hair behind her ears and revealed a surprised expression.

'Er, well. I'm not sure. What do you think, Jen?'

Jenny was completely bewildered but she knew if anything awful was about to break over her head then she wanted Lydia close by. She said, 'Stay with me, Lydia.'

Marcia let go of her arm and stood back.

'Go on then. You first. Lydia and I are right behind you.'

Jenny opened the door and then turned back and put out a hand to touch Lydia's hair. She knew it would bring her good luck.

The man getting up from Mr Cousins' chair

was old, probably seventy, maybe even older. He had too much skin for his face and hands and too many clothes for the rest of him. He seemed to be shrinking inside them even as he stood leaning on the desk. It was obvious even to Jenny's frightened gaze that he was not employed by the Social Services. But then he could be a judge. Judges had to be old.

Behind her, Marcia said, 'This is Jenny Price, Mr Marston. This is her friend, Lydia Brahms. Lydia and I are here just to help if we're needed – if you don't mind.'

'I dun't mind. 'Tis up to the lass.'

Jenny said nothing; at least it was now obvious he was not a judge.

The silence stretched itself out; Jenny looked at him and he looked at her. She frowned and bit her lip. Behind her she sensed Lydia pulling at her hair and beginning to fidget. Lydia hated silence.

Marcia finally cleared her throat. 'Shall I begin?' No-one spoke so she went on. 'I thought about your cottage garden, Jenny. It had to have an owner. And there was just a possibility that the owner would drink at the Lamb and Flag in the village. So I asked my husband to do a bit of detective work. Try to find out whether anyone had heard of a small girl called Jenny Price. You were six when you lost your parents, Jenny. Eight years ago. So your memory was from before then. Well, Mr Marston came in one night when my Tom was making inquiries. And he can remember you. Your grandfather was his friend. And when your grandfather died, your father came to tell Mr Marston what had happened. You were four at the time. It was late summer and there were hardly any beans left on the plants, so you were allowed to play between the poles. And you never forgot it.'

Jenny stared. Behind her Lydia whispered, 'That was ten years ago, Jen. Is it the same man?'

Jenny took a breath through her mouth and whispered back, 'No.'

And the man said, 'And you're not the same neither, my girl. Ten years is a long time.'

Jenny felt a little bubble rise in her throat and pop into her mouth. 'You sound the same,' she gulped.

'You don't.' He smiled suddenly and every crinkle on his face smiled with him. 'You'm different but you'm just as pretty. And as good as an apple.' He came out from behind the desk with some difficulty. Jenny noticed a walking stick hooked over the back of Cousins' chair. 'They tole me about Robert and Mary. Too bad. Bloody Jerries. An' you . . . poor little devil. All on your own, eh. Well, you en't on your own no more. You got me, now. Cantankerous they do call me, and that's when they're being polite. But you got me however I am. An' I 'ope I got you.'

Jenny made a sound that was like a long

ecstatic sigh. And behind her, Lydia Brahms, known for being tough, started to cry.

Harry Blackmore, like Jenny Price, had what his mother had always called 'a happy disposition'. His childhood before the war had been totally secure and predictable. Mondays, whatever the vicar said, started the week. His mother was up at six to light the furnace beneath the boiler for the weekly wash and it was Harry's job to make sure Ernest and William plied the facecloth behind their ears and round the back of their necks as well as over their faces, ate their bread and dripping, and were ready for school when his mother came in to collect the coloureds. Harry would then go out into the yard and mangle the sheets and towels before his mother pegged them out on the line in the small yard. Then he would take Ernest and William to the infants' playground while he went on round the sooty old building to the senior boys' playground.

Usually his dad was home from work when he brought the boys back at teatime. Dad was a guard on the Great Western Railway and left the house at five every morning. It was a good, steady job. People respected Stanley Blackmore; admired the way his wife kept the house and their sons, took in washing and still looked pretty. On Monday evenings when he got home early, Dad always cooked the tea: bubble and squeak and cold cuts from yesterday's joint, spiced up with a jar of tomato chutney or piccalilli and followed by yesterday's cake covered in custard. Personally, Harry liked it better than the Sunday joint which was always followed by stewed fruit. He liked the burnt bits from the frying pan and the way Dad pretended to be a waiter and called Ernie and Will 'kind sir' and Mum 'my lady' and then the way you could cut the cake so that the custard rushed into it and made it into a delightful mush. Harry never wanted his life to change; everything was just right.

At fourteen he left school and became a lamp boy for the GWR. He cleaned the brass lamps that were on the front of the engines and the back of the brake vans. He rubbed the soot off the inside of the glass and buffed the brass until it looked better than gold. He was in charge of the gas mantels which popped in the waiting rooms and the refreshment rooms. He saved the broken ones, powdered them up and took them home in a paper bag to clean the knives and forks for Mum. He swept the platforms and cleaned the gents' conveniences and ran a clean cloth over the leather seats in the waiting rooms. He fetched hods of coal for the station master's office, the porters' room, the waiting rooms and the inspectors' office. If he worked hard and kept his nose clean he would be a porter or a ganger or a signal boy and then one day he would be a guard like his dad. Everyone knew that; his life was mapped out.

And then horrid Hitler invaded Poland and the balloon went up. For a long time he imagined Mr Hitler walking casually into Poland all by himself and saying, 'This is mine whether you like it or not.' Dad put him straight on that.

Dad could have got out of the army because he was in what was then called a reserved occupation. But he didn't want it like that. He was a happy man too and the things that made him happy were worth fighting for. He told Harry this one night when they were out looking at the stars from the back yard.

He said, 'Mum doesn't understand. But you do, don't you, son? It's not as if I was leaving her all alone. You're sixteen now and you'll look after her.'

'Course I will, Dad.' Harry felt good. It was all rather exciting.

'It isn't going to last for long, son. But the more of us who pitch in to help, the sooner it will be over. Mum doesn't seem to realize that.'

'She'll see, Dad. When it's over and you come home, she'll realize then.'

'I reckon you're right there.' Dad grinned into the night sky. 'See that one there, Harry? The big one? Your gramps always used to tell me that was the star that looked over us.'

'Like the Bethlehem star, Dad?'

'Just like it. Keep an eye on it, son. And I will too.'

'All right, Dad. We'll both keep an eye on it.'

It helped, that did. When Dad was in France and then taken prisoner and shipped off to dig coal in Silesia, they would all look at the Bethlehem star and imagine him looking at it from somewhere else. They saved all they could to buy the Red Cross parcels and they wrote to him practically every day. Mum said, 'You hear awful tales about letters and stuff never getting through. But if we send enough, surely some of it will reach him.'

'Course it will, Mum,' Harry said.

When it was his turn for call-up, the African campaign had been under way for a year; he arrived in Libya just as Auchinleck was leaving and Alexander was taking over. They trained him to drive a tank in three days; a great many troops had been taken off the year before for the Greek campaign. It was obvious the new command was preparing an attack. At the beginning of October he joined a convoy of Churchill tanks and went into the desert to harass the enemy. It was a diversionary tactic that went wrong because Rommel was solidly backed by air power.

Harry felt good; he had his own tank with an officer and two other men who he was certain would become friends. When it was all over he discovered that he had forgotten their names.

He sat in front of the controls on a seat like an upturned bucket. His gunner was slung on a sort of hammock above his head and rotated with the turret at regular intervals; his co-driver and wireless operator was on his left and the officer in charge of the tank was seated behind them. They were attacked from the air on the second day without a sight of the enemy's ground forces. With two tanks out of action, the retreat was ordered. They kept in convoy when they could, separating when the Messerschmitts came over, bucketing down into wadis, ploughing a clumsy zigzag course through the sand to avoid the spitting guns. They could have been only a few miles from El Alamein just north of the Egyptian border when they were cut off from the rest of the convoy by a sandstorm. They sat it out; they could not sleep and the gunner had dysentery. By the time morning came and the storm had abated, he was dehydrated and beginning to ramble.

The officer went outside and had a look round; he reckoned he could see palm trees over the next dune, but Harry never really believed him. They lugged the gunner out and the co-driver tried the engines. Nothing happened.

'They're silted up with this bloody sand,' the officer said. 'We'll have to do a cleaning job.' He was the same age as Harry and looked terrible. 'Is there any water in any of the canteens?'

They marshalled the water between them. The

gunner was twitching ominously. There was a cupful, if that.

'We need some water if we're going to work on the engines – we're all drying out. Blackmore,' he avoided Harry's gaze, 'I definitely saw a palm tree over that dune. Can you investigate? Take the canteens and fill them all. We'll work flat out here. Might even have a result by the time you get back.'

Harry collected the canteens. The co-driver rolled his eyes at him. 'Poor bugger's got the runs as well. Don't hang about, Harry. Need you 'ere not there!'

He grinned up from a tortuous position inside one of the tracks. Harry never forgot that smile. It was the last time he saw any of them.

The palm tree must have been an illusion. Over the next dune was another dune. Harry looked uncertainly into the wadi and flailed his arms hopelessly. Already the tank and the three other men were wavering in the heat; they would not see him or his semaphores. He squatted, trying to decide what to do. If he left this ridge for the next one, he could be all day and he would never find his way back. But if he went back now, the others would expect him to have water for them.

He heard the familiar pulsing drone of enemy planes five minutes before they arrived and started back down the dune in giant strides, shouting and waving as he went. They dropped bombs; three of them. Just one was a direct hit. Harry knew it immediately because the cloud of sand was molten with burning petrol; later when he had trekked across the wadi floor praying that someone would be moving, he knew just how direct a hit it had been. The tank was like a giant Meccano set; there were a few shreds of uniform clinging to the mangled metal; no trace of bodies.

He spent fruitless hours searching and then sat for a long time, shivering in the desert night, unable to leave the place where they had been. And when he did, he had no idea in which direction to go. He tried to remember the position of the tank but in any case they had turned several times as they came down the wadi. Every dune looked the same; he was no longer certain which one he had climbed in search of water.

He started out at nightfall; he was so thirsty he knew he probably had only another twenty-four hours to find the British lines. He chose a star, a very bright star. And he walked. When the sun came up, he lay face down and tried to cover himself with sand. He might have slept or maybe he simply lost consciousness. He came to when the sudden darkness arrived again, dragged himself up and walked. Twenty-four hours had passed and he was not dead.

He had no idea that the Battle of El Alamein had started. When a patrol found him he was almost inside the enemy lines; he had been stumbling in the wrong direction completely. It was 25 October 1942 and the British had a new commander under Wavell; he was called Montgomery. Harry met him later. He said something about the spirit of the troops who could produce a soldier determined to continue the fight alone.

It was poppycock and he knew it but Harry was a useful mascot for a time. The trouble was, it was all based on a lie. Harry Blackmore was not a hero; he was a very domesticated man who loved his job of keeping the railway station clean and neat and the lamps all shining. All he wanted was to get back home and go on with the life he had left behind.

The trouble was that the raids on Bristol had driven his family into North Wales where a forgotten uncle had offered them a home. And when eventually he was demobbed and his father was repatriated, they were different too. Dad had lung trouble and the air in Wales was better for him so he went to live with Mum and the boys and they bought a house and did bed and breakfast. Harry had some lovely holidays with them. They wanted him to stay up there; the air was fresh and the sea was clear and he could probably find a job on the railways. But Harry's dream had always been constant, like the star. He wanted to be a guard, he wanted to forget Africa, he wanted a house and a family in the familiar surroundings of Bristol and a routine as regular as clockwork, with Christmas at one end and August bank holiday at the other.

By the time he was demobbed, it was 1946. He stayed with an aunt in Kingswood for a time and learned how to manage ration books so that when a railway house came up almost next door to Temple Meads, he was back into the domestic routine and thoroughly enjoyed furnishing it with bits and pieces from junk shops. His Aunty Ida was full of praise.

'Well, my lad, you've done well here, haven't you? Beginning to look like home. I think I've got some curtains in the loft for your doors – keep the draughts out. And I can let you have a couple of saucepans. Yes, you'll do very well. You're a quiet one, Harry. But you work hard. You'll be all right.'

And then he got on to the training scheme organized by Miles Pemberton. That was the biggest stroke of luck he had had since they picked him up in the desert in '42. He took to it like a duck to water. Lots of the others were frightened of the written work but he'd always been good at reading and writing at school. The signalling exam, the Rules and Regulations – he'd been brought up on all of them. It came to him like breathing. He was probably one of the youngest guards on Western Region. And the older men liked him instinctively; Wilf Pickering, Albert Priddy, most of the local signalmen who were always on the defensive, took to Harry Blackmore. He was one of the old school; he knew that the more you put into a job, the more you got out of it.

Aunty Ida came with a steak and kidney pie and more comments on his way of life. 'Doing all right, aren't you, Harry? Your mam and dad must be proud of you. Where you going from here then, my lad?'

And that was it. Where was he going from there? The stupid little incident with the stewardess, Corinne, forced him to sit down and work out what should come next.

Strangely enough, he did not know. Underneath his smart and capable exterior, there were things he did not want to think about. That business in the desert was the main one; and the fact that he had been fêted as a hero for a time, when he knew very well that he was not. And then, after keeping himself to himself all these years, to almost succumb to the cheap charms of blond hair and perfect nails . . .

He looked at his round English face in his shaving mirror and said aloud, 'Probably all the nice steady girls have been snapped up already. You'll have to take up a hobby, my lad!'

Five

Mary Morrison put her head against the white
linen cover still embossed with the entwined
initials of the old GWR, closed her eyes and
consciously relaxed her body bit by bit. The
sun through the window glass was warm on
her upturned face, then there was a chill as it
was shaded by various obstructions; then warmth
again. She correlated the heat and cold with a
faint flicker behind her eyelids. Yes, she could
still register light and shade. She smiled faintly,
then concentrated on her hearing. At first she
thought the only audible sound was the clatter
of the wheels as they passed over the rail joints
but then she discovered she could separate
other noises from the insistent rhythm. The
coach actually creaked when it took a curve; a
strange humming noise could be heard from
the telegraph wires – she remembered how
they appeared to sway and dip with each small
gradient. She smiled again with a certain

satisfaction; if she could associate sound with remembered sights, then she would be able to form pictures in her head. She ran her fingers along the arm rest, distinguishing the grain of leather and the strange roughness of the plush upholstery. And smells, what smells could she identify in this small container on wheels? Coffee? That would be from the buffet car of course. But there was something more pungent, a smell associated entirely with trains. Sulphur . . . soot . . . She remembered telling her father that trains smelled of salmon sandwiches. He had laughed – he had laughed so often with her. He had been happy with her. And then he had gone. Remembered grief flooded her for a moment as they passed through a station: shadows behind her eyes, a sudden chill on her face, the frantic clattering of the wheels as they changed their rhythm; then the train burst into sunshine again and she remembered that her father's desertion had been a kind of forcing-house for her affair with John Kenyon. She smiled again. She was certain that eventually John would have agreed that age made no difference; they would still have married and been just as happy. But when that telegram had arrived, it had literally precipitated her into his arms.

Dear John. All right, she had put him on a pedestal. Famous war artist, twenty years older than his young pupil – 'I'm just a father figure to you' – shy and full of self-doubt. Generous and kind beyond belief – 'I want you to be an artist in your own right, not in my shadow.' Such an ordinary-looking man. But when he smiled at her, the sun shone and she was warm, just as she was now as the train turned imperceptibly and the sun hit the window and warmed her face.

He brought her a kind of fame; he brought her security because when her father left, there was no money at all, just debts. He cocooned her with his love and when he had his nightmares and was back in the trenches, she was the one who would lead him to his studio and let him 'paint it out of himself'. They could have been happy for many years. He would not be seventy yet and these days seventy was not old. She could still be living in his house in Cornwall, painting her careful pictures, but he, too, had left.

And then had come Andrew. Andrew French. Electrician. Recently divorced from a wartime marriage; only son of adoptive parents. Blond, blue-eyed, like a Greek god. An Adonis.

She had fought the attraction half-heartedly; he was fifteen years younger than her and practically admitted that he was looking for his real mother in every woman he saw. And he loved John Kenyon's work. And she was John Kenyon's widow.

They were the talk of the village of course. Because she was an artist and artists lived in a different world, they were accepted up to a point. But they did not marry and he was probably considered to be her passing fancy, never an integral part of the household as she intended. Only Katy seemed to accept him completely. Dear Katy who had come with her from Cornwall and organized her and the house to perfection. It was Katy who had recognized immediately that he had 'fallen' for Mary. Katy had thought it was great; special and wonderful, fun, like nothing that had gone before.

Andrew French came to repair her washing machine one snowy February morning in 1947. It was, coincidentally, her forty-second birthday and she was setting up her many cards along the mantelpiece in the old study. He was in his mid-twenties. He was ridiculously beautiful; handsome was a word she associated with her father and photographs of her brothers. John had been good-looking – good to look at certainly. This young man was beautiful. Katy giggled at him and told him all the girls must be after him. He did not deny it. He fitted a new switch, put the tub back inside the casing and ran a test wash. The three of them sat, silently, watching water swill around the tub. Katy told him that no one else in the village had a washing machine; this one came from America. He nodded but made no comment.

'That'll do,' he said at the end of the cycle. 'If you get any more trouble, call me.' He handed a card to Katy and she giggled again and passed it on to Mary.

'Thank you so much. I've been lost without a washing machine.' She smiled at him and he looked surprised, then nodded. She got up and went to the door. 'I'll just write you a cheque.' She went into the study again and discovered that he had followed her. 'Oh.' She indicated a chair. 'Do sit down, I won't be a minute.'

He did not sit down but went to the mantelpiece to examine the cards. 'Your birthday?'

'Yes.' She wrote his name and asked how much.

'Twenty.' He looked round. 'Call-out. Parts. Labour.'

It seemed an enormous price but she knew he would not overcharge. She said, 'Do you do other electrical work? I have quite a bit of trouble here. It's an old house.'

'Probably needs rewiring. I could do that. Yes.' He looked at a card from Davis Bryson and grinned. 'You are almost exactly fifteen years older than me.'

She, too, grinned. There was a kind of safety about his youth. 'Old enough to be your mother,' she said.

His eyes widened, then he laughed. 'But too beautiful by half!' His teeth were white and very even. He must have a beautiful mother, no-one who looked like him could have anything less. He read her thought and said, 'I never knew her. I was adopted by a lovely, perfect Mum. But not beautiful.'

She handed him the cheque and said piously, 'Beautiful on the inside, by the sound of it.'

He was suddenly serious, nodding emphatically. 'Venus.'

She was unexpectedly touched. 'Oh. That's nice.'

'Not really. Just factual.' He smiled again. 'I can't imagine you using the washing machine. I thought you would be waited on hand and foot. You're famous, after all.'

'No. Not really. The people in the village know I paint. But in the art world I'm not famous.'

'You were married to John Kenyon. That's what I meant.'

She laughed. 'Oh, how immodest of me! Of course, I was married to John. And he was extremely famous in the art world. But not outside it. I'm surprised you know him.'

He moved to the window. 'I love his pictures. Especially the abstracts. They make me feel . . . happy.' He turned and looked at her. 'You must feel the same.' He glanced around. 'I thought you would have the house full of his stuff.'

She drew a deep breath and felt it vibrate in her throat. Surely she wasn't going to cry. Not in front of this boy.

'Actually, most of John's work is in a gallery.

I've got a few in one of the upstairs rooms. Would you like to see them?'

She went immediately to the door so that he would not see her face. Katy was vacuuming the hall and looked up surprised as they went upstairs. Mary forced a reassuring smile but Katy switched off the vacuum and listened as they crossed the landing and went into the oriel room. Mary could imagine her climbing halfway upstairs and staying poised in case of trouble. Dear Katy. Maybe she fancied the young electrician and would go out with him and . . . and . . .

She said, 'We call it the oriel room because of the window of course. Let me pull up the blind.' She did so and the paintings filled the room. The long, banner-like creation she had seen first in the Penzance gallery, an enormous canvas titled 'Sea and Land', thick oils applied with a spatula, interlocking waves and shoreline; another long painting of recognizably human forms, hundreds of them, marching.

Andrew went from one to the other and then stopped before the last. 'This is from the First World War sketches, isn't it? Retreat at Mons?'

She could not speak but she nodded once. He did not move for a long time, then he said, 'If he was in the trenches, and you are now forty-two years old, he was much older than you, wasn't he?'

She stopped wanting to cry. He had been

looking at the painting and doing sums.

She said, 'Is that relevant?'

He said slowly, 'I'm not sure. It might be. He could have been your father, and you could have been my mother.' He turned and stared at her. 'You're not my mother. Are you?'

She said, 'Of course not. And this is a stupid conversation.'

He breathed out audibly. 'Thank God.' Then he smiled and was so beautiful she blinked as if at a strong light. 'You are just about old enough to be my mother. You are exquisite. You are a painter. And you were married to John Kenyon. My God.'

She walked past him to the door, went through it, caught sight of Katy scurrying back downstairs and marched down them herself to the front door. He followed.

'We'll be in touch if we need the rewiring work,' she said.

He went into the porch. 'We?' he enquired.

She could have told him that she had meant herself and Katy but she did not. 'We,' she repeated and closed the door.

Behind her Katy exploded into giggles. 'I've never seen no one so smitten!' she crowed. Mary managed to laugh too.

The next night he telephoned.

'Did you know there was an exhibition of Marcus Doan's stuff at the West of England Gallery in Bristol?'

She did not have to ask who was speaking. She said, 'No.'

'Let's go! He's doing a talk as well. You could introduce me.'

She put a hand to her throat; so that's what this was about.

'I've never met him.'

'Well, I could introduce you then!'

'I'm afraid I'm busy that night.'

'Which night?' She did not immediately reply and his voice became subdued. 'It's tonight actually. I could call for you about seven. The talk is at eight and afterwards we could look at the paintings.'

'I'm so sorry—'

'Please. Please, Mary.'

'I don't think it's a good idea.'

'It's the best idea I've ever had. Please, Mary. I'm not a kid. I'm twenty-seven. I've been married and divorced and I thought there would never be anyone else for me ever again—'

'Don't be ridiculous! You came to mend my washing machine!'

'Ah! You used the singular. So there's no-one else.'

She replaced the receiver, then lifted it and laid it on her desk. But somehow she knew he would call for her at seven that night.

She had a sandwich when the light failed, then changed into black trousers and matching jacket. Promptly at seven, he turned up. On a motorbike.

It was an explosion of feeling. He wooed her passionately and she responded just as passionately. It showed in her work; she stopped being careful and ordered enormous canvases and laughed out loud as she tried new techniques. She loved pointillism; Davis Bryson, who had always exhibited her, told her she was 'quite the little impressionist these days'.

She painted a Cornish landscape from memory. In the centre was a long black line, like a fissure in the canvas. Andrew sat in front of it for a long time without saying a word. When he turned and held out his arms, she went into them and put her head against his neck.

He said, 'You are so lucky. Do you know that, Mary?'

She nodded somehow, her tears salting his skin.

He said, 'To be able to take something awful out of your head, put it on canvas so that you can look at it objectively and come to terms with it – yes, you are lucky.'

She whispered, 'How did you know?'

'It's obvious. There is your old homescape. I've seen it in John's paintings. Tranquillity and a kind of one-ness with everything. John always contrasted that with a wound in the landscape, like a tin mine. And you have done it too. That sudden scar. The black hole. The disappearance. It had to be that.'

'I've never painted it before,' she whispered. 'Everyone wanted me to but I couldn't.'

'Why have you done it now?'

'I suppose . . . because of you.'

They walked in the garden afterwards and watched the sunset; he was very quiet. When she asked him what was the matter, he told her, 'Nothing. I'm happy. Just . . . happy.'

Strangely, his reply had marked the first time she questioned his love for her. Had the fact that she had been able to paint John's death shown him that her love for him was growing each day, putting down roots – trapping him? Did it frighten him that their wild romance might be settling into something much deeper?

And then had come the difficulty with her sight. A year ago almost. And she had eventually gone to Henry Yorke, Andrew had taken her, and the cataracts had been diagnosed. There might be something else, something behind the cataracts. She had to wait for test results. Possibly she would have to wait until the cataracts could be removed and more tests were done. She had been terrified. She was still terrified. And part of the terror was to do with Andrew. Because if the attraction he felt towards her was connected with her talent and she could no longer use that talent, what would happen to the attraction?

She shivered in the warmth of the train

carriage. She could almost smell his love turning to pity and she could not bear his pity. But she could not bear to live without him.

How much easier her love for John had been. Based on respect and a deep admiration for his work, it had grown to include everything about him. They had the same interests; she was the daughter of older parents and the age difference seemed nothing. He loved her for her youth and beauty and latent talent but also for her understanding of his paintings. Sometimes she knew where he was going, what he was doing, better than he did himself. She let herself imagine how different her life would have been if John had not disappeared. She would still be living in Cornwall, watching him create his work like a diary of their days together.

She took another deep breath because it was so hard to imagine that life now. She felt a pang of guilt as she realized that her love for John had not been enough. It was Andrew who had brought her a flowering – a late flowering perhaps, but a true one. She was shocked by this sudden revelation, as if she was being disloyal to John. And yet he never seemed far away. He was part of her, always part of her. Behind her closed lids she brought up a picture of him. She smiled and thought he might be smiling back. As if he understood. It was so trite in a way; master and pupil, experience and innocence – hadn't he said those words? And would it have happened between them if it had not been for the other man in her life? Her father?

She turned her head slightly towards the window of the compartment so that the sun could warm her other cheek and confirm her sense of touch. She again felt the upholstery and registered the carpet beneath the soles of her shoes. She had always loved textures. As a child she had stroked her rocking horse, and then her pony. She remembered pushing her hands into the mud of the kitchen garden and asking the gardener whether she would take root.

Her memories took over and she was back to her childhood at Lynch End, the Georgian house on the Wiltshire Downs where the sky dominated everything and cloud shadows raced across the sheep-bitten grass and existence was timeless, no beginnings, no endings. Her mother was called Helena and her father Ian and her twin brothers were called Owen and Gerry. Her pony was called Acorn and there was a governess cart for trips to the village. Her father bought a car on her fifth birthday, a Morris which of course was called Mary. She tried to recall the registration number. GY4396. Everything, everyone had names and labels and were totally secure. She smiled slightly. The car came in 1910. The boys had loved that car. Her father hid the starting handle but they sat in the front anyway and pretended to roar along, waving to her as she sat on the old mounting block and tried to sketch them. She could draw before she could write; it was her second governess who arrived much later who had so cleverly told her that if she could draw of course she could write. Writing was drawing and drawing was writing. Letters were patterns that made pictures.

That had been four years later in fact. So she must have been nine. No wonder her father was worried; nine years old and unable to read and write. Her mother wanted her to go away to school like the boys had, but they could not send her anywhere until she could at least manage to write her name. The governess's name was Miss Pensford. Grace Pensford. Mary had never forgotten her; had never blamed her for what happened. Eventually, she had not blamed her father either.

Her brothers were ten years older than their sister, born rebels. Fun to be with but always in trouble. She knew them during school holidays when they let her help with damming the brook and then persuaded her to pretend to drown in the resulting pool so that they could rescue her. There had been a fuss about that. Not such a big fuss as when she started ballet classes and they got her to dance naked on the dining-room table. They had been eighteen, going in daily to a crammer near Swindon in a desperate effort to be ready for university the following year. But their hearts had never been in it and when war was declared the next August, they had both joined up immediately and on 4 September were killed at the Battle of the Marne.

Mary remembered that very well. Her father read out the telegram and she did not know what to do; there were no set rules for this. There never had been rules where the boys were concerned.

The silence went on and on and then her mother whimpered and her father turned and left the room. She had stood there uncertainly for a while and then put an arm round her weeping mother. They sat together on a sofa and Mary cried too but not for the boys because she did not understand about death at all. She cried for her mother. After what seemed like a long time, the cook came in and said tea was ready for Miss Mary in the kitchen. She sat at the big table with the gardener and the cook who were her friends, and gradually stopped crying. Somebody said the master had taken the car and driven off like a maniac. It did not occur to Mary until years afterwards that he could have stayed at home and comforted his wife.

But everything eventually fell into place – a different place but not at all uncomfortable. Her mother took up painting again and converted one of the rooms into a studio. She was there most of the day and, Mary found out later, most of the night too. She said her painting saved her sanity.

And then Miss Pensford came and life returned to its pleasant ways. Mary and her father and Miss Pensford had picnics on the Downs and went to look at Stonehenge and the Avebury circle. That was, quite literally, a magical time. Miss Pensford cast a spell over them; she told them she would make them happy again and she did. When Mary went to school at last, Miss Pensford stayed on as housekeeper and there were wonderful Christmases and Easters with pantomimes and egg hunts. When the Armistice was signed, they did not go to Salisbury and join in the celebrations; they went to Avebury instead and watched the sun rise and held hands. Miss Pensford said, 'Now we really can begin again.' Father said, 'Amen to that.' And Mary, who was thirteen, felt the solemnity of the moment like a knell and thought she might die then and there. When they got home she discovered she had started her periods and Miss Pensford talked her through that as well, making the messy business into something precious and wonderful.

It was six years later when it all blew up. She was studying art in Falmouth then; the Newlyn school was being reassessed and to be an artist in Cornwall seemed the best thing in the world. She had looked at art schools elsewhere and had known they were not for her. She was not adventurous. Some of the work exhibited looked like her mother's enormous garish paintings and that frightened her. She did not like the new flapper era either; her tutor told her she was not exactly old-fashioned, just from another place and time and she thought that was true too.

She had lodgings in a house overlooking the harbour and when her father arrived late one evening just before the end of her second summer term, she took him into the garden to watch the ferry cross to St Mawes. The scene was idyllic; hardly a ripple on the surface of the water, the swallows flying high for their supper.

She said, 'I'm glad you came early, Daddy. Can you stay a couple of days while I finish off the term?'

'Afraid not, Mary. I've come to tell you that your mother is not at all well. I think it's better if you stay here for the holiday. Will you mind?'

She minded very much; she adored Cornwall but Lynch End was home. But she said, 'Well . . . no, of course not.' It did not occur to her that she might help her mother. 'If that's what you want.'

'It's not what I want, darling. It's what is best.'

At last she asked, 'Is Mother really ill? I mean . . .'

'I know what you mean.' He met her eyes and then looked out at the ferry again. 'She has shut herself away for a while.' He cleared his throat and added quickly, 'I might manage a week in August. If I can work things out at the bank.'

'Oh, that would be lovely. Could Miss Pensford come too?'

'I'm not sure, darling. I'm not sure what will be happening in the next few months. Whatever it is, you must be brave, Mary. Will you promise you will try to be brave?'

She said, surprised, 'Of course, Daddy.'

After a long pause her father spoke again.

'My work . . . it's my work, Mary. I might not have it for much longer.'

That did not seem important. She murmured comfortingly, 'You're chairman of the bank, Daddy. I don't think they can manage without you.'

'No-one is indispensable, Mary. There have been . . . discrepancies. Nothing to do with me but of course I'm responsible for whatever happens. You understand that?'

'Well . . . it's not fair, is it? Who is responsible – what has happened?'

'Money has been diverted – yes, diverted. The chief cashier has borrowed in order to speculate. For a long time he paid back his unofficial loans so of course they were never discovered. But speculation and accumulation do not necessarily follow.'

'But you can't be held responsible for that.'

He shrugged.

He did not join her for that week in August

and she did not mind because she had met John Kenyon by that time and had erected another pedestal and put him on it. He had done the same for her. He saw her as Innocence and she saw him as Experience. They smiled at each other but neither would allow the other to come closer.

He had been a war artist and since then had turned to landscapes; damaged landscapes. Mary had admired his work for years, and when she was invited to the opening of an exhibition of his paintings, at which he would give a talk, she leapt at the chance.

He was a short man, prematurely grey, with brown robin eyes looking out at the world from beneath big brows. Always looking. He spoke about his latest work. It was to do with forgiveness, with learning to live again. If the land that we lived in could accept the evil of industrialization, absorb it, neutralize it, then so could we. She thought she knew exactly what he meant. If you could not love something, you could not paint it.

Afterwards she approached him shyly and asked whether he was only referring to the war or whether his philosophy could extend to everything in life.

He smiled at this twenty-one-year-old who looked like someone from an Edwardian garden party.

'Why did I paint the land if I hadn't meant

everything? Even the pettiest of sins is evil and unless we learn how to take each separate pain and earth it, then it will spread like a plague.'

'How do we learn to do that?'

He spread his hands. 'If only I knew. It's something to do with perfect love.'

She nodded eagerly; it was as she had thought.

She went to one of his classes and was disappointed when it was on still life. She expected the model to be a bowl, some fruit, a fallen flower against a black silk backdrop; in fact it was a jam jar of water on a table in the middle of the studio.

'You may tackle this from any angle. Whichever one appeals to you most or you see as most important.'

Everyone began to walk round the table, measuring, posturing. She stayed where she was. Behind the jar was a window framed by other paintings; to the left was a sink full of pots and brushes.

Two hours later he said, 'I think you should take a break, Miss Morrison.'

She looked up, startled. 'I'm sorry. I didn't realize. Has everyone gone?'

'Yes. They went at midday.'

'The class was until midday,' she said, dismayed. 'And I've kept you all this time. I do apologize.'

'Please don't. It has been a pleasure to watch you working. Will you talk about your painting?'

She sought desperately for words. 'There was so much to do, you see. If you frame it from here then you have the window and the sink – so much. The jam jar is almost irrelevant.'

'But it's there. Is it a blot on the landscape? D'you want to tidy it away?'

'No. From lots of angles it would be a blot. But not from here. Because there are so many muddles all to do with painting and it's just one more.'

'Why is it important then?'

'Just because it's in the foreground. It's not really important anywhere else.'

'Ah.' He smiled gently. 'Shall we walk?'

They walked along Fore Street and round the castle to the beaches. He asked her questions and encouraged her to say whatever she thought. It was a classic teacher/pupil relationship. They both thought it would stay that way.

And then as October turned into November and it was dark by teatime, she received a telegram from home.

'Come immediately stop Father gone stop Mother.'

She thought it meant that her father was dead.

It was six o'clock; there was no way she could get back to Salisbury that night. But John Kenyon had a telephone in his rented cottage and he would let her use it so that she could talk to her mother.

He opened the door to find her standing

there, hugging her coat round her and waving a yellow telegram like a flag. Her beautiful mass of hair was flying out from beneath her beret and her face looked drowned.

She said something like, 'It's my father. He's dead.'

He opened his arms and she almost fell into them.

She did not speak to her mother that night. After he had comforted her, kissed her, pushed her tangled hair from her eyes and kissed her again, she did in fact phone Lynch End. A strange voice spoke to her; somehow she assumed it was the local undertaker. It was a polite voice with just a touch of unction about it. It said, 'I think you should come as soon as you can. The car has gone of course, but there's a horse in the stable. I can arrange to meet you at Salisbury.'

She imagined her mother was prostrate with grief and did not insist on speaking to her. John was looking up train times and she told the voice at the other end that she would arrive in Salisbury at three fifteen. And then John gently took the phone away and held her again while she wept.

While he was with her, she coped wonderfully. And he was with her all the time and took her to Penzance in the morning for the train. But during the long journey she had time to think. It was impossible to imagine Lynch End without her father. She was twenty-one but she needed his approval to marry John – though he had not asked her to marry him. And what about her mother? Had she once again shut herself into her studio?

The governess cart was at Salisbury to meet her, driven by a man who could quite easily have been an undertaker. He wore a dark suit and bowler hat, took her bag from her and told her his name was Bennett. There was no conversation. She wanted to ask him how her father had died but it was difficult to turn and address his back.

He put her bag on the step and led the horse round to the stable. She picked up the bag and opened the door. She had always loved the hall at Lynch End, the curved staircase with the banister which was so gloriously smooth and ended in a very ornate newel post. Now, in the late afternoon twilight, everything was too big, empty and echoing. She stared around and then saw that her mother was coming slowly down the stairs. She reached the bottom and hung on to the newel, her free hand on her heart.

She said, 'I heard the cart arrive.'

Mary wanted to rush forward and fling her arms round her but there was something about her mother's greeting that stopped her in her tracks.

She said, 'Oh, Mummy, I'm so terribly sorry—'

She got no further. Her mother pointed a

finger at her and almost screamed, 'Did you know? Did he tell you what he was going to do?'

Mary dropped her bag to the floor and looked round for the familiar faces of the staff.

'He's gone!' her mother screamed. 'Gone!'

'Mummy, I know. The telegram said . . . Was it his heart?'

For a moment there was a silence, then her mother started to laugh. And could not stop. She clutched the banisters and swung herself back and forth. 'His heart! Oh my dear God! His heart. Yes, yes, yes, it was his heart.' She stopped laughing and stared. 'Did you think he was dead? I wish he were! How I wish he were dead!'

'Mummy! Don't speak like that! Nothing could be worse than—'

'He's gone with her! To Italy! He's embezzled money from the bank – he was chairman, Mary! People trusted him! He hasn't betrayed only you and me! He's betrayed his clients!'

Mary felt the blood drain from her face. She stammered, 'No! No, that wasn't Daddy! He told me last summer that there was someone using bank funds to speculate. It wasn't him, Mummy! It wasn't! He was going to sort it all out—'

'He sorted it out, all right! Used it to take her over to Italy – they've got a villa. Would you believe it? A villa!' Her own words seemed to drive her crazy. She put her head on the newel post and began to cry. Not as she had cried when the boys died; this was something different. She cried loudly with noisy sobs. A constant protest.

At last Mary went to her and put her arms round her. She said, 'There's got to be an explanation. He's not dead, Mummy! That's the main thing, he's not dead!' All the way up the country in the train she had tried to balance the paradox of her happiness about John with the loss of her father. But she had not lost him after all. Surely joy could now be uppermost – could be *appropriate*.

'Listen, Mummy. Listen!' She put her mouth close to her mother's ear. 'He's probably gone abroad to raise funds somehow. Be sensible. You keep mentioning a woman but Daddy hasn't got time to—'

Her mother looked up. 'You little fool! Surely you've known for years what's been going on. If *I* have known, then you . . . No, you're like an ostrich, aren't you? Won't think about anything unpleasant! Didn't it occur to you that your governess and your father got on better than either of them did with us?'

She protested instantly. 'No! Mother, you're wrong! Miss Pensford would never allow such a thing to happen!'

Her mother started to laugh again and swung out of Mary's arms to flop onto the stairs. 'You'll have to face it some time, Mary. Because there's no more money. The bailiffs have already been in. The house is to be sold to pay off some of the debts. The car's gone. Nelly's the only horse left. The silver, furniture . . .' She swept her arm round the hall.

'Oh dear God.' Mary followed the gesture, realizing that the large hall really was empty.

Suddenly her mother crouched in a huddle, head on knees. 'Someone has sent a man to see to things. I don't know who he is. It's horrible, Mary. Horrible. He was the one who met you. He – he's taken over, and it's not his house . . . What are we going to do?'

Mary was shocked into silence.

The man, Bennett, appeared in the doorway, dusting down the sleeves of his jacket and then the front of his trousers. He said, 'You can stay here tonight, miss. Two bedrooms are still in use. But tomorrow we shall need to clear everything.' He looked at Mary's face. 'She's told you, hasn't she? All assets seized against debts.'

Mary nodded numbly.

'Right. I'm off then. I can take you back to the station tomorrow if it's convenient. Or perhaps to a friend.' He waited for a reply and when none came he shrugged. 'It's my job, ladies.'

Helena Morrison choked on another laugh. 'You've got a car out there. You come and go in a car. And you meet my daughter in the governess cart!'

He paused by the door. 'I did not need to meet her at all, madam.' He closed the door carefully after him and was gone.

The nightmare went on and on. If her father had died, there would have been a funeral and a farewell. As it was, the farewell was to the house and grounds. Helena packed her painting equipment and they went to a hotel for two nights while Mary telephoned her aunt who arrived post haste and had to hear the sorry story. Helena and Dorothea had both made 'good' marriages and it was a great shock for Dorothea to hear that her sister's was suddenly not at all good. But she was marvellous.

'You must both come to the Grange.' The offer was instantaneous, made without thought. 'Darling,' she turned to Mary, 'obviously you can't go on at the college and you've nothing to keep you in Cornwall. Donald has two cottages in the grounds – he was only saying the other day he would have them done up for holidaymakers. Walkers and so on. You can choose which you would like. It will be such fun!' Donald Forrester, her husband, had made his money from coal in the Forest of Dean and had changed his name from Smith to Forrester.

Helena said, 'I doubt that, Dorrie. How are we going to pay rent?'

'Who has mentioned rent?' Dorothea tried to hug them both at once and lost her glasses. 'But Mary will need an occupation and Gloucester and Cheltenham are both within reach. I might manage to get you a teaching job at the

Cheltenham Ladies College, darling. Wouldn't you just love that?'

Mary thought of John and the cottage on the cliffs. But of course that could never happen now. 'Yes, Aunt Dorrie. It sounds marvellous. Thank you so much.'

'Book in here for another few days while Donald fixes it all up,' Dorothea said happily, settling her glasses higher up her nose.

Helena glanced at Mary who faltered, 'Aunt Dorrie, we can't stay here. We literally haven't a bean.'

'Don't worry. I'll have a word with the manager.'

Mary heard nothing from John. She wrote to him and rather tersely told him what had happened and what was going to happen. But she did not give him an address because that one night was all they had had and she could not presume anything at all from that. She finished her letter with, 'You will understand my mother needs me now.' It was as good as saying goodbye.

They moved into the Grange while Uncle Donald had one of the cottages 'done up'. Mary did not think it could possibly work; it was so small, two tiny rooms and a lean-to kitchen downstairs and two bedrooms upstairs. No bathroom, no hot water or central heating. But strangely, her mother took to it instantly. She made a great thing of keeping the fire going all the time for the rest of that winter and she converted one of the bedrooms into a studio for herself and slept downstairs in front of the fire. They walked up to the Grange each afternoon, through the elm trees full of squabbling rooks and in through the small side door by the pump. They used one of the bathrooms and came down for dinner with Uncle Donald and Aunt Dorothea and then he walked them back soon after eight and they went to bed. Christmas Day came and went and superficially everything was fine. But there were no messages from Italy and of course nothing from Cornwall.

And then a letter arrived. It was dated 20 November, two months previously; it was from John.

'Darling Mary. I have been in Wiltshire for the past week and I have traced you to the Swan Hotel at Lynch End but after that the trail is cold. The manager there tells me that your mother's sister has spirited you away but cannot say where and has no record of your aunt's name. I am addressing this letter to your old home in the faint hope that eventually it will be officially forwarded to you. My dearest Mary, if our love means anything to you, I beg you to get in touch with me. If you feel anything for me – friendship, anything – do not send me packing in this way. I have been in love with you since we walked and talked that first day though I did not intend to tell you so. I am old and you are young. But the night of November the second – two weeks and four days ago – broke all the barriers for me. And I thought for you also. Write to me, Mary. Or telephone. Or just arrive. I beg you.'

She talked to her mother. There was nothing for her in Gloucestershire; she had no qualifications so was useless to a school. They were dependent on the Forresters for everything; she would have to do something – take a secretarial course, anything.

Helena, used to her own space, said, 'Listen, Mary. Why don't you go back to Cornwall? You've got contacts there – you might get a job in a gallery. Or even as a model.'

Mary nodded. She said tentatively, 'Actually, Mummy, there is someone . . . I think – I'm certain – I love him. And he says he loves me.'

Helena said almost enthusiastically, 'There you are then! Go back and see what happens!'

Mary said, 'But you . . . on your own here . . .'

'Darling, be sensible. I like being on my own – you must have gathered that at least. You and me, we're not really close, are we? You were always Daddy's girl.'

There were other discussions, with Donald and Dorothea, and then with John.

He turned up out of the blue two days after she posted a reply to his letter. It had started to snow and when she opened the door to him he had icicles clinging to the brim of his hat. He enfolded her into his freezing overcoat and kissed her face until she begged for mercy. 'Come in by the fire – oh, you ridiculous man! Have you walked from Gloucester?'

'Of course not. I got a train to Cam and walked from there. Darling, it's beautiful. Not like Cornwall of course, but the trees and the snow and the little cottages – this one is wonderful. Can we come here for our holidays? Will your mother permit that? Have you asked her about us getting married? Will you have to get in touch with your father and ask him?' He talked about the whole situation in terms of their life together.

After a very short stay in Gloucestershire they went back to Falmouth and she and John were married within the month. Her family did not join them. The Forresters were too busy and Helena was simply not interested. For the first time, Mary could begin to understand why her father had not only fallen in love with Grace Pensford but had stolen money in order to spend the rest of his life with her.

John, determined to have all problems in the open, used to tease her that she was after a father figure and she would counter by telling him he was looking for a daughter. Certainly after her father's betrayal Mary needed someone to admire as well as to love and respect; and he needed someone who represented the future.

He often told her that the world was safe in her hands and knowing that in the very nature of things she would have to live for him as well as for herself one day, she would shake her head fiercely, telling him wordlessly not to talk like that.

They had ten wonderful years together, and then John, quite literally, disappeared. One second he was sketching the wheelhouse of Ladyhouse mine near the Lizard while Mary laid out a picnic on the springy turf around the car which they had so recently bought. The next he was gone. He had chosen a tiny dell in which to lie back and see the stack and the spokes of the wheel against the sky. Later, they told her that the dell was the beginnings of subsidence into old workings; he would have been killed in the fall, there was no question of a rescue operation. When, at last, they brought his body out, it was surprisingly undamaged. But he was not in it. She could look at it without emotion. He was part of her body now. It was quite simple.

The Forresters brought her mother for the funeral but she would not stay overnight. They explained that she was better at home in her studio. Dorothea said that some of her paintings were surprising – huge abstracts, quite frightening really. Donald took Mary aside and confided that he thought her mother was plain nuts. 'Happy with it, though. Can't say I blame your father.'

Friends told Mary to paint again, to take a daily walk, to eat healthily. But especially to paint again. That was the answer, she must paint again. She must 'get on with things'. But for the time being she preferred to look at John's work. After all, she could not compete with him.

The Munich crisis came and went without disturbing her greatly. Her friends thought it was marvellous, she was so calm. But she knew that her apparent calmness was self-centredness; she could not see past her grief, absolutely nothing else mattered.

After a few months, when winter began to give way reluctantly to a late spring, she visited a psychologist. It was a sign of her suppressed desperation.

At first the whole thing seemed ridiculous; the woman was elderly and rather brisk. 'Very few people can share grief,' she informed Mary. 'It's a very personal emotion. It can become an emotion that we jealously protect and cherish. That way it can never become part of your present life, simply a kind of blot. And that's not fair to your husband's memory or to yourself. So try to talk. I know it's difficult. But try.'

'A kind of blot' – where had she heard that before? She could not think of one thing to say. It was so obvious this woman was going to suggest what everyone else had suggested: physical and mental work.

'Tell me how you met your husband,' the woman said. 'First of all, where was it? What was the weather like? What were you wearing?'

Laboriously, hesitantly, Mary began.

'It was summer so I must have been wearing something light. Fairly formal too because it was the opening of his exhibition.'

She waited but the woman said nothing, in fact she seemed to be hardly listening. She had a pad and pencil in front of her and she was doodling. Mary sighed.

'Yes. Well. It was at Davis Bryson's gallery in Chapel Street, Penzance. He's left there now. Opened somewhere in Cork Street. London. He was going to do an exhibition of John's war stuff. But . . .' She looked to her right. There was a window framing a view of a Falmouth street. But on the window ledge was a blue pottery vase full of daffodils. It was a typical still life with extras. She half smiled. John described her own work as 'still lifes with extras'.

She blinked and looked round at the woman who still said nothing, still doodled. Mary sighed again. 'Anyway, he did his best with John's stuff. The space was too small really for John's later work, but there were quite a few of his pencil sketches from the war.'

She closed her eyes, remembering. Love was such a strange emotion, stranger even than grief. All she had known when she saw the small man standing next to one of his long banner-like abstracts was that she wanted to be near him; in his company; part of his life. She had turned to Davis who was presenting her with the usual glass of white wine, and asked him whether John Kenyon did classes.

Davis said, 'You admire him that much?'

'Of course. He's a legend in his own lifetime.'

'He's too old for you, Mary.'

She had reddened angrily. 'For goodness' sake, Davis! I'm supposed to be an artist! And he is a master.'

'And you want to sit at his feet?'

Davis Bryson was a cynic but he had bought several of her paintings and exhibited others. He was a friend.

She said, 'Yes. All right. What's wrong with that?'

He said, 'You like older men, Mary. Are you in love with your father?'

It was a flip remark and she had laughed. Now, sitting in the psychologist's small upstairs room, she realized that in spite of his desertion, she did understand her father. He had grabbed for happiness at any cost. And now he was probably paying the price: an alien in an enemy land. She did not repeat Davis Bryson's remark just in case it turned out to be Freudian and almost true.

She saw in her mind's eye, back in the gallery,

people coming in behind her. She remembered moving on, clutching her drink and re-shouldering her bag automatically. She could not take in the mass of work on display; her one idea was to find a chair and sit down. At one point John Kenyon passed close to her, conducting two Americans around the exhibition space. His voice was low and diffident. He had been shy with everyone – except with her. From that first day he had been completely relaxed with her.

She found a chair and sat down gratefully. She remembered drawing her sandalled feet beneath her chair out of the way. Oh yes, she had been wearing sandals, schoolgirl sandals, and her summer skirt was pale blue, her shirt white. A man's shirt. And a hat – so it was probably hot outside. Or maybe she had worn it just to contain her flyaway hair. A squashy straw hat. She still had it.

It was difficult in this sharp springtime to recall the drowsy heat of a Cornish summer. It had been August. It was April now, 'the cruellest month'.

She said quickly, 'It was a hot summer. You know how romances develop quickly in the heat – hothouse blooming—'

The woman said something and Mary looked up.

'Romances? It was a romance?'

'Yes. No. Romance makes it sound . . . too

light. It wasn't light. It was deep. Nobody really knew. The bit that showed was like the tip of the iceberg. Underneath, it was very deep.' There was a very long pause. Then Mary said with difficulty, 'He was more than a husband, you see. A brother . . . a father.'

The woman stopped doodling.

'Shall we stop there and go on another day?'

Mary stood up with alacrity. The woman also stood and held out a hand. On the desk Mary saw the results of the doodles: a cartoon figure in hat and full skirt with strappy sandals on the feet.

She said, 'That's me!'

The woman smiled. 'It's a representation. I find it more helpful than taking notes.'

Mary stared, she had not known the woman was an artist. She said, 'I – I don't think I can come again.'

'That is absolutely your decision,' the woman said.

But Mary knew no-one else so quietly objective, such an intent listener, and suddenly she wanted to talk, so she went back a week later and talked as if the woman were John Kenyon himself. Six months later, when Neville Chamberlain declared war on Germany, she was painting again.

*　　*　　*

Mary moved to the small village outside Bath in 1945. The war had ended at last and she felt she could face a move. She was exhibiting occasionally in the Cork Street gallery, and Bath was less than two hours away from London by train. She was forty; in her prime. She felt strong and sure. She wanted to visit Lynch End again; visit her mother and her aunt occasionally; start again. Winderslake was the ideal place to make a new home.

It occupied her for years. She moved from the house on the outskirts of the village into a big old house in the centre. It was roomy enough to put up all her friends, hold exhibitions for the local art group, help out with village fêtes and Christmas carol parties, and there was a stable which converted easily into the perfect studio. She knew that her mother's genes were lurking in her somewhere so she limited herself to four studio hours a day. It was terribly tempting to incarcerate herself for longer when she was in the middle of something that was going really well, but she managed to resist those temptations. Davis Bryson told her once that she had more inside her than landscapes and still lifes 'with extras'; maybe even great talents. But she refused to explore herself any further. There was no need; she had found an emotional plateau where contentment was the order of the day. Materially she was comfortable, spiritually she was also comfortable. Almost.

She had only acknowledged the 'almost' when she met Andrew. And then the word 'almost' disappeared from her life.

He told her he was obsessed with her and she knew exactly what he meant. They did not see each other during the day; he had his business to run and he insisted that she should spend more time in her studio. 'I want you to paint what you are feeling now,' he said to her. 'So that there's a record of our love.'

'You want me to paint you?'

'No. Paint the summer and the autumn and the winter when we're there.'

That was when the big canvases began. At last she could do what Davis had told her to do years ago; go within herself. All her experience could be tapped now. Perhaps unconsciously she had shared her father's love affair with Miss Pensford and she could understand her mother's phobia for solitude. Her love for John Kenyon had been a result of all that. And now, with a younger man, she seemed to be free to use all that in her work. Davis Bryson was startled. 'You're practically going off the edge of the canvas these days. You're painting with fire.' He narrowed his eyes at her. 'You're in love again, aren't you? And this time it's nothing to do with Daddy!'

But it had everything to do with Daddy. It had everything to do with love, and her father had been her first love. Her second love had taught her how to see. And her last love had shown her how she could share her visions.

And now . . . now the visions were threatened.

She breathed deeply and carefully. She remembered not only Henry Yorke's name now, but his very words.

'You have cataracts which can be removed. It is difficult to see past them. I would like to discuss your case with a colleague. Sensitivity to light is . . . exaggerated, shall I say. It could mean some damage to the retina or it could quite easily be light refraction because of the cataracts. We might need to do some more tests. And then you could come again to hear the results and discuss the treatment.' It sounded reasonable enough to Andrew; to her it sounded like a sentence. Her eyes were everything. Everything.

'It's just . . .' She thought Andrew would understand. 'I mean, if I can't paint . . . I just can't imagine not being able to paint.'

'Don't worry about it, darling.' Andrew was concerned but bracing. 'Nothing will ever stop you painting.'

She avoided his kiss. 'You're being ridiculous, Andrew. How can I paint if I can't see?' She was angry with him; was he being obtuse or was he simply not interested?

'I don't know. But you would.' He moved away from her. 'How did Beethoven write music when he was deaf? You'd be the first blind painter in the world!'

She did not think he was funny and told him so.

He said quietly, 'Can you see me?' He was standing by the bed, his arms held out to her. 'We can still make love, can't we?'

But she found she couldn't. They were oddly out of tune. Perhaps it was because she now needed a father figure again and the enormous age difference meant Andrew could never be that.

There had been no more discussion; if he opened the subject she made sure she closed it. He seemed almost unobtrusively to draw away from her. And this morning . . . Was she over-reacting by thinking he had abandoned her?

She opened her eyes suddenly and stared out of the window and saw nothing except light. It occurred to her that two of the men she had loved she had lost. Why did she imagine that the third might be different?

Six

Jeremy sat very quietly in his seat next to the
corridor and thought about Sylvie and what she
had said about a small incident illustrating a
big one. There were so many incidents, almost
anecdotes, that he could use; almost too many,
and it would hurt to recall them. Or would it?
He thought about Dougie Beech who had been
an inveterate gambler and had said one day,
'If I get through this lot I'll be paying off my
gambling debts for the rest of my life!' He had
been killed a week after saying that. Would it be
unbearable to use that small and ironic incident?

Jeremy frowned and bit his lip and then
noticed that the woman who had been sitting
next to Sylvie edged away from him. He
changed his frown to a smile and she smiled
nervously back at him. It came as a nasty shock
to think that nice ordinary people were frightened of him. How had he allowed himself to
get to this pass? And would it help if he wrote

about Dougie Beech? And the others. He forced himself to remember some names. Ted Wiley, Stan Clark, Fred Russell . . . and then further back, to his grandfather who had called him Joe. Was that when the bitterness had started?

He was twenty when war was declared. He was in his second year at Cambridge, reading English.

Until then he had had a privileged life; he looked back on it now as a long summer's day. A private school in Bath, then Queen Elizabeth's Hospital school in Bristol where he spent three nights a week with his grandparents in Clifton, then a state scholarship to Trinity.

He had always wanted to write, especially plays. He never sang in the bath, instead he declaimed long passages from *Lear*, *Othello*, the Comedies. He dreamed of living in a bedsit in Islington, writing far into the night and then roaming London through the fog, walking through Smithfield Market before dawn, Covent Garden when the flowers were being unpacked. He saw London as a giant heart being supplied from every corner of Britain, pumping energy back into the land. He was a romantic.

His grandfather was an aircraft designer and worked at Filton on the outskirts of Bristol. It was he who arranged for Jeremy to learn to fly. He got his pilot's licence when he was eighteen, flying a Sopwith Camel, his grandfather in the rear cockpit. When they landed he pushed his goggles to the top of his leather helmet and grinned round at the old man.

'It's living poetry, Gramps. You can see the words across the land – this sceptred isle . . .'

'Let's go and get some breakfast, Joe. That sounds more like poetry to me.'

Gramps had first called him Joe when he was a baby. His mother told him that he had visited her in the nursing home and absolutely snorted when she told him the name they had chosen for the baby.

'Jeremy? What sort of name is Jeremy?'

'Actually, it's George's father's name, Dad. So please don't be awkward about it.'

Gramps snorted again. 'Oh well. I suppose if it's a family name . . .'

Jeremy's mother had smiled lovingly. 'It's better than yours, Dad. I'm sure you'll agree.'

'You could have trimmed mine up a bit,' Gramps had protested. 'Algy's not too bad.'

'Jeremy's better,' his daughter had maintained.

'I think I'll call him Joe,' said Gramps. And he always had.

Because Jeremy could fly, the RAF swallowed him up and he was at Biggin Hill when the Battle of Britain began. He made friends easily, he wrote poetry for them when they needed to fill their letters with words that had nothing to do with the war. Even so, some of them were 'blue-pencilled'. He remembered once when he

164

was tired and out of ideas he had copied a Shakespeare sonnet for Ted Wiley to send to his girl friend. '*Shall I compare thee to a summer's day, thou art more lovely and more temperate . . .*' It had all gone by the time it reached its destination. He and Ted had laughed inordinately about that. 'Bloody fifth columnist, that Will Shakespeare,' Ted had said. Ted had been killed the next day when they were scrambled in the middle of a card game. That same week Jeremy had heard that his grandparents' house in Clifton had received a direct hit. They could not have known a thing about it.

By the end of the war, Jeremy discovered he had no friends left and he did not know what to do with the rest of his life. Very often he wished he had died with the others but he hadn't and so he had to live for them. And the only way he knew how to live was to write.

He got his dreamed-of bedsit, but in Kilburn where the trains thundered by his window and shook the table where he sat. He roamed the streets at night and discovered that the fog was killing people, the river stank and most of the population seemed to be slowly sinking into a mire of drudgery. He lost his ration book so he could not eat properly and when his demob suit wore out he could not afford another one.

His parents rescued him. They took him home, made him stay in bed for three days just as they had when he was 'overtired' as a boy, fed him, found him more clothes, and when he felt better, provided a room where he could write.

Strangely, sitting there warm and comfortable, he could not seem to put words onto the paper in front of him. He stared out of the window at the rooftops of Bath with the abbey at its centre and the amazing bowl of terraced houses which Nash must have originally seen as an amphitheatre surrounding the ancient hot springs, and he thought about the sheer unfairness of life. All those terrible deaths, all that grey misery that had gone on since, seemed almost irrelevant. The land had been here long before all the huge injustices created by its offspring. Should he not be digging back into those prehistoric times and trying to understand them so that today might make sense? Wasn't that what history was all about?

He chewed the end of his old-fashioned pen then looked at it and realized it must be the pen he had used for homework, even to the J nib; and the Indian ink pot was the same too. His mother had kept them all this time. She had probably kept his blazer and tie too. If he had been killed with all the others she would have needed those precious mementos of his past.

He closed his eyes and felt the usual burning sensation behind the lids. He dared not cry; it hurt his eyes too much. He sometimes thought he cried tears of acid.

So he went back to Kilburn and for the next

eighteen months he wrote acidic plays that tried to display the sheer awfulness of post-war life; to ask whether this was what all those young men had died for.

No one was interested.

That April with its annual message of resurrection hurt more than usual. He could not go on living like this; he knew it. For his parents' sake, if not for his own, he had to 'make something of himself'. Perhaps re-invent himself in some way. He left them promising he would be back in four weeks as usual. He hugged his mother and shook hands with his father.

'I might have some news for you next time,' he said as if, by committing himself, he would have to make something happen.

His father said nothing. His mother hugged him back and said, 'Just keep coming to see us.' He knew she wanted to tell him that she loved him, but they didn't talk like that.

He knew they would stand at the front door until he had rounded the bend of the crescent. Then they would close the door and she would go to make tea, although they had just had some, and he would shrug into his jacket and go for the paper while the kettle was boiling.

Maybe theirs was the right way. Once you opened floodgates, you couldn't close them.

Sylvie got along the corridor to the toilet with some difficulty. She found her leg was aching horribly and beneath her hat her scalp was itching. The nervousness was not far away. Perhaps she should have agreed to the young man coming with her to Westminster. It was obvious he was used to dealing with people in authority; he could have made sure she had a fair hearing. He obviously thought that Roger Hargreaves had set the whole thing up for his own ends. What if he had?

Sylvie shut the toilet door with some difficulty and leaned against it for a long moment, thinking about the young man – Joe – and wondering why somebody so aggressive and, at first, down-right unpleasant had made such an impression on her. Surely she wasn't attracted to him? It was simply ridiculous. Her face grew hot at the very thought.

She came out of the toilet and stood by the door and after a while she let the window down so that the air could blow around her face. She remembered what Pem had prophesied for her years ago when he first asked her to marry him. 'I know you don't love me, Sylvie. I know one day you will meet someone, someone very special. Until then, won't you stay with me? It won't be for long. And after . . . you'll have my pension. You'll have my travel facilities. Life will be that much easier for you.'

And Henry at the reading group, Henry who was old and blind and who liked her to read to him had said something similar.

'All right, you were married, I realize that, and you must have loved your husband a lot. But one of these days, mark my words, you'll fall in love properly. You'll savour that love. Roll it round your tongue and taste it. Smell it. I can't see but I can still do those things. Because of my Gracie. An' it'll happen to you too. You see.'

She had thought of Pem after that, thought of the love and companionship they had shared; she thought of him now. The scents from the damp earth flooded through the open window, promising a better summer, a better life, a much better world. Wasn't that what Pem had wanted for her? She closed her eyes and pictured him, tall and thin, prematurely grey with dark intelligent eyes and a narrow face.

She had admired him from the very beginning when he interviewed her for the post of his secretary. He had assumed from the moment she sat down opposite him that she would take the job. She had been on countless interviews and because employers imagined her leg would keep her off work quite often, she never got the job. Her confidence was low so this time she couldn't quite believe that something good seemed to be happening. She had to be sure so she told him that her shorthand wasn't that good and she could not manage the stairs to the upstairs office. He had immediately said, 'You will learn as you go along, Miss Angiers. And it is a simple matter to change my office to one on the ground floor. I think we will suit each other very well.' She had thought at the time he was taking her on because he felt sorry for her. But she soon knew there was more to it than that. He had liked her, genuinely liked her, right from the start. And she had liked him too.

She had been with him for a year when 'peace broke out'. He had been put in charge of re-locating the servicemen who were ex-railway and she had become more than a secretary. He had valued her ideas and encouraged her to voice them and develop them. He always, without fail, respected her opinion.

And then had come the bombshell. He had been taken ill in mid-November in 1946 and had been admitted to hospital in the middle of the night. It seemed presumptuous to visit him, so for a week she carried on the work at the office and telephoned on behalf of the staff and sent best wishes the same way. And then she saw from the staff records that it was his fifty-fifth birthday and with some embarrassment she took him flowers and chocolates and a card. His face lit up with pleasure as she came into his room. A man was already there and stood up as she came in.

She said, 'Oh, please don't go. I'm only from the office. I knew it was Mr Pemberton's birth-day so I popped in just for a minute.'

The man smiled. 'It's Sylvie, isn't it? Pem has spoken of you. I'm Marcus.'

He chatted easily for a while, then put the palm of his hand to Mr Pemberton's cheek, turned and walked through the door.

She knew it was a moment which she should not be sharing, even as an accidental bystander.

She said, 'I'm so sorry. I've come at completely the wrong time.' She was terrified Mr Pemberton was going to cry. 'Would you like me to leave and come back tomorrow?'

'No.' His voice was very controlled. 'No. I'm glad you've met Marcus. He was just about to go anyway. He's emigrating to Australia and if you'd been later, you would never have known him.'

She stared at him, willing the tears to subside. He smiled at her expression and nodded at the chair by the bed.

'Sit down, Sylvie. Put the flowers on the cabinet. A very nice woman comes round and sees to all the flowers. I think she's a volunteer. They rely on volunteers a lot in this ward.'

She did as he said and almost by a process of osmosis she gathered that he had a cancer feeding off his liver and his days were numbered.

He said, 'Marcus and I have been friends for years and we were intending to go to Australia together. It would be so silly for him to change everything now. He's got to make a fresh start. I wanted him to go before . . . well, before this cancer gets me. It will make it easier for him. And in a way he's doing it for me. Enjoying the sunshine and the relaxed life – everything.' He smiled. 'You need not look like that, Sylvie. It was my suggestion. Really. I think he's found it more difficult than I have.'

She thought: he could have stayed until . . . he could have stayed.

He picked up on that too. 'I didn't want him to see me getting really ill. Funny thing that, Sylvie. Bit of vanity left in me.'

'Please . . . Mr Pemberton.' It was she who was going to weep; tears were tightening her throat.

'Call me Pem. Everyone does. I want you to tell me how it's going in the office. The demob programme – are there many of them wanting to come back? We must get some sort of training going, Sylvie. So that these men have an opportunity to use the skills they've learned in the forces. Now that Churchill's been voted out of office again, the Labour Government will be nationalizing everything right, left and centre. We must be seen to have an established plan for re-staffing. You understand this, don't you?'

'Of course. Mr Carling from Paddington rang only yesterday. I've sent him a copy of your notes from the last meeting.'

'Any comments yet?'

She felt her cheeks warm. 'He said, "Good old Pem." Then he said that the old GWR wasn't dead yet and would lead the way as usual. Things like that.'

'Send him names as soon as you get them,

Sylvie. Men from railway families will want to come back. I'm sure of that.'

'Yes, sir.'

'Sylvie, please. Don't call me sir.'

'Sorry . . . Pem.'

He smiled weakly. 'Thank you, Sylvie. I would like you to use my name several times. To get used to it. I rather like it myself. Pem. It sounds like a character in a play. Don't you think?'

She choked on a little laugh. Anyone less like an actor than Mr Pemberton – Pem – it was hard to imagine. But she knew that he was struggling for some kind of ordinariness; a friendship.

She swallowed and nodded.

He said slowly, 'Sylvie . . . I want to ask you something. It's rather . . . well, shocking, I suppose. But please believe that I mean well and if you find it . . . disgusting, then just forgive me and forget it. Can you do that?'

She said stoutly, 'I would never find anything you said disgusting, Mr . . . Pem. And if there is anything I can do for you I should be really pleased. Really, really pleased.'

He closed his eyes and put his head right back on the pillow. His words emerged in a disembodied way. They seemed to have nothing much to do with him. She listened to them with no sense of the shock he had anticipated, but simply with disbelief.

'Sylvie, you are an unusual girl. Not exactly

innocent, not exactly naive, but you have a directness, a simplicity, which I find true. I know a little about you. You live in a hostel, you strive to be independent and you make a good job of it. You have no money except what you earn. You never . . . gripe.'

She made a little sound but he ignored it.

'What I am proposing is, quite simply, marriage. A marriage of convenience. I do not want to end my days in hospital. I would like to end them in my own bed with someone I like and respect looking after everything. There will be nurses, of course, people who will do the physical labour. But I would like you in charge. And the only way I can think of arranging that is with you as my wife.'

He did not open his eyes but he held up his hands as if he expected her to protest.

'It is one-sided, I agree. But my dear, we are friends. That is one advantage for both of us. I would gain your companionship, which gives me so much pleasure. Perhaps you could say the same. That is important, Sylvie, and if you cannot say it, then we cannot go ahead. But if you can say it, then we could move on to more practical matters.' He sighed. 'I hate this bit because it sounds like a bribe. But I have no-one – no family. As my wife and family you would inherit my pension and my house, and what little capital I have managed to put aside.' A faint smile appeared on the long narrow face.

'And of course my travel facilities.' He stopped speaking and waited.

She swallowed tears and whispered, 'I need none of that. I'll look after you anyway.'

His smile widened slightly but he sighed again. 'I knew you would say that. And I cannot accept it, Sylvie. Sorry.'

There was another long silence. Then she said, 'I think I had better go.'

He looked at her. 'Remember, you promised to forgive me and to forget what I said. Will you bring those names with you – the applicants for training – and come again?'

'Of course.' But she was already turning so that he could not see her face. There was nothing to forgive and she knew she would never forget.

There was a time of remission. They worked together as they had never done before, trying to set up a pattern for the future before it was too late. And during that time her respect and admiration for him flowered into love.

When he was ill again she kept the department going for a week and then went to see him at his home.

'There's nothing more we can do,' she told him. 'It either works or it doesn't work. We have to let it go now.'

He nodded. He was sitting in an armchair by a fire that was much too hot for that golden autumn day. There was a blanket round his shoulders.

He said, 'Thank you, Sylvie. I think it will be all right.'

She told him what she had done in the last week. She had been amplifying the filing system for some time and it now offered instant information to anyone who took over.

'I think it will be Gerald Smythe,' Pem said, nodding again with satisfaction. 'He'll carry on where we left off and make sure everything goes through.' He looked at the list she had given him. 'I know that name. Harry Blackmore. His father was a guard. He was like the captain of a ship.' The list slipped down his knees and onto the floor. 'Leave it, Sylvie,' he said.

But she picked it up and put it in her bag and waited until the spasm of pain abated. Then she said quietly, 'If you still want to get married, then . . . I am agreeable.'

He opened his eyes and smiled at her. 'Pity, Sylvie?'

'Of course. But that was always there. I needed to love you before I could marry you. And I do.'

His eyes widened incredulously. 'I don't think you understand—'

'I do understand. Perhaps you don't.' Her face blazed; the fire was much too hot. 'You see, I can never have children in case I pass on my withered leg. They don't know why I was born with it. Probably a great-grandmother or someone . . .' She glanced down at her caliper. 'So . . . that . . . side of things doesn't matter to me. But

I still needed to love you, Pem. I couldn't do it for money. But I can do it for love.'

He looked at her wonderingly and then started to tell her what a hopeless case he was and how thankless a task she was considering.

She said steadily, 'If you've changed your mind, please just say so. I think we both can be honest with each other.'

'Of course. Oh, of course, Sylvie.' He looked into the coals. 'I simply want you to know . . . certain things. I believe Florence Nightingale had quite a shock.'

'Actually, she didn't. But I don't see myself as Florence Nightingale in that sense, Pem. Just as a friend who will be with you.'

They talked for a long time until he was so obviously tired she told him she was going. When she came the next day he had asked his doctor to make all the arrangements and they were married by special licence the following week.

He often said to her, 'One day you will meet someone, Sylvie. I promise you that. And I think you will find that you are able to have a family.'

By that time she had made it ungraciously clear that though she would happily inherit his pension – 'I'm stuck with that, I suppose' – she would have nothing else and he must will his house and money to the hospital.

But that did not happen. Their marriage lasted just over a year and they were both surprised at the extraordinary happiness they gave each other. There was a tranquillity in the big house overlooking the Downs; Sylvie felt it each time she came in after shopping or after one of their short walks. She ran things unobtrusively. They had a twice-weekly cleaner and the cook who had been with Pem for years. They both liked Sylvie instantly and thoroughly appreciated what she was doing. She instituted a routine which they managed to keep up until that final winter. Mornings were the most difficult but by midday Pem was bathed and dressed and sitting by the fire with his lunch, which he rarely ate. Then there was a nap – a siesta Sylvie called it – and then the wheelchair and a walk through the leaves which were already turning orange and gold. Tea by the fire and then chess or draughts until that look of exhaustion came over him and she said, 'Pem, I'm really done. I think it must be bedtime.'

The end was blessedly swift. The routine finished just before Christmas and for three weeks Pem stayed in bed, literally fading away. Sylvie had engaged a nurse to help her with the washing and turning him in bed and one night in January when big, wet flakes of snow were beginning to stick to the windows, they lifted him into a sitting position between them and he gave a cry and closed his eyes.

His heart had given out. Sylvie talked into his ear for ten minutes while the nurse kept her finger on the pulse in his neck. She told him he was a good man and that she would always love him. She thanked him for making her happy, giving her confidence, just for sharing his life with her. And then she went into the next room and wept. It was 1948; they had been married for fourteen months.

His solicitor told her that he had, quite simply, wanted her to have everything. There was a letter for her and after she had read it she folded it carefully into her handbag and said, 'Then so be it.'

She could have sold the house and moved into a more functional flat but between them they had made the big old house into a home so she stayed on and kept the cook housekeeper because she had nowhere else to go. It was a temporary measure which somehow had lasted for almost three years now. She hardly touched his pension, living off income generated by his capital. She travelled third class on his first-class staff card. She felt he was close; she never thought of herself as a widow, but then, she had never thought of herself as a wife. Miles Pemberton had given her much more than a home and an income: he had given her a certain confidence. She knew that she had been able to help him through those last difficult months in a way no-one else could have done, not even his beloved Marcus. She was no longer ashamed of her limp and her walking stick; Pem had told her that if it had not been for her caliper she would not be the person she was. That was indisputable, but it had not occurred to her before.

He had said, 'This leg gives you a kind of passport into so many other lives, Sylvie. It gives you an understanding that other people might not have. Later on, love, let it take you to other places. Will you?'

She thought of that often. His words had taken her into the reading group and onto this train. And she had met Joe who was injured and angry and more crippled than she was, though he did not know it.

The guard was making a last walk through the train. She noticed his carnation. Pem would have approved of that. She pressed against the side of a compartment to let him past but he stopped by her.

'Mrs Pemberton, isn't it? Would you like some help when we arrive?'

She shook her head. 'I'm all right getting off and on. But thank you for the offer.' She hesitated. 'Is it Mr Blackmore?'

Harry nodded, beaming.

She said, 'I remember you on the list of demob applicants. Your father was a guard too.' She smiled. 'Are you happy following in his footsteps?'

'Very much.' He tried to modify his grin a little. She was of the old school and her husband had literally worked himself to death to get the staff re-established after the war. He said, 'I didn't think you'd remember me. I came to the office to do the signalling exam. You brought me a cup of tea.'

'Yes. I remember that too.'

They smiled at each other like old friends. He said, 'I'll be at this end of the train so if you change your mind, I could get you a taxi.'

'I prefer to manage on my own. But thank you. Thank you very much.'

She knew he would understand and he obviously did because he nodded and went past her into the front coach.

She stared at the view gliding past outside and breathed in the air, closing her eyes and letting the scent of summer to come flood her whole being. It was, somehow, like a rebirth.

Seven

The night of the fire, the Harts went to bed early. There was nothing unusual in that, but on that particular night there was a definite reason for it.

As a general rule, by the time Ray got home from work, Ilse had had enough anyway. Throughout the day she just about managed to cope with shopping and housework but it was never easy. She had to wait until the street was deserted before she could venture out of the house, her tiny frame half hidden by the hooded pushchair, a string bag knocking against her calves. She might have been pretty once; now her blond hair was completely colourless and her wary expression drained away any hint of beauty. The journeys home seemed to be even more fraught with danger as she went from doorway to doorway in order to avoid all passers-by. Ray knew that Ilse would never really get over the displaced persons camp in Berlin but sometimes he wondered how long he could cope with living behind drawn curtains and suspecting every other person of being a spy. The atmosphere of terror had got to him too over the years. He jumped almost as high as Ilse when the doorbell rang and he colluded with her about hoarding food. In the green-painted metal meat safe in the cellar there were tins of salmon and spam and baked beans and processed peas. Food they could have done with in those days of austerity rather than the mounds of potatoes and cabbage Ilse dished up daily, but food that might be vital in the weeks and months to come. Not that Ray believed that, not really. It was one of the things that the army doctor had warned him about when he offered to marry Ilse and give her a home back in 1946.

'There will be things she has to do compulsively. Let her do them – help her to do them. They will strengthen her sense of security and one day she will voluntarily give them up. But until then, if you oppose her, you will turn into the enemy and she will be worse still.'

Ray knew exactly what he meant. While they were still in Berlin and she had told him she was pregnant he had kissed her tenderly and said, 'Listen, Ilse, you don't have to pretend to be pregnant just so that we have to get married. We're going to be married anyway, my dear. D'you think I'd leave you here in this hellhole and swan back home without a thought?'

She had looked at him then; the sideways look he had come to dread.

'*Aber* . . . but . . . I have baby. It is true. It is good for you to be a father, *ja*?'

He remembered the words of the army doctor and smiled indulgently. 'Absolutely marvellous, Ilse.'

She moved so that she was looking at him properly. 'Ah, Ray. You are a good man. You will be a good father. You do not hit me therefore you do not hit baby.'

He was shocked though he knew only too well what went on in the so-called displaced persons' hostel.

He kept his smile in place somehow. 'I will spend my life trying to make you happy, Ilse. I want you to forget all the terrible things that have happened. Will you try to do that?'

'I cannot forget the rape, Raymond. I think it will stop me having baby but now . . .' She kissed him chastely and he was thankful for that. Sometimes when she tried to be a seductress he almost hated her. 'Caroline,' she whispered. 'We will call her Caroline.'

He held her head against his shoulder and smoothed her long hair. She had mentioned a child called Caroline before. Perhaps when they got home they would indeed have a baby and call her Caroline. He paused, staring over her head at the dirty grey walls of the dormitory she shared with twenty other women. The thought of a baby was not unattractive, but Ilse would have to be more . . . more settled.

She whispered, 'Do not stop, Raymond. Please do not stop.'

He blinked and then knew what she meant and resumed smoothing her hair. At some point during the last few terrible years, her head had been shaved. Now, she loathed short hair in women and would not even pin hers back.

She whispered, 'We will be safe in England, *ja*?'

'Yes, my darling. We will be safe. And there will be food and warm clothing and I will get my job back in the bakery and I might be able to get you a job in the front shop.'

'But I must care for baby!' she said, jerking her head up and eyeing him again. He kissed her face tenderly. 'I forgot. Of course, you will be at home looking after our child.'

He got his job back all right but there was very little warm clothing to be had and the food situation was bleak too. They rented a house that needed to be renovated and Ilse slipped into her previous role of a hunted victim. Ray understood, he always understood. And he never opposed her. When she thought he did, her eyes would slide sideways and he would try to explain what he had *really* meant. Ray had always been a 'good boy': his mother had told him so, his father had nodded agreement and his older sister had looked after him when their parents went to work. She had taken him shopping, holding his hand and wiping his nose and letting him listen when she met her friends. He began to grow when he was fourteen and by the time he went into the army he was almost six foot tall, almost broad-shouldered and almost good-looking in a brown-haired, grey-eyed way. His face was good-natured and that was what he was. He liked people to be happy. He felt that Ilse was his life work. If he could make her happy he could do anything . . .

His sister, Janet, who was sensible and down-to-earth and tried very hard, called their way of life 'Ilse's nuttiness'. She laughed at them when they went out together and he turned up his coat collar and pulled his hat brim almost over his eyes. She wasn't quite so amused when they dodged from cover to cover and flattened themselves against walls to let people pass. The house in the St Paul's area was the best they could do – they were lucky to get anywhere and she couldn't have them in her flat – but she could see that it did not help Ilse to lead a normal life. It was rundown and bomb-damaged and full of rather peculiar people; a lot of foreigners, other displaced persons, bereaved people – not a salubrious area at all. Anywhere else her brother and his German wife would have stood out like two sore thumbs but St Paul's accepted everyone. When Ilse occasionally wheeled out an empty pushchair, they assumed it was to carry home her shopping. When she pegged out squares of linen, they only noticed how white they were and sniggered about the Harts' social aspirations. They might recognize table napkins but no-one else in St Paul's would use them. Janet visited as often as she could and brought things like apple pies and jam tarts. Ilse was always pleased to see her, that was one thing. On a housewifely level they got on quite well.

For a long time before and after their marriage, Ray thought Ilse had had a daughter way back in her previous life and had lost her to disease and starvation. Another Caroline did not materialize and he was thankful because Ilse was no better. Perhaps it was not meant that Ilse should have anyone but that first Caroline.

It was Janet who discovered that both Carolines were imaginary. Janet, in her eagerness to help Ilse, encouraged her to talk about the first Caroline.

'We should know about your little girl, Ilse,' she said one day when she was helping to get the washing off the line. She flattened a linen square into the laundry basket. 'When did she die, my dear?'

Ilse spun round, the prop in her hands like a medieval lance.

'Die?' Her voice was high with fear. 'Is she dead? *Mein Gott!* Is Caroline dead? What have you heard?'

Janet sidestepped, the laundry basket held in front of her.

'Nothing. How could I? Do you mean . . . Oh Ilse, my dear, do you mean that Caroline is still alive somewhere?'

Ilse stood still, lance at the ready, eyes huge. She said nothing but her tension was such that Janet was afraid she would collapse.

She said swiftly, 'Listen. Ilse. Talk about it. Please. Tell me about Caroline. Tell me what she looked like. You're safe now. You have a husband and a home and a family. I am your sister. I love you and I want to understand you.'

Ilse very gradually relaxed; she replaced the prop and then walked back down the awful little concrete yard and into the house, with Janet close behind. Ray was making tea in the kitchen and Janet jerked her head at him. He immediately went into the yard and sat on the coal bunker staring up at the remaining cloths, knowing that they were nappies. He longed with all his soul for Janet to unlock something in Ilse so that they could start to lead a normal life. If only she would weep or wail or tear her hair; the silent terror was getting to him.

Ilse sat at the table and started scratching the chenille tablecloth with her fingernail. Janet put the basket down and sat by her, ignoring the fact that as usual she cringed away from any possible physical contact.

'Come on.' Janet tried to sound like her

mother used to. Encouraging but firm. 'Let's be having it. Bit by bit.'

She thought at first that Ilse was not going to speak a word. They sat there, side by side with the awful sound of the chenille being scraped until Janet began to count inside her head, simply to stop herself from screaming. She had reached a slow fifty-two when Ilse spoke.

'I am not family.' Her voice was quiet but convincing. 'Ray married me in order for me to come to England. When I tell him I have baby soon he no longer sleep with me. So I am not proper family. You understand?'

Janet put a hand to her throat. She loved Ray and naturally she had assumed that he and Ilse loved each other in every way. But she did not want to think about him co-habiting – if that was the word – with Ilse before their marriage.

'I didn't know,' she said lamely.

'He is a kind man. Some of the men were not kind. Even,' she flashed a quick look upwards, 'even the English men. We were German girls and they liked to hurt us.'

'Oh . . .' Janet put her hand from her throat to her mouth. This was terrible.

Ilse said matter-of-factly, 'There was not much food in the camp. He saved food for me. He does it still. We keep it in the cellar.'

Janet breathed deeply and consciously. Then she said, 'Yes, I can see him doing that.'

'He made me eat first. Always. Before bed, I

mean. So that it would not seem like payment. Then when he was due to be demobbed, he went to see the Red Cross people to ask about getting me out of the camp. Already he said he would marry me because then I could be sent to England. So we were married.'

Janet nodded. She was breathing very audibly behind her hand and forced herself to put it back on the table.

Ilse whispered, 'I was sorry for him then. Because, *natürlich*, I will never leave him. I could not live without him now. So always he has me. You understand?'

Janet felt an echo of Ilse's terror. 'Yes,' she whispered. 'I understand.' And she thought of Ray, her brother, and felt her heart contract with pity.

'So then . . . I had Caroline. For Ray.' Ilse's face suddenly creased into a smile. 'It was the only thing I could do for him. I do not mind. The nappies and the walks with the pushchair . . . I hear women grumble, but I do not mind. It is for my husband. He is a good man. A kind man. He deserves to have a child.'

Janet could not speak; she needed all her self-control to stop herself fleeing the room. When Ilse got up to make tea, she still sat there, watching her every move, more frightened by the minute because this woman lived with her brother.

Ilse went to the door and called to Ray that

tea was ready and Janet wondered whether Ray would allow her to tell the doctor all about this so that Ilse could be sent to an institution. Not a camp. An institution. And she knew he would not.

The only way she could deal with it and make it possible for Ray to deal with it, was to diminish it in some way. Almost trivialize it. That was when she started to talk about Ilse's 'nuttiness'.

'If you could see yourselves!' she laughed at them when she called next. 'You came creeping along the road like a couple of old age pensioners! And with that blessed pushchair full of shopping – well! D'you remember old Aunt Agatha, Ray?' She turned to Ilse. 'We had this dotty aunt who used to take a pushchair with her every morning to collect firewood! Her boast was that she kept a fire going all winter long without having to buy one piece of coal!'

Ilse didn't know what she was on about but when Ray laughed and hugged his sister gratefully, Ilse laughed too and forgot to point out that the shopping was dangling from the pram handle in its string bag while the pram contained . . . well, obviously it must contain a baby.

While she unpacked the bag, Ray ushered Janet into the front room and drew the curtains against the watery spring sunshine.

'Ilse thinks next door are spying on us!' he confessed sheepishly. 'Mind you, they are a strange pair. Sleep all day and out all night as far as I can tell.'

'Then they're not likely to be around now, are they?' Janet pulled the curtains back again. 'Listen, Ray, I know Ilse is a bit on the nutty side, but don't you go the same way, all right?'

He looked even more sheepish. 'You don't understand, Jan. The army doctor – the one who discharged her from the camp – he told me to go along with all her funny little ways for a while.'

'Yes. For a while. It's nearly four years since you brought her home, Ray. How much longer is a while?'

'Well, obviously not four years!' He tried to laugh and failed dismally. He spread his hands. 'I don't know what else to do, Jan. If I try to put her on the rails again she might turn against me. I'm really her only friend.'

The pathos of the whole thing was almost too much for practical Janet. She willed herself not to cry.

'Listen, Ray. I've got an idea. Let me try it. I promise you it won't turn her against you.'

'What is it?'

'I'm not going to tell you because it has to be as much a surprise for you as for her.'

'Janet. Be careful. You have no idea of the kind of hell she lives in. If you could have seen that camp – no more than an enormous brothel—'

'Don't tell me. I would much prefer not to know.'

'All right. Just take my word for it that I must know what you're going to do.'

Janet paced the little sitting room; she could hear Ilse clattering cups in the kitchen and hoped she would interrupt them soon. Ray read her thoughts and went to the door.

'Want some help, love?' he called through.

Ilse's voice was almost light. 'No, *liebling*. Talk to your sister while I make tea. I have cake here also.'

Ray turned back. 'Come on. Out with it.'

Janet said, 'I am going to look after Caroline for you. While you have a little holiday.'

The simplicity of it took him by surprise. He put his back to the door.

'She – she won't agree to it.'

'She will if I tell her that you need a break. And you do need a break.'

'I – we can't afford it.' He stared at his sister. 'Where would we go?'

'There's a place in Somerset. A girl at the office was telling me about it. Half a dozen chalets – quite separate from each other. You needn't speak to anyone else if you don't want to. Lovely seaside walks. Bus trips to Minehead and Dunster and – and other places. You'll just love it.' He did not immediately reply and she added, 'And so will Ilse.'

He was still silent, considering. Then he

sighed and said, 'She'll want to take the baby.'

'No children allowed,' Janet said swiftly. She had no idea whether it was true. She sat down on the hard sofa. 'Listen, how would it be if I booked it? A present from me. Belated wedding present if you like. Then she'd have to accept it and she'd have to let me look after the baby.'

He gnawed his top lip. 'I don't know . . . It would be an amazing break. Some nights she is up two or three times when Caroline cries.'

Janet hit the arm of the sofa with a balled fist. 'Listen to you!' She shook her head. 'Listen to me too! We're talking as if the baby were real!'

Ray said soberly, 'She is to Ilse.'

'Oh dear Lord. It's so awful.'

Ray was spared having to agree with her. Ilse came in carrying a tray and almost immediately Janet told her about the 'wedding present' and said that she had arranged to take time off work to look after Caroline. Ilse passed tea and cake, frowning prodigiously but Janet did not give her a chance to say a word. She reminded herself of one of the barrow boys at the Saturday market, no-one was allowed to interject one word of dissent. Both Ray and Ilse were well into their cake but she had not dared to give herself time for a single bite. Eventually, exhausted, she turned to her brother.

'Well, you're the head of the family. What do you think? Will you trust me with Caroline? I'm very good with nappies and – and Ilse will give me a list of the kind of food she has.'

Ilse said, 'Milk. Only milk.'

Janet turned to her, beaming. 'That's good. No wonder she's looking so well. We must persuade your husband to accept my present, Ilse. It will be such a treat for me to look after Caroline.' She went back to Ray. 'Please say yes, Ray. You need a holiday.'

Still Ray did not speak and it was Ilse who said, 'When for did you book the little cottage by the sea, Janet?'

'April.' Janet was improvising now. 'The middle of April. The flowers will be out but the crowds won't. You'll have the place to yourselves.' She only hoped her contact at the office could fix her up.

Ilse looked at Ray. 'What do you say, *liebling*? Would you like this holiday? It would be good for you, no?'

He looked at her wonderingly. 'Well . . . if you think . . . yes, I would like it.'

He said afterwards to Janet, 'I can't imagine it will make much difference, sis. When we come home she'll—'

'Don't look too far into the future,' Janet advised him. 'You never know what might happen.' She had already planned that future. One way or another Ilse had to face up to the fact that there was no Caroline.

*　　　*　　　*

195

Ilse seemed to enjoy the holiday in her own peculiar way; she would get up at the crack of dawn and go down to the muddy Bristol Channel and walk along pebbled shores and then clamber over rocks to the next little cove and explore that. At first Ray was terrified she might walk into the water and not walk back again. He got up just after her and followed her at a distance but when she returned at midday, apple-cheeked and bright-eyed, he realized that she had found some kind of happiness and he let her go. He had taken his fishing gear and he would set himself up on a headland and fish on an incoming tide. Twice he cleaned his catch and made a bonfire on the pebbles, rigging up an arrangement of old spars on which to hang the fish. She enjoyed that too and he told himself they were sharing something precious at last. Then he realized that the word sharing had never applied to them as a couple. They might do everything together but they never really shared their lives. He had time to think about their marriage; to think about the future. Sometimes he shivered with a kind of terror.

They returned home on a typically April afternoon; showers soaked them on their way to the bus stop, and then again from the bus station out to St Paul's.

There were people about, which meant that Ilse dragged him into doorways every few minutes; it took them over an hour to reach home. There was no sign of a pushchair. Ilse ran from room to room. No sign of Janet either.

'Where can she be?' Ilse asked despairingly, her wet hair hanging in rat's tails around her face. 'Where is Caroline?'

'No need to worry.' Ray was tired, wet and hungry. 'Let's get the tea and Jan will be round and we can tell her all about—'

And at that precise moment Janet appeared at the back door. Without the pushchair.

Her story was simple and so obvious that Ray wondered why he had not realized before exactly what she intended. Caroline had been as good as gold all week. Absolutely no problem. They had gone for walks every afternoon. One day they had got as far as the Downs. She had loved that. She had gurgled at the trees over her pushchair. Janet had started to wheel her back home straight after lunch. The nappies were packed in the bottom of the pram, together with a new bottle she had bought from Timothy Whites. Oh, and a pretty frock too. She had been crossing by the Belisha beacon in Gloucester Road when a lorry had come thundering down the hill out of control.

She wept as she spoke but her voice was steady and deliberate and she kept looking straight at Ilse, not once did she glance across at Ray.

'She could not have known a thing, Ilse,' she said, then paused to wipe her eyes. 'The lorry driver did not even stop – did not realize what he had done. When the police arrived—'

For the first time there was a sound from Ilse; a kind of hiss. Janet paused, suddenly doubtful. 'One of the witnesses dashed over to the phone box at the top of the street and . . .'

Ray found his voice. 'Go on,' he ordered grimly.

'They were so kind, Ilse. But there was hardly any . . . evidence. Everything . . . just everything . . . had gone.' She stared at Ilse and then broke down completely. 'Oh Ilse. I'm sorry. I'm so very sorry. She – Caroline – she didn't have a chance. Poor little scrap. Even the pushchair . . . gone.'

Ilse sat at the table, her nails trying to cut the chenille pile. Janet put her head down and wept but Ilse's eyes were dry, her face set. When Ray put his arm round her shoulders she looked up at last.

'We must go,' she whispered. 'Now. Tonight. We must leave Bristol.' Her eyes widened. 'Where can we go, Ray? Where will no one know us?'

'Why should we go, Ilse? This is our home. It was an accident, a tragic accident. We can comfort each other. And Janet too.'

'The police will come, Raymond. We must go before they arrive.'

Janet lifted her head; her face was streaked with tears. 'They won't come, Ilse. I promise. I told them she was mine – I didn't give your name.'

'They will find out. They always find out.'

Janet gabbled reassurances. Ray said, 'Listen. We will sleep on it. Nothing will happen tonight. In the morning we will decide what to do.'

Ilse hardly heard him. 'London. We go to London. No one knows us in London. There is a train from Temple Meads. Many trains, I believe.'

'Not until the morning, love.' Ray sounded completely certain of this. 'There's one at eight forty-five. Let's see how we feel when we get up, shall we?'

Bit by bit he led her upstairs and encouraged her into her bedtime routine. Janet waited downstairs, wondering what she had done. It was eight thirty which, even by Ilse's standards, was early for bed.

The fire started accidentally: Ilse swore as much to Ray. The can of paraffin kept in the outside lavatory had nothing to do with it. She shook him awake at two in the morning. She was frantically pushing things into a case and she was fully dressed.

'Hurry, Raymond. We have to leave. The house will burn down. Soon. Please hurry.'

He stumbled to the bedroom door and was beaten back by the smoke. He tried to remember his army fire drill. She flung clothes at him. 'Get dressed, quickly. We are quite safe. There is a ladder at the window. But please hurry.'

Even as he ran to the window to check, he started to question her. 'What do you mean? What ladder?' He flung up the window; it was their own ladder from the back yard, conveniently placed, wedged against the wall and a street lamp. Nobody was stirring. He shouted, 'Fire!'

'Raymond!' She grabbed him and pulled him back. 'There is no time. Put on your clothes. Quickly. Soon everything will be destroyed.'

He dragged on his trousers. 'What have you done, Ilse?' he groaned. 'Oh God, this will bring the police down on us right enough! Is that what you want?'

'We must go before then!' She rammed the case shut, went to the window and threw it out. 'Identity cards. Everything. In the desk. No one will know.'

'So you did do this?'

'Of course I did not. But it is so fortunate, Raymond. Can't you understand that God is giving us another chance?'

Somehow, gabbling at first and then silent, he put on the rest of his clothes and clambered down after her. The street was filling with acrid smoke.

'Take the ladder to the back. Quickly.' She picked up one end and started towards the back alley. He obeyed her; he had been indulging her for so long, it was automatic.

At the back of the house the fire could be seen

behind the windows; the curtains had gone and the flames were licking the ceiling. He shoved the ladder to the side of the shed and stood in horror as the whole of the downstairs was engulfed in an orange inferno. And then, without warning, the windows exploded and balls of fire sailed out, landing on the toilet roof. It was then that he saw that the house next door was also in flames.

'Oh God!' He turned frantically to Ilse. 'Listen, go and call everyone to get out. The whole terrace will go up! Call the fire brigade – ask the man on the other side of the alley to call them. Do you understand?' She did not move, she stood watching, her face in its usual tense lines. He grabbed her by the shoulders and shook her hard. 'Ilse. I have to go and warn that couple next door – get them out. Do what I say. Go back down the alley and knock on number twenty-five. Do it now.'

'Raymond. They do not come home at night. The house is empty.'

'You've thought it all out, haven't you?' His voice was grim. 'We don't know that for sure. I have to go and see.' He turned and gave her a shove in the right direction and then leapt over the fence and put his shoulder to the back door of their neighbour's house.

Inside, the scullery was full of dirty pots, a broken chair, a split and sagging mattress and several army blankets. He ran the tap and shoved the blankets beneath it. The stink of urine was everywhere. He wrapped himself in a blanket and left the others beneath the tap.

He never knew how he got up the stairs. On each tread the flames seemed to dance out of the sides of the lino covering and he danced with them, skipping from step to step just ahead of what he knew would happen. And it did. He was actually on the landing when the flames ignited the tinder-dry wood and the stairs exploded into flame. He opened the door to the first bedroom, went in and slammed it shut behind him. He ran to the window and lifted it and there, struggling from the back alley, was Ilse with the ladder. He leaned down and grabbed it as it wavered towards him, then turned back to the room. It was empty except for a cot in the corner. In the cot was a child, apparently asleep. He snatched it up and held it under one arm as he clambered through the window. He saw that the bedroom next door was a mass of flame; no hope for anyone who might be in it. He slithered downwards and was gathered up by Ilse – an Ilse who had changed. She was weeping, thanking God for deliverance, holding him and kissing his streaked face. She took the child, a girl, and turned to the people who were gathering. 'Is there somewhere we can rest until morning?'

Eventually they were in what he imagined was a church hall. They washed in a tiny cloakroom with a triangular basin and a string to pull the lavatory flush. Ilse washed the child too and combed the lank hair.

'Caroline has been returned to us,' she told him, smiling happily.

He stared at her. 'She must belong to that young couple.'

'The ones who spied on us?' Ilse still smiled. 'I do not think that is possible. In any case, they have gone. Disappeared. They had no child – you know that. She is Caroline.'

He wanted to cry, but he knew that soon Janet would hear of the fire and come round; she would take over somehow. Or the child's parents. They must have gone out and left the little girl there and they would appear and claim her at any moment.

But they did not.

The child was apparently deaf and dumb; certainly dumb. She did not speak or cry when the comb snagged on knots of hair. She looked about eight or nine years old but she was terribly under-nourished. Ilse went through a pile of clothes collected for evacuees in the war and selected a gingham frock and red cardigan. The child began to look like a little girl.

Breakfast appeared: cheese sandwiches and hot sweet tea. They all ate like refugees – Ray realized that they were in fact refugees. On the run. People asked questions and Ilse replied. 'Her name is Caroline. She is always good like this – yes, always.' At eight o'clock she said, 'We will go now. To my husband's sister. Thank you very much. We will deal with the insurance and all that when we have slept. I am afraid for our daughter . . .'

Nobody had the authority to order them to stay in the church hall and the police had not put in an appearance. They walked to the bus station and, as if waiting just for them, there was a bus to Bath. They got on it and at Bath they went to the station to catch the train.

'This is the eight forty-five from Temple Meads,' Ray said as it snorted alongside the platform.

'That is good.' Ilse could not stop smiling at the child. 'No-one knows we are getting a train. We have disappeared already.'

There was a slight mist of summer rain drifting beyond the canopy. What with that and the steam everywhere, they did in fact seem to be wrapped in invisibility as they clambered onto the first coach. The child had difficulty walking; Ray suspected she had rarely been allowed out of her cot and never out of the house. In the end he had held her beneath his mac. No one could have seen her.

He said, 'Ilse. We do not know where to go in London. And I must get in touch with Janet. She'll be worried about us.' It occurred to him that nobody else would be concerned; they hardly knew a soul in the neighbourhood.

Ilse kept smiling. 'No, we do not get in touch

with Janet. Not with anyone. We start a new life. We find a flat and a job and we look after Caroline.'

He felt as if prison gates were clanking shut behind him.

Eight

A few miles from Paddington, the train slowed at a signal box and then came to a halt.

Albert, eyeing the dropped signal from his cab, frowned slightly and Wilf shut the firebox with a bang and said, 'This will bugger us up completely.'

Albert said, 'They won't keep us waiting. Crack service like this.'

Harry Blackmore hung out of the brake van at the rear of the train and held up a hand to Albert ten coaches up. Albert waved back. Nothing doing yet.

Harry withdrew his head and looked at Jenny who was standing uncertainly by the connecting door to the first-class coach.

'Signal at danger. Could be anything. Give it the usual time then I'll walk up to the box and find out.'

Jenny wanted to stay with him but she said, 'I'd better go and reassure Miss Morrison.

She'll be wondering what's happened.'

He grinned approval and she glowed and went through to the coach. This trip was getting better and better. She felt she could cope with anything. She remembered Lydia saying to her, 'Lucky sod. Your own job – I'll never have that.' And Jenny had retorted, 'You don't want it. You're going to get married and have an enormous family, remember?' She knew that would never happen for her, in spite of her new grandfather and the wonderful peaceful school holidays in the cottage at Winderslake, learning how to grow vegetables and then gather them and cook them in the tiny scullery, how to wash up and put everything away 'Bristol fashion', as her grandfather always said. When he had mentioned her to Mr Beauchamp he had said, 'She's a good girl. Proper standards. Neat. Bristol fashion.' And Mr Beauchamp, still smarting after the awful Corinne, nodded approvingly as he looked at Jenny's reassuring figure and capable hands. 'That's what we want,' he said as if she were a commodity.

Not that Jenny would have minded even if she'd noticed. She was too happy for that. And even when she came under the critical eye of Ahmed, nothing could take away the deep contentment inside her. From the moment when she had met her new grandfather in Mr Cousins' office, she had known everything would be all right. She was conscious that there was a terrible battle with Social Services to allow her to make her official home with an elderly man who was no relative at all, but she never had any doubt that it would all turn out all right. After all, she had been searching for him for so long; God would not be unkind enough to stop them being together now that she had found him.

And now, quite suddenly, today in fact, though she knew no-one would want to marry her, there was nothing to say she couldn't fall in love, was there? She smiled as the connecting door slammed shut behind her. She was in love all right, and it was wonderful. When she stood within sight of Harry Blackmore, it was like standing in the sun. It was enough in itself, that was.

She swung down the corridor, perfectly steady now that the train was at a standstill. As she passed the second compartment, the newly-married girl signalled to her and she slid open the door and looked in.

'What's happening?' the girl asked, still clinging to her husband's arm. 'Has something gone wrong?'

'The signal is against us,' Jenny said professionally. 'We don't know why, of course. If it stays at danger much longer the rule is that the guard leaves the train and walks to the signal box to find out what's happening. But it shouldn't be long.'

'Everything has gone so well so far,' the

girl said apprehensively. 'I hope this isn't a sign . . .'

The young husband slid his arm further round her shoulders. 'Darling girl. You and your signs.' He looked up at Jenny, smiling indulgently. 'She can read palms, you know.'

At any other time Jenny would have been captivated but not now.

She said, 'Why don't you come along to the buffet? Have another coffee or something. Then you'll be on the spot when there is any news.'

They consulted each other and then nodded and began to gather themselves together. Jenny passed on, smiling to herself. Ahmed would have to open up again; he could hardly refuse to serve a first-class passenger. Serve him right for wanting to clear up so quickly instead of waiting till they arrived in Paddington. She stopped smiling, shocked at herself. It was the first time she had retaliated against the dictates of Ahmed – even in her thoughts. She must be following Lydia's advice at last. 'Bite back,' Lydia was always telling her. 'Give 'em as good as they give you, and better!'

Mary Morrison looked up as the door opened. She knew immediately who it was.

'Jenny. We're almost there, aren't we? Should I come into the corridor now?'

'Not yet.' Jenny sat down opposite her and leaned forward like Lydia had taught her. 'We've had to stop at a signal. I expect there's another train in front or something. I'll let you know when we're about to arrive.'

'Thank you. Thank you so much, Jenny.' That wide smile again. 'You're looking pink and happy.'

She was delighted that Miss Morrison could see that much. She smiled back and said, 'I think I'd prefer to be pink than peaky!' Miss Morrison laughed and Jenny could not believe she had actually made a joke that was funny. She felt confident enough to add, 'You've spoken to Mr Blackmore, haven't you? The guard.'

'He looked in briefly. He was the one who helped me onto the train at Bristol. Courteous.'

'Good-looking, didn't you think?'

'Yes. Very.' Mary's smile widened still more. 'Do I gather you are interested in him rather than Marvin?'

Jenny felt silly. She made a face. 'I'm not really interested in anyone. I'm so happy with my grandfather at Winderslake. Boys and . . . things like that, they're not for me.'

'No, perhaps not yet. What about your friend? Lydia – was that her name? Is she interested in boys?'

'Oh yes. She wants to get married and have a family. The sooner the better.'

Miss Morrison turned her mouth down. 'Sounds to me as if she thinks marriage is an escape. It's not, you know.'

'It might be for Lydia. Her parents are so . . . anxious. I'm surprised they let her go to a residential school like Winderslake. We were allowed to make our own rules – well, almost. I mean, if you weren't there for meals you didn't have them and you couldn't smoke and you had to go up to your room at half past eight unless something special was on and you couldn't actually hit people.'

Miss Morrison laughed. 'I have a feeling that was difficult for Lydia.'

'Yes. But she had her secret weapon. That's what she called it. She's a brilliant screamer.'

'Screamer?'

'She can scream longer and louder than anyone I know. She developed it when people thought she was deaf as well as blind.'

'Rather difficult for her friends, surely?'

Jenny said quietly, 'She's the best friend in the whole world. She screams for me sometimes. When she thinks people aren't listening.' She smiled. 'She wouldn't have to scream today, would she? I'm talking far too much.'

Miss Morrison put out a hand and found Jenny's. 'You have no idea how much you have helped me,' she said.

Just at that moment there was a blast from the engine whistle and the chuntering of slipping driving wheels and then they moved.

Jenny jumped up. 'I'll have to report to the steward now. But I'll come and help when we get in.' She smiled at the face framed in the mass of hair.

'Thank you,' Miss Morrison said.

There was no sign of Harry Blackmore; he had obviously moved towards the front of the train nearer to the signal box in case he had to walk up to it. The young couple were leaning on the bar talking to Marvin and drinking what smelled like port and lemon. Ahmed was in the kitchen examining the books. He looked up as Jenny came in.

'Ah, Miss Price, did you enter the complimentary drinks as I showed you?'

Jenny was immediately thrown. 'I was going to do it before we arrived,' she said, 'but then we stopped and I sat with Miss Morrison and—'

'Just because they are free does not mean they are not entered. We have to keep a check on all our supplies. You should know that. How many times do I have to explain?'

Marvin said, 'Oh, hello, Jen. Here's that list you gave me. Free drinks, wasn't it?' He passed her a piece of paper. He must have guessed the figures just as she usually did. The list was in his handwriting and was liberally decorated with scribbled flowers and hearts. He swung himself back to his side of the buffet and gave her an enormous wink. She swallowed.

Ahmed said, mollified, 'Oh, I see. You intended to copy your list into the ledger. Here you are then.' He smiled round at them.

'Another highly successful journey. Let's hope the return one will go as well.'

Marvin smiled at her and after a split second's hesitation she smiled back. The newlyweds smiled all the time.

At the front of the train, Ray Hart suggested to Ilse that it might be a good idea to take Caroline to the toilet before they arrived.

He glanced at the little girl who was smelling and obviously wet. He remembered the urine-soaked blankets in the kitchen of the next-door house and thought that perhaps it was a good thing that the child was now with them. But when he watched Ilse carrying her down the corridor, he knew that no child would really be better off with the two of them. A gout of sooty smoke obscured the windows and he had that feeling again of being trapped.

The guard suddenly appeared at the door and slid it back. This was it. They had been discovered and they would be charged with arson and probably murder too if that young couple had been in the other bedroom. Kidnapping seemed a minor offence in comparison.

The guard smiled. Ray could smell the carnation in his buttonhole and was reminded of schooldays with Janet, helping at the nurseries for pocket money.

'We shall be arriving in five minutes, sir. Are you on your own?'

Ray looked at him. Then he said, 'Yes.'

'Right. You're at the front of the train. Have your ticket ready for the inspector at the barrier.'

'Yes. Thank you.' Ray willed him to go away before Ilse and Caroline appeared.

'Sorry about the delay. We're not sure why it happened.'

Ray forced himself to speak. 'It wasn't for long.'

'No.' Harry smiled again, closed the door and went on his way.

Ray gathered up the bag containing the biscuits and Ilse's frantic packing of the night before and went into the corridor.

Sylvia knew she should go back to her compartment and gather up her papers and bag ready to get off the train but that would mean talking to Joe again and she was not quite certain whether she was ready to do that. He might try to help her with everything and it was so important to do everything herself.

She leaned out of the window and sooty smoke immediately blew into her face; she felt the sting of a smut going into her left eye. She blinked furiously and ducked her head and then grabbed at her hat. Too late. It was gone, flying away from her while the wind blew her hair everywhere and she lost any semblance of authority she might have had. Tears filled her eyes and she reached into her pocket for a handkerchief and dabbed quickly. At least the tears had washed away the smut.

She clung to the window frame and watched the engine, two coaches up, labouring for the last few miles. She told herself that it didn't matter two hoots about her hat, she could deliver her petition perfectly well without it. But somehow she did not quite believe herself; the hat had been a symbol, it had given her a bit of presence, even authority. She saw herself stepping out of a taxi with her hair all over the place, leaning on her sticks . . . Oh dear God. She felt like catching the next train home. With her hat gone and her hair a mess and doubtless soot all over her clothes, what chance did she have of convincing anyone of her cause? She almost wept again and leaned further out so that the wind would dry her face. And then something very strange happened. She had what she thought must be an optical illusion. The engine, the huge locomotive called the *Prince Albert*, was leaning to the right. Leaning, and leaning, and leaning . . .

Further down the train, Jeremy Kemp, his mind completely taken up with what Sylvie was going to do at Westminster, hardly noticed the camber of the coach until his fellow passengers began to slip and slide against him. And then his first thought was that Sylvie was higher up the train, nearer whatever was happening.

He got to his feet and managed with enormous difficulty to push back the door to the corridor.

'Sylvie!' he bawled as the whole train began to jar and bump and keel over almost in slow motion. 'Sylvie, I'm coming!'

Albert wished he knew what that signal had been all about. Another two minutes and Harry would have set out for the signal box to find out. But this was the eight forty-five and it was already going to be over ten minutes late into Paddington so he nodded to Wilf to fire her up and he opened the valves and gave the engine everything he could. It seemed to take a long time to get up speed and they made a lot of smoke, which wasn't like Wilf. As usual when anything wasn't absolutely smooth in the driving cab he mentally talked to Walter, his father. 'Come on, our Dad, give us a hand here.' He eased the drive handle forward and at last the *Prince Albert* settled into a steady fifty. He looked out and saw the usual view of the canal with boats moored ready for the April weather to turn into summer. And then his eye flicked to the curve of the rail ahead of them and he frowned sharply. The sun was properly out now and he had seen a flash. Something on the line? He leaned out and fixed his gaze on the arc of rail ahead. And saw it. What all drivers dreaded. A broken rail, askew from the line, making an angle where there should be the smoothest of curves.

He leapt for the handle. 'Brake. Wilf! Brake! Broken rail!' he shouted.

He knew it was too late when he felt the driving wheels begin to slide onto the ballast. And then as the coaches followed, the locomotive keeled fatally. The fire door flew open and coals spewed out. He leapt across the cab and shoved Wilf out of the other side. The last thing he registered was the coaches zig-zagging across the sleepers and onto the ballast, beginning to rear like startled horses. He knew from his father that they would then start to concertina as if they were made of tin.

To anyone who might have been watching, the scene was incredible. The sophisticated locomotive, so perfectly engineered, so splendid and magisterial on its rails, was reduced to a crazed monster as it left the permanent way and careered helplessly across the down line into the embankment where it continued to travel on its side, spewing fountains of fire and sparks, steam and smoke. The tender behind seemed to disappear, crushed like a nut between crackers as the first coach mounted it, before it broke in half and continued to climb all over the locomotive. This was the coach in which Ilse and her Caroline, Ray and his guilt were escaping their pasts.

Behind that first coach the other third-class coaches made desperate attempts to deal with what was happening. The next coach, the one in which Sylvie was standing in the corridor, mounted the two halves of the first coach and then began to break up, splintering like matchwood. The next two were compressed to a third of their lengths, just as old Walter Priddy had described to his son years ago. And they provided a kind of mounting block for the next coach, in which Jeremy Kemp was shouting the name of a girl he had just met.

The other coaches were flung over the lines almost casually, breaking up, twisting, squashing and coming to a grinding rest on their sides, their tops wrenched off as if by some giant can-opener, glass showering them.

Sights which in the order of things simply should not be were accompanied hideously by sounds that could have come from hell. A woman walking her dog along the opposite embankment put her hands over her ears and closed her eyes. When she opened them, the sound was still there and went on for a long time as metal settled against metal and flames spurted and more windows cracked and the terrible hiss of the cracked boiler grew louder.

The eight forty-five Bristol Temple Meads to London Paddington derailed at precisely ten forty on that April morning in 1951.

The buffet car climbed to a ninety degree

angle. Jenny and the newlyweds standing on one side of the bar were hurled backwards into the first-class accommodation, through the swing door and down the corridor as far as the brake van. The urn crashed onto Ahmed's head, throwing scalding water along the other side of the bar. Ahmed, blessedly unconscious, and Marvin were trapped in the tiny kitchen and bar area with the crockery and broken glass and, quite suddenly, the exploding gas cylinder. Ahmed's body was across Marvin's head and shoulders. Far, far away, Marvin heard the explosion but he did not feel the weight of the bar and its contents on his legs, and before the flames reached him, he too lost consciousness.

Mary Morrison, in an effort to relax as the appointment with Henry Yorke drew closer, had put her legs up, donned her silk scarf and kid gloves, put her head back and was counting her breathing in and out. Even when the jarring began, she forced herself to screen it out and concentrate entirely on loosening her tense muscles and keeping her thoughts strictly away from Andrew French.

And then with a kind of terrifying inevitability the world started to turn upside down. The awful sounds of screeching, tortured metal seemed to pass her by. Afterwards it was the movement she remembered; the lurching upwards and from side to side as the coach tried to climb over the one in front. Then the inside of her compartment began to disintegrate; the windows exploded, then the walls began to cave in and she had to swing herself sideways because the compartment was two feet wide instead of six and was collapsing on top of her.

The door splintered and was gone. She vaguely watched the corridor crumple like paper and then tear apart at the weakest point and fold in towards her. It seemed to go on for a very long time, writhing and twisting as it changed shape, yet still her tiny space cocooned her, threatening but not yet snuffing her out. And then a whoosh of flame swept past her and seemed to gather itself up before leaping from the broken window. She waited for it to come again, knowing that that would be the end; and then the coach gave up the battle and broke into two pieces. Mary felt herself rolling, her head hit something which could have been the luggage rack, her arm was held in a vice between the armrest and the side of the coach, her legs were flailing against the roof and the seating collapsed suffocatingly on top of her. The half-coach came to rest at last on its side. Mary kept very still and wondered whether she was dead. She should be in pain but she wasn't. She must be dead. She wondered what would happen next.

Further down the half-coach the jumble of bodies was also very still. The ball of flame from the gas container in the buffet had scorched their clothing and hair but had shot out of the window just before it reached them. It was obvious that the newlyweds had broken limbs but they had cushioned Jenny's impact and she lay in a foetal position, hands over her head, apparently uninjured.

Through the smashed window came sounds as if from an animal. The *Prince Albert* gasped for breath. Its scattered firebox had started small fires everywhere along the grass embankment; a more serious one burned in the front third-class coach. The other coaches groaned and rocked as they settled into their own debris. Torn metal and glass added their own percussion. And then came the worst sound of all: cries for help, screams of pain, the uncontrollable hysteria of shocked human beings. And it was these that brought Jenny back to consciousness.

She fought her way upwards slowly, almost unwillingly, as if she knew what awaited her. The pain came gradually at first; and then was there, omnipresent, taking all her energy. She lay very still, head pillowed on the bride's dress, and fought it quite deliberately just as she had fought the awfulness of her parents' extinction. She, Jenny Price, against the pain. She had to separate it, get it outside herself where she could deal with it. First she had to locate it, isolate it. Her head was the worst, in two places: one behind her ears, the other where skull joined neck. And then her left arm; that was easy to identify because it had happened before on the hockey pitch at Winderslake. She had dislocated her shoulder.

She waited until she had the head pain right outside her body, then she rolled sharply onto her left side. She shouted out loud. But she knew she had done it, the bone had clicked back into place.

For a long time, she lay waiting for her shoulder to stop screaming at her. And then, eyes closed, she lifted her head and almost immediately vomited. And began to cry.

'Oh, I'm so sorry, so sorry . . . I've just ruined your dress . . . and it's your honeymoon dress.'

But there was no reaction from either of the newlyweds and by the time Jenny's tears had dried she was certain they were dead.

She tried to think; her head felt loose and thoughts would not stay inside it. Ahmed, Marvin . . . same coach as this. Harry Blackmore . . . at the head of the train, next to the engine, the point of greatest danger. She sobbed again and then wondered why. Something to do with Harry Blackmore? Or perhaps Marvin?

The corridor ahead was hardly recognizable, its floor against her right shoulder, the shattered windows letting in gusts of April air; and other smells. She knew instinctively that she had to get out and find Ahmed and ask him what she must do. She began to clamber along the line of inner windows and doors, all broken and mangled beyond recognition. Some of the compartments had been compressed to the size of shoeboxes and where businessmen had been sitting there was . . . She shifted her gaze quickly so that all she registered was blood. And then she came to Mary Morrison's compartment.

Mary, trapped beneath the line of seats, saw her crouching above and whispered, 'Are you dead, Jenny? Or are we both alive?'

Jenny was so pleased she began to weep again.

Mary forced strength into her voice. 'You must be alive because I can feel your tears on my face.' She gave a tiny laugh. 'And I think it's your blood too.'

Jenny said, 'It's my knees, they're bleeding a bit. My stockings are ripped, gone almost. I've been clambering through all this glass.' She hiccoughed another sob.

Mary moved experimentally. 'I think my arms and legs are working almost as well as yours. Shall we try to get out?'

'Yes. I was going to try to get to the buffet. But it's gone.'

'Is there a gap at the top of the coach?'

Jenny was lying almost full length in the corridor. She tipped her head with great difficulty and pain shot through her shoulder. 'I can't see. But it gets narrower and narrower.' She looked down at Mary again. 'I think the window back there is broken enough for us to get through. I could pull you up to me and we could work our way back and try.'

Mary said, 'Yes. Let's do that.' She tried to extricate herself from the armrest. 'I might be fixed here rather too firmly, Jenny. If I can reach you with my other hand, have you got the strength to pull me?'

Ignoring the pain in her shoulder, Jenny pulled while Mary pushed, feebly at first, then with the energy of desperation. Eventually Mary was standing on the offending armrest, her head and arms through the inner window. She said, 'This compartment feels like a matchbox.'

'I know. Poor train.'

Mary said, 'Like the *Titanic*. All that engineering. Gone.'

Jenny had never heard of the *Titanic*. She began to wriggle back the way she had come. Her skirt tore and she felt a slice of pain on her thigh.

'Be careful. Glass everywhere.' She reached the smashed window and tried to haul herself through. It was impossible. 'I'm going to lie on my back and try to break some more away,' she panted. 'Can you stay where you are for a bit?'

'Of course. But is there room for me? I'm wearing gloves.'

Jenny wanted to laugh at that but was afraid she might weep again. They were both sharing the job of trying to pull away the toughened glass when the bells of the ambulances came into earshot. They put their arms through the gaps they had made and waved.

Mary said, 'If I'm going to hospital, you must come too. You're bleeding terribly and I'm perfectly all right.'

'The lady's right, miss. Hop in with her and sit on one side, will you? We're going to stretcher in the couple behind you.'

Jenny said, 'They're dead.' But the ambulance men did not hear her. She turned to Mary. 'I have to go and find Ahmed. And Marvin and the guard. I'm all right, honestly. And I'll be at the hospital as soon as I've finished my job.'

Mary could not stop her. She watched her disappear into the chaos, then sat back and closed her eyes. She knew that her calmness was part of the shock and that soon she would shake and probably weep. But first she wanted to think about Jenny Price who had pulled her out of that awful trap and was now going to see what had happened to everyone else.

Nine

The ambulance went to St Mary's Hospital in Paddington, which must have been a good omen for Mary Morrison because after a check-up by a young doctor, she was immediately discharged. She asked whether she could sit in the reception area of the casualty department so that she could keep track of who was being admitted. Someone brought her a cup of tea and a cheese sandwich and someone else sat by her and told her that these things always looked worse than they were and human beings were amazingly resilient.

She said, 'I can't go until I know how Jenny is. And that young couple who were in the ambulance with me. Jenny thought they had died on the train, but they'll be all right, won't they?'

'Would you like me to make some inquiries?'

'Would you? Thank you so much.'

She sat there, holding her tea as if she were at a party. Other cases were arriving now and the atmosphere became more urgent. Mary could see none of them and would not have recognized any of them anyway. She wondered about the boy Marvin. Had he told her his other name? She could not remember. Her head ached, her eyes were more unfocused than usual. The guard, the one who had shepherded her aboard the train at Temple Meads, Harry Blackmore. Where had he been when the train left the track?

The young nurse who had got her tea did not come back and Mary was not surprised. 'All hands to the deck now,' the receptionist said conversationally. Then she leaned over her desk towards Mary. 'Please don't slip away without telling me, will you? And try to drink your tea.' She smiled and put her pen down. 'I love your pictures. I paint a little myself. Some of your pointillistic work is so – so comforting.'

Mary almost dropped her cup and saucer. She stared at the receptionist, speechless.

The woman went on, 'I loved your still life period but your landscapes are wonderful, especially the country scenes. *The Bluebell Wood* is my favourite. I intended to go to your exhibition this afternoon but,' she grimaced at the scene in front of them, 'not much chance of that now.'

She picked up her pen again and began to write down the particulars of the latest arrival.

Mary sat back and sipped her tea. This kind of

thing had only happened once before and that was when Andrew had come to mend the washing machine. And he had been interested in her work only because she was the wife of John Kenyon. John had called her work 'still lifes with extras'. Andrew called the later paintings 'nostalgia with a difference'. 'You offer the comfort of the past with the endless possibilities of the future,' he had said. 'You take people back to before the war. Picnics with thermos flasks and wasps. Look at that milk jug – those beaded covers are practically Victorian.'

She had smiled. '*I'm* practically Victorian,' she told him.

He had laughed but he hadn't really understood. She had been born in 1905 but her father had been a Victorian; and so had her husband. They had been protective and she had been submissive. She remembered her brothers Owen and Gerry all those years ago telling her to take off her clothes and dance for them, and she had done it without a thought.

She recalled the sheer exhilaration of that first evening with Andrew. She had been flattered of course, but it was more than that. Like being a girl again and putting her pony over that first fence. She had sat behind him on the pillion seat of his motorbike and wrapped her arms round his waist, and during the ride down to Bristol she had sometimes put her face between his shoulder blades. She was old enough, experienced enough to know the effect she was having on him. And to know that for the first time in her life she was fully in control of an emotional situation.

That had changed now, and she knew exactly when he had started to pull away from her. It was after the eye test. He might enjoy living with an older woman who was talented and independent. But he was not going to enjoy looking after an older woman who was losing her sight and therefore her talent. And it was not what she wanted either. Not at all.

She looked up as a nurse approached.

'You were enquiring after Mr and Mrs Tamworthy?'

She swallowed. 'I'm not sure. I don't know their names.'

'The couple who were in the ambulance with you. They have multiple fractures but I'm sure you'll be glad to hear that they are both stable.'

Mary managed a shaky smile. 'Jenny will be pleased,' she said.

At the impact, when that first coach climbed over the tender and then folded sideways, Raymond Hart was catapulted to the front next to the toilet where Ilse was cleaning Caroline. His forehead connected with a glass case containing a fireman's axe. He was then sent backwards, flying over the angle of the break and landing with sickening force against the far end. He was completely winded and quite unable to co-ordinate his movements but when he saw that the external door was gone, he somehow willed himself through it and fell face downwards almost on top of the broken rail which had derailed the train. Flames leapt just behind him. With a separate part of his mind he knew that Ilse was in the midst of those flames. He did not move.

The ambulance men found him nearly an hour later. He was conscious but somehow disconnected. His eyes were open and the sun was warm on the back of his head and he felt a kind of disappointment that he was alive and all the difficulties of his sterile life were still there. But not yet . . . not quite yet. He could lie and watch a weed growing between the chippings on the ballast and feel the sun and know about Ilse and Caroline but have no feelings about them.

The ambulance men ran their expert hands over his body and asked him whether he could feel his legs, then whether he could stand with their help. When he did, they asked him whether he could walk to the ambulances which were lining up at the top of the embankment. They took an arm each but he shook his head.

'I can do it. I'm all right.'

One of them said, 'My God, you were lucky. The first coach took the brunt of the crash.'

The other one said, 'You need to be checked for concussion, sir.'

Ray shook his head. 'I'll come in a minute. I must look for my wife.'

He realized suddenly that there were firemen everywhere, hoses playing over the crumpled train. He began to walk jerkily towards the engine and was waved back.

The ambulance man said urgently, 'It's not safe yet, sir. Where was your wife?'

'The toilet . . .' He was about to tell them about cleaning Caroline but thank God did not.

The men exchanged glances. One of them said, 'It's possible she was thrown clear.'

Even in his dazed state Ray knew that the front half of the coach and the tender had simply disappeared.

He said woodenly, 'She's gone. Hasn't she? I must know. She's gone.'

'I'm afraid . . .' The ambulance man caught his arm as he fell. 'We need a stretcher here,' he called, and added to his mate, 'Worse than we thought, poor devil.' But Ray was not unconscious. He could not use his legs but he could hear what was being said and he understood what had happened. He had escaped. The trap had opened. He was going to live normally again.

'I have to stay for a while. Just in case,' he said.

And in the end they left him because there were others who needed them more.

*   *   *

Sylvia Pemberton, leaning out of the window in the second coach, saw the leaping flames from the firebox of the locomotive, she saw Wilf thrust from the cab, sailing through the air, she saw the first coach begin its fatal climb. As her own coach began to twist, she clung to the window frame rather than fall back inside; it was a movement she made every day, using her arms to compensate for her legs. The narrow opening of the window held her waist firmly while the coach bucked and twisted its wheels free of the track so that they spun uselessly and dangerously.

She thought at first that she would be broken in half like the coach; there seemed to be no way she could get control of what was happening. Her body was in the grip of this juggernaut and she was being crushed and then forced over then pulled back, as if some giant hand were playing with her.

At some point she must have lost consciousness because the next thing she registered was that the wheels, now turning idly, were level with her shoulders and, at what had been the front of the train, a fire was raging. She watched it and knew it would devour her quite soon. She put her hands on the jagged metal either side of her and pushed down. Her arms were not broken and her shoulders were intact. She could hardly believe it. She sat on the side of the train, reached down and pulled each leg through. The caliper clattered down into the wheel; it was in several pieces. She inspected both legs. They looked the same as usual, though her sticks were gone – her briefcase too. But she was alive.

She half slid, half fell along the side of the coach, catching her skirt and bare arms on the remains of door handles, broken glass and ridges like pleats in the metal. The whole coach had buckled and squashed to a fraction of its normal width. She held one of the wheels and let herself swing to the ground only a few feet away; nevertheless she landed painfully and lay in a crumpled heap, suddenly very conscious, smarting all over and wanting – ridiculously – to cry. When the firefighters found her, she was in fact sobbing uncontrollably.

'Come on now, love, you're all right. And you're going to be more than all right soon. You're alive!'

It was a clarion call but had nothing to do with how she was feeling. As they picked her up and began to carry her towards the embankment, she said, 'Joe. Where is Joe?'

The man had seen her wedding ring.

'Hubby, eh? Where was he? Down a bit?' He was thankful when she nodded. The first coach was a charred wreck, no-one could have survived in it. 'All right then, love. Keep your eyes peeled. Anyway, he'll turn up in the hospital. Just you wait and see.'

'He wanted to help me and I wouldn't let him.

I should have gone back . . .' She was barely comprehensible. 'I was so . . . unforgiving.'

The fireman hurried her past the next coach which was still full of people and suddenly she gripped his shoulder.

'There. He's there!'

Perhaps she did not actually say those words because the man took no notice of her at all. But the prone figure curled into itself was Joe. She twisted her sore neck to see him properly. He was holding something; clutching it right into himself. Bits of straw sprouted from his hands. And a flower.

She gave a small cry. Joe was holding her hat. How on earth had it come to be in his possession?

Jenny made for the front of the train. People, trapped inside the coaches, were silent and waiting with a kind of stoic resignation. She heard someone call out, 'Like the bleedin' war again, eh, love? Keep smiling!' All the services were operating: police dealing with the general public and helping the 'walking wounded' to the ambulances, ambulance men everywhere with stretchers and chairs, firemen making sure the fire would not start again. She recognized Sylvia Pemberton as she was carried up the embankment. Was Harry Blackmore in her coach when the crash happened? It wasn't something she could ask, not at the moment.

She came to what remained of the front coach. No-one could have survived in the tangled mass of burnt-out metal. The firemen were gathered round the locomotive itself and the coach lay derelict and abandoned except for one man who stood back a little, looking at it.

Jenny approached him. 'Are you all right, sir? The ambulance people want everyone to be checked. And then I'm sure taxis will be laid on to take you home when you feel able.'

The man looked at her and shook his head slowly.

'I'm quite all right. I must wait for a while longer. Till they've finished looking for . . . bodies.'

Jenny felt her heart contract. 'Did you have someone in this coach, sir?'

He said vaguely, 'Not really. Not any more.'

She frowned; this must be a case of shock. 'Let me help you to the ambulances . . .' He let her take his arm and lead him away, then he stopped.

'I forgot. The guard. He was going into the next coach.' He shook his head. 'No. It's all right. He didn't know, did he?' He looked at her. 'He didn't know about Ilse. So it's all right.'

A fireman came up. 'OK, miss, I'll take him. You staff? No-one in the first coach. Woman got out of the second. And there was a bloke too.'

'Have you seen the guard?' Jenny relinquished

the man's arm. 'This passenger says he was in the next coach.'

'Yes. He's all right. Up by the loco.'

Jenny sobbed with relief. Harry would know what to do. She had to find him. She immediately forgot about the strange man and his Ilse.

She scrambled up the embankment; a fireman shouted at her but she ignored him. On the other side of the cab, which was half buried in the turf, two men were crouched over a third. Jenny recognized Wilfrid Pickering, the fireman. The second man was Harry Blackmore. The third must be the driver, Albert Priddy. His head was on Harry's chest; Harry was supporting him with one arm, protecting his face with the other. Jenny could see why. There was no face. It had burned off.

Jenny stood back; it was a moment she could not share. Wilf's head was right down, he could have been praying or weeping or both. Harry's uniform had almost gone, ripped to shreds by whatever had happened to him. A huge gash across his shoulder was bleeding profusely, staining his white shirt to the waist. She saw he was holding something in the hand protecting Albert's face. It was his carnation. She began to cry.

At last he looked up and saw her.

'Ah. Jenny.' He managed a smile. 'Can you walk?'

'Yes.'

'Then see what you can do, will you? Just a word to the passengers who are trapped. Tell them it won't be long. See if Ahmed and Marvin are alive. They will help you. I'll see you at the hospital.' He looked back at Albert. 'I shall be with Mr Priddy if you need me.'

'Is he . . . ?'

'Yes. He must have died immediately.'

Wilf looked up. He was covered in soot. 'He saved my life. That's what he did. He saved my life.'

Jenny held out a hand. 'Why don't you come with me, Mr Pickering? Go to the hospital and let them have a look at those burns.'

Wilf took her hand and got to his feet some-how.

Ahmed was dead, there was no doubt about that. The firemen had managed to crawl to within three yards of him and saw that his body had been almost incinerated. But in the tiny box which had been a full-size buffet car with kitchen, his body had protected Marvin's from the fire and it was just possible that Marvin was alive.

After taking Wilf to an ambulance, Jenny had gone up and down the train for an hour doing exactly what Harry had told her to do and had watched as the firemen took the coaches apart bit by bit and released the passengers. The crane was being manoeuvred into position when she came upon what remained of the buffet car. One of the firemen explained what was happening.

'If we can raise the whole coach – even a foot would do it – then we can get people out. We can see inside the kitchen and there seemed to be some movement from beneath one of the bodies.'

Jenny said, 'I could get through there. I'm the other steward. I could crawl under the coach where the window has gone.'

'You'd cut yourself to pieces, miss. No point anyway.' He looked at the small bloodstained face beneath the hastily scraped back dark hair and tried to smile. 'As soon as we can cut away the side of the coach, the ambulance men will be inside. Try not to worry. There's nothing you could do if you went in.'

But there was; she knew that. She could talk to them; tell them that help was on the way and they had to hang on. She thought of Ahmed, tall and dignified; she thought of Marvin with his acne and his brace and knew suddenly that the personal remarks, smirks, winks and meaningful looks had all been hopeless attempts at flirtation. She had to try to reach him.

The fireman moved away to direct the crane and she seized the opportunity. Her torn knees protested yet again as she dropped onto them to ease herself beneath the roof of the coach; she chose the place where it had buckled into an inverted V shape but then discovered that molten glass from the windows had formed a solid mass that blocked her way. She had to lie down and twist her body to the left, then to the right, looking for a broken window that was wide enough to let her crawl through. It seemed to take a very long time before she was actually inside the coach, and then the business of fighting her way on hands and knees through the smashed interior towards the buffet area seemed endless. Inch by inch she pulled herself through the ghastly debris, sobbing audibly with horror as glass shattered above her and a human arm suddenly swung in front of her face. She stopped and squeezed her eyes together and then opened them wide as if she thought the arm might have been part of a nightmare. But it was still there, still idly swinging. Without a shred of clothing, and without skin.

Jenny turned aside and closed her eyes again; she had never fainted in her life but perhaps she did momentarily lose consciousness because she became aware that the yells of the firemen were coming to her as if from a long way off. They made no sense; she stayed where she was, very still, and then a voice she knew said, 'Jenny. It's me, Harry. They're going to clamp the crane onto the roof of the coach in a minute. It will lift slightly, not enough to throw you one way or the other but it will help you reach the kitchen.'

There was a pause, then he said, 'Can you hear me, Jenny?'

She whimpered, 'Yes. Oh, Harry . . . you left the driver . . . oh, Harry . . .'

He said urgently, 'Listen to me, Jenny. Are you all right? Hang on to something. There's bound to be a jerk. Do you understand?'

'Yes. Thank you . . . yes.'

It was the sounds that came first. Through all of them, Harry's voice came to her, fragmented but always reassuring. When the claws of the crane were clamped to the roof, when the ghastly groaning of tortured metal exploded into more breaking glass, he was near at hand.

'I can see you now, Jenny. There's a way ahead. The men are going to wait until you can get through into the bar. Can you do it? Just an inch at a time and then through that opening and the shelves . . . can you manage to ease through the shelves?'

She knew, even at that moment, that she would never be clumsy again. She put her left leg through first and she was quite confident – determined – that the rest of her body would follow. And it did. And there, the other side of the smashed crockery, was what was left of Ahmed, spread-eagled as if trying to protect the boy behind him.

She could not bring herself to touch him. There was just room for her to ease her own body between his and the edge of the bar. She blinked and forced herself to look at what was next to her. She made a sound, half horror and half relief. She could at least recognize Marvin; his hair and eyebrows had gone but his spots were, blessedly, still there and his mouth, parted in a rictus of pain, showed his silver brace quite plainly. But the burns that had scalped him were livid lines already twisting his skin into a mask that would change his appearance for ever.

She crouched over him, not knowing whether he was still alive when, suddenly, the grinding noise crescendoed and the coach lurched higher. Marvin's head moved, whether with the coach she could not tell. But then his eyes flickered.

She turned instantly. 'Harry! He's alive! Marvin is alive!'

Harry's voice said, 'Thank God. Are you all right, Jenny?'

'Yes. Yes, of course.' She did not listen when he told her that it would not be long before the rescuers would reach her. She put her head very close to Marvin's and started to talk to him. She'd seen a film with her granddad not all that long ago and Hedy Lamarr had kept talking and talking to Charles Boyer to stop him from dying. Granddad had said it was a load of nonsense, but Jenny had wept and believed every word of it.

Mary was still sitting near the reception desk when Jenny and Harry brought Marvin in. She was no longer alone: Wilfrid Pickering had had his burns dressed and was sitting beside her waiting for the ambulance to take him back to Bristol. And a girl in a wheelchair was waiting for a caliper to be fitted to her leg. They had struck up some sort of conversation and Mary knew that the driver had saved his fireman's life but had lost his own; she knew that no-one had been saved from the first coach but the girl had got out of the second coach. The guard, caught between the front and second coach, had miraculously escaped with his life. They had both seen Jenny crawling as close as possible to the surviving passengers and reassured Mary that she was all right. Wilf said, 'The guard told her to reassure everyone, so she did.' He heard his own voice shaking like a schoolboy's and clamped his jaw shut. He remembered how he had gone on and on to Albert Priddy about the gossip he'd heard from the office. Why had he done that? He'd never do it again.

Sylvie said, 'She was very good at her job, wasn't she? Dedicated.'

Mary nodded. 'We must mention that. To her superiors.'

Wilf risked his voice again. 'And Albert. Dedicated.' He saw their incomprehension and croaked, 'The driver. Albert Priddy.'

They both nodded. Wilf thought that Albert would enjoy that, the two beautiful women nodding agreement about him; Albert had liked women, he'd always admired them. Put them on pedestals really. He'd put lots of people on pedestals; his old dad for instance, Walter Priddy. Wilf could remember him well. There was a phrase he'd heard once that applied to Walter Priddy – what was it? Morally self-righteous. That was it. Yes, now there was an old hypocrite if ever there was one, but Albert had thought the world of him.

Sylvie spotted Harry before the other two and waved frantically. He touched Jenny's arm and peeled off towards the desk.

'Are you all right? Wilf, what's happening?'

Sylvie could not wait. 'We're all right. The three of us. But what about everyone else? The man I was with – do you remember him? I saw him lying by the side of the train. I don't know what happened to him.'

Harry shook his head. 'I'm sorry. I have no idea. But as soon as we see our young steward into the theatre, I will make some inquiries.'

She was profuse with her thanks. Mary spoke above them. 'Do you mean Jenny? Is she hurt?'

'No. She appears to be all right apart from cuts and bruises. I meant Mr Bramley. Marvin Bramley. He was trapped in the buffet car.'

He tried to smile at them all. Then he hurried after Jenny and the stretcher, and was surprised to find how much it hurt. He hoped he didn't look too much of a sight and glanced down at his carnation. It was a shock to see that carnation and jacket were both missing and his shirt was torn and blood-soaked.

Transport came for Wilf Pickering just as one of the nurses arrived with news of Joe Kemp.

'We're going to keep him in tonight,' she said. 'He seems to be concussed and he's not co-operating at the moment.'

Sylvie said, 'He – he gets angry. With . . . things.'

The nurse rolled her eyes. 'That could be it. He won't release the hat.'

'Hat?' Sylvie queried.

'He's clutching some awful old hat. Won't let it go.'

Sylvie smiled.

The ambulance driver wanted to wait for the two women but Sylvie said firmly, 'As soon as I've had a new caliper fitted, I must keep an appointment. But thank you for the offer.'

Mary hesitated and then shook her head too. 'I don't think so. I'm perfectly all right. I still have time to go to . . . where I was going.'

Sylvie smiled at her. 'Where do you have to go? Perhaps we could share a taxi.'

Mary was delighted. It would be good to have the company of this pretty girl for a while longer; it didn't much matter what time she arrived at the gallery. And Sylvie thought contentedly that after what had happened today her interview with the MP held few fears.

Ten

Andrew French parked the hired car outside the tall building in Harley Street and prepared for a very short wait; he knew he could not have beaten the train but was relying on Mary having taken some time to secure a taxi. He had hired the car because the van with his name emblazoned along the side – 'French Electrical' – would give him away immediately. Mary could still recognize shapes and colours and the glaring white of the van would attract her attention and then she would stand still in that way she had and work things out for herself. He could have driven her car; he usually did these days because she had not driven it herself for the last six months. It was black and unobtrusive and would have blended in with the other parked cars. But somehow he couldn't do that. Her car was . . . her car.

So he hired one of the new bulbous Vanguards and wedged it between a Daimler and a Rolls.

He sighed; that was another difference between them, their attitude to money. She had always had it so could totally ignore it. He had to work physically for every penny and never took it for granted. There were many other differences, and, until this eye business, they hadn't mattered in the least. They could tease each other about them, make them positive rather than negative. But she seemed to think that when it came to the sickness and health bit, she was the only one allowed to be a carer. Every time he tried to help her she pushed him off. Every solitary time. When he took her arm at a kerbside, when he told her about the snowdrops emerging in the garden and then the primroses, she had a way of saying tensely, 'Will you stop it, Andrew! Right now!'

He had known only too well how it would be this morning at the station and he had planned his exit carefully. He would take her down, see her onto the right platform and then he would go. He wouldn't wait for the usual dismissal, he would just leave. It would suit him well anyway, because he could collect the hired car and be on the road before the train left Bristol.

So here he was, in good enough time, sweating in spite of the cool April air, wondering what on earth he could do to salvage their wonderful relationship before she said something irrevocable. 'I'd like you to leave now, Andrew. We had something and now it's gone. We both know that.' He had seen the words practically hovering on her lips a dozen times in the last few weeks and had talked long and loudly to stop her saying them. At first she'd had a way of listening to his blatherings with a kind of stupefied interest; lately she had simply turned away from him.

He'd planned today so carefully. He'd let her have her precious independence as far as he could; then he'd drive up to London and wait for her to emerge from her appointment so that he would know the instant she appeared exactly what the verdict had been. Then he would get home before her so that he could meet her at the little side gate and not even mention the appointment; just say, 'I've got a surprise for you, it's in the shed – come and have a look.' And he would link his arm through hers affectionately and lead her along the brick path and say, 'See? It's your next thing, Mary Morrison. Put your hands on it – feeling is so important . . .'

How would she react? Would she see it as a loving and thoughtful gesture? He didn't know any more; they had always been so straight with each other, discussing everything – 'flat out', as he put it. But this was different. This was horribly, horribly different.

He clutched the steering wheel of the Vanguard and lowered his head slightly. He was losing her and he could not imagine life without her. He remembered that first meeting when he had been stunned by her, literally stunned; he hadn't known what he was saying or doing. If she hadn't come with him that night to see the exhibition of Marcus Doan's work, he would have had to camp outside the house, or send her flowers every day, or keep phoning. Something. He could not have let this wonderful heaven-sent woman go out of his life. But she had been there, waiting for him. He had known from that first evening that they were made for each other. She must have known it too though she pretended never to take him seriously. Every time he asked her to marry him she would laugh and tell him he saw her as a mother figure. He usually replied that she had fallen for a father figure in John and what had been wrong with that? Only once had she treated his question seriously and replied, 'Nothing. But . . . *am* I a mother figure to you? I'd be . . . interested, that's all.'

He had been completely honest. 'I don't know, Mary. I can't analyse things like you do. You've just . . . burst into my life. You're there all the time in my thoughts, the last thing I think of when I sleep and the first thing when I wake. I've lived half a life up till now. You make it whole – more than whole. Overflowing.'

And she had said with tears in her eyes, 'I know. I'm the same.'

*   *   *

248

By midday his neck ached from craning round to see whether she was coming down the street or up it. She was never late for an appointment, what on earth had happened to her? He went through a list of scenarios: she had fallen getting into the train and was even now in Bristol Royal Infirmary having surgery on her legs. She had been unable to find her way to the taxi rank at Paddington and was still wandering around, lost and terribly, terribly vulnerable. Or the train was late. He spoke the last one aloud to try to convince himself; after all, it was by far the most likely.

By one thirty the most obvious answer of all occurred to him: she had arrived really early, gone into the building and waited for her appointment. But he had to be sure. He got out of the car and crossed the road to the glistening black-painted door with its brass furnishings. He had been here before, they knew him, probably thought he was Miss Morrison's chauffeur. She hadn't introduced him, she hadn't wanted him to come. The hall was big and square, the waiting room on the left, consulting rooms upstairs via the twisting staircase. The receptionist sat behind a leather-topped desk flanked by two vases of fresh flowers. She was the same one as before.

He gave his small smile. 'Hello. I'm Andrew French. Accompanying Miss Morrison. I'm meeting her here after her appointment. Has she come down yet?'

The receptionist looked at him and pulled down her mouth.

'You haven't heard – why would you? I'm so sorry, Mr French.' She did look genuinely upset. 'We heard on the wireless. Miss Morrison's train from Bristol was derailed at about ten thirty this morning just outside Paddington. We've heard nothing from her. Nothing at all.'

He could not take it in. The fact that a train had been involved in an accident seemed to have nothing to do with Mary. He concentrated, frowning like a schoolboy.

The receptionist said, 'Please sit down for a moment, Mr French. It must be quite a shock.'

She got up. He moved back a step and felt the edge of a chair against his legs. He sat down.

She said, 'Can I get you some water?'

He shook his head. It was connecting now; the train had been Mary's train. From Bristol. And she had not telephoned Henry Yorke to explain why she could not keep her appointment. That probably meant she could not use a telephone. He swallowed convulsively.

'Do you know anything more? Where they might have gone?'

She leaned over him sympathetically. 'I believe most of them were taken by ambulance to St Mary's at Paddington.'

'St Mary's.' It wasn't a question; he and Mary had walked past it last year when they'd had a day in town to do Christmas shopping.

She said, 'Almost next door to the station. Down the Edgware Road.'

'Yes. Yes, I know.' He looked up at her. 'I'll go.' He was already halfway out of his chair and the receptionist leaned back to give him more space even as she protested that he should sit for a while longer.

He turned at the door. 'What were the results? Did Mr Yorke say? Mary's test results.'

She bit her lip. 'I am not actually permitted . . .' She looked at him and said, 'It's operable. She could have been cured . . .'

He was across the road before he realized what she had said. 'She could have been cured.' The woman – probably the whole practice – they all thought Mary was dead.

It took him an age to get into Edgware Road; he took a wrong turning and got caught up with other traffic. Eventually something told him that a taxi in front of him was going to the station. He did a U-turn and followed it and managed to park in Praed Street. Then, for another precious ten minutes, he sat in the driver's seat as if turned to stone, terrified of going into the hospital and discovering she was in fact dead. And then at last he got out of the car and began to walk up the road towards the gates of the hospital.

Inside the enormous courtyard he saw at once there was an emergency. Ambulances were everywhere, more came past him, their bells still ringing. They made him panic; he began to run, not reading the signs properly and finally having to follow a stretcher into the emergency area. He went to the desk and had to wait another interminable age and then at last he was asking . . . the question.

'Mary Morrison. She was on the train. Is she here? Can you find out—'

'She was here.' The woman behind the desk smiled. 'She left. Not long ago.'

'Left? For another hospital?'

'No. She was discharged almost immediately but she wanted to wait to see whether a friend was all right. As soon as she knew that, she left.'

'So she wasn't actually injured?'

'No. She was checked for concussion. She seemed to be in shock but she sat quietly for a couple of hours and then left by taxi with another outpatient.'

He drew a shuddering breath. 'She was with someone?'

'Yes, a lady who was also on the train.'

He was so relieved that it did not occur to him to question why Mary needed a taxi to travel the few yards to the station. All he knew was that she was safe and was on her way home. He smiled his thanks to the receptionist and made his way back to the car. And there he sat, his head in his hands, knowing at last that nothing mattered more to him than Mary's life. If he had to give her up, then so be it; he could face that as long as he knew Mary was all right.

Tom Marston heard the news on his pre-war wireless which was as good as it had been when it was bought in 1936. He put on his cap to go to the Lamb and Flag to use their telephone. There was a public phone box in the village but he wasn't much good with the buttons and he knew the landlord at the Flag would get the number for him.

Sam Beauchamp answered almost immediately.

'Sam?' Tom heard his own voice going up and down like a choirboy's. 'Listen, Sam. Just had the wireless on and the train what our Jenny is on 'as 'ad a crash.'

Sam's voice came back, instantly reassuring. 'I know, Tom. Heard it myself. I've been in touch with Paddington and they've promised me news as soon as they get it. Thought it was them. Been sitting by the phone ever since.'

'Nothing so far then?' Tom asked.

'Well, nothing about Jenny. No.'

'What then?'

'The chief steward, that Indian chappie. He's bought it.'

Tom groaned an oath. 'Dead?'

'Aye. But that doesn't mean the others have come to any harm. These things always look worse than they are, Tom. You know that. The fireman is all right so there's hope for the driver. But Ahmed . . . a crying shame. There was a woman in the toilet compartment of the front coach but her husband seems all right. See what I mean?'

'Aye.' Tom's voice was heavy. 'But until we know for definite—'

'Where are you? The Lamb and Flag? Can you wait by that phone then? I'll be back with you as soon as I can be.'

He was as good as his word and ten minutes later, Tom knew that Jenny was safe and a heroine to boot.

'The other youngster, Marvin Bramley, is badly burned. He's still unconscious. Jenny stayed with him till they could get him out. She's still with him now.'

'And she's all right herself?'

'Cuts and bruises, but nothing serious. You know Jenny. She'll heal quicker than most.'

Tom said, 'Thank God. Oh, thank God. If she'd gone as well as her folks . . . oh God . . .'

'Take it steady. She's going to be all right. Might not be back tonight by the sound of things, but she's all right. Get that into your head.'

'It's there, Sam. It's there.'

'Listen. Go back home and make yourself a cup of tea. Sit down. When the pub opens tonight, give me another ring.'

'Don't be daft. I'm going to London.'

'How?'

'Train of course.'

'Which one?'

'Don't try and put me off, Sam. I shall get the bus to the station and wait till there is one.'

'You can't get through, Tom. The line's blocked.'

'Then I'll thumb a lift. I've done that before. I'm going to be with Jenny and bring her home.'

'You silly old duffer! Stay put and give her a proper welcome.'

'You don't understand. Families, they got to stick together. And Jenny and me are family. So long, Sam. And thanks.'

'Hang on there. Look, I'll take you. Be ready in an hour. I'll go and see Ahmed's family, and Mrs Pickering, the fireman's wife, and Mrs Priddy, the driver's wife, and the Bramleys. They might want to come too. Till you said, I never thought. But I should be there with them too.'

Tom Marston nodded. 'Aye. You ought, Sam. They're your staff, when all's said and done.'

'Don't rub it in. They – the hospital – they probably won't want us cluttering up the place. I shall tell 'em it's your fault!'

Both men made an attempt at a laugh. Then Tom went back home to make some sandwiches for Jenny. She liked his cheese and onion sandwiches and she'd be hungry by the time he reached her. And he filled a thermos with strong sweet tea because he knew that was good for shock. Then as he sat in his little front room waiting for Sam's big car to draw up at the gate, he started to cry. If he'd lost her, what would he have done? He blew his nose with a sound like a trumpet. 'Silly old fool,' he muttered into his handkerchief.

Gertie Priddy wasn't a great one for the wireless and in any case she'd spent a lot of time that morning with Janie McEvoy at the shop. The strangest thing had happened that very morning and she needed to talk to Janie about it; also she had wanted to have a look at something in the shop.

Albert had left for work at seven thirty, pecking her on the cheek, thanking her for his sandwiches which she had packed in old Walter's black satchel, then wheeling his bike down the yard and stopping at the back gate as per usual to wave to her and blow her kisses. He was such a romantic old so-and-so, was her Albert; it was hard to keep up with him without feeling soppy and she never knew what role he had cast her in for that day. All right, she had accepted that That Woman next door would always be Lili Marlene because she was really no better than she should be, which, Gertie understood, was how Lili Marlene had been. Mind you, in a way that made her all the more dangerous. But as she said to Janie, if Albert could call her Lili Marlene then he knew what she was really like

and he wasn't a complete fool. Besides, after . . .
the time in the kitchen, Gertie did feel different.
Sort of special. Sort of wicked too. Sort of
desirable. So, assuming she was Hedy Lamarr
that particular morning, she half closed her eyes
and made a moue of her mouth in Albert's
direction. And then felt stupid and went indoors
quickly. She thought she heard Albert laugh and
she stood in the middle of the kitchen floor
and blushed. How could a man who was your
husband and not even there make you blush?
But Albert did. And even though by that time
he was in the back alley and scooting his bike
down to the road, she felt . . . certain things.
Her breasts were heavy and rather itchy and
something was going on below; she went upstairs
to spend a penny.

From the bathroom with its ancient geyser
and rough painted bath, she heard Janie
washing her face ready to go to work. Sometimes
she was appalled at how easily sounds travelled
the length of the terrace; no wonder Janie knew
when her special fertile times came round, she
couldn't miss them. Maybe that was why the
angry and passionate . . . *session* . . . on
the kitchen floor was so amazing. Because the
basement kitchens had thick walls and stone
floors and the sounds could not possibly have
got past the gas stove. Perhaps she would
suggest to Albert that they repeated that . . .
session. Although how on earth she could ever

broach the subject to him again, she had no idea. Maybe he could be encouraged to repeat the whole thing if she really took on the Hedy Lamarr role. She bit her lip as she pulled up her knickers. Since January everything had gone a bit haywire really; she hadn't kept her temperature graph and it seemed ages since the last visit of her 'girl friend' but they really ought to be trying again.

Janie pulled her flush and clattered down her lino-covered stairs. Gertie pulled her chain and made up her mind that as soon as she had cleaned up she would go to the shop and give Janie a hand and try to have a proper woman's talk with her. She made the big double bed and then sat at the dressing table adorned with the alabaster powder bowl which had belonged to Albert's mother, looking at her face to see whether she could make it more like Miss Lamarr's.

It was after she had painfully plucked her brows and outlined her mouth with lipstick that the knock came at the back door. Gertie frowned because people who came to the back door did not knock; if they were knockers then they went to the front door.

She ran downstairs in her stockinged feet and opened the door. She only just stopped herself recoiling. Wendy Watkins stood there. Brazen wasn't the word for it; she was grinning from ear to ear, her blouse was open almost to her waist and her make-up looked as if it had been put on with a garden trowel.

She said, 'Kin I come in a minute? Something rather interesting to tell you.'

Well, what could anyone say to that? Gertie chose to say nothing. But she did move her body very slightly sideways so that Wendy Watkins could slide past her into the kitchen. Gertie could feel her heart sinking as the woman drew out a kitchen chair and sat down on it as if for a lengthy visit. If she'd come to say that she and Albert were having a fling, then she could think again. Gertie looked round for a saucepan. She'd get it right across the head.

Wendy said, 'Well now. Something very funny 'appened yesterday. Never took no notice 'cos as you know I mind my own business. But then I thought, why not tell Mrs Priddy? She'd be interested and it might do her a bit of good.' She dropped the smile and leaned forward. 'You probably don't realize this but I'm very fond of you, Truda. You and Albert. You're reliable and honest and I appreciate that. Being on my own, like.'

Gertie almost did a double take. What a thing to say. And calling her Truda too. She drew out a chair slowly and sat on it. 'Well, that's nice to know,' she said lamely.

'Yes. Well. Sometimes these things 'ave to be said.' Wendy Watkins sat back and smiled again. 'Anyway, where was I?'

'Nowhere.'

Wendy laughed heartily. 'That's me, innit? Never get nowhere! Anyway, I works in the bakers as you know – that's why I keep funny hours. And sees things other folks don't see, probably.' She laughed again. Her meaningless laughs usually annoyed Gertie but today, for some reason, they didn't.

'There's this woman. She's always by 'erself. German she is, talks to 'erself in German. Mad as an 'atter. Wheels a pram around with nothing in it – blankets and a pillow and baby clothes. But no baby.'

Gertie was wide-eyed. 'Poor soul,' she said.

'Yes. If you look at her closely you can see she's gone through the hoop.' Wendy sighed. 'The war's over, we all know that, but it's not really, is it? For some poor folks it'll never be over.'

Gertie felt sudden and unexpected tears behind her lids. What on earth was the matter with her? This was That Woman with a bit of gossip!

She swallowed hard. 'I don't think I've ever seen her. I would remember.'

'Yes, you would. She's out early mornings or late nights. Sneaks from doorway to doorway. Terrified, she is. Anyway, the thing is, her sister-in-law 'ad the pram last week and came into the bakery and got talking to the manageress. Well, that woman couldn't keep a secret if she'd done a murder, so of course we all knew within a day or two that this sister-in-law was trying to make the poor soul with the pram face up to the fact she didn't 'ave no baby in it!' Wendy Watkins made a face. 'You could laugh if you didn't cry, couldn't you?'

Gertie nodded; she could still taste salt at the back of her throat.

Wendy sighed and resumed her story. 'The plan was, on the day she was supposed to take the baby back, there was going to be an accident. A lorry was going to run the pram over.'

Gertie gasped. 'But the poor woman! If she really thought . . .'

'Exactly. But maybe the sister-in-law knew her best. She did it. Yesterday they came back from holiday and she went round to tell them.'

'What happened?'

'Don't know. But what I do know is that the pram and all the clothes went to your friend's shop.' Wendy leaned back triumphantly.

'Well I never,' Gertie said. 'Janie never mentioned it.'

'Only 'appened yesterday, she wouldn't have known, and when she sees the stuff she won't have any idea of where it came from. But I know. And I can assure you, Truda, that those clothes and blankets, and the pram, was all first-class stuff. I don't know where she got it all from but there was a shawl there that I wouldn't mind myself. Lovely, it was.'

Gertie said, 'Oh. That's nice.' She did not know what to say. She wondered about the woman and the woman's husband. What did the pram and the clothes matter?

Wendy Watkins leaned forward again. 'Save you a lot of money, they would,' she said, nodding her head meaningfully. 'And you don't get such good stuff in the shops anyhow. Worth your while to go and see your friend this morning and snap it up before anyone else does.'

'But why . . .' She stared at Wendy's knowing eyes and felt her own widening incredulously. 'You think . . . you actually think that I might be . . .'

''Sobvious, innit?' Wendy grinned delightedly. 'Don't think I didn't hear you and your 'usband that night! Gawdalmighty, you made Greta Garbo and John Barrymore sound like Jack and Jill. I was that jealous! If you didn't make a baby between you then, you never will! And look at you! Twice as big round the bust as you were at Christmas. Bet you 'aven't seen anything for the last three months, 'ave you?'

Gertie stammered, 'I don't know . . . haven't noticed . . . think so. I'm sure so. No, it can't be.'

Wendy kept grinning. 'Oh yes it can! Lots of women go on having a bit of a show. You're expecting all right. I can tell.'

Gertie stared at her. She couldn't believe it, yet she had felt so different. And that day – that day when Albert had practically ravished her, it had been different too, full of passion.

She whispered, 'Oh dear Lord. Could it be? Oh . . .' She put her hands to her face and burst into tears. The next thing she knew, That Woman had her arms round her and was stroking her hair and saying comforting things into it. Of all people. That she should know before Albert – before herself even!

'How could you know before I did?' she sobbed into Wendy Watkins' shoulder.

The laugh was high like a schoolgirl's giggle, not in the least like Lili Marlene.

'Gran was a bit of a midwife and she always took me with her. I can deliver a baby with the best of them – do it for you, if you like. I can lay people out too, make 'em look real nice.' She sighed. 'Gran was a wonder and she taught me lots.' She sighed again. 'It was nice being Lili Marlene but it's not me at all really, I'm too humdrum. But . . . well, you know, a little bit of daydreaming never hurt no one, did it? You and your Albert are like that, so you understand.' Gertie went on crying more than ever so Wendy Watkins went on talking in that soothing voice of hers. 'When I heard him call you honey, I knew you must be good at romancing.'

Gradually Gertie calmed down and let the joy take over. She was pregnant. At long, long last, she and Albert were going to have a baby. It was somehow part of the 'romancing' and it made her feel all the more wonderful because it had come from that evening of 'romancing' and sheer, raw, passion. Without knowing it she had been Hedy Lamarr that evening and Albert had most definitely been Charles Boyer. All right, she had been ashamed of herself at the time. Her father-in-law would have been ashamed too – perhaps that was why *she* had been ashamed. Not for herself and Albert but for old Walter Priddy. As if he'd been standing there, thumbs in his waistcoat ticket pockets, face drawn down in disapproval and stomach girthed with the chain of his turnip watch. Part of Albert's charm had always been his stable background; she had no-one and to belong to this strong and upright family meant a lot to Gertie. But Albert had his own charm. He had dreams and she had become part of them.

She made tea and nodded when Wendy Watkins suggested an immediate visit to the shop to secure the pram at least. 'You might not fancy the clothes, though they are beautiful, but you couldn't object to the pram, could you?'

'Not a bit. I'm not proud like that. Though . . .' Gertie mashed the tea and smiled at her neighbour. 'I do feel proud. Proud to be Albert's wife and the mother of his baby. Does that sound boastful?'

'Yes, but it's how it should be, innit?' Wendy watched the dark brown tea going into her cup and smiled mistily, 'There's a bloke at the bakery. He never talks about a wife so I'm hoping for the best. He had a rough time in the war and he never smiles. But I got him to smile at me the other day. I did the can-can for a row of cob rolls an' he clapped and said they appreciated the floor show!' She sipped her tea. 'I think I could make him happy.'

Gertie said, 'You've made me happy.' It was a huge step for her to take. She drank her tea and looked at the table and thought that she and Janie must never ever be catty about Wendy Watkins again. And as she listened to Wendy, she knew she was the luckiest woman in the whole world.

George and Mabs Kemp did not hear the news until the one o'clock broadcast. Their morning followed a set pattern, as it had done since George retired, and the wireless was never switched on until they had finished lunch.

After Jeremy disappeared round the bend of the crescent, Mabs switched the kettle off and on several times while George went for the papers. She needed to pull herself together and think about Jeremy's parting shot when he had as good as promised that things would soon be better. She whispered, 'Please God, please God.' The thought of Jeremy travelling back to Kilburn and his awful little bedsit was unbearable so she hung on to his last words much too tightly. She stood and watched the steam hissing from the kettle spout and tried very hard not to weep. The moment she heard George's key in the door she straightened, put on a smile and poured the boiling water into the teapot as if she hadn't a care in the world.

George wheeled the trolley onto the tiny balcony so that they could watch Bath waking up. It meant she had to go and put on another cardigan and a coat too because the mist was what her father had called a sea fret. They sat at the iron table with cushions on the seats to take off the chill and smiled at each other because it was so ridiculous to be sitting out in April.

Mabs sighed. 'It's nice though, isn't it, dear? To be outside again after the long winter. Like coming out of Box tunnel!' She laughed then sobered. 'How I wish dear Jeremy could enjoy this sort of thing. The small pleasures of life are always there. They don't let you down.'

George cleared his throat and slapped the paper on the edge of the table as if reprimanding himself and said stoutly, 'He'll come to it, Mabs. Never fear. It's Festival of Britain year. New beginnings and so forth.'

'So forth and so on,' Mabs said smilingly; it had been one of her mother's sayings.

George nodded, understanding. 'You still miss your parents terribly, don't you?'

'Can't help it, George. They were great ones for special routines, weren't they? Like we are now.'

He said musingly, 'Took us some time, remember. You have to build these little – what are they?'

'Ceremonies?'

'Yes. Ceremonies. Afternoon tea, morning coffee, a walk before bedtime . . .'

'You need a companion for that.'

He looked at her and saw the terrible grief in her eyes and quite suddenly he put down his cup and his paper and reached for her hands.

'Of course you need a companion, my Mabs. We didn't think much of tea ceremonies before we had each other, did we? And Mabs, he'll find someone. I know it.'

She smiled, her mouth trembling. 'I know it too, George. It's the one thing I've always been sure of. He will meet someone who needs him as much as he needs her. He'll respond instantly.'

He squeezed both her hands, agreeing with everything. And then, his voice slightly hoarse, he said, 'Mabs, you do know that I still love you as much as I did at the beginning?'

She said, 'Yes, George. I know that. And I love you too.' He released her hands and she stood up and said, 'I'm going to start lunch now so that we can put our feet up for half an hour afterwards. You remember we've got the Jamiesons for afternoon tea?'

He made a face and they both laughed.

So it was not until they switched on the wireless after an early lunch that they heard about the crash. The number of confirmed deaths so far was eight, including the driver; several passengers were critically ill in St Mary's Hospital; rescue operations were still proceeding.

They stared at each other wordlessly for what seemed like a long time. Then George leaned forward, switched off the wireless and said, 'I'll get the car out, Mabs. You'd better telephone the Jamiesons.'

She moistened her lips. 'Couldn't we telephone Paddington first? To find out . . .'

'They won't have names yet. Would you rather not come?'

She stood up. 'Nothing would stop me.'

She watched him leave the room and knew that he had turned down her suggestion because he did not want to know that Jeremy was dead. She put a hand to her throat. Jeremy had escaped so much during the war; was it because his time was now? She closed her eyes for a second and then went into the hall and lifted the receiver.

Eleven

The taxi came at two thirty; Sylvie and Mary
climbed into it with some difficulty. 'The halt
leading the lame!' Sylvie quipped and then
remembered that Mary had told her about the
appointment in Harley Street and put a hand on
her knee in silent apology.

Mary, released from the awfulness of thinking about her appointment with Henry Yorke
– she had completely forgotten about it until
now – laughed and said, 'The blind leading the
blind!'

Sylvie smiled, relieved; after all, they were
both alive and so was Joe Kemp.

'Where to first? Did you say Cork Street?'

Mary said, 'There's no hurry. Let me see you
off at Westminster first.'

Sylvie smiled again; it was strange how
nothing seemed to matter. 'I doubt whether Mr
Hargreaves will have waited. I was due there at
midday.'

Sylvie had explained about the petition while they were waiting for news of Jenny and Joe so Mary knew what she was talking about.

'He'll know about the crash, Sylvie.' Mary looked apologetic. 'It's an awful thing to say but it may well have done your cause a lot of good. We'll leave a message and just wait in the taxi until someone comes.'

Sylvie blenched. 'It'll cost the earth!'

'I'm paying for this taxi and frankly I don't care what it costs. We're here, we're alive, and you are going to do what you came up for. And I'm going to go to the exhibition at Bryson's. I might have missed my doctor's appointment—' she took a sharp breath. 'Oh Sylvie, I forgot to phone!'

It was Sylvie's turn to say, 'They'll know about the crash, Mary.'

'But they'll fear the worst because I haven't rung. They might ring my home!'

Sylvie put a hand on Mary's. 'Don't worry. It'll all be all right in the end. You'll see.'

Mary stared at the face so close to hers. The outlines were fuzzy but she could see that the pretty face was full of understanding and reassurance.

She said suddenly, 'Sylvie, afterwards but not too long afterwards, while I can still see something, I'd like to paint you. And Jenny too. And maybe that nice guard.'

'Harry Blackmore.'

'Is that his name? He was wonderfully brave, wasn't he?'

Sylvie said, 'My husband welcomed him back when he was demobbed. We arranged for all the old employees to come into the office and we worked out with them what sort of choices they had. Harry remembers me getting him a cup of tea . . .' Her eyes filled with tears quite suddenly but they'd told her at the hospital this might happen. Shock, apparently.

Mary said, 'You worked with your husband?'

'He was my boss. He took me on when no-one else would. Then we got married. Then he died.'

Mary swallowed fiercely. 'Oh Sylvie. I'm so sorry.'

'It's all right. We knew it was going to happen. And . . . there are other things. You know what they say, life goes on.'

'Of course it does. And it will.' Mary sat up straight. 'There must be other things a blind artist can do. Andrew said that, he said I might well be the first blind artist.' She smiled wryly, remembering.

Sylvie did not know what to say about that. 'With help perhaps?' she murmured. 'The halt leading the lame?'

And Mary followed up meaninglessly with, 'The blind leading the blind.' And they both laughed.

In the end they did not have long to wait. As they drew up outside the Houses of Parliament, a policeman opened the door for Sylvie and newspaper photographers appeared from nowhere. The policeman escorted her along the footpath and almost into the arms of Roger Hargreaves. A ragged cheer went up, cameras were held high; it was obvious that whatever the outcome, Sylvie was going to get plenty of good publicity for her reading group. She looked wonderful standing there in the full April sunshine against the ancient backdrop of Westminster. Her skirt had ripped at the waistband and dipped in front and all her clothes were filthy but she had tremendous dignity. Mary, who by this time knew that it was quite possible Joe Kemp would figure in Sylvie's future, thought how proud he would be when he saw the newspapers the next day.

She leaned forward and asked her driver to take her to Cork Street. 'Bryson Gallery please. And then can you come back and wait for this young lady? She will be invited into the House but then she will want to be taken back to St Mary's.'

'I'll do it, lady. But I don't think she'll need a cab.' He grinned into his mirror. 'I've got a feeling they'll lay on a limousine to take her wherever she wants to go!' He caught her eye and turned his grin upside down. 'Turning out to be quite a day out for you two!'

'Yes.' The horror of the crash seemed to have separated itself from everything else now and she was thinking only of meeting Sylvie and Jenny and Marvin. Mary sat back and watched the receding figure of Sylvia Pemberton and knew this was all part of being in shock. But she seemed to be understanding . . . something . . . better than ever before. If only she could put a name to the something.

Sylvie was amazed at how easy it all was. It turned out that Roger Hargreaves had telephoned the hospital and knew that she was on her way. He hurried forward immediately when the taxi drew up and met her before she was halfway down the path to the visitors' entrance.

'My dear lady! I heard that you were safe – what a terrible experience! I've laid on drinks in the Members' room but if you feel up to it, the papers could make a lot more out of us meeting like this, straight from the crash, as it were.'

He was in the same suit he had worn when he had visited the group at home. That put her at her ease and she was suddenly glad she was no longer dressed up and wearing her hat. She'd washed her face and combed her hair at the hospital, which meant it was probably standing on end and her skin was shining like Pem's collection of copper warming pans. But it didn't matter. This was how she always looked. This was her.

She reassured him. 'I'm all right, honestly.

And I'd really prefer a nice cup of tea anyway.' Then she produced the petition and turned quite naturally towards the cameras and smiled.

With some resignation, tempered by amusement and admiration, Hargreaves took one end of the paper and posed expertly, aware that she had stolen the show. He knew he had no choice now but to make damn sure that this proposed swimming bath incorporated every single suggestion made by this group.

'May we have a picture of you by yourself, Sylvia?' the journalists asked cheekily and she leaned on her sticks and limped forward and hardly noticed the pain in her calipered leg. A woman took her arm to help and said, 'I'm Bella Anderson from the *Forum*. Please lean on me. I would very much like to do an article about you, Mrs Pemberton. After you've spoken to Roger Hargreaves, may I have a few words?'

Sylvie smiled. She thought: how about this, Joe? And I haven't even had a chance to tell them how I drew the plans by proxy!

Eventually she was escorted into the House as if she were royalty. She looked around her carefully. She must remember every little thing. So that when she got back to the hospital she could sit by Joe's bed and tell him. He might have regained consciousness by then. But even if he hadn't, she would still tell him.

* * *

Mary paid off the taxi and made for the glass door with the large gilt six and seven on it. As usual her gait was hesitant and several passers-by had to avoid her. Before she reached the step, Davis had flung open the door and put his arms round her.

'Christ, you frightened us to death! Look at you. Have you come straight from hospital? Should you be here at all?'

'Do I look that bad? I thought I'd done rather a good repair job.' Mary stared down at herself, concerned. Her navy suit had several small tears in it but compared with everyone else who had arrived while she was in the reception area, she looked absolutely fine. She looked up at him again. 'Would you rather I didn't come in? It was just that it was something I could do, you know, even if I can't see. I can do talks and things.'

'My dear, dear girl. Of course you must come in! Everyone who is anyone has been in to find out if you're all right and they're still here. You've got twice the viewers you would have had. You couldn't have planned better publicity—' He realized what he was saying and shut up quickly. He hugged her again. 'Listen. Come in and say hello. Then I'll get you some tea and you can put up your legs and just relax.'

'Oh, but Davis, I don't want to do that. Talking to people about my pictures – I want to start now. I had to stay on at the hospital to see how the others were. I missed my appointment with the eye specialist but I wasn't going to miss this.' She thought he hadn't heard her and she repeated emphatically, 'If I can't see to paint any more, Davis, then I want to be able to communicate in some other way.'

He hesitated, looking at her searchingly. Then he squeezed her arm. 'Isn't that what I've been saying to you these past few weeks?' He beamed. 'Come along, Mary Morrison. Let's hear you do your stuff!'

He flung open the door and ushered her inside and to her absolute astonishment a round of applause rippled through the gallery. She recalled Jenny's lovely simplicity and said, 'Oh, how wonderful! Thank you so much. There was a time this morning when I did not think I would be here. And now I am. How could anyone ask for more?'

Jenny was swabbed and bandaged in so many places she looked like an Egyptian mummy. Harry was the same. They met in the waiting area and for a little while did not know what to do. People brought them tea and they were seated in comfortable, upholstered chairs which caught on some of the dressings and made them both wince. Jenny had managed a word with Miss Morrison after Marvin had been brought in and was glad to see that she had now gone home. Harry felt the same about Mrs

Pemberton; some of their responsibilities were being taken off them.

Harry said uncertainly, 'I suppose we should report to Paddington and try to get a train back.' He gnawed his lip. 'The line will be blocked for a while. Perhaps they'll put us up in London.'

'I can't go yet, Harry.' She wondered when she had stopped calling him 'sir' and taken the enormous liberty of using his Christian name. 'As soon as Marvin is out of the theatre I must stay with him.'

Harry dropped his head. 'I'd forgotten. I'm so sorry. I can only think of Albert Priddy and Ahmed. Oh Jenny, I thought it was going to be such a good trip. Oh, dear God.'

Jenny did not look at him but she knew he was weeping. She said fiercely, 'We've got to think of the ones we can still help. It's not over yet.'

'Marvin . . . yes. Of course.' He controlled himself with obvious difficulty and straightened. 'And Mrs Priddy. I remember Marvin calling her Gert. When she gets here, we must be . . . ready.'

He turned his head with difficulty and looked at her. His dark eyes were drowning. 'Jenny. Jenny Price. You are so . . . special.'

She smiled wryly. 'Yes. That's what they called me. Special.'

He moved his head again, experimentally. It still hurt. 'Listen, Jenny. When this is over . . . oh God, will it ever be over? But when it's properly past, may I take you out? To the pictures? Or the theatre in Cheltenham? Would you come with me?'

It was what she had dreamed of. She looked at him and between the bandages he still had that wonderful boyish English face. Straightforward and honest, with white teeth and clear skin.

She moved her head slowly from side to side. 'I don't know, Harry. I just don't know. I'm so happy with my grandfather and seeing my best friend Lydia at the weekends . . .' She swallowed and added, 'Eighteen isn't very old, really, is it?'

At eighteen he had learned how to drive a tank and fire a gun. Yet at twenty-eight he had fallen flat on his face for Corinne the stewardess with the nails. He thought perhaps he wasn't very old either.

He said, 'Don't turn me down flat. Let me – let me—'

She thought he was going to cry again and she said quickly, 'Would you like to come to tea at my grandfather's house? We've got such a pretty garden and there are some lovely walks over the hills.'

It was all strangely formal. They sat there with cups and saucers in their hands and people scurrying around them, and talked about the Cotswolds and gardens and what sort of soil was best for roses and kidney beans. Harry was an authority on the first because, as he said, 'You can cut slices of clay from my allotment. Roses and spuds. They go best for me.' Jenny was definitely better on the latter. 'Our soil is quite light. You wouldn't think it would hold things that grow so tall. But it does. We pick from August till October. Kidney beans are my very most favourite vegetable,' she said contentedly. He snorted a little laugh, put down his cup and took her free hand. She didn't pull away.

'How come? I thought most kids hated beans but it sounds as if they've been your favourite vegetable all your life.'

'Yes. Since I was four. Or maybe five.' She looked at him. 'I'm not very good at remembering. It's called suppression, or so I was told.'

He raised his brows, obviously puzzled; she saw that the tears had almost dried.

'How do you mean?' he asked.

She knew it would be good if he didn't think about the train, or about Mrs Priddy, just for a little while. So she said, 'Before Mum and Dad were killed in the bombing, they took me to see a friend of my granddad's. My granddad had died and they wanted to tell this friend about it. He lived in a little cottage in the country, not far from Bristol. And he let me play in his kidney-bean tunnel. It was like being an Indian in a wigwam. I was fostered when I was six. But I kept trying to find the kidney-bean cottage again and I always ate kidney beans because they might help me to remember where it was. And then . . . I found the cottage and I found my grandfather's friend. And he wanted to adopt me as his granddaughter. And he did. And I live with him now in the kidney-bean cottage. Lydia called it kidney-bean heaven. And it is. Heaven, I mean.' Jenny stopped talking because her eyes were filling with tears and Harry was holding her hand much too tightly. She reclaimed her hand and sat back smiling. 'I told a bit of this to Miss Morrison. She was so understanding.'

'Haven't you ever told anyone else?'

'Lydia. My friend at school who is blind.'

'And now me.' He looked at her, his eyes pools of kindness. 'Can you remember your parents, Jenny?'

'Oh yes. Of course. Mum was very dark. Dad called her his gypsy girl. When the gypsies come to the village selling pegs in the winter and daffodils in the spring, I wonder if any of them are related to Mum.'

'Your father was probably just teasing her,' Harry said.

'Yes. But . . . you know. It's like a game I play.'

'I do that. I used to anyway. I used to pretend there was an accident – not a crash, just a little accident. And I saved someone's life.' He sounded bitter. 'It didn't work like that, did it?'

She said, 'No-one could have saved Mr Priddy's life, Harry. You stayed with him. Some-one he knew. Mr Pickering told me about it. Mr Pickering said you were wonderful.' She swallowed. 'I wasn't going to tell you this. Not ever. But I couldn't have got to Marvin and stayed with him if I hadn't known you were just outside the coach. It was your voice that . . .' She started to hiccough on a sob and then broke down completely. He took her cup and put it with his then leaned over and tried to dry her streaming face with his bandages. The nurse on the desk came over with some tissue and mopped expertly.

'Don't worry about this, dear. It's the shock, you know. Why don't you go in the next taxi? They'll run you back to Bristol in a couple of hours and you'll feel so much better once you're home.'

Harry looked up. 'We can't go yet,' he told her. 'We're still on duty, you see.' He turned back to Jenny, smiling gently. 'Thank you for telling me that, Jenny. Now tell me about your father. Was he dark too? Was he tall? What did he do for a living?'

So, for the first time in her life, Jenny Price began to talk about her father, her mother, their home together on the outskirts of Bristol, and then about her days of truancy and her blind quest to find her special haven. And Harry Blackmore listened to every word and knew that one day he would be able to tell her about the desert and the wadi where his tank was shelled and how he had thought nothing could be worse than that. Until now.

At four o'clock, after three hours in the

operating theatre, Marvin was admitted to the burns unit and Jenny was allowed to sit next to him and put her bandaged hand over his bandaged hand. Even his eyes and mouth were bandaged, with just a space for a drinking straw. No sign at all of acne or brace.

He had a special nurse who whispered that her name was Julie and she would never be far away. 'But he's going to be all right, you do know that, don't you? And he can probably hear and understand what you're saying, so do talk to him. Just for a few minutes.' She smiled reassuringly. 'You can have a bit longer tomorrow and even longer the next day.'

Jenny registered that she was expected to visit daily. She bit her lip. Already she was yearning for the kitchen at the cottage, the sound of the brown enamel kettle hissing gently on the gas stove, the garden smells coming in through the open door, her grandfather scraping his boots just outside . . .

She said, 'I must find somewhere to stay.'

The nurse lifted her brows. 'Of course. You don't live in London, do you? There's a spare room at the nurses' home. Shall I make inquiries?'

Jenny nodded, feeling as if a door was slamming shut somewhere. And then she turned to the inert figure on the bed. 'It's me again, Marvin. Jenny. We're out. We're safe now. I'm going to stay in the nurses' home so that I can see you every day. And you're going to get better. Did you hear Julie telling me that? Julie is the name of your nurse . . .'

The afternoon crept on. Three miles away, the lines in and out of Paddington were closed and a fleet of buses was taking passengers to Reading where they could pick up the services to Bristol and the west of England. The control offices in Paddington and Bristol had located rolling stock and locomotives and were arranging for them to be marshalled at Swindon. From the reports coming in, it looked as if all the passengers were now out of the eight forty-five and arrangements were being made to take them to their destinations. The situation, in the words of the BBC newsreader, was contained.

Ray Hart wandered along Praed Street and then Edgware Road and eventually sat beneath Marble Arch and watched the traffic. He did not feel contained in any way at all. If his arms and legs had suddenly flown off with the pigeons, it would not have surprised him. For so long his only real concern in life had been Ilse: what she was doing and what she would do next had been constant fears. And now those fears were laid to rest in the crashed train and he discovered that he had no idea what to do with himself. They'd patched him up at the hospital and told him to wait in reception but he hadn't waited, he'd drifted out and gone where his legs had taken him and quite suddenly they wouldn't take him any further.

He might have been sitting for ten minutes or an hour when a policeman stopped in front of him. He knew it was a policeman from his shiny shoes, and sure enough when he lifted his head, there was the reassuring helmet and the white gloves which probably meant he had been on point duty.

He said, 'Are you all right, sir? I've been watching you. Wondered whether you'd come from the crashed train.'

Ray squinted slightly against the lowering sun. Young bobbies these days, they were bright. He said, 'Yes. That's right. Well done.'

'Where are you going, sir?'

'I don't know. I can't remember.'

'Do you live in London?'

'No. I live in Bristol.' He shivered. He didn't want to go back there. 'My house burned down,' he confided.

The policeman frowned. 'Is there someone you could get in touch with? Wife? Parents? Other members of your family?'

Ray smiled suddenly. Of course. There was Janet.

'I could telephone Janet. She's my sister. She'll still be at work. And they don't mind me phoning because they know she doesn't take advantage. And I don't take advantage either . . .'

He found he was being escorted to a

telephone box and given quite a few pennies; he recited the number and the policeman, who was very kind as well as very bright, got it for him and pressed button A and handed him the receiver.

'Janet?' he said, much too loudly. 'It's Ray. I'm in London. I was on the train and it crashed. What shall I do next?'

There was a flurry of voices at the other end and then suddenly Janet's voice, also loud, hit his ear. 'Oh Ray! I've been so worried! The house has gone, and next door too, and I traced you to the hall at St Werburgh's Church and then *you'd* gone! Oh Ray – thank God. I thought I'd lost you.' She was crying with relief. 'Tell me where you are. I'll come straightaway. There's a five o'clock bus from the bus station. Meet me at Victoria, Ray. Can you do that?'

'Yes.'

'What about Ilse?'

'She's dead, Janet.' He heard his sister's indrawn breath in his ear. 'She was in the toilet with Caroline and the train was derailed and the whole of the front of the coach was squashed and then caught fire and they're both dead.' It all came back to him and he leaned against the glass of the phone box. 'I don't know what to do, Jan.'

Her voice dropped to a whisper. 'Caroline? What do you mean, Caroline? She isn't real, Ray. You know that.'

He said, 'Oh, she was real. But no-one knows about her. No-one at all. I haven't said anything. What shall I do now, Jan?'

There was a long pause, then she said, 'See if you can find us a bed and breakfast place somewhere, Ray. We'll talk it all over tonight.' She dropped her voice suddenly. 'Who knows, we might decide to go to Australia.'

He stared into the tiny mirror above the coin machine. Australia. Was that possible? A new start, a really, really new start?

The policeman said, 'All done, sir?'

'She said I should get bed and breakfast somewhere while she catches the bus.'

'Well, that's not easy, sir. People are booking early because of the Festival. How about if I take you back to the station with me and see if anyone there knows of a place.'

Ray said, 'The station?'

The policeman smiled indulgently. 'The police station, sir.'

Ray nodded dumbly.

After Jenny had gone, Harry kept his eye on the entrance, wondering how he would identify Mrs Priddy. His head was throbbing and without Jenny there he was conscious of pain in his chest and back, his legs and arms; in fact everywhere. They had given him aspirin but he longed for bed and silence and lack of . . . scurry.

He looked around the room at the others

there, nearly all of them bandaged, and knew they felt the same. Like animals they wanted to crawl away and lick their wounds. Deep inside himself he shuddered. The war, now this; what might come next? He wished he could be like Jenny Price who seemed to have lived on the edge of things since she was six years old; if she had agreed to come to the pictures with him, gradually slide into his life until they were one, might that have helped? But she was right, she was eighteen and held her youth high like a precious banner. He had been robbed of his youth; what right had he to take hers?

He squeezed his eyes tight shut in an effort – paradoxically – to keep them open, and there, coming through the doors, was Sam Beauchamp who ran the experimental buffet car, and he was ushering in three other people: an elderly man and two women. Harry held up a hand. Sam saw him and came across.

'It's the guard, isn't it? Harry Blackmore? You look more wounded than walking! Who's co-ordinating this –' he waved his hand helplessly around him – 'operation?'

Harry tried to grin reassuringly and with great difficulty he stood up; he must have stiffened while he sat talking to Jenny.

'I don't know, sir. Jenny Price and me, we've tried to keep in touch with as many people as possible.'

Sam said urgently, 'Jenny Price. Is she all

right? I've got her grandfather with me.' He moved his head slightly to indicate the old man standing uncertainly with the women, holding the back of a chair. 'And Truda Priddy. She's brought a friend, thank God. If anything has happened to her husband . . .' He saw Harry's face. 'Oh God. Has he bought it?'

Harry said the words he had said before. 'He couldn't have known anything about it.'

'Christ,' said Sam Beauchamp fiercely. 'I gather she might be pregnant. And he doesn't know. Didn't know. Oh Christ.'

Harry said, suddenly quite sure of his facts, 'Well, he knows now, sir.'

Mr Beauchamp gave him a funny look. Harry knew all about shock, and the way he had been in a black funk just now and was gloriously in touch with everything at this moment were symptoms of shock, he knew that very well. But he didn't care.

He walked steadily across to the three people waiting for him; he felt no pain anywhere and he hardly heard the cacophony of a busy accident ward. He said, 'Jenny is all right. She's with the other steward who has suffered severe burns. She's been wonderful, sir. I wouldn't be surprised if she got a . . .' he fumbled, trying to find the feminine equivalent of knighthood. 'I wouldn't be at all surprised if she got a lady-hood,' he concluded with great dignity.

Jenny's granddad, who probably also knew

from personal experience what shock could do to a person, took Harry's hand and shook it painfully.

'She's spoken of you,' he said hoarsely. 'Thank you, son. Thank you. To be honest, I wouldn't be surprised if you got a lordhood.'

Harry turned and looked at Albert Priddy's wife. He'd heard about her from Wilf Pickering; bit of a termagant at times, so he understood. Straight as a die though, quite literally at the moment because her back was like a ramrod and she looked him in the eye and dared him to soften any blows he might be about to deliver.

He was going to say that Albert hadn't known a thing but he didn't because how could he possibly know what Albert knew?

He said, 'He saved Wilf's life, Mrs Priddy. When the firebox blew back, he shoved Wilf out the other side of the cab and took the full force . . .' He stopped because he heard her tiny whimper. Then he said simply, 'He'll always be with you. You know that, don't you?'

She nodded, speechless. And then she rested her forehead carefully on his bandaged shoulder. He wrapped his arms tightly round her and stared over her shoulder at the other woman, who had put her hands to her face. How right Jenny was when she said their job hadn't finished. He bent his head and touched Mrs Priddy's hair with his lips. She was shaking, but she did not cry.

Twelve

Eventually Mary allowed Davis to hire a car
to take her back to Winderslake. He suggested
that she should stay in a hotel overnight, but
suddenly she was very tired and needed the
peace of Winderslake. She thought of the oriel
room in the old house, full of John's paintings,
and wanted very much to wander around the
walls and look again with the inner eye she
seemed to have acquired today. Hadn't she said
something like that to Davis and all the others
only an hour or so ago?

'We look at paintings, any kind of art, with two
types of vision. We look at what we see and we
look at what we do not see but what we feel. A
very dear friend tells me that I paint nostalgia.
Certainly my landscapes with figures are how
I remember the countryside. But I am also
painting what I see in front of me. So am
I looking for subjects that I already recognize
from the past? Or does nothing really change?'

She had smiled. 'That's for my viewer to decide perhaps.'

There had been questions, lots of them, until Davis had said, 'Ladies and gentlemen, as you know, Miss Morrison was in the train that was derailed this morning and although she is obviously safe and well, I think she should finish now.'

The applause had been long and loud. And she had thought that, yes, she could do this sort of thing. Perhaps talk to the children at Winderslake. Perhaps even give some lessons. The first blind artist . . .

But before that could happen, she needed to look at John's paintings again. Was there some sort of clue in the later ones about John's feelings for her? He had fought the age gap and he had won the fight. It seemed that somewhere along the line, she had lost a similar fight with Andrew. Might she find some help from John as to how she could free Andrew?

She rang the hospital from the office at the back of the gallery and asked after Jenny.

The person on the other end said, 'Would that be Jenny Price?'

Mary recognized the voice; it belonged to the receptionist who had intended to go to the viewing that afternoon. She said, 'Yes. The stewardess on the train.'

'Is that Miss Morrison? Are you all right?'

Mary reassured her. 'I'm still at the

exhibition,' she said. 'And it's done me so much good.' She gave a small embarrassed laugh. 'It's as if I'm seeing everything, even my own stuff, with new eyes.'

'Accident victims often say that. And of course it's true, isn't it? In a peculiar way, to survive an accident is to start a new life.'

'How – how clever of you!' Mary was struck by the truth of this; it was exactly right. 'I'm going home now but first I wanted to have news of Jenny and Marvin Bramley. And I wondered too about someone called Joe Kemp. Mrs Pemberton was with him but he wasn't conscious.'

'Let me see . . . yes, Jenny Price is with Mr Bramley and she is staying in the guest room at the nurses' home tonight. They think Mr Bramley will make a good recovery though it will be a long process.' There were sounds of paper being handled. 'Joe Kemp, Joe Kemp. There's a Jeremy Kemp in one of the side wards. Head injuries. His parents are with him now. They identified him as Jeremy Kemp.'

'That must be the same one. I thought Mrs Pemberton called him Joe.'

'He is going to be all right. His injuries are not serious.' Mary could hear a smile arrive in the voice. 'He's clutching the remnants of a straw hat and, unconscious or not, he will not let it go!'

'That's him,' Mary said. 'Mrs Pemberton will be relieved.'

'Just a moment, Miss Morrison. Hang on.' Mary heard her talking to someone else. Then she came back. 'Apparently Mrs Pemberton called in about ten minutes ago when I was taking tea to one of the other patients. When she heard that Mr and Mrs Kemp were with their son, she left.' She cleared her throat. 'There was a car waiting for her. It looked very important, my colleague tells me.'

Mary smiled to herself. 'So she will have gone back home. That's good. I think Joe will find her. Eventually.'

'I'm sure. Was the exhibition good, Miss Morrison?'

'From my point of view it was a life-saver. And now I'm going home too. Thank you for looking after us. You were all absolutely marvellous.'

'It's our job. We just do it. Like you going to the exhibition.' She laughed. 'Thank you, Miss Morrison. I'm very glad I met you.'

Mary replaced the receiver and allowed herself to be ushered back through the gallery and outside to a waiting car.

'Front or back?' Davis asked.

'Back, I think. I'll probably sleep.' She smiled through the glass, hoping the driver would see. 'I'm sorry. I don't think I can talk.'

The window was wound down and a girl's voice said, 'Please don't worry about that. Make yourself as comfortable as you can. There are cushions and a rug.' She added tactfully,

'And I can stop wherever you like if you need a break.'

'Oh, a woman driver.' Mary was delighted. She turned to Davis. 'How clever of you. I can snore with impunity!'

They all laughed and as Davis tucked her in and then waved goodbye, she thought how odd it all was. Seven hours ago she had been trapped in a splintered train carriage with a very real likelihood of being burned alive. And now she was taking leave of her old friend as if nothing untoward had happened.

Sure enough, once they were clear of the city, she was asleep. The driver was good, she kept at a steady forty miles an hour and as the sun sank into evening she wound down her window so that Mary could smell the scents of Surrey and Berkshire and eventually Wiltshire and Somerset and incorporate them into her dreams. Whether they fired her imagination or not she never knew of course, but for the first time she dreamed of her father and her two brothers; then of John Kenyon as he might have been before she knew him: a young man in the trenches of the First World War, sketching feverishly, recording everything he saw. Just as that psychologist had done in Falmouth. One person's view . . . another person's view . . . the words thrummed a rhythm through her head and she smiled in her sleep and thought that she must paint the people she knew so that they would know themselves. If she had painted her parents and Miss Pensford, would that have changed anything? Too late now. Her mother had died just after the war and there had never been any word from her father. And if she had painted Andrew, it would have been obvious to him and the whole world that she could not manage without him.

She sighed in her sleep and turned her head away from the setting sun.

They skirted Bath and took the road to Wells and then diverted into the heart of the Mendips and there, far above Bristol, they ran through Winderslake. Past the school with its ivy-covered walls and primrose-studded gardens, down into the village, past the Lamb and Flag and the church and then home with its lych gate and the modern five-barred gate which allowed cars right up to the front door. Mary had been semi-conscious since Bath and now she roused herself completely and sat up.

'What a wonderful drive. Thank you so much.' She waited for the driver to come round and open her door. 'I'll just go inside and get my other cheque book. I'm afraid I've lost my hand-bag.'

'Mr Bryson saw to the fare, Miss Morrison. I know you lost your bag in the train crash.' The girl smiled. 'I would have done it for nothing, you know, but he wouldn't let me.'

'Of course he wouldn't.' Mary stood there

hesitating. Even her own front door posed a challenge these days. She said, 'Will you come inside and have a cup of tea or something?'

'I'd better not. I'd like to get to Marlborough before it's completely dark. Thanks all the same.' She went ahead of Mary and knocked on the door. 'Is there someone in? You've lost your keys as well, I take it.'

She was answered when the door was flung open by Katy who cast herself onto Mary in floods of tears. 'We didn't know what had happened to you! We kept phoning and no-one knew anything and Mr French went looking for you and didn't know where to look and I said by the time you get back home she'll be here but you weren't and we didn't know what to think!'

Katy had always been a friend, never criticizing or gossiping when Andrew had moved in. Since Mary's sight had deteriorated, their roles had changed; Katy had taken over the kitchen as well as the cleaning and she would have taken over Mary herself had she been allowed. Mary extricated herself now with some difficulty, and with one arm hugging Katy to her side she said goodbye to the driver who was smiling mistily, unaware that it should be Andrew out here frantic with anxiety, welcoming her home. The two women stood there, Katy gradually recovering, until the sound of the car engine had almost gone, then Mary said quietly, 'I was quite safe, as you see, and there's no mystery about it at all. I went to Cork Street. Mr Bryson was putting on a retro for me. I didn't intend to go but then when I realized how lucky I'd been it seemed the right thing to do.'

Katy's tears were finally checked by Mary's calm voice. She said wonderingly, 'You sound so much better than when you left this morning. Did you pop in to Harley Street to get the results?'

Mary hesitated. Then she said, 'As a matter of fact, I did. They're good. Really good.'

Katy wept again. 'And that was when you thought you should go to see Mr Bryson. Because you knew you'd be painting again. Oh, I'm so glad.' She pulled away and tore into the house and Mary could hear her announcing to Andrew that everything was fine, she would be in the kitchen if needed and supper would be an hour and was that all right. Mary did not hear Andrew's reply. She went slowly down the tiled hall to the old study where they usually spent an hour when Andrew came home from work. He was sitting by the window which meant he was in silhouette and she could not see his face.

She said in the most neutral tone she could summon, 'Katy has a way of summarizing everything, hasn't she?' She smiled at the shape in the window. 'As you see, I really am all right. I was rescued by the stewardess.' She swallowed suddenly. 'D'you know, it was the strangest coincidence, she went to Winderslake school!

She hadn't left there long. She was so sweet, Andrew. She had a kind of wisdom and a kind of innocence and they went together perfectly.'

'And you're sure you're OK?' Although the words were concerned, the tone was as neutral as her own.

'Yes. Tired of course. I slept in the car – Davis arranged a car – but not very deeply. I could smell summer. And the past.' She sat down in a Victorian spoonback, a replica of one that had come from Lynch End. 'Can you smell the past, I wonder?'

'Probably.'

He did not move. She knew he was watching her though she could not see his eyes. Why hadn't he put his arms round her and kissed her and thanked God and Jenny Price for her rescue?

He cleared his throat. 'Your clothes . . . and your hand is bandaged.'

'We were cut quite a bit, Jenny and I. There was a lot of broken glass and we had to crawl through it.' She closed her eyes. 'We were so very lucky. A sort of fireball ran along from the buffet car and exploded through one of the broken windows. We could so easily have been burned to death.' She laughed a little self-consciously. 'Sounds melodramatic, doesn't it? I suppose all near-misses sound like that. We're all right. That's what we need to remember. We've got a second chance.'

He said nothing for a very long time. She thought: I wish I didn't still love him, it's going to be so difficult . . .

When he spoke, his tone had changed and he sounded curt.

'What did old Yorke say?'

She had to make a conscious effort to switch her thinking. Hadn't she already told Katy that she'd been given the all-clear? He must have heard. Perhaps he just wanted to hear it from her.

She said, 'I'm all right. Can you believe it?'

'Not really.' He was still curt. 'Not when you can't see the way to the front door.'

She would have to elaborate. 'Well, obviously I need new specs and he's going to test me himself.'

'Why didn't he do it then?'

'Because I wanted to get on. The exhibition opened at two . . .'

'You didn't tell me there was an exhibition.'

'I didn't think you were interested.'

'You did not think I was *interested*?' he repeated slowly and incredulously.

She said wearily, 'We've grown apart, Andrew. Face up to it. You've stayed because you thought you should. Very tricky to end a relationship when one of the partners is going blind. Now . . . things are different.'

'You mean you can tell me to go now? You can

manage without me, thank you very much? Is that what this is all about?'

She felt the stirrings of anger. 'I don't think I need to tell you to go, Andrew. You've made it all too obvious that my failing eyesight has irked you. Well, now it need not.' There was another long pause and eventually she filled it by saying, 'I want to go and look around the oriel room before supper. Will you excuse me?'

She made to get out of the low chair. To her amazement he leaned across and pushed her back down.

'No, I will not excuse you, Mary. Not any more. You're not going to slip into the past again and leave me standing outside. You're going to stay in the present and tell me exactly what is going on.'

She protested vigorously. 'I'm not hiding anything from you, Andrew. And as for escaping into the past, you think that because of the age difference.'

He said triumphantly, 'I knew we should get to it eventually. The age difference. Fifteen little years.' He put his face close to hers and she registered the pain there. 'Unless people share a childhood they cannot share a past completely, Mary. But they can try. They can talk about it, let each other in. When do you talk about your marriage, your parents?'

She said defensively, 'You've never told me about *your* marriage! I just get anecdotes about you and your brothers climbing trees, pinching apples. I've told you how my brothers and I dammed the stream in our garden . . .'

'You've never taken me to see Lynch End. Or your cottage in Falmouth. And how could I mention my disastrous marriage? Yours was successful and – and obviously wonderful, but you never talk about it! How could I suddenly mention Miranda and all that mess?'

She said, 'I think we're getting away from the point. Which is that we have . . . drawn away from each other.' She did not want to start hurling accusations. 'To be blunt, had my diagnosis been otherwise, you may well have felt duty bound to stay and look after me. But, as I just said, you're now quite free. Don't let's quarrel. It's been a wonderful few years—'

'When did you get to Harley Street?' he interrupted. 'After your rescue you were taken to St Mary's and then presumably discharged. So did you go and see Mr Yorke then, even though it was long past your appointment time?'

'I just had a word with the receptionist. She had the results of the tests.'

'On the telephone?'

'No. I called there on my way to—'

'Stop it! You did not call there and you did not telephone! I was there before midday and left at two o'clock after I'd found out from the receptionist that your train had been derailed and they had heard nothing from you! I went to

St Mary's after you'd left there – no-one knew where you were going – and I came straight home hoping to find you here. When I didn't, I spent the rest of the afternoon telephoning Harley Street!'

She stared at the shadowed face so close to her own. And then she whispered, 'But you left me at Temple Meads. The guard had to help me onto the train.'

He frowned; she could see that. 'You wouldn't have allowed *me* to help you, would you?' he said. 'Just as you never let me help you around the house. Just as you've let me know that I'm not welcome in your bedroom any more.' He took her hands and thrust his face even closer so that she could see it. 'If we've drawn apart, Mary, it's because you keep pushing me away. And now you're lying about your appointment. To give me my freedom, according to you. Or is it really because you want yours?'

She whispered, 'So when you left me you drove straight up to London?'

'I'd hired a car and—'

'Why? Why not drive our car?'

'Nothing seemed to be *ours* any more. And the van would have shown up like a sore thumb.'

'What did you plan to do?'

'I would have known what the results were by the way you walked down the steps. I can tell just how you are feeling from the set of your shoulders, Mary. If the results were good, I would simply have driven back home. If not, I had worked out a way of making you see it as a new life, and I would have begged you to let me stay and help you.'

She swallowed.

He said very quietly, 'What would you have said, Mary? Would you have told me to pack my bags?'

'No.' She tried for one of her smiles but her mouth wouldn't co-operate. 'I don't know what I *would* have said, Andrew. What I *am* saying is please will you stay and help me into this new life?'

He gripped her hands so hard she could hardly bear it.

'Do you mean that, Mary? What about all our differences – age, talents? I don't know anything about my real mother – I could have a lot of problems. You had an idyllic childhood with a big family—'

'Oh my God, Andrew. My mother practically locked herself away and my father embezzled money from his bank and ran off with my governess.' She gasped a little laugh at his expression and then said, 'Can you let go of my hands, darling? They're hurting.'

He fell to his knees and drew her forward onto his shoulder.

'I'm sorry, Mary . . . my dear, dear Mary. I thought . . . all the wrong things.' He stroked her flyaway hair and held it to the nape of her neck. 'I can't manage without you, and I thought that if you were losing your sight you would have to rely on me more but it didn't seem to be working that way.' He kissed her forehead.

She closed her eyes. 'Have I really pushed you away?'

'You wanted to take a taxi this morning. You didn't even want me to drive you to the station.'

'Oh, Andrew. I'm sorry. But try to understand, darling. When you're my age, I'll be over sixty. You'll probably end up looking after me anyway. And this business with my eyes brought all that closer.' She sighed. 'Pity. It's not a good basis for a relationship, is it?'

'I don't pity you, Mary. I admire and respect you more than I can ever say.' He smoothed her hair again. 'If you had been going to lose your sight, I would have been so *honoured* to be able to help you, darling.'

'Oh Andrew . . .' She stopped, registering his words. '*If* I had been going to lose my sight? We don't know yet, darling.'

He moved slightly so that he could see her face. She opened her eyes. 'I got to London in good time for your appointment,' he told her. 'I waited until two o'clock and then I went into Mr Yorke's place and I caught the receptionist off guard because she was so anxious about you. Darling, your condition is operable. The cataracts can be removed. Your life need not change, Mary. You'll be able to go on painting.'

There was another silence; she stared at him as if trying to find the truth in the elaborate mesh of lies they had made between them.

At last she said, 'Maybe I'd like something else. Something different. To justify this second chance.'

'I thought you would be ecstatic.'

'Of course I'm ecstatic. But not really about my sight, though that's wonderful, absolutely wonderful. But I'm ecstatic because I haven't lost you.'

He tightened his mouth against tears and she put a hand to his face and cradled it comfortingly.

He kissed the palm. 'You've always done that, haven't you? Touched objects that you're going to paint. That's why I wondered . . . I've bought you a present, Mary mine. It might help with your new life.'

She smiled. 'How marvellous. I can't wait. But I've got something in mind too. A new start for us both.' She stilled her hand and said, 'Andrew, will you marry me?'

Much later, after he had told Katy to cancel supper and had carried Mary over the threshold of their room, she told him about wanting to look at John's pictures.

'I wondered if I would find a message there. He was so much older than I was. How did he cope with that?'

'Do you want us to go to the oriel room now?'

'No. You told me how he coped with it, darling. He shared all those years with me through his paintings.'

He hesitated, looking at her in the dim room. 'But you've painted ever since I've known you, and long before. And somehow that didn't bridge any gaps.'

'Darling, I've always been such a careful painter. You told me I painted nostalgia and John said I did still lifes with extras! But I'm changing. Davis says at the moment I'm going right off the canvas! And now I want to give some lessons at the school. What would you say to that?'

'I'd say, good for you.' He swung his legs off the bed. 'We're going to share everything from now on, Mary. We're going to be married.' He flung his hands into the air and made a whooping noise. 'We're going to be married! You're going to be Mrs French. Oh, I know you'll have to stay Mary Morrison for your work, but legally you will be Mrs French!'

'My old work will bear my old name. But from now on anything I do will be signed Mary French.'

He made the whooping noise again and scooped her up.

'Listen, before we go to bed – I know you're tired – but you need to eat something and have a hot drink, and I want to show you my present. Can you manage that?'

She giggled into his neck. 'The way you say that, it's so portentous! What on earth can it be?'

'It fits in so well with our new beginnings policy! Come on – shoes, cardigan, because we have to go outside and it's still only April after all . . .' He held her to him in sudden terror. 'I thought I'd lost you today for good, Mary. And I dare not risk a cold carrying you off. Promise me you will take care of yourself, always.'

'I promise. Outside?' She thrust her feet into shoes. 'Surely it's not a car?'

'No. You already have a car. That's sheer greed!' He armed her down the stairs and through the back door into the garden. 'It's in the shed. I can move it later, but I didn't want you to see it.'

She forgot she was tired; the night air was sharp and she drank it in and clung to his arm as they went down the path to the kitchen garden and the shed. She thought of Jenny Price and her kidney-bean heaven and Sylvia Pemberton who might well be experiencing new beginnings soon and poor Marvin Bramley who was so obviously in love with Jenny who was in love with the guard . . .

Andrew undid the door of the shed and they both squeezed inside. It was solidly dark here and she waited for him to produce a torch or at least strike a match. But he did not.

'I came here last night when it was dark,' he said in a low voice. 'I thought this is how it would

307

be for you. Blackness. So I tried using my hands to see.' He took one of hers and placed it on something – a rough surface. 'It's a block of limestone, Mary. I've put your left hand right at the top of it – it's the same height as you. Give me your other hand, I need both of them now, and start working down. What do you think?'

He stood there expectantly, his hand in the small of her back. She knew instantly what he had in mind. Limestone was easily carved. She brought her wrists together, then fanned her hands out and started exploring the bumps and crevices of the stone until she was crouching at its base. It was an enormous lump, apparently shapeless, but promising the full excitement of discovery.

She knelt on the rough wooden planking floor and put her arms right round the stone and held it to her.

She whispered, 'The first blind artist, Andrew . . . the first blind artist.'

'It was a stupid thing to say.'

'It was a wonderful thing to say. And you were going to make it happen.'

He said, 'It's a bit redundant now. But I wanted you to – to confront it. So that you would know . . .'

'Yes.' She could feel tears damping her collar. 'You thought if I couldn't see to paint I could feel to sculpt. Oh Andrew, I've always wanted to sculpt. How did you know?'

He was amazed. 'I didn't. I couldn't think of anything else that could be accomplished by touch. Do you really like it? Could you work it, d'you think? I haven't bought tools. We could go together. Then you could choose which ones.'

She stood up. 'It's the most wonderful present I've ever had. The new beginning.' She put her hands at the top again. 'This head is so familiar.'

'What head?' he laughed.

'Oh, it's there. Just underneath the stone.' She turned to him, glowing. 'My God, it's your head! This is you, Andrew! I'm going to find *you* underneath this stone!'

After an incredulous moment, he started to laugh. And then so did she. Katy found them twenty minutes later, still laughing and dancing around the shed.

'You're mad,' she informed them. 'Come along in and have a sandwich, for heaven's sake! My goodness, this has been a day and a half!'

Andrew sobered suddenly. 'It's been much more than that,' he said. 'It's been . . . all our lives!'

They walked back to the house together. Mary knew she must tell him about today. But not yet. Tonight they must savour this happiness to the full.

She smiled up at the moon. 'I think there might be a ground frost tonight,' she said. As if in complete agreement, an owl hooted from the woods. They laughed again.

Thirteen

There were no owls hooting around the wrecked remains of the eight forty-five. As darkness fell around the train, the arc lights illuminated the disaster in stark detail. The enormous crane swung half a coach high above the rest and onto the embankment. Just for a moment the protesting screech of metal could be heard between the scream of saws and the roar of acetylene torches. The passer-by of this morning who had covered her ears was walking her dog again and now stood and surveyed the scene more objectively. It was like a gargantuan dental operation: the drilling, the sawing, the extraction. She shuddered and pulled on the dog lead. The six o'clock news had reported eight dead; four in the front of the train had died instantly, the others in hospital. The most recent body, protected by another, had been that of a child. The woman shuddered again. Poor little devil. At least the kid couldn't have known much about it. She tugged her dog back onto the path and made for home. It was a chilly night; she would make some toast by her gas fire and stop thinking about the accident.

Back in the hospital, the night staff had come on duty and it was as if the very building itself was settling to sleep. The receptionist who had missed the retrospective exhibition of Mary Morrison's work was saying goodnight to Jenny Price and her grandfather. Sam Beauchamp was sitting nearby next to Janie McEvoy; they were waiting for Harry to bring Gertie Priddy back from the mortuary. She had been there a long time.

Jenny took her grandfather's arm and led him back to the line of chairs.

'Gramps, I have to stay. Really. I'd love to come home but if the Bramleys aren't coming to sit with Marvin, then I must.'

Tom Marston sighed deeply. 'This family business isn't easy, my girl. How can I be expected to keep an eye on you if you're stuck up here for the next week?'

'You'll just have to have a bit of faith in me, Gramps!' She grinned, meaning it as a joke, but he suddenly realized it was no joke. She could look after herself, could his Jenny. She'd gone out into the world and she'd . . . dammit, she'd conquered it. He couldn't ask for more.

Sam Beauchamp leaned forward. 'I can take you home, Tom, or I can pay for a bed and breakfast up here for the two of you. I reckon your Jenny could do with a good night's sleep and you'd probably sleep sounder if you knew she was next door. How about it?'

'I'm fixed up at the nurses' home. But thank you, sir. It's very kind of you.'

'We can unfix that I expect, Jenny.' He looked from one to the other. 'Come on. You could have a couple of hours together tonight and odd times throughout the day. Give you the chance to get to know a bit of your capital city!'

Jenny looked at her grandfather. Suddenly the prospect of being stranded up here was not so difficult. She said diffidently, 'How do you feel, Gramps? Long time since you slept anywhere else but the cottage.'

Tom smiled slightly, knowing how she was feeling. 'Bit of a change. Make something good out of something terrible. Eh?' He winked. 'Get something out of your boss too, eh?' He looked sternly at Sam. 'We don't want no doss house mind, Sam!'

'There's a place in Gloucester Terrace.' Sam began to lever himself up. 'Let me go and phone. They know me from my brewery days.' He lumbered off and Tom took his place and patted the seat next to him. Jenny subsided gratefully.

Tom turned to Janie. 'How about you, Mrs

McEvoy? Will you want to get back home tonight?'

Janie nodded. 'We're waiting for Truda to come back. And the guard.' She pleated her skirt nervously. 'I would have gone with her but he said it would be best if he went. He'd seen . . . Albert's body before.'

'I doubt very much if she will actually see the body, it will be covered.'

Janie bit her lip. 'You don't know Truda. She will see him.' She took a small breath and began to cry. 'It's so awful. They've wanted a baby for ages and now . . . he didn't even know about it! She didn't know! It was her next-door neighbour, the other side, came in this morning after Albert had gone to work and, well, she just knew somehow. It's so terribly, terribly sad.' She found a handkerchief and blew her nose.

Tom glanced at Jenny, hoping she would take over, but she was sitting there with her eyes half closed, obviously punch drunk with exhaustion. He leaned forward and patted the older woman's arm and told her how Mrs Priddy would rely on her in the future.

Janie snuffled a laugh into her hanky. 'Truda rely on me? Not likely. Truda never relied on anyone in her life.'

Tom looked at the bent head curiously. People so rarely understood people; that was one thing he'd learned over the years. That was why he and Jenny had hit it off straightaway.

When they'd met again after so many years, in that Mr Cousins' office, looking at each other across the desk, they had understood so much. He sighed and thought: poor Mrs Priddy.

Sam came back just before Jenny was fully asleep. He and Sam got her to her feet and they trudged out of the hospital. They crossed the road and took a turn to the left and then to the right and Sam left them clinging to railings while he climbed four steps and rang the door-bell of a terraced house. There were more stairs and a landing and two small rooms at the end of it.

'They're for children really – I've got two other single rooms but they were taken earlier.' The landlady smiled at Sam. 'Afraid the beds are only two foot six but your friends don't look very big.' She stood aside while Jenny went into the first room and sat on the bed. 'Oh, my dear girl. You do look tired. What a day you must have had. I'll lend you a nightie and a face flannel and you can buy a toothbrush tomorrow.' She bustled around Tom too, promising pyjamas and a razor from her husband. 'We've finished dinner but I can do you a little supper down-stairs. Some soup and cheese and a nice cup of cocoa.'

Jenny smiled wanly. Tom nodded. 'You could do with something, lass. Help you to sleep.' He inclined his head to the window: the faint sound of traffic came through it. After Winderslake it was noisy. Tom went downstairs again with Sam, pumped his hand, thanked him for everything.

'I shall be back of course,' Sam said. 'The boy – Jenny's boy – is still on the staff. Telephone me if I can bring anything up for him – or for you.'

Tom said, 'What do you mean, Jenny's boy?'

Sam shrugged. 'Bit obvious, isn't it? She'd hardly want to stay with him otherwise.'

Tom was taken aback. He went into the first room down the hall where the landlady was laying breakfasts. She glanced up. 'Take your granddaughter into the lounge, Mr Marston. There's a fire there. You can have your supper on a tray nice and cosy.'

He nodded and went to fetch Jenny. She was sitting exactly where they had left her on the edge of the bed but she stood up when he came in.

'Gramps, this might be all right, mightn't it? It's a lovely house. And it was so kind of the landlady to say we could have some supper. I was reading in the paper that some London landladies are really quite strict.'

'You and your newspapers. Bringing one home every night and going through it with a fine-tooth comb!' He thought: perhaps I don't understand as well as I thought. She's too young to be falling in love . . .

She went ahead of him down the stairs. 'It's Lydia's fault. She made me read them so that I could tell her anything of interest. She taught me to read in the first place!'

'Aye, that young lady has a lot to answer for.' Tom often teased Lydia about this but his voice was not teasing now. 'I remember the second or third time she came to tea she asked me what I thought about her getting married. Talking about getting married at her age – silly, it is!'

They went into the lounge which was empty except for a couple sitting well away from the fire. Tom nodded in their direction and the woman nodded back; the man seemed not to see them.

Jenny said soberly, 'She wants to be independent, Gramps, make her own choices. You know what I mean. Getting married is the biggest, most shocking thing she can think of!'

'Red rag to a bull,' Gramps said glumly.

Jenny laughed. 'Exactly. That's why she screams and swears and is so cheeky to everyone.'

'And it's why you love her,' Tom said.

'I suppose so. She's so brave.'

Tom sat down in an armchair with a bump and burst out laughing. 'And you think you're not!'

Jenny flushed deeply. 'I know they're going to start saying I am. But Gramps, it wasn't like that. I just did, I don't know, the next thing I had to do. And when I was trying to reach Marvin, it was Harry encouraging me outside that did it.'

She looked at her grandfather very seriously. 'He's a wonderful man, Gramps.'

Tom groaned aloud. He could see he'd got a lot of problems coming up. Not only the young steward, but the guard as well! 'Old enough to be your father!' was all he said.

Jenny sighed. 'Not quite. But, well, he's seen things, done things I can't imagine. He really is a hero.'

The sandwiches came and Tom watched her tuck in with her usual healthy young appetite. He was teetering between being horribly anxious for her and trusting her completely.

At the table by the window the woman said, 'I know exactly what it said on the news, Ray. All right, they've found the remains of a child and that's going to get a lot of publicity. But there's nothing at all to connect that child with you.'

Ray spoke in the monotone she was fast getting used to. 'If we'd caught another train . . . stayed where we were . . . the child would be alive now.'

'Listen, Ray. If you hadn't rescued that poor little girl, she would have been burned in the house. The fire was obviously started by Ilse and if you hadn't caught the train, she would have been arrested. So, let's face it once and for all, Ilse was mad. This whole business is because of her.'

'The child would have been alive,' he droned.

'If you're trying to take the blame, look at it this way. If I hadn't had my splendid idea of killing off Ilse's imaginary baby, then none of this would have happened.'

'Not your fault.'

'It's as much my fault as yours. And I don't intend to spend the rest of our lives hauling around a terrible weight of guilt. So much happened, Ray. In the war and after it. Let Ilse – and her Caroline – rest in peace. Please.'

He blinked hard and focused on her at last so she knew she had said the right thing. She reached over and took his hand very gently and almost wept when he tried to smile at her.

She whispered, 'Ray, let's go away. While all the fuss is still on, let's go to the authorities and find out about emigrating. The war is still with us here. Perhaps it always will be. Let's get right away from it. I expect there will be a lot of forms to fill in but we could get one of the assisted passages to Australia. Have you thought about it?'

He nodded twice. 'Now?' he whispered.

'Tomorrow. We'll start tomorrow.'

He repeated, 'Now. Now, Janet. The stuff you brought . . . let's take it with us and go now.'

She frowned. 'Don't be silly, Ray. Everywhere is closed. It's almost ten o'clock. Besides, you need a good night's sleep. You're still in shock.'

He dropped his eyes and leaned right forward. 'Jan, that girl by the fire. I've seen her before. On the train. They know and they've sent her to find us. We must go now.'

Janet looked across the room in astonishment to where Jenny and her grandfather were chatting and eating cheese sandwiches. 'Don't be daft, Ray. Even if she was on the train she doesn't know you were—'

'She came up to me afterwards. I'm remembering it all now. She was something to do with the train, she wore a uniform.' He flipped his eyes sideways. 'She's still wearing it.'

Janet nodded. 'All right. But we live in England and the war is over and we won it. Nobody spies on anybody else. She's with an elderly gentleman and they're probably putting up for the night here just as we are.' She was still holding one of his hands and she gripped it very hard. 'Ray, listen to me. Ilse was mad but you are not. Stop behaving as if she were still here. She's gone. You're free now.'

He closed his eyes and dropped his head further. 'That was exactly what I thought straight after it happened, sis. I thought the trap had opened and I could get out of it. But perhaps it opened and I stayed in it of my own free will.'

She shook her head. 'You haven't been really free for years. It will take a bit of getting used to. That's all.' She smiled brilliantly and leaned back in her chair. 'Listen, Ray. Stop worrying about everything in the past. Let's think about the future. We'll have to work if – *when* we get there. What shall we do?'

He shook his head. 'I don't know. I've worked for the flour people for so long, since I left school . . .'

'Exactly. So what you don't know about flour isn't worth knowing!' She leaned back triumphantly. 'Let's open a shop, Ray. Between us we can raise the money. Let's open a cake and bread shop. Homemade stuff. You do the bread and I'll do the cakes. We'd be self-supporting – our own bosses, Ray. Whether we managed any holidays or not wouldn't matter because we'd be really free of anyone else. What do you say?'

He stared at her, his attention caught at last. 'I – I'm not sure, Jan. Finding premises and signing leases, it's right out of my ken.'

'I can do that. When I looked after Dad he showed me all the papers concerning the house. I paid the mortgage. I got repairs done when no one else could get hold of a workman. I'm up to all that, Ray. If you'd let me take it on. I don't want to push you into anything. I know I'm the typical older sister, bossy and all. But I'd love to look after you, Ray. Be a proper family again.'

He felt his eyes filling. It sounded like heaven. He whispered, 'Oh Jan. We've always got on well, haven't we?'

She pressed her lips together in an effort for control; then she lost it. 'Ray . . . I said we mustn't talk about it but I have to say this. I'm so sorry, so terribly sorry. Poor Ilse. What you told me about the displaced persons camp and the men ill-treating the girls . . . she must have gone through hell. I shouldn't have interfered. She must have trusted me to let me take . . . her baby. And I killed it.'

It was his turn to be strong. He said very seriously, 'Listen, Jan. War makes everyone guilty – no-one can come away from a war without guilt. I tried to expiate mine by looking after Ilse and it didn't work, did it?' He closed his eyes momentarily. 'You just said we've got to let her rest in peace. And that's what we must do. The little girl too. They must both rest in peace. Take the guilt with them. Sort of . . .' He frowned, thinking. 'Sort of act like lightning conductors and earth it. Does that make sense?'

She thought about it, her mouth still working. At last she nodded.

He nodded too. 'Good lass. It's the only way we can make a new start, Jan. If we keep the guilt with us, then we have to go back and face the music. So let it stay here when we leave, all right?' He actually managed a proper grin and when she managed another nod, he said again, 'Good lass. So tomorrow morning, we'll start the ball rolling. How's that?'

After all that she had said since she arrived at Victoria, now she had no words for him. For a third time she nodded and when he stood up, so did she. They passed the girl and the old man who both looked round to say goodnight, and Ray could see that the girl did not recognize him. He smiled and nodded his head. And thought of the single room upstairs where he would sleep, blessedly alone.

At midnight Mabs Kemp leaned over her son's bed and said, 'Daddy's going to stay, my darling. I'm going to lie down for a bit. Then I'll be with you while he rests.' There was no reaction; Jeremy lay on his back with a tube up his nose and another one going into his arm and yet another appearing discreetly from beneath the sheet. In his right hand there were still a few pieces of straw and a single artificial daisy.

Mabs turned to her husband. 'George, I know they say he'll be all right, but why doesn't he regain consciousness? I can't help worrying.'

'No need for that, Mabs. If they say he's going to be all right, he's going to bc all right.'

Apparently she did not hear him. 'And what on earth is he clutching so obsessively? Oh George, he doesn't lead a normal life at all. We've been foolish not to take a firmer hand with him, then none of this would have happened.'

'He's almost thirty years old! He's fought in a world war. We can't tell him what to do, he does what he feels he has to!'

'I know. Oh George, I know.' She spoke so

sadly that he felt bound to put his arm round her.

'Chin up, old girl. When he comes round he doesn't want to see the Bristol Waterworks spouting over him!' He piloted her to the door. 'Find that night sister, Mabs. She'll show you where the side room is and you can get some sleep. Off you go.'

'All right, dear.' She glanced over her shoulder. 'Goodnight, Jeremy. Sweet dreams.' She'd always said that to him and he had clutched his teddy bear and smiled at her. Now he clutched a few pieces of straw and his face did not change. She controlled a sob with great difficulty and went up to the night sister's desk, dimly lit by a green-shaded lamp. The night sister reminded her of Mrs Danvers in *Rebecca*; grim was the only word. But she led her wordlessly to a tiny room equipped with a camp bed and a car rug and two pillows. While Mabs stood and watched, she plumped up the pillows and turned down the rug. Mabs wondered whether she looked as helpless as she felt.

'I'm not usually . . . so useless.' She was almost crying again and tried frantically to joke. 'Where's my teddy?'

The sister reached behind her to the tall cabinet and picked up a stuffed dog. 'We keep it for our younger visitors,' she said without a smile. Then she switched off the light with a definite click and left the room.

'Please call me at four o'clock!' Mabs bleated. 'Or before if anything happens!' There was no reply so she just hoped her words had actually been spoken.

Back in the dimly lit ward George stared down at his son and tried not to listen to the groans around him. Thank God Mabs had left at last, this was no place for a mother. He glanced at his watch. Good grief, Jeremy had been unconscious now for over twelve hours; why weren't they doing anything? George reached for the left hand lying loosely on the top sheet. He knew better than to touch the right; when Mabs had tried to undo the clenched fist, it had tightened into a spasm and the whole arm had gone rigid. He turned the left hand over and gently straightened the fingers. It was still a young hand, well-kept, the nails trimmed, no grime in the lines of the palm or knuckles. He looked at it intently. The last time he had looked at this hand had been when Jeremy was about six years old and they had played a game which began, 'Round and round the garden, like a teddy bear . . .' It had been a child's pudgy hand then; now it was thin, the knuckles prominent as if with arthritis. George's eyes filled suddenly. This hand belonged to his son and it had been on the controls of a Spitfire and the trigger of a machine gun. This hand had killed, but his son was not a killer. Was it any wonder that since then he had not been able to find another life?

He began to talk in a low voice. If Jeremy was not going to wake up perhaps he could still hear. 'It's Dad, Jeremy. The old codger. Mum's gone to lie down – she did tell you. I just want to say . . . no-one could have had a better son, Joe. Yes, I'll call you Joe like your grandfather used to. You loved him, didn't you, Joe? D'you know, there were times when I was jealous of him because he was so close to you. And then I felt ashamed . . . small. He was such a big man, wasn't he? Big-hearted. Big hands – I remember his hands. They were so capable. And big . . .' George paused and thought he heard a sound from the bed. He leaned over but Jeremy's face was motionless.

'Anyway. We had something too, you and me. Those walks by the river, remember them? You used to tell me about your week at school and with Granddad and Grandma. I appreciated that. Being put in the picture. You never wanted me to be left out. Nor Mum. You said once that the grandparents were great but they weren't like us because we knew each other well enough not to bother to explain things. You were right there, Joe. We've never done a lot of talking, have we? Because we haven't needed to.'

There came another sound and again George leaned over the bed. This time, although the expression was the same, he could have sworn that Jeremy had just smiled. He felt his heart do a little trip. He whispered, 'Joe? Did you say something?'

And, incredibly, Jeremy shaped his lips carefully and murmured, 'Mouth. Big mouth.'

George sat back in his chair with a bump, not sure whether to laugh or cry. He leaned over the bed again. 'All right, so he was a bit opinionated at times. But listen, Joe. Don't mention to your mother that I said anything like that, will you?' He held his breath as Jeremy said in a thread of a voice, 'All right, Dad.'

George Kemp sat back and began to cry.

Janie McEvoy pulled herself upright once again. She couldn't let herself go to sleep on this chair in the entrance of the hospital; she'd probably fall on the floor and knowing her luck she'd break something and have to stay in this place indefinitely. She felt like a fish out of water here. The memory of her cosy home next door to Truda, even if her old man was probably seething with indignation at arriving home to no tea, no nothing, seemed like a wonderful dream. She pictured it now: the brass-railed guard round the range where she dried off the washing when it couldn't go out in the yard, the rag rug she'd made when she and Cyril got engaged, the rocker that had belonged to Granny McEvoy from Ireland, the Toby jugs along the high mantel; and Cyril sitting there with the newspaper, mumbling quietly to himself because that was how he read. To her horror she felt tears running down her face. Next door, the kitchen that was so similar to her own would never again house a man who read the newspaper and talked about what was in there. And Albert had been such a lovely man, different altogether from Cyril, full of ideas and plans. And so full of love.

Her tears stopped when she came to that thought. Yes, she'd hit the nail on the head there. Albert Priddy had been full of love; not just the sex kind because Truda wasn't really that sort, but the kind that didn't criticize other people, that saw the best in everything, people, places, everything. Janie swallowed convulsively. He would have been a wonderful father. What a waste. What a bloody awful waste.

She put a hand to her mouth and was glad to find she had not spoken the words aloud. She never swore; she and Truda were above that sort of thing. The woman next door, Wendy Watkins, she swore and used very common language. But Truda was refined. And Janie tried to be the same. But now and then, circumstances called for a swear word, and this was one of those circumstances.

Mr Beauchamp came back in and stood for a moment, hand at his waist, trying to get his breath. He was steaming like one of the trains; it would be a ground frost tonight, that was for sure. He came over to her.

'Ah. Mrs McEvoy. No sign of Mrs Priddy yet?'

'No, sir.' Janie was in awe of this man who drove a big expensive car and could find lodgings in London at the drop of a hat. It had been a boon when he turned up at Truda's front door saying that the Bramleys could not go to London so there would be room in the car for herself as well as Truda. Janie hiccoughed on a little sob and he put a hand on her shoulder.

'Come on now, Mrs McEvoy, bear up. For your friend's sake. She'll need you over the next few months.'

Janie said, 'She's very independent, sir.'

He sat beside her and took one of her hands in both of his. 'You don't have to do anything or say anything much. Just make sure you see her each day. Let her know that you're always there if she needs you. There's no need for you to worry about what you can do – no-one can do anything. That's how it is. But it's good to have friends very near.' They sat there for a while and she began to feel embarrassed and to wonder whether she should withdraw her hand and pretend she needed it to find a handkerchief. Then he started talking again. 'I lost my wife five years ago. Just as the war ended and we could have enjoyed life again.' He sighed. 'That's why I started the buffet car service. Thought to myself that something new would help. In one way it did. But in another . . . the only thing that could have helped me was if

Margaret was back by my side without that rotten cancer inside her!' He released Janie's hand and sat back. 'Sorry. Sorry, Mrs McEvoy. You see, you don't get used to it.' He tried to laugh at himself and then took another deep breath. 'Take no notice of me. Everybody's grief is different. She might be better than you think.'

Janie fished – legitimately – for her hanky and dabbed her eyes. 'I didn't know. I'm sorry, sir. I'm so lucky . . . too lucky really.'

'Ah!' He shook his head. 'That's another thing. You mustn't feel guilty because you've still got your husband. He'll be able to help Mrs Priddy too. Little jobs. Light bulbs and tap washers. That sort of thing.'

Janie said sturdily, 'Oh, he'll do anything like that.' And she thought to herself that if he doesn't he'll get the rough side of my tongue, that's for certain.

Harry Blackmore slowly approached the trolley on which lay the sheeted body that had belonged to Albert Priddy. He had given Mrs Priddy the privacy she had asked for, retreating into the corridor outside the mortuary and finding a clock so that he could time himself exactly. One hour. He thought one hour was ridiculous really after they had had ten years of marriage together, but the nurse who had brought him down here had said to him, 'She'll want to be on her own but don't let it go on longer than an hour. It won't do her any good. An hour is long enough. And impress upon her not to try to remove the sheet.'

Harry thought that was ridiculous too; he hadn't mentioned the sheet. Of course she would have to look at her husband and if she fainted with shock then she would faint with shock. There was no way he could make rules for her. So he had pushed the swing door an inch or two every ten minutes just to make sure she wasn't lying on the floor. And she hadn't been. And as far as he could tell she had not moved the sheet. Indeed she had found herself a chair, pulled it close and seemed to be sitting at Albert's feet.

And she was talking. Of course. What a fool he was. Obviously she would be talking to him, maybe saying goodbye, maybe thanking him for the time they'd had together.

He halted in his tracks, embarrassed to be intruding. And she turned and, incredibly, smiled at him.

'A little longer, please, Mr Blackmore.'

He stammered, 'Of course. Are you all right?'

She looked faintly surprised. 'I think so.'

'I was afraid you might be . . . overcome.'

'Not yet. There's still such a lot to say. Perhaps later . . . I don't know. He says he will be with me. Always.'

Harry almost blubbed. 'Of course. Of course he will always be with you.'

'And thank you for staying with him. He knew.'

Harry could not control himself any longer; his body was racked with sobs.

She said, 'It's all right. I wanted you to know that. Because he spoke of you sometimes. You had a nasty experience in the desert in the war.'

He dropped his head almost to his chest. 'I told him once . . .'

'He wanted to help. He always wanted to help.'

'He did. It was good to be in his train crew. He was so – so reliable.'

She said nothing, looking at him, waiting for something else. And suddenly he realized what it was.

He said earnestly, 'Listen, Mrs Priddy. It wasn't his fault. The signal was at danger and he brought the train to a halt. It delayed us. I was just about to leave the train and go to the box to find out what was happening when the signal came off and we proceeded.' He heard himself prosing on, as if he was making some official report. But she had to understand, it was vital she should understand.

She said very quietly, 'Thank you, Mr Blackmore.'

'Call me Harry.'

'And you must call me Gertie. That's what he called me. Always. Gertie. I didn't like it, Harry. I preferred Truda and everyone else called me

Truda. But someone somewhere must go on calling me Gertie.'

He couldn't stop shaking now. He whispered, 'I'll call you Gertie. I would be honoured to call you Gertie.' And he turned and went back to the shadows.

Gertie sat on. Her left hand was beneath the sheet and she was holding her husband's foot. She had wanted to kiss him but there was no face left. She had had a terrible job not to scream out and fall down on the floor. But then she continued to lift up the sheet along the length of his body and at last had found something recognizable. His boots had protected his feet and though they had been burned away, the feet and ankles were almost perfect. They were so comfortably familiar. How often she had used his razor blade to scrape away at the hard skin under the ball of the foot. And regularly she had trimmed those toenails and made sure the cuticles were pressed back. She was proud of those feet.

She said now, 'That was Harry Blackmore, Albert. He didn't know about your feet. He couldn't see.'

And Albert would have replied, 'Good job, my girl. He might have thought we were a funny pair, you holding my feet instead of my hands.'

She waited in case he might have said something else. Then she whispered, 'Albert. How am I going to manage?'

And he would have said, 'You will, my girl. You will.'

And she said, 'But the baby and all, Albert.'

And he would have said, 'It'll be all right, my girl. You'll have each other, you and the baby. We managed that in the nick of time, didn't we, my apple?'

And she said, 'When I think of that time . . . I still get embarrassed.'

And he most certainly would have said, 'Don't you ever be embarrassed! And don't ever be ashamed of anything again. Play games, pretend to be Princess Elizabeth – we know she does it, don't we? Just look at that little Charles, three years old and already knows he's in line to the throne! Gertie, you'll always be my princess.'

She tasted her tears and said, 'I'm no good at games and pretending.'

And suddenly, into her head, came his voice and it said, 'Then ask Lili Marlene next door. Go on, Gertie. My Gertie. She'll teach you to pretend.'

She sat very still, wondering if she had conjured up those words or whether Albert had put them there in her head. They were so . . . unlikely. And if it hadn't been for this morning, they would have been almost offensive. But Wendy Watkins had made friends with her this morning and changed that. Did Albert know?

She held on to his foot and spoke without a sound and without a movement of her lips.

'Albert . . . are you there? Really?'

And he said, 'You just told Harry Blackmore that I said I would stay with you always. You've never told a lie in your life, Gertie. So it must be true.'

She said, still soundlessly, 'I love you, Albert. I wish I'd told you face to face but it wasn't my way, was it?'

'I knew. I always knew.'

'Thank you.'

And then she lifted the sheet right away and she leaned over and put her face against those precious feet.

Harry came in again, lifted her gently and held her against his shoulder.

'It's all right,' he murmured. 'It's all right to cry. There, there, Gertie. There, there, my apple . . .'

He was surprised by his own words. He had never called anyone an apple before; he had never held a woman to his shoulder and encouraged her to sob her heart out.

He felt as if he might be holding all the women in the world.

Fourteen

Jeremy Kemp lay very still in the bed his father had shoved against the big sash window in the sitting room of the Marlborough Crescent house in Bath. He had not felt so content since . . . ever. His whole body was perfectly relaxed to the point of melting into the mattress; his headaches had gone at last and his eyes were focusing properly again. The night sky far above the old Roman town was exactly how it should be, velvety, pricked with stars; above all, kind. The skies could be so cruel, hard and frosty, heavy with cloud, thick with snow. This sky caressed the planet, wrapping it in a dark blue blanket just as he was wrapped now. His mother had come in two hours ago with hot milk and sponge fingers. She had glanced at the wireless on the window ledge and grimaced.

'You've been listening to the latest about the train crash,' she said. 'I should have come and talked to you, taken your mind off it.'

'It hasn't depressed me, Ma. It happened. They interviewed the fireman. It was awful about the driver. And the chief steward. They don't know much about him – the steward, I mean. The fireman said he was an Indian prince but I doubt that somehow.'

Mabs sat by the bed while he drank his milk. She felt guilty for being so happy. To have Jeremy at home would have been joy enough, but to have him comfortably and so safely in bed in the sitting room and obviously content to be there, that was a treat indeed.

She smiled and said inconsequentially, 'Every cloud has a silver lining.' He lifted one eyebrow and she shook her head apologetically. 'It's all so awful, Jeremy. But good things somehow . . . emerge. Have you noticed that? When you are knocked flat by life, sometimes – not always, I know, but sometimes – something nice comes out of it.' She knew she sounded unbelievably trite and laughed. 'I'm a silly old woman, my darling, and I'm so sorry for the people who were injured and the families of the ones who were killed, but you're here and you're safe and you seem better somehow.' She waved her hands helplessly. 'Not angry any more.'

He reached for one of the flapping hands and held it gently. 'I think I am better. I mean, I'm not angry. That went before the crash, when I was still on the train.' He made a face. 'You would have been ashamed of me, Ma. I picked on a woman. With a bad leg – she wore a caliper and used sticks. It must have sounded awful because the ticket collector sent that girl down to check that the woman was all right.'

Mabs clung to her son's hand, trying not to feel horrified by his behaviour. She could imagine it only too well.

'What girl?' she asked.

'The girl steward. The one they're making such a fuss of. She's just a schoolgirl but she put me to shame. I sort of saw myself. Not that I hadn't realized before what a useless so-and-so I've become, but I saw it.' He grinned wryly. 'My anger became shame. I wanted to help this woman then. But she wouldn't let me. She explained about the importance of being independent. She wouldn't even let me help her along the corridor to the toilet.' He finished his milk and put the cup on the table by his bed. 'That was the last I saw of her. But I know her name and so far it hasn't been given out. So she might still be alive.'

The implications behind this confession were so vast that Mabs was silent for a long time. Obviously the main one was that Jeremy's bitterness had somehow disappeared and instead of hating himself for being alive he was thankful. That was amazing; that was stupendous. But Mabs, being Mabs, went beyond that. He had met a woman.

'What *was* her name, darling?'

He was watching with some amusement as a hansom cab drove round the crescent. Some enterprising firm had found a couple of old cabs, done them up and hired them out. Jeremy was tickled to see a bag hanging under the tail of the horse. He wondered who had decreed that there must be no droppings in the elegant city of Bath.

He pointed it out to his mother. 'See, Ma? That would have made me really ratty before. Such ridiculous pretension! Now it makes me laugh. That must be good, mustn't it?'

'Absolutely,' Mabs said enthusiastically. 'What was her name, Jeremy?' she asked again.

'It was Sylvia. Sylvia Pemberton. Mrs Sylvia Pemberton.'

She was dashed. 'Oh. Married.' Then she smiled. 'I'm silly, I know. I can't help it.' She frowned. 'Did you say Pemberton? There was something in the paper the day after the accident. I can't quite remember . . . outside the Houses of Parliament.'

'That was her! She was delivering a petition on behalf of a group of other crippled people. Thank goodness she's all right. Have you got the paper? See if you can find it, could you? If I could get her address I could get in touch and tell her I've still got her hat!'

Mabs stared at him. The straw . . . the artificial flower. A hat?

She said, stunned, 'I'll go and see. Your father

gives the papers to the salvage people, but it may still be around.' The accident was three weeks ago; it was extremely unlikely the paper was there.

He relaxed, leaning back on the pillows, smiling idiotically.

'Don't bother. Pa will have got rid of it, you know that. And it doesn't matter. Really. Just to know she's safe and well is enough.' He looked at his mother. 'D'you remember what the piece said? Did she get her message across?'

'I'm sure she did, Jeremy. I remember the picture now. Her skirt was torn and her hair was flying about her face but she looked sort of, I don't know, triumphant almost.'

'Good.' He grinned. 'I told her to take a small anecdote and use it to illustrate a large theme. I bet she didn't have to bother with that after the accident!'

She said suddenly, 'That's what you should do, Jeremy. A small tale. About one of your friends. It's like – like the tip of the iceberg.'

He stared at her. 'The tip of the iceberg?'

'Yes. The little bit that shows tells you about the enormous lump of ice that doesn't show.'

'My God, Ma. How did you know that was what I've been working on?'

'I didn't. I don't know what made me say that. It just came.' Her gaze sharpened. 'What do you mean, working? Have you been working while

339

you're supposed to be resting? You know what the specialist said.'

'I can't stop thinking, can I? And today I really feel my old self. I'm enjoying being bedridden now. D'you remember when I was little and got those awful feverish bouts, you always told me to hang on and soon I would enjoy being ill?'

'Of course I remember. Do you think I forget anything about you?' She could feel her eyes filling which they did a lot lately. It was her age of course. She stood up briskly. 'Now, no more chatting. I'm going to help you into the bathroom and while you're there I can make your bed, then I'll tuck you up and leave you in peace.'

He chuckled as she pulled back the bed-clothes. He was wearing his father's pyjamas and the trousers had rolled up, showing a pair of legs that were not a bit elegant. But they were serviceable and would improve in time. Maybe he could help Sylvie and her group with these legs. You never knew, there might be a use for him yet.

He went to the bathroom and dutifully cleaned his teeth and washed his face. Then he 'snuggled down', as his mother put it, and let her tuck the sheet and blue blanket comfortably around him. She chatted on as she did so, about the opening of the Festival and the new hall that the London council had provided on the South Bank and then told him if he was good he could get up for lunch tomorrow and listen to his father's new record. Caruso singing at the Metropolitan. Bit scratchy but still very moving.

'And Jeremy dear,' she said as she left the room, 'I'm glad. About Mrs Pemberton and everything.'

He turned his head and smiled at her wickedly.

'I know what you're getting at, Mabel Kemp,' he said. 'And just to put you out of your misery, Sylvie Pemberton is a widow.'

She said, a little too quickly, 'Oh Jeremy, I'm *so* glad!'

She went downstairs and checked that George was deep in the *Evening Post* and then she shut herself in his study and lifted the telephone. Directory Enquiries informed her that there were more than a dozen Pembertons listed for the Bristol area, of which four featured the initial S. She would need an address. Thinking quickly, Mabs requested the number for St Mary's.

She was in luck. The receptionist who eventually dealt with her query knew all about Jeremy Kemp. 'I remember you arriving, Mrs Kemp. How is your son now?'

'So much better. Today has seen an enormous improvement.'

'It often happens like that. The neurologist was quite certain he was going to be all right.'

'This is an odd question, I hope you won't

mind me asking you. Before we arrived, was there a Mrs Sylvia Pemberton who sat with my son?'

The voice was bright and reassuring. 'Oh yes. She stayed with him until just before you and your husband arrived.'

'Ah.' Mabs smiled into the twilight. 'I would like to get in touch with her to say thank you. I wonder, do you have an address?'

'Well. Yes. But I'm so sorry. We're not allowed to disclose that kind of information.'

'I know. It was wrong of me to ask. Thank you so much.'

She rang off and sat for a while, thinking back over what Jeremy had told her about Sylvia Pemberton. A caliper – she wore a caliper. That meant she must have had treatment somewhere, most probably in the Bristol area. Mabs had done a great deal of voluntary work in her time and had many contacts. She rang the ortho-paedic hospital just outside Bristol and asked to speak to Sister Medway who might be on night duty. She was not but she would be on duty tomorrow at eight o'clock. Mabs said she would ring then. George had told her once she should have been a detective. He was right.

Jeremy continued to lie contentedly watching the sky and thanking God that he would never again have to fly into its vastness hunting for someone to kill. Instead he could write about Dougie Beech, the inveterate gambler, who had lost a game of cards just before he took to the skies, and lost his life too. Dougie Beech, who would never have to pay back his gambling debts. He would write it as a story first of all, then, if it sold, he would talk to people about making it into a play. Dougie would love that.

Better still, Sylvie would love it. He'd write it and then type it out and take it to show her. It should be easy enough to find her; the Bristol telephone directory would be the obvious place to look and if that was no good, he could try asking at the railway station. Her husband had worked at Temple Meads, she had told him that. He imagined phoning her and saying, 'Have you missed your hat?'

What would she say? Had they really got on so well together or was he imagining it? He tried to recall her in detail but all he could remember was a shy girl with flyaway hair and unsophisticated clothes and that ridiculous hat.

Before he slept he thought: I won't wait until I've done my story, I'll get her phone number tomorrow. And then he thought: no, I mustn't do that. I have to show her that I can do something right . . . And then he was asleep.

Sylvie was quite glad to see the rain when she got up the next morning. Yesterday's beautiful day had tugged at her heartstrings in the strangest way. She had done her usual Wednesday job of cleaning the brasses; she had a light lunch with

Mrs Carey, the cook housekeeper who had been there when Pem was alive, and then she had visited Henry who was in the reading group although he was blind; she read the newspaper to him from cover to cover. He had been lugubrious.

'No more about the accident then? Who are they blaming? Poor bloody signalman, I bet you a dollar.'

'I think it must have been the signalman,' Sylvie said, going back over the article she had just read. 'It says here—'

'Never mind what it says there, my girl. He'll get the push. No pension. Everyone looking at him as if he's a murderer. He was acting on information given him. And the pressure was on from the control office to push on into London on time – or as near on time as possible.'

Sylvie said, 'Do you know him, Henry?'

'Course I don't know him.'

'You sound quite heated about it all.'

'My dad was a signalman on the Somerset and Dorset. Signalmen always get the blame. I'm telling you.'

Sylvie sighed. 'I'm sorry, Henry.'

The old man was silent for some time then he said quietly, 'Guilt is a dreadful thing, Sylvie. If anything had happened to you on that train, it would have been our fault. We pushed you into that job and you did us proud. But if anything had happened—'

344

'You're low today, Henry. Nothing did happen. Mr Hargreaves took our petition. I think he'll fight a good fight for us.'

'I think he will too.' Henry cleared his throat. 'You say nothing happened. Something did, that's for sure.'

'Well, of course. I meant I was lucky enough to escape.'

'I know what you meant. I still say, something happened. To you. Personal like.'

She did not pretend to misunderstand. 'You could be right, Henry. But . . . well, three weeks have passed and I haven't heard from him. So I rather think it was all on my side.'

'Hmm. More fool him then.'

She could have told Henry that Joe had been hurt, unconscious when she left him. She could also have told him that she had telephoned St Mary's every day and heard that his parents had stayed with him until he had been discharged a week later. Surely he could have found her telephone number by now if he had really wanted to? But then she could just as easily have found his. She frowned, trying to force the next thought out of her head . . . The last time he had seen her was when she was hobbling down the train corridor. It was also the first time he had seen the full extent of her disablement.

She walked back home. The May sunshine lit up the young leaves on the trees around the Downs. The mixture of light and shade, continually changing, suddenly struck her as too beautiful to bear. She stood for a moment, leaning on her sticks, and watched an aspen dance for her. She thought: is this to be my life then? From now on am I just to be doing 'good works', counting my blessings because there are people so much worse off than I am? Not sharing this joy, not letting this excitement flower into ecstasy?

A dog ran towards her and she braced herself against it; a male voice yelled sternly, 'Heel, sir!' and the dog stopped two inches from her caliper. A man came towards her. He was tall, well-made, about the same age as dear Pem, with silver hair and a military look.

'I'm awfully sorry. He wouldn't have knocked you down or anything but he could have jumped up and that might have had the same result.' He smiled, leant down and clipped a lead to his dog's collar.

She said, 'I can't help being a bit nervous. Silly of me.'

'Not at all.' He straightened and held out a hand. 'Mark Goring. I recognize you from newspaper pictures. Congratulations. You did a good job there.'

She managed to release her stick long enough to shake his hand. She recognized him too; he was a councillor and had agreed to visit the group and listen to their suggestions. He never had.

He said, 'Listen, I've got my car over on the road. Let me give you a lift home.'

She thanked him. 'It's not worth it. Really. I wanted to walk, it's such a beautiful afternoon.'

'Then I'll walk with you. Perhaps we could call into a teashop in Clifton. A cup of tea would go down well. And Leonard could do with some water.'

'Leonard?'

'Winston Leonard Spencer Churchill.'

'Oh. Yes. He does have a look of Churchill.' She surveyed the dog without pleasure. She had always been frightened of the unpredictability of dogs.

'Will you, dear lady?'

'Will I what?'

'Take tea with me. I'd be honoured.'

She felt bound to agree and then wondered if this was the start of something. But when she left him to go home, she knew it was not. He wanted to see her again but she had said she was too busy. And the beauty of the world had seemed to mock her.

So when she saw the rain on Thursday she was glad and said so to Mrs Carey when they ate their toast at breakfast time. 'I've got the miseries, Mrs Carey. This weather suits me!' She laughed but the cook housekeeper knew she was serious.

'It's not surprising you're a bit flat, is it? Not really. The accident shook you up proper, then

347

the newspaper people following you around all week getting interviews. An' that nice woman from the magazine—'

'You mean life is now going to be one long anti-climax?'

'Oh, I hope not, Mrs Pemberton. We all has our ups and downs. This is just a little down. I heard that the group are going to have a coach trip up to London to see the new Festival Hall. That'll set you up again.'

'I'm not keen. The accident put me off London.' She held up the jar of marmalade and let the light shine through it. 'I thought of getting in touch with that artist I met, Mary Morrison. I'd like to see her work. She talked a lot about colour and light. That's what I need. Colour and light.' Yet she had had colour and light in abundance yesterday among the trees on the Downs and all she had felt was lonely.

Mrs Carey was unexpectedly enthusiastic. 'You might start a little art group then, mightn't you? If this artist lady would come and give you a few lessons—'

'Oh, she's much too famous for that!' But Sylvie knew that Mary Morrison would do it; she had talked of teaching. Now that would be something. An art group. She herself had always wanted to paint.

'You could ask her. Nothing to be lost. You could ask her to lunch. I could do one of my steak and kidneys. And a bakewell tart for afters with nice hot custard. And real coffee like Mr Pemberton used to have. And them little biscuity things – what was they called?'

'Petits fours.'

'That's right. Petty what's-its. It would be really nice, Mrs P. Like old times before Mr Pemberton was ill when him and Mr Marcus gave dinner parties.'

'Oh, Mrs Carey . . .' Sylvie felt the weight of the past suddenly press on her heart.

'Now, now, Mrs Pemberton. Come along. Life's got to go on and you never know what's round the corner. Mr Pemberton would be just delighted if he thought you was getting properly started again.'

'Started again . . . I thought I had started again.'

'Well, course you have. But there are stages, aren't there? I reckon we're on to the next stage.' Mrs Carey cleared the table onto a tray. 'I'll try the butcher's in Whiteladies for some skirt and a bit of kidney as soon as I know when your artist friend is coming.' She looked roguishly at Sylvie. 'We're not registered with him but he keeps me a bit back now and then. I told him I'd go to the pictures with him one of these days.'

She went through to the kitchen and after a moment Sylvie laughed.

And then the phone rang.

*   *   *

She scoffed at herself for taking so long to choose a suitable outfit, tame her suddenly electrified hair and find a mac that was light enough for summer but would keep the rain out. Mrs Kemp had introduced herself as Jeremy's mother, which confused Sylvia for a moment until she remembered that that was in fact Joe's real name. Mrs Kemp had said that the only visitors Jeremy had had were all elderly and it would do him good to see someone his own age. Somehow she sounded exactly like Sylvie would have imagined Joe's mother to sound. She gave a little gasping laugh.

'Oh, Mrs Kemp. I'm so glad to hear from you. How is he?'

'He's very much better, Sylvia. He wants to get up.' Mabs' laugh was rather shaky. 'He has to rest of course. But otherwise . . .'

'Oh, I'm so pleased. He looked so awful lying there unconscious hanging on to my hat.'

She could hear Mrs Kemp swallowing.

'I know. But he's on the mend now, and not just from his injuries. He's so much better in himself, Sylvia. He lost all his friends, you know, in the war. And it made him bitter and almost ashamed of still being alive.'

'I can understand that. It puts such a responsibility on him, doesn't it? He has to do a lot of living. For them.'

'My dear girl! That's it exactly! I must remember those very words – to tell my

350

husband! Oh, Sylvia! No wonder he wouldn't let anyone take your hat!'

They both laughed and then Mabs went on, 'All that bitterness has gone. He is so . . . content. And he was proud that you accomplished your mission. That's what he called it.' She paused and then said, 'Will you come to see him?'

Sylvia said, 'Does he want me to?'

'He doesn't know I'm telephoning. I got your number from a friend at the orthopaedic hospital. That sounds as if I'm being underhand and interfering, I know. But I just think it's important for Jeremy to see you, Sylvia.'

'Please call me Sylvie. And I call your son Joe.'

'His grandfather called him Joe.' The voice was full of tears.

'Clearly you already know I'm lame. Perhaps Joe would prefer to remember our meeting as, well, just a little cameo in his life.'

There was a pause while Mrs Kemp dealt with the tears. Then she said strongly, 'Everyone calls me Mabs. And I'm just asking you to visit Joe. That's all, Sylvie. You need only come once.'

'Thank you, Mabs,' Sylvie said without hesitation. Now that she had been invited, she knew nothing would keep her away. 'I'll be with you some time this afternoon then. Will that be all right?'

Mabs said, 'We'll have crumpets. I've got a fire in his room and you can toast them.'

Sylvie said, 'That would be nice.'

Crumpets sounded autumnal and it was still only May. She went slowly through the few hangers in her wardrobe: there was the deep orange and brown dress she'd worn to the register office when she and Pem had married. The hem of the skirt covered her caliper completely. And she was, after all, partly what Pem had made her; it would be good luck to wear the dress. She slid it over her head and it dropped past her satin petticoat and sat on the heels of her schoolgirl sandals. Mrs Carey was full of approval. 'I remember you on that day,' she said sentimentally. 'I already knew it was the best thing Mr Pemberton ever did. And now you're off to meet your young man. What could be better?'

'Steady on, Mrs Carey. There's no young man about it.'

'We'll see. We'll see. And don't forget to phone up that other new friend of yours. The artist.'

Sylvie felt dreadfully nervous as she laboriously clambered onto the bus. The conductor was kind and tried to help her into a seat but got tangled up with her sticks and nearly fell on top of her. She had to reassure him several times that she was all right but the little incident reminded her unpleasantly of how difficult it was to fit into a world built for people who could walk without difficulty, see and hear properly. And how difficult it was for able people to make the adjustment. She stared out of the window as they passed grimy old Temple Meads station. Could Joe make that adjustment? Would he want to make it . . . and did she want him to make it?

The bus lumbered past the Two Lamps and went on up the Bath Road. She pleated the skirt of her wedding dress then, unwisely, ran a hand through her hair and immediately held it down as it crackled into a life of its own. As they negotiated Keynsham she started to recite the Hamlet soliloquies. By the time they ran into the ancient grandeur of Bath, which took an age, she was on to *The Lady of Shalott* and even the twelve times table. And then there, waiting, looking anxiously along the line of bus windows, was Mabs Kemp.

Sylvie would have known Joe's mother anywhere and of course Joe's mother knew her immediately too. Mabs came to the step of the bus, smiling mistily, and simply held out an arm for Sylvie. Sylvie transferred her sticks to one hand and used the arm. They were almost the same height. They fitted together somehow. Sylvie said, 'I'm so glad to meet you, Mabs.' And Mabs said, 'You look lovely, Sylvie. As I hoped you would look. Natural and sincere. I think we'll be friends, don't you?'

'Oh, I hope so. Even if . . .'

'Yes. Even if.' Mabs squeezed the arm in hers

and laughed. She already knew there would be no even if. She had hired one of the hansom cabs because she thought they were romantic; now she wished she had been more practical. But with help from the driver Sylvie got into it quite easily and was simply delighted to be boxed in and to look up through the small trap at the driver on top. 'This is such fun!' she exclaimed as they clip-clopped up the hill towards the crescents. Mabs felt herself relaxing properly for the first time for years – literally years.

'Isn't it?' she said. And then, 'I have to say, Sylvie, I do so admire your confidence. The way you cope is so simple and easy. You make the rest of us look hopelessly clumsy!'

Sylvie said, 'It's you. I was a nervous wreck coming here.'

'I was too.' Mabs smiled at the open face so close to hers. 'Perhaps we're good for each other.'

She was conscious that Jeremy and maybe George would see the arrival of the cab and their descent from it. She proffered her arm as before and was delighted when Sylvie leaned on it quite naturally and let the driver take her weight to the pavement. Nothing awkward about that little manoeuvre. The steps had to be negotiated one by one but then George was at the door, eyebrows disappearing into his hair at the sight of them.

They stood in the hall; ahead of them was the curved staircase and each stair rod gleamed in the grey afternoon.

'This is a friend of – of Joe's,' she said to her husband. 'Sylvie Pemberton.'

George got it. Immediately. His face dissolved into a slow smile and he held out his big hand. 'I believe Joe would like to return your hat,' he said.

Mabs opened the door on her right and went into the sitting room. Jeremy had not seen their arrival for the simple reason that he was out of bed, wearing grey flannels and a shirt and sitting at the small table, writing. She was horrified.

'What on earth are you *doing*?' she cried.

He looked up; his face was animated. 'I've started my story, Ma.' He stabbed at a pile of papers. 'Look. It's going so well. This is what I wanted, right from the beginning. As I write about Dougie I can feel it sort of coming out of me at last!' He laughed. 'Oh Ma, I know you're cross but don't be. I'm all right. Is it time for tea? I'm suddenly hungry, Ma. I haven't felt hungry for six years!'

She wanted so badly to cry. She said, 'Yes. And we've got crumpets today. But first, you've got a visitor. Lots to talk about with her, I think. Pull the bell when you're ready for tea.'

She left. She had to. Sylvie went in and George leaned past his wife and closed the door and then held Mabs to him.

She wept as quietly as she could and then they went downstairs to the kitchen to listen for the old-fashioned bell. She said, 'Oh George. I do love you.'

And he said, 'Come on now, old girl.'

And she said, 'Yes, but George, we might be dead tomorrow and you wouldn't know. Not properly. And I've always loved you.'

And at last after a lot of throat-clearing, he said, 'You know I love you too, don't you, Mabs?'

And she said, 'Oh, you silly old thing! Of course I know that! I've always known that!' And they hugged and then separated and sat down at the kitchen table to smile at each other foolishly.

Sylvie said quietly, 'Hello, Joe. How are you?'

Jeremy, who had still been riffling through his papers, furious with his mother for inviting someone to visit him just as he was in full flow, visibly jumped. The resultant pain in his head was momentarily excruciating. He winced and pushed himself back into the chair physically. 'My God. Sylvie. How on earth – why – when – how did you know?' He heard himself gibbering and stopped speaking abruptly.

She was horrified at his reaction and stood in the middle of the room leaning heavily on her stick and wondering whether she should call for his parents, but then he blinked and smiled up at her.

She clenched her free hand. She had assumed

Mabs had told Joe she was coming to visit. 'I'm so sorry, Joe. Making you jump like that. Is it bad? Would you like me to help you onto the bed?'

He said, 'I'm all right. Any sharp movement . . . I'm all right. Honestly. You look different.'

'Well, yes. I suppose I do. My hair is all over the place.'

He managed a grin. 'You're missing a hat, of course!'

'Yes.' She smiled too and then was silent again.

He said, 'Sorry, Sylvie. I – I'm so surprised to see you. And pleased. Of course, pleased.' She made no comment and he rushed on, 'I missed seeing the pictures in the paper but Ma said you did it! Congratulations. After all that happened, you know they won't dare just let that petition sink without trace. You'll get the new plans through. I'm sure of that.'

'Yes. I think you're right.' It occurred to her suddenly that she could have used yesterday's meeting with Mark Goring to some advantage. What a fool she was; what an absolute fool. She should go back home. Now.

He smiled again and there was the sweetness that she had been so certain was there when she first met him on the train. She thought, if only he can be happy, nothing else will matter; I don't mind if he doesn't like me any more, just let him be happy.

He said, 'Sit down, Sylvie. Please. My neck is cricking looking up at you. Sit by the fire. It's such a nasty day and the hem of your dress is wet.'

She sat in a small Victorian nursing chair and spread her skirt carefully. She shouldn't have worn this dress; it would spoil in the rain and it was her wedding dress.

He said, 'That's better. It's so good of you to come. My mother tracked you down, did she?'

'Yes. She has a friend in the orthopaedic hospital. I go there sometimes for treatment.'

'Do you?' He looked surprised. 'I know so little about you, Sylvie. I was going to look up your number in the phone directory but I wanted to do something first. A story. That's why I got up today.'

Sylvia nodded. 'Probably you wouldn't have found my number. It's under M. Pemberton, for Miles. My husband's name was Miles. And there are loads of Pembertons. So your mother used her contact . . .' Her voice petered out. They were talking but they were not communicating.

He said, 'I put it off because I wanted you to know that you had . . . well . . . *inspired* me. That sounds so pretentious, doesn't it? But it's true, Sylvie. I had been so – so content since I got home. Like an animal in its den. And then I thought that if I could show you some work, you might realize what you have done for me. Sorry, I am talking rubbish.'

'No.' This was much better. 'Please. Tell me about your work. Unless you don't want to. Now that you have seen me again.'

'I do want to. Oh yes, I do want to. It's just that . . . you look so different, Sylvie. So smart and confident and in control.'

She did not know whether to laugh or cry. 'It's the dress, isn't it? I should have worn the same clothes. But they were ruined, of course.' She looked down at her silk-covered knees. 'This is my wedding dress.'

There was a long pause, then he said, 'Why did you choose to wear your wedding dress to see me? Have you come to tell me that you could never love anyone else but your husband?'

She looked up at him. Her eyes were full of tears.

'There's so much you don't know. My husband was a wonderful man. Yes, I loved him and he loved me. But as friends love each other. I think I wore this dress because I needed his friendship to give me courage.'

'Am I still frightening?' He tried to laugh. 'I'm sorry, Sylvie. Really sorry. Thank God we made friends before the crash.' He put out a hand towards her. 'We are friends, aren't we?'

She nodded, willing the tears to subside. But she did not reach for his hand.

He left it where it was. 'Sylvie. Will there be a time for you to tell me about your husband? Have we got time?'

She said nothing, just stared at him, knowing without a single doubt that she had fallen in love.

He tried again for a laugh but it sounded more than ever like a sob.

'Yes. Rather a silly question after the crash. But . . . if we have time, can we spend a lot of it together? To talk. And to be quiet. To be . . . everything.' He dropped his head, shaking it helplessly, then stopped abruptly and held himself still.

She took the hand and gripped it hard. 'Is it very bad?' she asked.

'No. Yes. It goes though.' He looked up at her and managed a grin. 'I'm not saying anything properly, Sylvie. Perhaps I should shut up. But you must know – surely you know – that I love you completely? Surely you know that? Otherwise why did you come here today?'

She blinked the tears away. 'Oh, Joe. Why do you think I came here today? Because I love you too. Completely.'

Somehow they stood up and held on to each other as if they were in danger of drowning.

She whispered, 'I was so full of doubts and fears. They rattled about inside me. I didn't want you to tie yourself down to someone who wasn't . . . you know.'

'And then you knew that the boot was on the other foot. I would not want you to tie yourself down to someone who is probably always going to get headaches and who hasn't done much with his life and—'

She silenced him by putting a hand over his mouth. He stared down at her. And then, as she removed her hand, very tentatively he kissed her.

It was some time later that Mabs and George felt bound to tap gently on the door and bring in the crumpets and the toasting fork, by which time Jeremy was sitting on the edge of his bed and Sylvie was drying the hem of her dress by the fire. They were both flushed, bright-eyed, smiling inanely.

Mabs smiled too. 'Don't feel awkward. It's just that George would like his tea. And I would like to get to know you better, Sylvie.' She handed over the toasting fork and a crumpet. 'Shall we have our tea here by the fire? Jeremy dear, why don't you sit here next to Sylvie. And George, pull out that little table – be careful, that's Jeremy's book!'

She kept talking. George smiled. Jeremy caught Sylvie's eye and they very definitely communicated.

Unexpectedly, Sylvie thought of the old eight forty-five and knew that she had reached her destination at last.

Fifteen

The ship belonged to P & O and was called the
Alexandra. It had been converted from a troop-
ship without difficulty: the women used the
officers' quarters and the men the rest. They met
during the day for walks on deck and meals but
were strictly segregated before lights out. For
some this was a real hardship; for others it was
not.

Ray Hart enjoyed the discipline; it took him
back to his army days before Berlin. He liked
rules, you knew where you were when there were
rules, and usually, within their perimeters, you
had your freedom. And there was the sea air too.
He had not realized how much he had pined
for the sea air. When he and Janet walked on
the deck and leaned on the rail facing the
south-westerlies, he filled his lungs with it and
felt his heart lift. After a few days it was warm
enough to discard his hat and gloves and he let
the wind comb his hair and wash the inside of

his body. After another few days he borrowed a pair of shorts from one of the men in his cabin, rolled up the sleeves of his shirt and let the sun get at the outside. He liked everything about the ship: its workaday atmosphere, queueing for the heads and the laundry room and meals; the food was the sort he was used to, good substantial fry-ups and stews. Everyone else grumbled about eating hot food when they were in the tropics, but it suited him. It made him sweat profusely, sweat out all the old poisons and terrors. There was a tatty-looking swimming pool set in the deck at the stern, and he lowered himself into it and did two lengths each morning and evening when the heat was unbearable.

Janet was not as keen as he was but she knew it was a necessary process to get them where they wanted to be and she made the best of it. The walks and the dips in the pool compensated for the meals and the queueing. And the distance from England and Bristol and the awful train accident became greater each day. She liked that. It had been terribly hard work to organize the emigration; she had felt sometimes as if she were physically manhandling her brother up the gangplank. Each time a signature was needed she had to practically stand over him; it was she who provided the financial details, sold her house and negotiated the insurance claim on his, and let elderly aunts and uncles know what was happening.

There had been no repercussions from the police; in fact both of them had received unexpected sympathy and help. The few people who knew Ray understood why he wanted to get right away; everybody wished them well. There was a girl at the bakery, rather a common piece, who had wept on Ray's chest when he gave in his notice, and Janet was inundated with presents and compliments. Ray had said, 'I had no idea people thought anything of us at all,' and she had replied, 'Ray, you are so modest. Always have been.'

She had managed to screen him from one or two tricky things. There had been no trace of any bodies in the house next door to his and a week later the odd-looking young couple had turned up and claimed a place on the council housing list. They said they had been on holiday and had heard nothing about the fire. The child was not mentioned. Janet was aghast. Half of her felt they should be punished for leaving a helpless human being all alone to starve to death; the other half felt almost thankful that Ray had taken her from her cot and given her at least a few hours of undiluted love from Ilse. And to herself she used the phrase that everyone had used that day: the poor little thing could not have known anything about it.

They found what were probably Ilse's remains and Ray asked them to bury them in the small churchyard almost next to the railway line and the derailed train. Two other people chose similarly for their dead and there was a short and poignant service a week later. It poured with rain and nobody else attended. Janet held her father's big black umbrella over the two of them and stood by the open grave, feeling only thankfulness that Ilse was now at rest.

The authorities kept the remains of the small child, expecting that someone would report her missing. When nobody came forward after two months, Janet heard that the charred corpse was to be released for burial. She said nothing to Ray but she contacted the young vicar at the church where Ilse was buried.

'My sister-in-law was unable to have children. It was a great grief to her. I wondered, Vicar, whether you could put in a word and have the child buried next to Ilse. When we leave for Australia, Ilse will have no one to visit her grave, and neither will the child. Might it not be good if the two of them were side by side?'

She had to be careful not to arouse the young priest's suspicions. But the abandoned child had touched a lot of hearts and he was grateful that someone was practical enough to give the awful business some coherence.

Janet had actually gone to the funeral; the weather had been glorious and several local people had turned up too. Luckily, media interest had moved on from the story and although one lone reporter and cameraman were there, nothing appeared in the press the next day. Janet did not mention it to Ray.

She watched him on the voyage and saw the healing process beginning. She was sure it was doing the same for her too; sometimes she would lean on the rail and watch the wake of the ship and think of Ilse and that poor little girl and her tears would be cold on her face. Then she would talk to herself briskly, about Ilse and her living nightmare, about the malnourished child and her chances in life. 'Let them rest, dear Lord,' she would murmur. 'They couldn't have known what was happening. Let them rest now.' And very gradually her grief would subside, going from her head down through her body and out through the soles of her feet.

Jenny went home for Ahmed's funeral. Mr Beauchamp took her and Harry in his car. The funeral had had to wait for relatives to arrive from India and Jenny privately wondered what they had done to keep the body. She banished the thought instantly and tried to pay attention to what was happening.

The four weeks had proved difficult. Gramps had stayed for the first two and they had managed to see the Tower of London and the new Festival Hall but he tired easily and complained that the pavements were too hard and the smells were rank.

She said, 'That's a good one! We're used to cow dung, remember!'

He said, 'You know what I mean, my girl. I'd rather smell natural animal smells than human beings.'

She persuaded him to go home. Marvin was beginning to undergo skin grafting and she wanted to spend more time with him. Gramps agreed and went back the next day with Sam Beauchamp who had brought Marvin yet another basket of fruit.

Jenny missed Gramps; the hospital seemed to claim her body and soul and she was reminded of the hostels where she had been sent when she ran away from her foster home. She stayed on at the Paddington bed and breakfast but moved into a bigger room when the other two visitors left. After they'd gone, she learned with surprise that he had been on the train too. She did not remember him; parts of that day were mercifully gone from her mind.

Marvin could speak through the slit of his bandages and he told her that he would not have to wear a brace any more and he probably wouldn't have acne. His dark, bold eyes watched her when he made these announcements. She knew why. But all she said was, 'Strange, isn't it? And I'll probably never be clumsy again.'

Mr Beauchamp told Marvin about Weston-super-Mare. 'You're going there to convalesce. I've booked three rooms. One for you, one for

Jenny and one for Harry Blackmore. He needs a break too. I had a chat to your surgeon chappie. Beginning of September, he said. How does that sound?'

Marvin nearly split his bandages he was so overjoyed. Jenny said not a word. She knew she could not share a holiday with Harry Blackmore; she had not seen him since that night. She still loved him quite desperately. She wanted to slow everything down but to be in a hotel with Harry and Marvin together would be out of the question.

'I'm not sure,' she prevaricated.

Marvin said, 'You've got to come! I'm not going if you don't come!'

'I meant, I'm not sure that Mr Blackmore will come. He hardly knows us, Marvin.' She glanced at Mr Beauchamp who seemed to understand everything. 'I wondered, could my friend Lydia come with us? That is, if Mr Blackmore turns it down?'

'Of course, my dear! Would you rather I didn't mention it to Harry?'

'Oh no. I couldn't ask you to do that.'

But Harry did turn it down. She didn't know how she felt about that either.

It turned out that Ahmed had a big family: a wife, a mother, uncles, aunts, cousins . . . They had a proper Hindu funeral pyre in a corner of a field Kingswood way. There was a great deal of wailing. Jenny could not associate any of it with the super-particular Ahmed. It started to rain just as they lit the straw around the pyre and the whole occasion was marred for her when they poured paraffin a little too liberally and he practically exploded.

Harry jumped. He would always be nervous now where there were flames.

'My God! Are they all right? Those saris will go up in a puff of smoke if they're not careful.'

'They're fine, Harry, don't worry.' Mr Beauchamp was like an uncle to all of them now. He was really excited about the holiday and had met Lydia and communicated some of his excitement to her. And Marvin thought it would be the nearest thing to heaven to be in Weston-super-Mare with Jenny.

After the funeral, they went back to the tiny house in Montpelier and ate spicy triangular things and round oniony things and drank tea that did not taste at all like the tea Jenny had at home. Everyone was very nice to her and told her that Ahmed had thought she was a very good girl. She did not believe them. She told them she thought Ahmed had been wonderful to work for. Another lie. But she knew that sometimes you had to lie. People needed lies as much as truths.

Mr Beauchamp left quite early and Harry walked her down to the bus station and told her that she was looking better and how was Marvin.

'He's getting better. Slow but sure. Poor Ahmed knocked all Marvin's teeth out – did you know? They're fitting him with a denture and he won't have to wear a brace any more. He's very pleased about that.'

'What about the skin grafts on his face?'

'Well, it's all very slow of course. But by September, when we go to Weston-super-Mare, he should be able to leave off the dressings.' She smiled at him shyly. The moments of intense closeness back in the hospital were over now and she almost caught herself calling him sir. 'I've told Lydia all about him. She's dying to meet him. I think they'll get on really well together.'

'If they don't, it could be awkward for you, Jenny. Are you sure about going?'

'I've got to go. He's so looking forward to it. Lydia will make it all right.' She was wearing a new navy-blue linen dress for the funeral and it had slit pockets in the skirt; she put her hands into them like men did. It made her feel rather rakish. She giggled. 'You don't know her. She's so quick and cheeky. And Marvin is the same in a way.'

He turned his head to stare at her in surprise. 'You're not match-making, are you?'

It had not occurred to her. She said, 'Of course not. But now you mention it, Lydia would love a boy friend and Marvin would love a girl friend . . .'

370

'It's you Marvin wants,' Harry said glumly. 'No-one else.'

'Don't be silly.' She blushed deeply and half turned away from him. 'I told you before. I want to learn to look after myself. Gramps lets me do that. I can make perfect Yorkshire puddings now.'

He grinned. 'How long did that take?'

She looked at him in surprise. 'I've never heard you joke!'

'You must think I'm a stuffed shirt.'

'No. I don't think that at all.' The blush deepened until she thought she might explode like poor Ahmed almost had. 'I think you're . . . marvellous.'

He felt humble. 'Don't think that, Jenny. Please. I'm a fool. Haven't you heard about how I hung around your predecessor?'

She just about knew what predecessor meant but she hadn't heard a thing.

'Her name was Corinne. She was glamorous. Like a beauty queen. And I was like a – a stupid sheep! Following her around. She knew it too.' He shrugged helplessly. 'In the end she made me feel cheap.'

She said fiercely, 'You could never be cheap! You're a gentleman. A real gentleman.'

He was deadly serious. 'All I'm saying, Jenny, is, don't put me on a pedestal. Everyone is telling us how brave we are at the moment. But I know I'm not brave and never have been.'

'I'm not either!'

'Yes you are.'

'No, I'm not!' She looked at him and smiled unwillingly; they were like a couple of kids arguing. 'I just did the next thing . . . you know. Whereas you—'

'We did our duty.'

'Yes. But yours was harder.'

He said, 'I didn't climb through torn metal and shattered glass that might have collapsed on me any minute.'

She found she was hanging on to his arm. She said, 'I know that in the war you survived after your tank was blown up and you crawled towards enemy lines.'

'Jenny, I didn't know what I was doing. I was delirious. I thought I was crawling towards the British lines.' He put his other arm round her and held her close. People glanced at them and then away. He said, 'I wasn't a hero then and I'm not one now.'

She looked up into the round, open face, vulnerable, already so dear to her. She whispered, 'All I know is, I love you.'

Someone said, 'Is this your bus? It's going any minute!' And Harry almost lifted her up the step and then followed her and they went up top which was almost empty and sat at the back holding each other tightly.

By the time they got to Keynsham, they had told each other almost everything about themselves and she had promised that some time in the near future she would go to the pictures with him.

'But I still have to go to Weston,' she told him. 'Marvin is depending on it.'

He looked at her glumly. 'You wouldn't start going out with Marvin because you're sorry for him, would you?' he asked. He didn't wait for an answer. 'Yes, you would. I already know that.'

She said, 'I might have to go to the pictures once or twice.'

He groaned and she said quickly, 'I shall tell him about you, Harry.'

'He'll laugh. I'm old enough to be your father!'

She said seriously, 'Listen, Harry. In a lot of ways I'm much older than nineteen. And you, you're younger than thirty – '

'Twenty-nine, if you please!'

' – because you lost five years of your growing up. In some ways you're an old man,' she pretended to cower away from him and was glad when he laughed, 'but in others you're the same age as me. That's why we get on so well.'

The bus lurched round a corner and he pressed her against the window. They seemed to exchange body heat; suddenly they were aware of each other in what Jenny could only call 'a grown-up way'.

She said, 'Harry. Would you kiss me please?'

He stared at her. 'Why?'

'Because I know jolly well that Marvin will. Once the bandages are off he won't be able to wait! And I'd like you to be the first.'

'And you'd like to see which you prefer!' He was laughing again and then serious. He did that a lot, she noticed. It made him so special.

He kissed her quite gently at first, small butterfly kisses around her eyes and down the bridge of her nose before his lips touched her full ones. And then the kisses intensified, becoming slower and more positive. By the time the bus arrived in Bath, he could not stop. Everybody had got off and the passengers for the return trip to Bristol were getting on and they were still clinging to each other.

Eventually they stumbled down the stairs and stood waiting for the bus to Winderslake, unable to tear their eyes away from each other.

As they walked through the door, Tom Marston knew.

He said crossly, 'What d'you think you're doing here, young man? You've missed the last bus back to Bristol and if you think you're getting free board and lodging here, you're much mistaken!'

Harry gave him a sweet smile. 'I'm all right, Mr Marston. I'll walk back to Bath and get a train.'

'It'll be midnight by then. Ten miles, it is!' Tom could have hit him; if he thought he could get round him with a soppy grin, he had another think coming.

'There's always the milk train.' Nothing could go wrong for Harry now; he kept smiling and smiling, first at Jenny and then her grandfather and then at Jenny again.

Jenny said softly, 'He could sleep on the sofa in the parlour, Gramps.'

'So he could!' Tom could have knocked their heads together, she was as bad as he was. 'And there's plenty of food in the larder, isn't there? Our meat ration and a bit of butter . . .'

'He could have an egg for breakfast, Gramps. You said Mrs Miller sent down half a dozen of her big duck eggs for when I came back home.' She was wheedling him; she was good at that. She was looking just like she'd looked five years ago in that Mr Cousins' office. As if she was standing at the gate of heaven.

Quite suddenly, he surrendered.

'All right. But how you're going to sort out that young Marvin Bramley, I don't know. I feel sorry for you. But I feel sorrier for him.'

Jenny went to him and kissed his cheek. He smelled of Lifebuoy soap and earth. She said, 'What have you been planting?' and then leaned back to look into his eyes. 'The beans! You've planted the kidney beans, haven't you?'

He looked sheepish. 'Didn't know what to do to welcome you back home.' He glanced at Harry. 'Kidney beans is very special to my Jenny,' he said in a proprietorial voice. 'We started with kidney beans back before the war.'

Harry nodded. 'She told me. She said this was her kidney-bean heaven.'

So then Tom Marston knew. It was something she would only share with special people: Lydia was one; it seemed Harry Blackmore was another. Well, it could have been worse. They might even live here with him for a bit.

He said to Harry, 'Not much for supper. I generally have bread and cheese and a raw onion.'

Harry kept smiling. 'We are a bit peckish, sir. The food after the funeral was . . . different. Not really to my taste.'

Jenny went to the bread crock and fetched the bread. Already she felt like a proper housewife.

The front at Weston seemed endless and neither Marvin nor Lydia could walk very far without sitting down for a breather. Jenny longed to stride out from Anchor Head right the way round Madeira Cove, past the Winter Gardens and the Grand Pier and the row of Victorian hotels to Uphill and the sand dunes and then take the ferry over to Brean Down. She had boundless energy; she wanted to run into the wind and jump and scream at the top of her voice. She thought she might burst out of her clothes and her skin; she was so happy that even the thought of Ahmed and Albert Priddy could not dim the wonderful incandescence surrounding everything. She said, 'Let's go a bit faster and a bit further. Come on, Marvin, step it out!'

He said, 'Dammit, Jenny. I got out of hospital two weeks ago! I'm not used to this!'

'Let's get as far as Knightstone. We'll sit there and I'll buy you both an ice cream. How does that sound?'

Lydia said, 'Unless you want me to scream, you can drop the condescension, Miss Price! I do not want an ice cream because when the weather improves I want to wear my bathing costume.'

'Wow!' said Marvin dutifully.

'Quite,' Lydia responded. 'I know I've got a good figure and it's only fair to share it around.'

'Which piece can I have?' Marvin asked.

'My big toe, I think. Yes, I think my big toe will do very well for you.'

'I'll settle for that.' He looked more cheerful. 'Your friend is a good sport, Jenny.'

'No she's not,' Lydia contradicted. 'Good sports are good losers and I'm not that nor ever shall be. I can't see very well, so I scream and show off and expect to be spoiled all the time.'

Marvin had found Lydia difficult at first with her enormous eyes that never quite looked at him and her hair that she pulled down like a curtain when she didn't want to talk any more. But she walked slowly like he did and never pulled away when he took her arm. Jenny seemed to be on springs all the time and she was

377

incapable of going slowly. And this conversation was making him feel rather rakish.

'I wouldn't mind spoiling you,' he said now as they sat in the lee of the wind while Jenny queued at the ice-cream shop.

'My God, I haven't had an offer like that for a long time.'

Marvin sucked in his cheeks and felt the new skin tighten warningly. For the first time he ignored it; he felt he was an actor in a play, something by Noël Coward with lots of . . . repartee. He said, 'And when was that? And who was it?'

'A dirty old man. Friend of my father's. Married of course, kids of course. But he still wanted to spoil me – quite literally actually.'

He was silent, temporarily aghast at her comprehension and her brazen truthfulness.

He stammered, 'I didn't mean like that. I meant look after you. Fetch things and help you go places and—'

'I know. I know all that.' She smiled at him and then stuck out her tongue and waggled it at him. That was another shock; he didn't quite know what she meant by it but she meant something, that was for sure. She said, 'Tell me, Marvin, what are you like? Jenny hated you, you know, at first. But even then, when she told me things you said, I thought you sounded interesting.' She leaned towards him and whispered, 'I've got big hips too, you know.'

He was appalled. Jenny must have told her . . . and he hadn't meant it like she was taking it. He remembered confiding his ill-judged remark to Mary Morrison and how well she had taken it. Lydia was deliberately making it into something else – she was using it as an invitation.

He forgot about smart repartee. 'I say things . . . don't always mean them . . . they come out the wrong way . . .' he stammered.

She leaned against his shoulder, shaking with laughter.

'Oh, Marvin. This is going to be such fun. Believe me, this is going to be such *fun*!' She was giggling so much he found his arm going round her waist to support her. And then the most amazing thing happened. Still laughing, she reached down and moved his hand upwards. He had never felt a brassiere before but he knew quite well that he was touching one now. And then Jenny arrived with the ice creams and he had to move his hand and try to avoid Jenny's accusing stare. But it was not directed at him.

'Lydia, stop it.'

Jenny knew only too well what Lydia was up to. She wasn't taking Marvin seriously at all. She was flirting outrageously and it would probably result in Marvin asking to be taken home.

Lydia laughed more than ever and Jenny leaned down to her and said seriously, 'Look, just because he wears a uniform at work and is in a position of authority, does not mean you can walk all over him!'

Lydia was strangely confounded. Jenny had used her own words from years ago – she wanted to marry someone in authority who wore a uniform – and being Jenny that had to be guileless. She stared in the direction of Jenny's voice and allowed an ice cream to be put into her hand. Then she said almost wonderingly, 'Of course. A uniform. My God, Jen. I hadn't thought . . . but you're right. *And* he's in a position of authority!'

'Never mind that.' Jenny tried not to smile because sometimes although Lydia could not see her face, she could hear a smile in her voice. 'Just eat your ice cream and then we can get on.'

Marvin was busy coping with his ice cream and had not understood the exchange at all. He spoke with a definite whine in his voice. 'What's the point of all this walking, Jenny? We must have gone two miles yesterday and now you want us to do the same today. I don't get it.'

She said patiently, 'You're convalescing, Marvin. You need to get your strength back and some good fresh air into your lungs. Don't keep grumbling all the time.'

Lydia came to life again. She said, 'That's not fair, Jenny. He's been at death's door. He's entitled to a little grumble now and then.'

Jenny thought of the hours she had sat

with Marvin, reading to him, encouraging him, listening when he told her how awful it was at home with all the kids and his dad getting drunk every night. Suddenly she had had enough; for two pins she could have turned on her heel and walked away from the pair of them. And then she thought of Harry and how wonderful it would be if they were together now. It didn't have to be here. It could be on Temple Meads platform with her scurrying back and forth with sandwiches and him checking that the train windows were up and the door handles secured. They had both started back to work in July and though it wasn't quite the same with the new chief steward and his assistant, the powers that be had made sure she was always on the same train as Harry. She loved going to work. This holiday was an unwelcome interruption.

She said, 'Tell you what. I'll leave you two here to have your ice creams and I'll have a short walk by myself. How does that sound?'

'Fine!' Lydia said enthusiastically. And Marvin nodded. Once the ice creams were gone, he might be able to put his arm round her again. If Jenny was definitely going out with Harry Blackmore, then it would be up to him to look around for someone else. Plenty more fish in the sea, when all was said and done. And there was something about this unpredictable and very forward girl that was interesting. For one thing, she felt the same as he did about walking in

Weston's prevailing winds; he'd had enough of them to last a lifetime.

As soon as Jenny had gone, Lydia turned to him, licking her ice cream furiously and looking very serious.

'Listen, Marvin. I didn't know, didn't realize . . . I mean, of course I knew you wore a uniform and you had authority. But it's Jenny's fault, she always talks about you as if you're just a kid.'

'I'm twenty-three. Mr Beauchamp says I can have my own buffet car team in a couple of years. That *is* authority. Plenty of tips, good money to start with too.'

'I thought he'd be looking for a married man.' She said it so innocently, he smiled at her as if she could see him.

'That might help,' he said.

Lydia tried to focus his face. It looked beautiful to her; the slight contortion from the grafts were visible, the loose false teeth looked as if they belonged to Errol Flynn. She had wanted to be married as a gesture of defiance; but there were other reasons, more personal reasons. She thought with shocked surprise: might I be falling in love?

When Jenny came back, they were sitting holding hands, talking like normal people. She loitered, watching them incredulously. She had never heard Lydia chattering nonsense before; and Marvin had only ever wanted to be clever-clever.

She heard him say, 'Will Jenny mind?' And Lydia reply, 'Don't be daft. It's exactly what Jenny wanted.'

It was October and the nights were drawing in. Mr Churchill was running the country again so things were bound to improve soon. Gertie, huge and cumbersome, lumbered around the kitchen laying the table for two, stirring the stew so that it didn't catch on the bottom of the saucepan, prodding the potatoes, waiting for the click of the back gate before she put in the dumplings. She was overdue with this baby and didn't she just know it. Must be a boy; they always said a boy was lazy. Well, if he was anything like his father he wouldn't be that. Albert had taken his turn at most things and would have done more if she'd let him. She did not let the thought surface properly but, well, if it could possibly be a boy, then it might . . . just a little bit . . . compensate for losing Albert.

Not that anything could; not really. She missed Albert in all sorts of ways and always would. He had understood her so well; and he had sort of respected her too. Loved her and respected her. There would never be another Albert. But she had to admit that Janie's hubby had been very good. Wouldn't let her sit out on the windowsills upstairs to clean the windows, always put her dustbin in the alley on a Friday morning. Everyone was good; everyone did their best. She was very lucky. She put a hand on her abdomen; she was very lucky indeed.

The back gate clicked and she put a spoon under the first floured dumpling and lowered it into the stew; then the next. It was a rich stew, the leftovers from the beef she had cooked on Sunday when Harry Blackmore had brought that Jenny Price to dinner. There was a nice girl, so natural and easy; she had told her all about that chief steward who'd been burned like Albert; then about the other assistant, Marvin Bramley. Gertie knew about the Bramleys. Not a good lot, not a good lot at all. Not that you'd wish anything like that train crash on anyone. She sighed deeply just as there was a knock on the back door.

The next minute Wendy Watkins was behind her at the cooker, giving her a peck on the back of her neck. It had shocked Gertie the first time that had happened and she had actually flinched; but Wendy had taken no notice and every time she came in, which was every day, she managed to get in a swift kiss. Gertie was used to it now though she never reciprocated. She found it very difficult to show affection.

'What's the weather like outside?' she greeted her neighbour without turning from the stew. 'I've put a fire in the front room. Been cold all day.'

'Oh, that sounds nice.' Wendy went through into the hall and hung up her coat. 'It's not exactly bitter out but it's raw. D'you remember in *Brief Encounter* when it was always raining and she used to wrap her coat round herself? It's like that.'

Gertie bent to take the hot plates from the oven. It was amazing how Wendy could say something like that and it was as if Albert was in the room. Gertie put the plates on the table and carried the saucepan over.

'Let me do that.' Wendy took the saucepan gently from her. 'Sit down. You look tired out.' She scooped out the dumplings first just like Gertie would have done and then piled the carrots, swedes and onion around them, followed finally by the small bits of beef.

'There's some potatoes as well,' Gertie said.

Wendy strained them and put the saucepan on the table. 'We'll help ourselves, shall we?' She picked up her knife and fork. 'My God, this looks good, Gertie.'

'Good enough to eat, eh?' Gertie asked as Albert would have done.

'Certainly is.' Wendy spoke with her mouth full. She still had plenty of bad habits: she swore and she spoke when she was eating. Gertie didn't mind any more. Three times a week they shared a meal. Wendy called in every morning to make sure she was all right; she brought yesterday's bread from the bakery and the jam tarts that got broken; she talked so openly that sometimes Gertie was embarrassed. She'd had a crush on one of the bakers and he'd gone off to Australia last month; she'd cried about that but then she'd said life had to go on. There was something about her that Gertie liked. It might even have been the same thing that Albert liked. She didn't know.

Wendy took a piece of bread and mopped her plate and then sat back with a huge sigh.

'The food in this caff gets better 'n' better,' she said. She grinned wickedly. 'We had a bit of trouble today – customer reckoned there was a fingernail in his bread.' Gertie screamed and put a hand to her mouth and Wendy laughed. 'It wasn't. This bloody national flour has all kinds of chaff and stuff in it.' Gertie made another sound and Wendy sucked her bottom lip apologetically. 'Sorry, Gert, I forget how delicate you are just now. Have a drink of water – go on.'

But Gertie shook her head. 'Not that. Something sort of . . . I don't know . . . shifted.'

'Did it hurt?' Wendy asked, instantly alert.

'A bit. Not like the midwife said though. It didn't last.'

'Midwife,' Wendy commented scornfully. 'Come on, let's get you by the fire and I'll make you a cup of tea and see if that sits all right.'

Gertie half sat, half lay in Albert's armchair; the fire had settled into a cavernous glow and she surveyed it without pleasure.

'What's the betting it'll come tonight and that

nice fire will be wasted?' she asked as she sipped her tea.

'Worth the price of a bucket of coal,' Wendy said, fetching a footstool. 'Besides, we've got to have somewhere to burn the afterbirth.'

Gertie shuddered at that and then shuddered some more. 'Oh . . . oh . . .' She put down her cup and saucer quickly and clutched the arms of the chair. 'Oh dear, oh my good Lord, oh Lili . . . it's coming!'

Wendy clapped her hands. 'Marvellous. *And* you called me Lili. Even better.' She held out her hands. 'Let's get upstairs, our Gert. Then I'll nip up the phone box and ring the midwife.'

But Gertie could not get out of the chair and certainly would not let Wendy go anywhere. 'You've done it before. You told me. You can do it. Oh dear Lord . . . knock on the wall for Janie . . . oh, Lili!'

Wendy knocked, then knelt and stripped off Gertie's undergarments and had a look.

'Christ,' she muttered. 'No time for an enema nor nothing else. The little bugger's here almost! He's in a bloody hurry, by the looks of things. Slow down, Gert. No pushing for a bit. Might give him a headache.'

Janie arrived at a trot and Wendy gave orders and laid newspapers and towels and then, without any more fuss, she knelt again and received a good-sized baby boy who slithered into her arms just at the right time, accompanied by a loud grunt from his mother and a scream from Janie. Wendy scooped the caul from his face, turned him expertly onto the palm of her right hand and pressed his back. He too grunted, as if with surprise, then began to cry without any distress.

'My God, he's lovely,' Wendy said, holding him for Gertie to see. 'Another little Albert.'

Gertie was so surprised; she couldn't get over it. 'There was hardly any pain,' she said over and over again. 'It was just like shelling peas!'

Janie came forward with a towel and wrapped him up while Wendy sterilized scissors, cut the cord, washed him gently then bound his abdomen with a penny.

The three women looked down at him as he snuggled into his mother's arms.

'Everything's there,' Janie marvelled. 'Look at his nails.'

'They're long.' Wendy nodded wisely. 'He was really overdue. No wonder he came in such a hurry. Look, he's real happy to be here.'

Gertie looked at them. 'We'll call him Bertie.' Wendy started to laugh and Gertie said, 'What's wrong with that?'

'Gertie and Bertie,' Wendy said. 'Aww. Wouldn't Albert love that, eh? Gertie and Bertie.'

And after they had finished laughing, Janie went to ring the midwife and Wendy went upstairs to pull down a mattress because, as Gertie said, they didn't want to waste the fire.

Much later, after the midwife had tidied everything up and the doctor had been to do some 'embroidery', Gertie lay on her side and looked at her son cocooned in a blanket, and waited for Albert to talk to her inside her head. She knew he would. He was a long time coming so she put in her two pennyworth first. 'The happiest evening since you know when,' she said without moving her lips. 'Same thing too – I didn't know that was happy till it was over. Then I didn't want to admit it. This time, I thought it would be awful, Albert. I was that frightened deep inside myself. But you were here, weren't you? Will it always be like that, Albert? Will you always be here when you're needed?' There was no reply. She whispered aloud, 'Albert, I'm so tired . . .'

He still said nothing and within three seconds she was asleep. Janie and Wendy looked in four times during the night and each time stood, smiling sentimentally at the mother and baby, fast asleep together.

'I reckon she can be happy again now,' Wendy Watkins said. And for once Janie agreed with her.

Sixteen

A year after it all happened, one or two passengers from the ill-fated eight forty-five went to the church just outside Paddington, which had once been the landmark of a small and separate village called Sellingford. It was as if they could not quite go on with their lives until they had looked at it all again, maybe even relived the actual accident.

Gertie never went there; she had never seen the crashed train anyway and Albert's charred body had been brought back to Bristol for a decent burial next to his parents. She took Bertie to the graveside in the pram sometimes and told him little things about his daddy and his grandfather. She wanted Bertie to have a good sense of his family; goodness knew she had no-one to be proud of on her side.

The people who visited the graves outside Paddington also looked at the scars on the embankment, which were already healing with fresh grass, nettles, cow parsley.

'Wonder anyone survived,' they murmured as they watched trains thundering past and tried to imagine one of them coming off the rails and piling up on itself as it slithered along the April-wet grass. Then they looked around the church and put a few coppers in the plate at the back. It was a sort of pilgrimage for them. Much later they might well have identified the visit as a psychological 'closure'. All they knew in the spring of 1952 was that they'd had to come just once more. And if they fitted it in with a trip to London, it would make it worthwhile.

Lydia thought it was ghoulish.

'You three go if you must,' she said. 'Leave me out. The aged pees have given in and got a television. They're going to show a bit of the Queen's trip to Africa – you know, when she heard about her dad dying.'

'She's not Queen yet,' Marvin objected. 'Coronation's next year.'

Lydia intoned, 'The King is dead, long live the King.' Marvin looked uncomprehending and she rolled her eyes. 'I don't know how long this can last, Marv. You've got to try and keep up.'

Jenny also wondered how much longer Lydia and Marvin could last together. They argued all the time.

The next time their day off coincided, Jenny, Marvin and Harry caught the eight forty-five and then took a bus back to Sellingford. They got out on what had been the village green; the pond had long gone and to one side of it was a fish and chip van. Marvin brightened. 'We could have our dinner here,' he suggested. Harry and Jenny ignored him; their thoughts were already back with the eight forty-five. Harry reached for her hand and she clung to it.

They had thought that the graveyard would hold no real interest for them, as Ahmed and Albert had been brought back to Bristol, but when they reached the two end graves they both stopped and looked frowningly at them.

'I remember the man and his wife,' Harry said. 'They got on at Bath. But there was no child.'

Marvin said, 'You read to me about them, Jenny. In the hospital. They expected someone to come forward to say the kid was missing. No one ever did.'

'I was just leaving that coach when it happened.' Harry's frown deepened. 'I chatted to him. He was nervous, very nervous.'

'Wife travelling without a ticket, hiding in the lav?' Marvin speculated.

'We had old Misery Guts on board that day. No-one but no-one would have got away without a ticket.'

'Why didn't he follow up for the child's ticket then?' Jenny said.

'Maybe they had one.' Harry looked at her. 'If the child was with them, they would have had a ticket for her. There would have been no mystery about it. Then.'

Jenny said suddenly, 'I remember him now. The man. He was absolutely shell-shocked. Staring at the front of the train.'

'Well, he would be, wouldn't he?' Marvin asked reasonably.

'Perhaps the child was theirs,' Jenny said slowly. 'His and his wife's. And the shock made him just . . . forget her?'

They were all silent. Then Harry said, 'The only person who might have seen the child getting on the train would have been Albert. He was leaning out of the cab at Bath. He would have seen who got on that front coach.' He tightened his mouth. 'Ah well. We'll never know.'

They wandered down the single street to where the road turned and ran above the railway track. There were some pipes piled along the top of the bank and they sat on them and looked down. The sun was shining, the blowing grass looked polished, the ten ten from Cardiff panted along the up line and passed the two thirty on the down line going to Swindon, Purton and down the Golden Valley to Stroud and Cheltenham. They were all silent, remembering.

Harry said, 'Poor Albert.'

And Jenny said, 'Poor Ahmed.'

Marvin sighed. 'The last I remember was seeing the urn go and knowing Ahmed had copped all that boiling water.'

'It was such a good trip too,' Jenny said sadly. 'There were one or two really nice passengers. Mrs French – you met her at the school, the Easter bazaar, Marvin. D'you remember her?'

'I remember her from the train. She was so nice to me. Took an interest. No-one took any notice of me. But she did.'

'And the young honeymooners. What happened to them? They were badly injured, I believe.'

Harry actually laughed. 'I think she broke an arm and he might have been concussed. But the last I heard they had a lawsuit going for compensation. She had an eye to the main chance, did that young lady.'

'Well . . . they were probably hard up.'

Marvin was following his own line of thought. 'I told her how I felt about you, Jen. She understood. She said I was an artist.'

'You? An artist? I didn't know you could draw, Marvin! You never said anything.'

'Well, I can't draw. But she said I had an artist's eye – a way of looking at things. At least I think that's what she meant.' He said, 'They do art at the evening institute. I wouldn't mind having a go.' He laughed. 'I bet Lydia would pose for me. You know, in the nude.'

'Marvin!' Jenny protested.

'Well, I bet she would.' He looked at Jenny. 'Actually, it's good coming here like this. Makes me realize . . . certain things.'

'What?' asked Jenny.

'Never you mind!'

'Things about Lydia?'

'Yes. I reckon so. She's vinegary. Real vinegary.' He chuckled. 'I have vinegar on everything. Drives my mum mad.' He stood up, suddenly impatient to be away. 'Come on. Mustn't get morbid.'

Harry and Jenny watched him go back down to the road. 'Good job he can't remember the actual crash,' Harry said. 'This has helped us, Jen, hasn't it? Got it out of our systems. Wish I could go back to that damned wadi and get that out of my system too.'

She said tentatively, 'Couldn't you wrap it all up together, Harry? The wadi and the train and all the bad things? Let Albert take them away?'

'Oh Jen . . .' He looked at her, his eyes alight with love. 'You're right, aren't you? Albert would want to do that – take it away.'

'D'you know, Gertie said to me that Albert was with her when she had little Bertie. It could be, Harry, couldn't it? That he's still around, sort of helping us.'

'Well, I don't know about that.' Harry hugged her to his shoulder. 'Like Marvin said, we mustn't be morbid. But if he is around . . .' He gazed over the scene of the accident as if he expected Albert to be there. 'If he's anywhere at all, I hope he can do something about it for us. Just take away the horror.'

Jenny tucked her head into his neck contentedly. She was sure he would.

Mary and Andrew French drove home that way after Mary's last appointment with Henry Yorke. There had been three operations at monthly intervals and Mary was still at the stage where the intensity of colour simply amazed her.

'Look at that grass! My God, people who think grass is just green . . . they're not looking, are they? It's silver and gold and there's blue there too. Can you see, Andrew? It's so wonderful!'

'I can see,' Andrew said happily. 'And it *is* wonderful.' He drew up next to the fish and chip van on the old green and they walked round the church and into the graveyard. 'D'you remember that chap who was at the school bazaar with Jenny Price?'

'The guard that day. His name is Harry Blackmore and he and Jenny are going to get engaged the minute she's twenty-one.' Mary laughed. 'I thought she would eventually make a match of it with the other young steward.'

'Apparently the three of them came back here last month. Just to look at it and sort of close the chapter.'

'I can understand that. Perhaps that's why we're here, darling.'

'Perhaps.' From sheer force of habit he took her arm and guided her around the ancient tombstones to the short row of newer ones at the back. He loved it that she never pulled away from him now. He said, 'I love you, Mary. It's wonderful that you've got the all-clear from Yorke, but we would have been all right, you know. Whatever happens, darling, we'll be all right.'

She turned to him. 'I know. I don't look into the future in that way any more, Andrew. I am just so delighted with each day as it comes.'

'Was that what John was saying to you in his paintings? That whatever happens – the awfulness of the trenches, death and destruction – that joy cannot be beaten?'

She put her arms round his waist and her head on his chest. 'You always had a feel for John's work, didn't you? And you're right. He would be so pleased about us.'

They held each other gratefully for a few more minutes, then moved on to look at the graves and to wonder, as did everyone, about the un-named child next to Ilse Hart. Then they, too, walked along the path above the embankment, and Mary sat on the grass and reached inside her bag for her sketchpad. Andrew settled beside her, smiling.

She said warningly, 'It'll only mean something to the people who were actually there.'

'I wouldn't put money on that if I were you,' Andrew said.

A few weeks before, he had met Sylvie Kemp at the art class Mary took in Bristol. She had talked to him about how she had met her husband on the eight forty-five. 'He's writing about it,' she told Andrew proudly. 'A play. It's going to be amazing. He's discussing the special effects with the director. They'll have to be mostly off stage of course but it will be really something. If you want to know what it was like for your wife, you should go to see it.'

Andrew had promised he would. 'And when Mary paints it, I'll let you know.'

'Is she going to do a picture?'

'She hasn't mentioned it, but I know she'll do one eventually.'

Sylvie had been excited. 'They should collaborate in some way!'

Andrew closed his eyes against the sun and his smile widened. It was quite possible they would collaborate.

In a strange way, Joe and Sylvie did not particularly want to close that chapter of their lives and for some time they held out against going back to the scene of the accident. But then Mary told Joe about the child's unmarked grave and Joe's curiosity was too much for him.

It was raining and they stood looking down at the sodden grave and felt undeniably depressed.

'We shouldn't have come,' Sylvie said. 'It's almost voyeuristic.'

'We shouldn't have come because it means I've got to change my script,' Joe said glumly.

'Why? It's complete as it is.'

He sighed. 'Come on, Sylvie. How can I leave her out? Nobody knows her, obviously nobody cares tuppence about her. But she was there. Part of the story. She's important.'

Sylvie stared down. 'Perhaps it's the first and last time she was ever important,' she breathed. 'Joe . . . make her important.'

He nodded. 'I will,' he promised.

He had no idea then that the shoe would be on the other foot. Caroline Hart, as Ray Hart would always call her, would make him important. Very important indeed.

Just beyond them, from the direction of the crash, came the sounds of building work; it seemed to be going on everywhere these days. The screech of metal as a saw ripped into it, the thud of a demolition ball as it swung from a crane. They both were still, listening.

It was like an echo; a dirge for the old eight forty-five.

THE END

A SELECTED LIST OF FINE NOVELS
AVAILABLE FROM CORGI BOOKS

14685 4	THE SILENT LADY	*Catherine Cookson*	£5.99
14451 7	KINGDOM'S DREAM	*Iris Gower*	£5.99
14895 4	NOT ALL TARTS ARE APPLE	*Pip Granger*	£5.99
14538 6	A TIME TO DANCE	*Kathryn Haig*	£5.99
14771 0	SATURDAY'S CHILD	*Ruth Hamilton*	£5.99
14820 2	THE TAVERNERS'S PLACE	*Caroline Harvey*	£5.99
14868 7	SEASON OF MISTS	*Joan Hessayon*	£5.99
14603 X	THE SHADOW CHILD	*Judith Lennox*	£5.99
14773 7	TOUCHING THE SKY	*Susan Madison*	£5.99
14823 7	THE PATHFINDER	*Margaret Mayhew*	£5.99
14872 5	THE SHADOW CATCHER	*Michelle Paver*	£5.99
14905 5	MULBERRY LANE	*Elvi Rhodes*	£5.99
12375 7	A SCATTERING OF DAISIES	*Susan Sallis*	£5.99
12579 2	THE DAFFODILS OF NEWENT	*Susan Sallis*	£5.99
12880 5	BLUEBELL WINDOWS	*Susan Sallis*	£5.99
13136 9	ROSEMARY FOR REMEMBRANCE	*Susan Sallis*	£5.99
13756 1	AN ORDINARY WOMAN	*Susan Sallis*	£5.99
13934 3	DAUGHTERS OF THE MOON	*Susan Sallis*	£5.99
13346 9	SUMMER VISITORS	*Susan Sallis*	£5.99
13545 3	BY SUN AND CANDLELIGHT	*Susan Sallis*	£5.99
14162 3	SWEETER THAN WINE	*Susan Sallis*	£4.99
14318 9	WATER UNDER THE BRIDGE	*Susan Sallis*	£5.99
14466 5	TOUCHED BY ANGELS	*Susan Sallis*	£5.99
14549 1	CHOICES	*Susan Sallis*	£5.99
14636 6	COME RAIN OR SHINE	*Susan Sallis*	£5.99
14671 4	THE KEYS TO THE GARDEN	*Susan Sallis*	£5.99
14747 8	THE APPLE BARREL	*Susan Sallis*	£5.99
14867 9	SEA OF DREAMS	*Susan Sallis*	£5.99
14907 1	SONS AND DAUGHTERS	*Mary Jane Staples*	£5.99
14846 6	ROSA'S ISLAND	*Valerie Wood*	£5.99